I0731304

Dancing with God's Grace

ഔൽ

JC Conrad-Ellis

©2022
Provision Press

DANCING WITH GOD'S GRACE

Copyright ©2011and ©2022 by JC Conrad-Ellis
Cover Design by Valerie Connelly

All rights reserved. Printed in the United States of America. No part of this book may be reproduced or transmitted in any form or by any means, electronic or mechanical, including photocopying, recording, or by any information storage and retrieval system without written permission from the publisher, except for the inclusion of brief quotations in articles and reviews.

If you purchased this book without a cover, you should be aware that this book is stolen property. It was reported as "unsold and destroyed" to the publisher, and neither the author nor the publisher has received any payment for this "stripped book."

For information about ProvisionPress please
visit our website at www.blackdiamondseriespress.com.

Library of Congress Cataloging-in-Publication Data

Conrad-Ellis, JC,

DANCING WITH GOD'S GRACE/ JC Conrad-Ellis
ISBN 13: 978-1-957593-03-6
Teen Fiction

Copyright Registered: 2022
Published by Provision Press in the USA

Printed in the USA

January 2022

10 9 8 7 6 5 4 3 2

DEDICATION

This book is dedicated to:

Bailey Jeanette
Blair Jessica
Brian Wardell "Newby"

ACKNOWLEDGEMENTS

Writing is a solitary vocation with hours spent giving voice, texture, meaning and life to words, characters and dialogue as though choreographing an intricate group dance routine. The words are then required to establish a rhythm that seduces even the most rhythmically challenged reader onto the dance floor. Once the reader is tapping along with the author's cadence, the hope is that the final written effort produces an unforgettable literary dance experience.

With that, I acknowledge the authors of the thousands of great books that fueled my love of reading as well as the mediocre writers whose work I read anyway because it gave me the "I can do better than that" courage and arrogance necessary to bravely walk the writer's plank.

Most importantly, I humbly acknowledge each of you for reading my work, dancing to my tune, and coming back for more. Thank you. jc

CONTENTS

DANCING WITH GOD'S GRACE

*"Do you not know that in a race all of the runners run
but only one gets the prize?
Run in such a way as to get the prize."*

*1 Corinthians 9:24
NIV Bible
New International Version*

Dancing with God's Grace

Chapter 1

Grace: Project Strong

Her head throbbed, like the ride at a carnival where the walls gyrated faster and faster until the floor dropped, pinning the riders' frozen bodies against the sides, their feet dangling like noodles. She took a deep breath and rubbed her neck. Her neck felt stiff too. That silly ride always made her dizzy. Dizzy was not what she wanted to feel. Her heart beat wildly while her palms dripped with perspiration. Her fingers and palms dragging along the carpet, she took another deep breath, not knowing what to say. The air stung her nostrils.

Grace shrugged her shoulders and dug her big toe into the shag pile throw rug at the foot of the bed. Her toe became entangled in a loose fringe that Maria's cat Sugar had unraveled. A nervous smile shadowed her face.

Grace wanted to tell Maria that it was okay, that she didn't expect her to remember his name, especially since she'd asked her friends not to bring up his name. She wanted to laugh and acknowledge that it had been months since they'd talked about the information that Teenie's Aunt Helen had shared about him. She wanted to take a deep breath and proudly state that she was now ready to confront the mystery that had haunted her for the past two years. She was ready to meet Charles Lovett, her biological father.

But as usual, the words were caught in her throat, swimming in a river of fear. She chewed on her bottom lip as her thoughts battled in her head. *What's wrong with you, Grace? What are you afraid of? These are your closest friends! In fact, they are your only friends. They love you and are on your side. They want to help you. Talk to them! Say something, stupid!*

"Oh my God!" Maria realized slowly. "I am so embarrassed. That's right!" she paused. "Charles Lovett is your birth father!" she repeated slowly. "No wonder his name sounded familiar," she confessed. "Is that why you were kicking me, Teenie?" Maria whispered. Her hand covered her mouth. "I'm so sorry, Grace," she offered as she smiled softly at her friend. Her apology was weak, yet sincere. Her face blushed crimson.

"Tanisha Denise Carlson," Maria groaned. "If you kick me one more time, I'm going to smack you silly!" she shrieked. "Why'd you kick me this time? I just apologized to Grace. What else did I do wrong?" she demanded as she rubbed her shin. "You know that I'm fragile. My bones are delicate, and I bruise easily, you bully," she whined.

Tanisha laughed at her friend's dramatics and waved her hand dismissively. "I kicked you that time because you used God's name in vain," Tanisha admonished. "Even though Lori isn't here with us, we have to honor her memory, remember?" Tanisha reminded. "And as one of Lori's Angels, I cannot in good conscience let you blaspheme in my presence."

"Blaspheme?" Maria repeated. "That is so not a word. The word is blasphemy, smarty pants," Maria gloated.

"Blaspheme is a word, genius," Tanisha teased. "It's a verb, and it means to curse or dishonor. Blasphemy is a noun," Tanisha laughed.

Staring at Tanisha in disbelief, Maria looked to Rashanda for support. Rashanda shrugged and smiled. "She's right, Maria. Lori would not approve of any of us loosely using God's name, so Teenie's right. And for the record, blaspheme is a word," she continued. "I remember it well because it was the word that I misspelled in my third grade spelling bee," she shared. "I spelled blasphemy instead of blaspheme," Rashanda sighed. "I should have been the third grade spelling champion."

Tanisha's eyes grew wide as saucers. "Oh my, God! I still remember the words that disqualified me from my fourth and fifth grade spelling bees at Mahala Elementary!" Tanisha offered excitedly. "In fourth grade, the word was hostile, and in fifth grade it was lullaby," she remembered.

She crisscrossed her legs at the knee like a pretzel and sat up straight, her hands waving in the air for emphasis. "I studied my spelling review list backwards and forward," she beamed. "I was ready, and just knew that I was going to win," she explained, her posture stiffened as though a board had been placed against the back of her chair. "The prompter said hostile, but she pronounced it with an A sound or a short "i" sound like dull. I thought it was pronounced with a long "I" sound like smile," she continued. "So I said, 'Do you mean hostile?' I pronounced it with the long I sound," Tanisha explained.

"The prompter looked at the second prompter who shook her head and repeated the short "i" pronunciation. I took a deep breath and spelled it the way she said it. Hostal, h-o-s-t-a-l, hostal. The first prompter looked at me with sad eyes and shook her head. 'I'm sorry, that's not correct.' She knew that I knew how to spell the word," Teenie sighed. "I just didn't know how to pronounce it correctly. I came in fourth place and cried for days!" Tanisha confessed slumping in her chair, the invisible board now removed from her spine. "I stuck around until the end, and I knew how to correctly spell all of the words that eliminated the other contestants," she offered glibly. "I was so angry! My mom even tried to meet with the people in charge to plead my case, but they said that I should have used a dictionary to confirm pronunciation while I was studying the words," she groaned. "I still get angry every time I hear that word!"

"So you become hostile when you hear the word hostile?" Rashanda giggled.

"Boo hoo hoo," Maria groaned. "How come no one just kicked you for using God's name in vain?" Maria asked sarcastically.

Rashanda rolled her eyes into the ceiling, ignoring Maria's question. "How did you spell lullaby incorrectly, Teenie?" Rashanda asked. "That's an easy word."

"I added an "e" to the end of lullaby at the last minute," Tanisha said. "For some reason, I remembered it as lullabies and thought that the root word for lullabies was lullaby with an e on the end," Tanisha continued. "It was a rookie mistake, but I wasn't as upset about this one because I hadn't studied my word list as hard," she said. "A year later, I was still upset about my hostile spelling debacle," she sighed. "Maybe I need to join a hostile support group," she teased.

Grateful for the distraction, Grace smiled softly as her friend's reminisced about their spelling bee disappointments. *Did they not hear me? I thought I said that I was ready to meet Charles Lovett aloud, but maybe I whispered it. No. I said it out loud. That's why Teenie kicked Maria, because Maria said 'Oh, my God.' Maybe they don't realize that I really want to talk about it this time. What am I supposed to say now?*

As Maria ranted about Teenie not getting kicked for taking the Lord's name in vain, Rashanda nudged her gently and motioned to Grace. Maria stopped mid sentence. "Enough about the spelling bee drama you two, let's focus on Grace now," Maria encouraged. "Sorry about that, Grace. Teenie and Rashanda can continue to skip down spelling bee memory lane, but I want to talk about Charles Lovett," she said gently.

Tanisha covered her mouth with her hand and gently smacked herself across both cheeks. The other girls stared at her quizzically. "The first swat was for my God faux pas," she explained. "See, Maria. I'm not above the law and will punish myself if I violate our Lori's Angels' covenant," she offered. Maria smiled approvingly at Tanisha and winked. "The second swat was for ignoring Grace's life changing statement and reminiscing about a silly spelling bee," she finished.

Sugar, the cat, jumped on Maria's bed, extended his paws as far as possible, arched his back and snuggled into her pillow as though settling in to hear Grace's story.

Distracted by the ticking clock on Maria's nightstand, Grace found herself once again losing her nerve. She smiled weakly at her friends and stretched her fingers. The ticking clock seemed to be getting louder and louder. Grace hadn't paid attention to the sound before, but now it seemed deafening. She pretended not to notice as her friends stared at each other silently. They too were confused about what to say next. They had yielded the floor to her, and now she didn't know where to begin. She took a deep breath.

"Take your time, Grace," Tanisha offered.

"In fact, we don't have to talk about this now if you're not ready," Maria suggested gently.

Grace smiled warmly at Maria, surprised by her compassion. Sometimes Maria could be downright brash, insensitive and callous, and other times, she was as gentle as a lamb.

"No, I want to talk about it now," Grace said. Surprised by the strength in her voice, she continued. "I think it would be good to get it over with and try to contact him," Grace said. "My parents said that they'll do whatever they can to help me."

Crossing her legs like a pretzel, the nervousness slightly

contained, the unscripted path looked less frightening. "I thought that the first thing that I should do is write him a letter?" Grace suggested in the form of a question. Her eyes widened seeking their approval and validation.

"That's a good start," Tanisha encouraged.

Maria furrowed her thick eyebrows. "I thought you said that you have his address **and** phone number," she stated. "Why don't you just call him so you can hear his voice?"

Grace dropped her eyes to the rug again, her voice but a whisper. "I don't want to call him because I'm scared," she stammered softly. "I'm afraid that if I call him, he will hang up on me or pretend not to be who he is."

"It's 'whom' he is, Grace," Teenie corrected. "He might pretend not to be whom he is," she finished, as the other girls stared at her icily. "What?" she shrugged. "You guys know that I can't help it. I come from a family of teachers who constantly corrected our grammar," Teenie explained. "Sorry, Grace. I will try not to give out any more grammar citations."

Her expression unchanged, Grace continued. "Or I'll get so tongue tied that I won't know what to say to him. If I'm afraid to talk to my girlfriends, how am I going to talk on the phone to the father that I've never met?" she trailed.

"Actually, I like the idea of writing him a letter," Rashanda agreed. "This way she can write it, rewrite it and read it several times to make sure that she likes the message," she finished.

"She could also include a photo of herself so that he can see his face in hers," Tanisha suggested.

"I hadn't thought of that, Teenie," Grace brightened. She twirled her hair, glad that it was growing back. She missed her long hair and regretted getting it cut so short. "But I like that idea. I look like my mother, so if he gets a picture of me, it will be hard for him not to acknowledge who I am," she shared. "I'll send him a picture of me with long hair."

Sugar arched his back again, digging his claws into the bed. Maria leapt from the floor and lunged at the fluffy, fat cat. "Sugar!" she squealed. "You're going to shred my new bedspread!" Ignoring her, the cat snuggled into her pillow and purred softly.

Maria plopped to the floor, the unmistakable look of defeat plastered on her face. "I give up!" she groaned. "I love that cat, but he is such a little terrorist. His claws are like razor blades! Look!" she screamed, raising her hands to display the fresh cat marks on her skin. She opened her palm to silence the group. "And before you ask, my mother wants to wait until he's one year old before we have his claws removed. Liz has this silly idea that cats shouldn't be de-clawed until then," she giggled. "I guess in a past life she was a veterinarian. Anyway, we can help you write the letter, Grace," Maria offered. "I'll get some paper and we can start drafting it right now."

Rashanda tossed Maria a notebook with a pen in the binder from the school books on her desk. "Here's some paper," she said.

"Let's write a draft first," Maria suggested. "Teenie, you're a good writer. You dictate, and I'll write down what you say," she continued. "I'll write as fast as I can, but speak slower than you normally do."

Grace was sitting on Maria's bed, gently rubbing Sugar's back. Tanisha glanced at Grace for approval. "Grace, have you thought about what you want to put in the letter?" she asked. "Why don't you start dictating to Maria, and then we can all add on to what you say," Tanisha suggested.

She continued to rhythmically stroke Sugar's fur, giggling as he purred softly to her touch. "I've been trying to think of something clever to write in a letter, but I haven't come up with anything," Grace admitted. She looked softly at Teenie. "Maria's right, Teenie. You're a good writer, so help me come up with something."

Tanisha rubbed her palms together and stretched her fingers. "All-righty then, let's get started!" Tanisha stood up and paced the floor. "We want the letter to be heart warming yet pithy," she said. "What do we know? We need to write down all of the questions that we want to answer and then write down the answers. Write these questions down, Maria," she ordered. "But first, we need a title for our project," she said.

The girls looked at each other and shrugged. "Why do we need a title for it?" Rashanda asked.

"Because assigning the project a title will help us focus and give it a life of its own," she explained. "I got it!" she squealed quickly. "Let's call it Project Strong." She made quotation marks with her hands. "Write Project Strong across the top of the page, Maria." Tanisha ordered without waiting for a response from the group. "Charles Lovett lives in Strong, Arkansas, and it takes a lot of strength for Grace to reach out to him. Get it? Project Strong," she repeated. "It works on several levels." The other girls obediently nodded in agreement.

Maria printed Project Strong on the first line of the paper. "Now. What do we know?" Tanisha continued. Her index finger and thumb stroked her cheeks gently. "Question number 1: Did Charles Lovett know that Lydia Moore was pregnant? Question 2: What was he told by Northwestern regarding why he was not receiving tenure? Question 3: Did he ever receive any correspondence from Lydia Moore? Question 4: Did he try to get in touch with her? Question 5: Is he still married? Question 6: Did his wife know about his dalliance with the college co-ed?"

Maria dropped her pen and waved her hands. "Teenie, you're

talking way too fast. I'm still writing question number two. I can't write that fast. Slow down!"

"I'm sorry, Maria," Teenie laughed. "I just get so excited that my mind starts racing. I feel like Nancy Drew," she giggled.

"Teenie," Grace said softly. "How are these questions going to help us write the letter? I don't understand."

"The way I see it," Teenie said. "Is that the more we can find out about him, the easier it will be to draft a letter that will touch his heart and make him want to contact you. For instance, if he's still married and his wife didn't know anything about their affair, the letter may scare him. Or his wife could open the mail and decide not to give it to him," Tanisha continued. "There are several different scenarios that could occur just based on the answers to some very simple questions."

Rashanda stretched across the foot of the bed and fanned her legs in the air. "But how are we going to know if he's married or not?"

"Well, before we write the letter we could call and ask to speak with Mrs. Lovett," Maria suggested.

"Brilliant, Maria!" Tanisha encouraged. "You see. This is more than just dropping a letter in the mail. We have to be very strategic in how we word the letter and try our best to understand Charles Lovett's current situation so we can anticipate the outcome," she finished.

Grace smiled widely. "I never would have thought of that. I would have just dropped a letter in the mailbox and hoped for the best."

"Nope! You should always get as much detailed information as possible before embarking on a journey. It's like being a lawyer. A lawyer only asks the witness questions that she already knows the answers to," Tanisha explained. "We want to eliminate any surprises. Grace, do you have any idea if he knew that your mother was pregnant with you?"

Grace bit her lip. "I have no idea. All I know is that when my grandparents found out who he was, they had the university fire him."

Tanisha scratched her head and fluffed her hair. "This is going to take some research. We'll all have to get involved," she suggested. "Maria, I'll repeat the questions in a second. But first, I have to ask Grace the most important questions of all." Tanisha sat on the bed with Grace, her face soft and concerned. She cupped her chin in her hand. "Grace," she paused. "First, have you thought about how you'll feel if he's known about you but hasn't tried to contact you? And second, what if he decides that he just doesn't want to meet you?"

"Teenie!" Maria barked. "Why would you ask her that? That is negative thinking! I can't believe you would ask her that!"

As Tanisha pursed her lips to explain, Grace spoke. "It's okay, Maria," Grace said quickly. "I'm glad Teenie asked me. To tell you the truth, it's all I can think about. It's why I've been so scared to contact him," she said slowly.

Maria tapped the pen on the notebook and stared cautiously at Rashanda who shrugged and leaned in closer.

"That's what I thought," Tanisha said. "These are the two worst case scenarios, and if you're prepared for the two worst case scenarios, then anything else that happens won't be so bad," Tanisha said. "I always say that you should expect the best, but prepare for the worst," Tanisha offered.

Glad that her private fear was now part of the discussion, Grace felt her heartbeat slowing down. "Honestly, I don't know how I'll feel if either of these scenarios happens, or what I'll do, but I'm glad we're talking about the elephant in the room," she shared. "I'm scared, and I'm hoping that you guys will help me get through this."

"Of course we will, Grace," Rashanda offered gently. "That's what friends are for. You're not going through this alone. We'll be with you every step of the way!"

"Exactly," Maria chimed in. "If he rejects you, he's rejecting us too," she said tenderly. "We'll be there for you no matter what!" she encouraged. "But if he does reject you, we may have to road trip to Strong, Arkansas and rough him up a bit!" she giggled, her arms shadow boxing playfully.

Rashanda laughed loudly. "She's right, Grace. You know we have your back. We're all in this together," she agreed. "If we have to road trip, I'm sure Ian will come with us to add a testosterone shot," she teased.

"Great idea, Rashanda! Since Ian goes to Northwestern, he could borrow the Willie the Wildcat mascot costume. If Charles doesn't give us the result that we want, we'll let Willie deal with him," Maria giggled. "Then he'll be able to say that he really got beat down by Northwestern! Literally beat down by Northwestern!" Maria finished.

Tanisha chuckled at her friends' silliness. "Okay ladies, Willie the Wildcat will not be kicking anyone's tail, and we're not going to have to road trip to Arkansas." She stood up and stretched her arms to the ceiling. "We're going to research Project Strong so thoroughly, that Mr. Charles Lovett will want to meet Grace," she paused. "Let's stay focused and get serious. This is a big elephant. We have to subdue it and slay it with finesse!" Tanisha clapped her hands and wiggled her fingers in the air. "The only way to eat an elephant is to chew it one bite at a time!" Tanisha encouraged. "Who's hungry?"

Chapter 2

Justine: Lake Shore Guilt

The bruise on her head was barely noticeable. Nonetheless, she brushed her bangs across her forehead to conceal the small knot. She didn't want her mother to freak out when she saw her. It was a stupid rookie mistake. A suburban, pumpkin head snafu. Once again, her mother had known best. She took a deep breath and creased her forehead gingerly. She thought her mom was just being too careful. Treating her like a baby. She was almost seventeen now. She wasn't a baby. She'd been warned not to ride her bike along the lakefront, alone, but the warm weather beckoned her like a siren, enticing her like a conniving friend. It's a beautiful day! The sun is shining. The tennis courts are less than two miles up the path. You don't have anything else to do. Go for a ride.

Without hesitation, she heeded the voice of the warm wind and dragged her bike down the stairs for a ride. She was lonely and missed her friends. She thought she knew where she was going. She'd seen the tennis courts from Lake Shore Drive so many times. Entranced by the sun beaming on the glistening lake, she rode past the tennis court exit. When she realized her mistake, she turned her bike around but it was too late.

Tag. She thought they were playing tag, the way one raced ahead of the other. When the first teen ran onto the bike path, she instinctively maneuvered the bike out of his way. She was from the suburbs. She didn't have the street smarts to know that it was a ploy. When she swerved left, she saw the sinister look in his gaze as his hand grabbed for the handle bars. His eyes glared at her like a wild animal.

The next thing she remembered was waking up and walking. But the lake was on the wrong side of her body. The lake was on her left side. Not knowing where she was, she knew that in order to get home, the lake had to be on her right side. This much she knew. Still dazed, she turned around and walked the other way. Her head hurt.

Like an alarm clock awaking her from a deep slumber, was the homeless man's question.

"Hey, pretty lady," he yelled. "Where's your pink bike?" he asked.

Justine stared at him blankly. She was not fully conscious. She kept walking. She realized later that it was nothing but God's grace that led her safely to her building. She didn't remember crossing the street or watching for traffic. She dreaded hoisting her bike up the stairs. It was heavy. She fumbled in her pocket for her bike lock key. Once in the vestibule of her building, she stared at the bike lock key. That's when it hit her. She'd been riding her bike. Where was her bike?

The veil was lifted as she used her key to enter their apartment unit. She unlocked the door and ran inside. She raced to the back porch. Her new pink Schwinn was not locked on the porch next to her brothers' bikes. The bikes had been moving gifts from their dad. Her brothers' new bikes were still there, but hers was gone. She shook her head in disbelief. In broad daylight, on a sunny, Sunday afternoon, she had been mugged.

"My mother is going to have a fit!" Justine groaned loudly. She raced into the bathroom to look at herself. She placed her hand to her forehead and could feel a tender spot from where her head slammed to the ground. She must have fainted. The memory was rushing back like a wave.

When his hand grabbed the handlebars of her bicycle, and she looked into his eyes, the air left her lungs. That was the last thing that she remembered. She looked down at her leg and saw a scrape on her left calf. She touched it and black oil smeared her fingers. Oil from the bike chain. I must have fallen on the bike, and they pulled it from under me. My mother is going to wring my neck. No she won't, Justine. She'll just be glad that you weren't hurt. True. But later, she's going to ring your neck. She told you not to ride south on the lake. I should have ridden into Evanston like she said. It was a stupid, suburban, pumpkin head mistake. You're not in Kansas anymore, Dorothy!

She splashed water on her face. Her gold necklace was still on her neck as was the gold bracelet. More gifts from her dad. She knew that the generous presents were his way of buying back his children's trust and affection. The gifts weren't necessary. Justine forgave him for his infidelity. He was her dad. He'd made a mistake, but she still loved him. At least all they took was my bike. Justine took a long, deep breath.

The clock struck five o'clock. Her mother would be home in a few hours. She squinted. Why do the numbers on the clock look so small? My glasses! Oh, no! I was wearing my new glasses! Her heart rate increased again. Why would they steal my glasses? She walked slowly into the kitchen, glad that her brothers had gone to a movie with the neighbors. She needed time to think. She really missed her friends from Newberry East. She needed someone to help her figure this out. The ringing phone interrupted her thoughts.

Fearing that it was her mother, she didn't want to answer it.

But she knew that if it was her mother and she didn't answer it, Andrea would worry. She decided to face the firing squad.

"Hello," she said somberly.

"Uh, hello. May I speak to Justine?" the male voice asked.

"Speaking," Justine replied. Who could this be?

"Hey, Justine," the voice smiled. "It's Ian. Rashanda's boyfriend."

"Oh! Hey, Ian," Justine smiled. "What's up?"

"I was just calling to get your address so that I can pick up Rashanda next weekend when she comes," he explained. "I have midterms next week, and I'll be pretty busy, so I thought I'd call now so I could cross it off of my things to do list," he paused. "Are you okay? You don't sound too good."

Justine burst into tears. Gasping for breath, she quietly explained to Ian what she remembered about her mugging experience.

"That's horrible!" Ian said. "Have you called the police?"

She blew her nose into a tissue. "The police?" she asked. "I hadn't thought about that." She wiped her face with her hand. Talking about her ordeal felt surreal. She loved that pink bike. Thinking about what happened to her made her angry.

"You were robbed, Justine. You need to file a police report," Ian explained. "The guys who mugged you may still be in the park ready to attack someone else. You have to get the law involved. Plus, this way, if you have a police report, your mother can claim it on her renter's insurance to replace your bike."

Justine perked up. She hadn't thought about that. "Ian, you're a genius."

"In fact," he continued. "You shouldn't be alone right now. I'm on my way. I can be there in eight minutes," he explained. "We'll call the police together when I get there. I doubt they stole your glasses. They probably just fell off of your face when you fainted.

Once we finish with the police, we'll go and see if we can find your glasses before it gets dark."

Her head still throbbed, but she was grateful that she wouldn't be alone. "Ian, before you hang up," Justine said. "I was going to call my mom. Should I call her now or wait?"

"Wait until I get there," he instructed. "Once we finish with the police, I'll take you to the hospital where she works. Since your head hit the ground and you blacked out, you may have a concussion," he said. "If you call her with this news, she's going to flip out and rush right home," he paused. "I think it would be better if we tell her what happened at the hospital," he finished. "I'll be right there. I can be there in less than ten minutes."

Fudge sauntered into the room and rubbed against Justine's leg, purring softly as though sensing that something was wrong. Justine reached down and picked up her beloved cat. *Ian is so awesome. Rashanda is lucky to have someone like him in her life.*

She used the bathroom and poured herself a glass of water. She wrote a note for her brothers in case she was gone when they returned from the movies:

Hey guys, I have to take care of something and will be home with mom. Just eat cereal for dinner and watch television. No company and no cooking! J

Justine had barely finished writing the note and taping it to the refrigerator door when the door bell rang. It was Ian. She buzzed him upstairs. He gave her a friendly hug and dialed 911.

Ten minutes later, two police officers arrived. Justine wondered how they'd gotten into the locked vestibule. One of the officers was a woman. Justine had never seen a female police officer before. The female officer asked her questions, and the male officer took notes as Justine told them what happened.

"It sounds like you fainted," the female police officer agreed.

"Good thing you didn't struggle with them," the male officer offered casually. "We've had a lot of reports of bicycle theft along that bike path, and sometimes they use two by fours of plywood to knock the riders off their bike," he finished. "You're lucky, kid."

Justine's jaw dropped open. I could have been knocked off of my bike with a two by four? My mother is going to kill me!

Ian smiled softly at her. "Justine, you're blessed by God's grace," he said confidently. As though reading her mind, he continued. "You're safe. Now you know better, and next time you'll be more careful. But you'll always travel with God's grace and mercy, so don't think about what could have happened. It'll drive you crazy."

"Grace, luck, mercy, hocus pocus," the male officer repeated sarcastically. "Call it whatever you want. But at least she wasn't seriously hurt this time."

This time? He says that like I should plan on getting mugged again! Justine looked at Ian who waved his hand and shook his head dismissively at the officer's careless statement.

Until then, Ian hadn't spoken a word during the police investigation. Justine was glad that he was there for moral support.

"Can you describe them at all?" the female officer asked. She stared softly into Justine's face.

"I wish I could, but all that I remember is that one was white and one was black," Justine offered. "By the time I realized that they were chasing me, I fainted," she offered softly.

The female officer patted Justine's hand softly. Her hands were soft and warm. "Well, you did the right thing by calling us. We're going to send more foot patrol officers to that area." She read the police report aloud and asked Justine to sign it, leaving a copy with her. "Be careful out there, Justine. Chicago is the third largest city in the United States. It's not like Newberry East," she cautioned. "The crime rate in the city is no joke."

Once the officers left, she and Ian drove along Lake Shore Drive to the area where she thought the mugging had occurred. He parked along the grass and they fanned out.

"Ian! I found them," she yelled a few minutes later. Ian ran toward her and laughed when she picked them up. "Wow!" he said. "I honestly didn't expect that we'd find them. I just didn't want you to worry about them or come out here by yourself to try to find them," he admitted. "I came out here to humor you." His eyes shifted as he looked at their surroundings. "I can't believe that you found those glasses and they're in perfect condition," he paused. His eyes studied the surrounding area. "You are so blessed, Justine. I don't mean to scare you," he said. "But they could have dragged you behind that little beach shack and really hurt you," he paused. "It's so sad that you were mugged less than twenty feet from Lake Shore Drive and yet no one stopped to help you. What kind of world do we live in?"

He'd been right. Her heart sank into her chest and her eyes welled with tears. Her head tilted to the sky, she said a silent prayer thanking God for his grace and that she'd only suffered a minor scrape on her calf. She smiled as she thought about Lori Perkins serving as her guardian angel in heaven.

Ian patted her back lightly. "Let's go back to the car so we can head to Evanston Memorial and tell your mom. I think they should give you a CAT scan since you blacked out, but they may not listen to me since I'm just a lowly chemistry/pre med student. But if you were my patient, I'd give you a CAT scan to ensure that you didn't suffer any serious head trauma."

Justine shook her head. Like a knight in shining armor, Ian had arrived at her apartment in exactly eight minutes, just like he said. He had been her life saver. Before he called, she was scheming about the lie that she would tell her mother regarding how her bike had been stolen. In an effort to avoid the lecture and trouble that she feared would result from her deliberate disobedience, she was prepared to lie. She'd partially crafted the scheme that her bike was stolen while locked in front of a store in Evanston. But with Ian there, she wasn't as afraid to tell her mother the truth. The fear was still there, but she knew that she had to face her mother.

Ian hummed along to the radio as he drove down Sheridan Road to Evanston Hospital. "I'm glad your mom is a nurse," he said. "You won't have to wait long in the emergency room since your mom works there. This works out well because her shift should be ending in an hour anyway. Does your head still hurt?"

"A little," she admitted. "But it's not throbbing like it was," Justine smiled. "Thanks, Ian. I don't know what I would have done if you hadn't called when you did," she said. "Truthfully, before you called, I was concocting a story to tell my mother so that I wouldn't get in trouble," Justine confessed.

"No worries, my friend," Ian said as he steered the car onto the busy street. "You suffered a traumatic experience and weren't thinking clearly. Sometimes we all need someone to help us readjust our moral compass and guide us to do the right thing," he said casually. "But you should always tell your parents the truth. Always!" he emphasized. "The truth is unconditional just like your parents' love. I'm sure your mom will probably give you a thirty second lecture, but she'll be so glad that you weren't hurt, that the lecture won't sting. Trust me," he smiled. "Been there done that."

Justine settled into her seat. Her head throbbed more, the closer they got to the hospital. I need a knight in shining armor. I need an Ian.

Chapter 3

Tanisha: Lavender, Lace & Lies

The lavender fabric complimented her golden, bronze skin. She stared at the price tag one more time in disbelief. One hundred and sixty dollars! Tanisha sighed loudly. That was over two weeks of pay from her part-time Save Mart job. She groaned. Her heart sank into her stomach. She couldn't afford to spend that much money on a dress. My life sucks! Why can't I ever catch a break!

Prom talk dominated the girls' lunchroom banter. Everyone was excited about finding the perfect prom dress. Rashanda's mother was an accomplished seamstress and was making her dress. Still trying desperately to buy her affection, Justine's father told her that she didn't have a budget for her dress, so Justine was ordering a dress from the bridal salon of Marshall Field's on State Street. Although she hadn't shared the cost, Tanisha imagined that ordering a dress from Marshall Field's couldn't be cheap. Grace didn't have a date and wasn't going to prom. Tanisha frowned and wondered if Lori were still alive if she would have had to pay for her own prom dress. Probably not, she concluded. As usual, Maria seemed to have an endless clothing allowance budget. She boasted that her prom dress was being shipped from an exclusive boutique on Rodeo Drive in California and cost over three hundred dollars. Her wealthy aunt was buying her dress as a birthday gift. Maria had sent her measurements to the boutique to ensure that the custom gown was a perfect fit. Tanisha scrunched her face just thinking about it. Maria doesn't even really know this aunt. She never talks about her the way I talk about Aunt Helen. And when she does talk about her, it's only to brag about the expensive gifts that she sends her. I don't even know this aunt's name. Maria just refers to her as her "sponsor!" How disrespectful is that? It's not fair! Why am I always the Good Times reject? I hate being the 'have not' girl in the group! This is supposed to be the most important dress of my life. Aaaaargh! She wanted to scream. But she knew that screaming would not change her sad reality. She would have to buy her own prom dress.

Twirling in the mirror, Tanisha thought about asking her dad to help her. She quickly dismissed this thought knowing that he would groan and mumble that one hundred and sixty dollars was way too much to spend on one dress. She unzipped the dress and checked the fabric tag. Polyester and Rayon. The dress wasn't even made from natural fibers. He would ask her if the dress was at least made of silk, and she would have to tell him that it was made of polyester. Her dad would definitely not support her decision to spend that much money on a polyester dress. In fact, he would suggest that Grandma Bootsy make her a dress.

Tanisha shook her head. She loved her Grandma Bootsy, but Grandma Bootsy was not a seamstress. She could knit up a storm, and made the most beautiful blankets, sweaters, hats and scarves. She could also cook better than anyone in the world, but Grandma Bootsy was not a skilled dressmaker. Tanisha played the scenario in her head. Never one to turn down a request to help one of her grandchildren, Grandma Bootsy would be more than happy to make something for her to wear. It would turn out average looking, and then Tanisha would feel obligated to wear it. She would hate to offend her Grandma Bootsy by not liking the dress. And no matter how the dress turned out, if she didn't wear it, she would be insulting her grandmother. No. She couldn't involve her dad. She knew him too well. By involving her dad, she might hurt her grandmother's feelings, and she loved her Grandma Bootsy far too much to even dream of that. If the dress looked like a sack of potatoes, Tanisha would wear it. She would have no choice.

Her dad was right. Prom was just one night. Just using simple math, she would be working over fifty hours just to pay for her dress. Why can't my mother be more like the other mothers? Doesn't she know that she's supposed to buy my prom dress? She's supposed to work overtime to earn the money to buy my dress, or at least to help me pay for the dress. Why doesn't she know this? Maybe I can find a nice dress at another store.

"How's it going in there?" the salesclerk asked. "I saw you when you twirled in the three way mirror, and I think that dress looks beautiful on you," she offered. "The color looks good against your tan skin."

"Thanks," Tanisha said. She opened the dressing room door and stepped into the hallway. "I'll take it," she blurted out before she could stop herself. She felt her heart rate increase.

Calm down, Tanisha. You have the money in your checking account. Maybe when I show Mommy the dress, she'll offer to pay for half of it. Anything would help. What am I thinking? Who am I kidding? Billie will look at the price tag and ask me to loan her some money. Stop it, Tanisha! You promised yourself that you would stop criticizing Billie! She's doing the best she can! Isn't that what he said? She's doing the best that she can.

"Great!" the clerk chirped. "Just bring it to the register, and I'll go ahead and wrap it so that it's ready when your mother gets back."

"When my mother gets back?" Tanisha asked.

"Yes. Don't we have to wait for your mom so that she can pay for the dress?" the clerk asked casually. "Wasn't that your mother in the yellow sweater?" she asked. "The lady you were talking to earlier in the mirror?"

Walking out of the dressing room to view her reflection in the three way mirror, an attractive lady in a yellow sweater approached Tanisha and admired her dress. Upon request, Tanisha twirled obediently as the woman commented on what a good fit the dress was and how well the color complimented her skin tone. The woman had shared that she was previewing prom dresses for her daughter who would be attending the Homer Glen High School Prom. Thanking her for the compliment, Tanisha shared that she would be attending River North's junior prom with her boyfriend. She loved saying the word boyfriend.

"Yeah, right," Tanisha lied. "My mom went to the shoe store to see if they have any cute shoes that might match this dress," she stammered. "But she's already added extra money to my checking account, so that I can buy whatever dress I want," Tanisha fibbed. "She told me to just meet her at the car when I'm finished. We're going to drive to the Moorland Park Mall to see what kind of shoes they have there too." Even the clerk thinks that my mother should be paying for my prom dress!

"Super! It must be nice! I wish my mother would let me write a check for anything I want!" she smiled. "My name is Margaret. I'll meet you at the register," the clerk finished, her long, red ponytail bouncing on her shoulders as she walked away.

Tanisha closed the dressing room door and puffed her cheeks like a blowfish. She stared at herself in the small dressing room mirror. Liar, liar, pants on fire! When are you going to stop lying? She shook her head dismissively and shrugged. Who cares! I'll never see this sales clerk again. She doesn't need to know that I'm buying this dress myself. Let her think that I'm a spoiled, little rich girl who can write a check for whatever my heart desires. I'm going to prom with Glen Horton! She laughed animatedly.

She rubbed her hand along the soft fabric one more time and smiled. If I look stunning enough, maybe Glen will finally kiss me!

She subtracted the total and stared solemnly at her new balance. Writing the check wiped out almost one third of her hard earned money. It was her most expensive purchase. I'll just have to keep saving to build up my nest egg again. I'm sure I'll get more hours at Save Mart next month. She watched as the clerk gently draped the dress in white tissue paper and placed it in a plastic dress bag, pulling the hanger through a small hole in the top of the bag. Her first dress bag. Tanisha carefully laid the garment bag over her arm. Grinning, she walked back to the mall entrance to wait for the bus. She glanced quickly at her watch. The bus would be arriving in fifteen minutes. Tanisha groaned and sat on the bench, careful to not let the white dress bag touch the ground.

Tanisha was scheduled to take her driver's education test in two weeks. She couldn't wait. She hated taking the bus. Her mother had dropped her off at the mall, but had told her that she couldn't pick her up because she wasn't feeling well and needed to rest. "I'm sure you'll pick out something pretty, Tanisha," Billie Mae said sweetly. Tanisha mumbled thanks and scowled angrily at the car as it drove away. She doesn't get it. Why doesn't she know that she's supposed to help me select my dress, and she's supposed to pay for it? Why is she so clueless? Stop it, Teenie! She's doing the best that she can. She's doing the best that she can. Thanks to Glen, this had become her personal mantra.

A few weeks before, Tanisha found herself talking to Glen about Billie Mae. She hadn't planned to discuss her mother with him, but he unexpectedly asked her about their relationship one day over lunch, and she found herself telling him about Billie's mental illness. Surprised at how comfortable she felt discussing it with him, the details flowed from her mouth like a waterfall. She shared what Dr. Dudley had explained to her about Billie's bipolar disorder and how her condition could be treated with medication. Tanisha even found herself detailing Billie's unpredictable mood swings and the postpartum depression that she'd suffered after her pregnancies. Throughout the disclosure, Glen listened intently and nodded, occasionally stopping her to ask a question. When she finished her Billie tale, Tanisha stared at him curiously, unsure how he would respond. Never having discussed Billie's condition with anyone except her brother, Jack and her father, she braced herself for his reaction.

"That's quite a story," he said. "I'm glad you told me. That helps explain why you and your mother aren't that close," he acknowledged. "But mental illness is more common than people realize," he stated. "People don't talk about it, but a lot of folks have someone with a mental health condition in their family," he suggested. "My dad's sister is schizophrenic," he shrugged. "My dad doesn't talk about it much," he paused. "It's nothing to be ashamed of. I'm sure your mother is doing the best that she can. Remember that," he comforted. "When you find yourself getting angry with her, just tell yourself that she's doing the best that she can. I'll pray for her," he said. "We'd better go so we're not late for the matinee."

Tanisha had stared at him curiously. She'd expected him to start treating her differently, but he hadn't. He'd been the same predictable Glen Horton. He hadn't pulled away or judged her or her mother. He'd only told her that her mother was probably doing the best that she could. Tanisha had never met anyone like him, and she suspected that his values had everything to do with his religious beliefs. He was a church boy.

The day of their first date, he'd gone to church before picking her up at Save Mart. She thought that it was sweet how he bowed his head and said grace before every meal that they shared. His faith was very important to him. She liked that about Glen. It was different. On Sunday afternoons, most of the guys his age were glued in front of the television set watching a sporting event. Not Glen. When she asked him if he missed the Sunday afternoon sports marathons, his reply stunned her. "I like sports a lot," he said. "I'm an athlete. But I love the Lord. And since every morning I awaken expecting God to sit on the throne of my life to guide my day, the least I can do is go to God's house to praise and worship him exclusively for a couple of hours one day a week," he explained. Tanisha had merely smiled weakly, not knowing how to respond.

Aside from Lori Perkins, she'd never met anyone whose life was a living testimony to his faith. Tanisha understood the importance of Glen's faith, but she wasn't prepared for how his faith would impact their budding relationship. Glen still hadn't tried to kiss her. Instead, after each date, Glen would give her a hug and tell her that he would call her later. After their third date, when Glen didn't try to kiss her, she asked her friends for their opinion.

"Tell me the truth," she pleaded. "Do I have halitosis? I can take it. Just tell me! Is my breath bad?"

Her friends stared at her and laughed. "Teenie, you have the freshest breath of anyone that I know," Maria explained. "You are the only person that I know who brushes her teeth after lunch," she paused. "And you don't even have your braces on yet! Besides, you're always sucking on a mint. You do not have halitosis, trust me! I would tell you if you did."

Tanisha exhaled. "Okay. I believe you. That Brian Kraft guy that I kissed at camp would have probably said something if my breath was foul," she said. "Well, what is it? Why hasn't Glen kissed me yet?"

"Have you asked him?" Rashanda asked flatly.

"I'm too nervous," Tanisha blushed. "I don't want to seem too forward."

"Just ask him," Grace encouraged. "He clearly likes you or he wouldn't be hanging out with you every chance he gets."

"I'll wait until prom," Tanisha stated. "If he doesn't try to kiss me on prom night, I'll ask him."

She stared at her watch again. Prom is only two weeks away, so I'll find out soon enough. If he doesn't kiss me at prom, I'll ask him what's going on. Where is that stupid bus! She stood up as the bus turned into the mall parking lot. "Finally! I'm ready to go home," Tanisha said aloud. She smoothed the garment bag over her arm.

"Hold the bus," a voice yelled animatedly. Tanisha glanced over her shoulder and saw a long, red ponytail racing down the path. It was Margaret, the sales clerk. Tanisha held her breath and lowered her gaze. Too late. Margaret recognized her and stared at her curiously. Her gaze asked a million questions. Wishing that she were invisible, Tanisha paid her fare and quickly walked to the back of the bus. She prayed that Margaret didn't follow her. She made herself breathe only when Margaret sat in the front of the bus. Staring aimlessly out the dirty window, Tanisha slumped in her seat, her prom dress cradled like a newborn. Liar, liar, pants on fire!

Chapter 4

Maria: The Root of All Evil

Startled, she quickly slipped the bank statement back into the drawer and continued her homework. Seconds later, her brother's bedroom door slammed. The muffled sounds of The Police bounced from the walls as Sting's voice serenaded her from the hallway. Her eyes roamed the newly decorated office with a newfound clarity. Her mom had hired an interior designer to transform the small room into a study sanctuary. The interior designer, the new furniture and draperies, it all made sense now.

The handmade sign tacked to the room's bulletin board stared at her. Quiet Room Rules: No food, no music and no talking. The sign dangled like a comma, her mother's trademark smiley face signature stamp grinned knowingly at her. She reached to straighten the sign, repositioning the thumbtack and carefully realigning her mom's handiwork.

She squeezed the knob on the top drawer, her mother's drawer. No longer a student herself, Mrs. Wesley used the office to manage the household finances, keeping the family bills in the top drawer. Maria rubbed her hand along the cherry wood desk, the books neatly arranged in alphabetical order atop the matching hutch. She fingered the keyboard of the new Apple computer that was purchased as a surprise for her brother.

When her dad lived in the house, the tiny fourth bedroom had been a storage room, home to abandoned electronics equipment, seasonal clothing and broken toys. Due to the unorganized clutter, the door was seldom open which made the hallway dark. Now the room was painted a soft yellow. The custom draperies matched the colors in the upholstery of the small chair and ottoman that sat in a corner next to a reading lamp. The sun from the south facing window now streamed lovingly into the hallway, illuminating the hall with a soft, warm glow. Mrs. Wesley often read in that sunny corner, curled up in the chair like a cat, an afghan draped across her slim legs. The quiet room had become Mrs. Wesley's favorite room in the house.

Maria carefully moved the interior designer's plans to redesign her mother's bedroom and slipped the bank statement into her notebook. She rolled the desk chair to the window and crawled along the ottoman into the matching chair. She gently pulled the statement from the envelope and stared at the account balance again. $66,122.43. She scratched her head. Her thoughts spun like a top.

I know that she makes decent money at the bank, but they don't pay you your annual salary in cash! Do you get a wad of money when you divorce your husband? Did she get a bonus? Where is she getting all of this cash?

She quickly fumbled through the envelope and noticed deposit slips dating back for the past two years. Each deposit slip was in chronological order and showed the same deposit amount. Seeing a deposit amount that was different, her eyes bulged like a fly. She pulled the deposit slip to her face in disbelief. A deposit for fifty thousand dollars had been made to the account on her mother's birthday, just two weeks before.

Her shoulders tensed as she felt the vibration from the garage door. Standing, she peered out the window and watched as her mom pulled the car into the garage. Maria quickly tucked the bank statement back into the drawer, her heart beat fast like she'd run a mile.

How are you going to ask her about the money, Maria? You weren't supposed to be looking in that drawer anyway. Isn't that the rule? Isn't that what Mommy said? ' I just need one private drawer in the desk, and you and Neal can use the other drawers. But please respect my privacy and don't rummage through my drawer!' Isn't that what she asked? What lie are you going to concoct to ask her about all of that money?

"Maria and Neal!" Mrs. Wesley's voice bellowed at the bottom of the stairs. "Come down here and help get the groceries out of the car, please," she ordered loudly.

"Here I come, Mom," Maria replied.

"Maria, knock on your brother's door and make sure that he heard me," Mrs. Wesley instructed. "And tell him to turn that music down, Sweetie!" she shouted.

"Will do," she replied, turning the knob on her brother's door.

The music blared through the open door. "What is wrong with you?" Neal demanded. "How many times have I told you to knock before you open my door?" Neal shouted. "One day you're going to get an eyeful!"

"Whatever, dude," Maria groaned, still not comfortable with the idea that her baby brother was now a young man of fifteen, complete with facial hair and muscles.

"Speak your piece," Neal ordered.

"Mom wants you to turn down the music and come downstairs to help bring the groceries in," Maria finished. She took a half step back and then changed her mind. "Come now,

Neal! I'm not going to bring them in by myself again," she whined. "That's not fair, especially since I have to put the groceries away!" she explained. "Since you eat everything in the house, the least you could do is tote them from the car!"

"Beat it!" Neal barked, slamming the door, barely missing his sister's face.

Maria stopped in the hall bathroom. She stared at her reflection curiously, wondering if her mother would know that she'd been snooping. She felt guilty. Will Liz be able to see the guilt? She brushed her hair and smiled widely. Too fake. Just be natural.

"Neal! Maria! Get down here now!" Mrs. Wesley's voice bellowed from the bottom of the stairs.

Startled, Maria dropped the hairbrush into the sink and frowned. Seconds later, the thud from Neal's gigantic feet hit the stairs. She peeked, trying to steal a glimpse of his technique, still perplexed at his ability to descend the stairs two at a time.

He'd started the two stair descent trick a few weeks after his twelfth birthday. The first time she'd seen him do it, Maria had stared in amazement. She begged him to teach her.

"It's just a feel. I really can't explain it," he'd shrugged.

She pleaded with him for tips, determined to try the trick herself. "But when you're skipping a step on the way down, how do you know where to land your feet so that you don't trip?" she'd asked.

She remembered him laughing and shaking his head casually. "The stairs aren't moving, knucklehead! They don't have legs," he'd said. "And each stair is the same distance apart, so you should be able to feel where the next step is," he'd boasted, running down the stairs two at a time backwards this time.

"Show off!" she'd screamed. "Teach me how to do it the basic way, Neal! I know I can do this! I just have to watch you closely. Do it again, Neal," she'd pleaded. "Do it slower this time."

He complied at least half a dozen times. She tried it half as many times. Each time, she ended in a heap at the bottom of the stairs. She agreed to try it one more time, her ankle paying the price for this last bit of bravado. Maria winced like a wounded fawn, too proud to let her younger brother witness the crocodile tears that pooled in her eyes. Gripping her throbbing ankle, she could feel it swelling like dough when the yeast is added. As she lay in a crumpled heap, she felt an arm around her shoulders and one under her knees as her legs were swiftly hoisted into the air. She remembered being amazed at how quickly and effortlessly he had picked her up. She weighed almost one hundred pounds. Placing her gently on the sofa, he tucked a pillow under her ankle and brought her an ice pack. "Just chill, Maria," he'd said. "I sprain my ankle playing ball all the time. If it were broken, you'd be screaming. Just keep it elevated and iced," he ordered.

"Mom and Dad are going to kill me!" she groaned. "They left me in charge, and they told us not to horse around," she whined. "They're going to peel my head when I tell them how this happened!" she screeched hysterically.

Rummaging through the refrigerator for his tenth snack of the day, her brother shrugged his shoulders. "We'll just tell them that you twisted your ankle playing basketball with me on the driveway," he'd said. "That's a safe, parent approved reason to have a sprained ankle," he said casually. "Whose sandwich is this?" he asked studying the contents of a doggie bag in the refrigerator. "It's mine now," he chuckled without waiting for a response. "I'm going outside to work on my jump shot," he mumbled in between bites.

Standing at the top of the stairs, she held the banister, missing the closeness that she and Neal had once shared. She remembered being so excited to have a younger brother. When she was five, and he was three, he'd been her living doll. They were inseparable. But as they got older, their closeness thinned, becoming like a vapor. It was her fault. When she turned ten, she thought that his desire to play Uno and board games with her was trivial and childish. At eleven, she banned him from following her around the park. "You play with your friends, and I'll play with mine, but don't follow me around, scumbag!" she'd mocked. He'd complied. When she turned twelve, she banned him from entering her bedroom, placing a "Keep Out Neal" sign on her door. It seemed that each year, there was a new restriction placed on their relationship. Now a muscular, young man of fifteen, Maria struggled to remember the last time that she and her baby brother had said anything civil to each other or teamed together to demonstrate a united front against the common enemy that was their parents. The sprained ankle caper was the last one that she could recall. Now all they did was fight. If they weren't fighting, they were tattling on each other. Neal is over six feet tall now and strong as an ox. I still only weigh about one hundred pounds, so I know he could pick me up like a sack of potatoes if I fell down the stairs again, but would he? Of course he would, Maria. He's your brother. Should I tell him about the bank statement? Maybe he knows why Mom has so much money in her account.

She listened as their mother scolded him. "I called you down here five minutes ago. You know I don't like to repeat myself, Neal Wesley! It's warm outside, and there are perishables in the car," she scolded. "I shouldn't have to shop for the groceries and tote them into the house too, especially since you eat everything in the house.

The least you can do is bring the food inside. You're a young man, that's your job," she ranted. Maria counted to ten and tiptoed down the stairs

"Sorry, it took me so long, Mom. I had to use the bathroom," Maria explained. "Did you get me a new toothbrush?" she asked.

"Hi sweetie, I did," her mother explained. "When you put the groceries away, Maria, please remember to separate the meat in the plastic bags so we don't freeze the large portions," she yawned. "I'm pooped. I'm going to take a quick nap," she explained.

Maria's heart raced, and her courage hid behind her fear like a child hiding behind her mother afraid to meet a clown. "I forgot to ask you what you got for your birthday," Maria stalled. "Did your aunts take you out to lunch like they normally do?"

Mrs. Wesley pulled groceries from the brown paper bags. "Yes. You know they never forget my birthday. We had a nice lunch, and they gave me my usual perfume and bubble bath gift sets," she offered, rinsing grapes in a colander.

"That's so thoughtful. I'm glad that they still treat you special on your birthday after all these years," Maria offered sweetly. "Tell me again how you became so close to your aunts."

Mrs. Wesley stacked the groceries on the counter, inspecting the egg carton carefully. "Well," she said slowly. "Once my mother died, her sisters just naturally stepped in and did all of the special things that my mother used to do. They baked me and your uncle Emmett our favorite cakes for our birthdays and made sure that we had the proper clothes to wear to different family events," she paused. "If we needed treats at school, they took care of it. They just filled the gap," she continued. "They were raising their own children too, mind you, but they also mothered your uncle and me," she finished. "They were wonderful. I don't know how I would have turned out without them," she sighed. "Now don't get me wrong," she offered quickly. "Your grandpa is a great dad, but he couldn't be a mother too."

Maria smiled softly. "Grandpa is awesome," Maria agreed. "What did he get you for your birthday?" she asked sweetly.

Pulling her head back, she frowned as her brother's large frame leaned into her space, his cheek against her ear. "Brown noser!" he whispered as he brushed by her. She smacked his arm with her free hand.

"You know your grandpa isn't big on gifts. He never has been," Mrs. Wesley said. "Why are you so curious about my birthday gifts anyway?" she asked.

"No reason," she lied. "We just haven't had a chance to chat, and I was just trying to make small talk while we put away the groceries," she offered casually. She reached for the gallon size plastic bags and repackaged the meat, rinsing the pork chops in the sink first. "Mom, since I'll be a senior in the fall," she stuttered. "The business economics teacher suggests that we learn how to write checks so that we're comfortable balancing a checkbook when we go to college," she continued.

"Wash your hands, Maria," Mrs. Wesley instructed. "I don't want you to get sick handling raw meat."

"I will, Mom," Maria said. "I'll wash them after I repackage the chicken. But let me finish what I was saying. The next time you balance your checkbook, can I watch you so I can learn how to do it?"

Mrs. Wesley shrugged. "Sure, baby. I think that's a fine idea!" she agreed gripping a head of iceberg lettuce and tossing it into the colander. She turned slowly, her finger resting on the tip of her nose. "On second thought," she offered. "Why don't I just open an account for you so that you can have your own checking account now? I was going to open one for you your senior year in high school anyway," she said.

"Oh," Maria said surprised. "I guess that's cool. But my checkbook won't have that many entries since I don't have any bills to pay, I won't have a reason to write any checks," she offered quickly. "And I want to learn how you reconcile the account."

"Good point," Mrs. Wesley agreed. "I hadn't thought about that."

Maria watched as Neal ripped open a bag of cookies and grabbed six, shoveling them into his mouth whole and chewing noisily. "That was the last bag from the car," he groaned. "My work here is done, people. I'm going back to my room to chill," he stated flatly. He peeked his head around the corner. "I'm expecting a call from Lisa so don't get on the phone, Maria!" he ordered as he walked away.

"You can't tell me not to get on the phone, you creep," Maria screamed behind him. "If I want to use the phone, I'll use the phone! Besides, I can't believe you're dating that scummy girl anyway."

"Who said anything about dating her?" Neal yelled back laughing loudly.

"Mom! Did you hear that?" Maria asked. "Did you hear what he said? He should not be hanging out with Lisa," she stated. "She's trailer park trash!"

"Maria!" Mrs. Wesley scolded. "Why would you call her that?" she said. "We know Lisa's family. They don't live in a trailer. They live in a nice home. Besides, he said that they're not dating," she continued. "Neal and Lisa have known each other since pre-school. They're just friends."

Maria stared at her mom in disbelief. "Mom, are you really that clueless? Did you hear how he said it? 'Who said anything about dating her?'" she mocked, her eyebrow raised suspiciously. "Lisa isn't the same little Lisa from pre-school. She has a really bad rep," Maria paused. "You know what, never mind."

"She has a really bad what?" Mrs. Wesley asked. "I didn't hear what you said. Finish your thought, sweetie."

Maria slanted her eyes and continued. "She has a really bad reputation, Mom. And you shouldn't want your son getting caught up with her," Maria whispered.

Mrs. Wesley continued to put groceries on the counter. "That's so cute," she cooed. "You're protective of your little brother. That's so sweet to see," Mrs. Wesley finished. "I was the same way with your Uncle Emmett. Once he started showing an interest in girls, no one was good enough for my little brother."

"It's not that, Mom. But Lisa is really bad news now," Maria stressed. "I don't even want to tell you some of the things that I've heard about her."

Mrs. Wesley stretched her arms to the ceiling. "My back is really hurting. I really think I'm going to lay down and take a quick cat nap. I'll be in the quiet room."

"Mom! Did you hear me?" Maria groaned.

"I heard you, sweetie," Mrs. Wesley said softly. "People have been making up stories about other people for years. They especially like to make up stories about pretty girls once they start dating. It's as old as time. You can't believe half of the stuff people say. They may just be jealous of Lisa, so they're making up stories about her," she paused. "Remember, unless you've seen her do something despicable with your own eyes, you can't believe it."

"Mom, no one uses the word 'despicable' anymore," Maria sighed.

"Why not? Did they remove it from the dictionary?" she asked. "I dare say they did not. So, as long as it's still in the dictionary, I'll use it at my pleasure," she giggled, waving her hand in the air. "And next you're going to tell me that no one says 'dare say not' anymore either," she teased. "Now did you personally witness Lisa doing anything despicable or dastardly?" she asked.

Maria shook her head. "No," she admitted. "I didn't see her do anything, but the people who told me are reliable sources," she pleaded. "And don't say dastardly, Mom. It makes you sound old."

"Tsk, tsk," she scolded. "The people who told you," she repeated. "And they probably didn't see her do anything either. It's just a malicious rumor like I suspected. People are crucifying this poor girl without any evidence," she stated flatly drying her hands on a dish towel and turning to face her daughter. "And by the way, I am old, so I can say 'dastardly' if I choose," she quipped. "You must learn to rise above such pettiness, Maria," she sang. "Just rise and soar like an eagle above the petty gossip and rumors! Soar!" she roared, her fist pumping the air. "Pledge that you will not give any energy to slanderous gossip!" she chirped. "But seriously, that makes me so sad. Things haven't changed much since I was in high school. It sounds like the school is blaspheming Lisa and crucifying her like they did Jesus. But at least Jesus had a trial," she said softly.

Maria laughed. "Mother! You are so dramatic! How can you compare Lisa to Jesus?" she asked. "And is blaspheme the new word? Everybody is using that word lately."

"It's a great word," Mrs. Wesley defended. "And I'm not comparing Lisa to Jesus. I'm merely suggesting that she's being convicted without the benefit of a trial. At least Jesus was tried," she paused and studied Maria's face. "By whom, Maria?" Mrs.

Wesley asked. "Let's see if you've been paying attention in Bible study. Who put Jesus on trial?"

"Pontius Pilate. Everyone knows that, Mom," Maria groaned.

"That is correct!" her mother exclaimed.

"Okay, Mom," Maria groaned. "I get it. But please spare me the religious lecture right now."

Mrs. Wesley hugged Maria's waist, and gave her a quick peck on the cheek. "I'll be in the quiet room. Don't let me rest for more than an hour, okay? I don't want to sleep the day away."

"When are you going to teach me how to balance your checkbook?" Maria asked quickly.

"That's right. That's what we were talking about before we started crucifying your brother's friend, Lisa," she remembered. "I should be getting another bank statement next week," she yawned. "We'll sit down and you can watch me do it. It's quite boring actually."

"Perfect!" Maria said excitedly.

"I dare say, Maria. You seem awfully excited about this," Mrs. Wesley noticed. "I didn't know that you had such an interest in banking and finance. What brought this about?"

"Who knows?" Maria said. "It's my newfound curiosity! Neal's interested in girls now, and I'm suddenly interested in money and banking!"

Chapter 5

Rashanda: College Chill

The rain beat on the roof in a steady stream. Pitter patter, pitter patter, rat tat a tat tat tat tat. The soft, comforting rhythm resembled the sound of Gregory Hines' tap dancing feet. Rashanda watched the rain stream down her window pane. Breathing through her mouth, she sighed. She liked the sound of rain. It soothed her like a blanket warmed in the dryer, hugging her shoulders protectively. She snuggled into her blanket and inhaled, missing the smell of the fabric softener that her mother used in the laundry. She breathed harder this time. She smelled nothing. She tried it again. Still nothing. Rashanda blew her swollen nose, tossing the tissue into the growing stack at the foot of her bed. Too tired to walk across the room and fetch her wastebasket, she kicked the soiled tissues to the floor, creating a tissue pyramid. She didn't care that her mother would lecture her about the germ tower that she was building.

She dialed Ian's number once more. The phone rang eight times. She let it ring three more times before hanging up. She'd been trying to reach him for the last few days, but hadn't been able to catch him in his dorm room. She knew his class schedule by heart. He had Advanced Biochemistry on Mondays, Wednesdays and Fridays at eight o'clock a.m. followed by Advanced Circuits at ten o'clock. He usually worked out in the gym or swam laps in the pool between eleven and noon. At twelve thirty, he had lunch in the cafeteria before heading to his biology class. Tuesdays and Thursdays were his light days, and he only had an English class and his science labs. He tutored every day until five o'clock in the afternoon, had dinner in the cafeteria, and relaxed in his room for an hour before heading to the library to study. Ian sometimes studied until well past midnight. She memorized his schedule his first week at Northwestern. She often found herself daydreaming about him and liked glancing at the time and knowing what he was doing. But this week was different. She hadn't been able to catch him during his usual routine. She glanced at the clock. It was eleven thirty two. Too late to call. Besides, the phone was probably unplugged anyway.

Ian's roommate was an early riser and preferred to study in the morning. He went to bed at eleven o'clock every night. He awakened at six o'clock each morning for his lakeside run before heading to the library. Ian had nicknamed his roommate AM. Rashanda didn't know what his real name was, she only knew him as AM. When they were getting to know each other, Ian and AM had established a series of roommate rules, one of which was a no phone calls after eleven o'clock practice. AM had explained that anyone calling that late was calling with bad news, and bad news could wait until the morning to be shared. Ian had laughed and agreed. Rashanda knew that AM religiously unplugged the phone at eleven o'clock to ensure that his slumber was not disturbed. She twirled the phone cord and placed the receiver back in its cradle. She wanted to talk to Ian.

She had the flu and wanted to hear his voice. She wrapped her blanket around her shoulders and climbed out of bed, toppling her tissue tower. She stepped into her slippers and stumbled into the kitchen for a snack. Feed a fever, starve a cold. Is that how it goes? Or is it feed a cold, starve a fever? Well, I have a fever and a cold, and I'm starving!

She made herself a mustard sandwich, squeezing brown and yellow mustard on the bread and spreading the concoction sloppily. Licking the glob around the crust, she swirled the mixture in her mouth, her taste buds barely awake. With her free hand, Rashanda tossed the knife into the sink. A glass rattled. Cringing, she peered into the sink, praying that she hadn't broken the glass, her mother's nagging reminder about tossing flatware into the sink echoed in her ears. Wrapping the gooey sandwich in a paper towel, she took a bite, and shuffled back into her bedroom. She savored the tangy flavor combination. Her secret treat. She always craved this comfort food when she was sick. As far back as she could recall, she remembered dipping her spoon into the mustard jar and gulping the spicy spread. One time, her mom caught her and made her spread the mustard on bread, insisting that she add a piece of ham or turkey. She refused. Mustard sandwiches became her trademark. She didn't recall when or why she decided to add spicy brown mustard to the sandwich. But the spicy mixture always made her smile and sometimes served to open her sinus passages. She took another bite and rested her hand on the phone. Maybe his roommate is out of town and the phone isn't unplugged. The phone rang. Startled, she dropped the sandwich on her bedspread.

"Hello," she said quickly, her voice but a whisper.

"Hey, you," Ian whispered. "I didn't wake you did I?"

"Ian!" she said loudly praying that the one ring hadn't awakened her parents. "No. I was awake," she said softer.

"I'm glad," he said. "I was afraid to call this late, but if your parents had answered, I was going to hang up," he confessed. "I didn't even hear the phone ring."

"It only rang once," she shared. "I was sitting by the phone trying to decide if I should call you again," she whispered softly. "I've been trying to reach you for the past few days," she whined. "Where've you been?"

"I'm sorry, Shanda. I've been crazy busy getting ready for finals, and spending a lot of time tutoring my chemistry students," he said. "I miss you."

Her heart skipped a beat. "I miss you too," she sang into the phone, not caring if her parents stormed into her room at that moment.

She picked up her sandwich and frowned at the yellow, sticky stain on her bedspread. She slipped her head under her bedspread and listened as Ian shared the details of his busy week.

"And so since some of the students are willing to pay double to be tutored extra hours," he paused. "I've been squeezing extra tutoring time into my already jam packed schedule. That's why I haven't been in my room after dinner. I've been hustling the cash, baby!" he teased.

She smiled widely under her blanket tent. "I understand. I just missed you," she whined.

"You sound congested. Are you sick?" he asked.

"Yes," she pouted. "I have the flu. But hearing your voice makes me feel better. Where are you calling me from now?" she asked taking a bite of her sandwich.

"I'm in my room. AM is out tonight if you can believe that," he laughed. "I came home from the library, and his bed was still made, and his shower slippers were in the corner. I don't see his backpack, so he may be studying," he surmised. "Either that or he's out creeping," he laughed. "I hope he's creeping. He needs to lighten up and live!"

"Ian!" Rashanda scolded. "That's so not nice. What if he comes back and hears you?"

Ian laughed loudly. "I don't care if he hears me," he boasted. "I'm always telling him that he needs to lighten up and hike to north campus and hang out at a fraternity party on Wednesday nights," he said. "But he's so not into the frat boy thing. He's such a study nerd," he teased. "I should talk, right? I'm an egg head pre-med chemistry geek. But at least I have a girlfriend. He doesn't have a life at all," he shared. "Are you chewing? What are you munching on this late?"

"A mustard sandwich," Rashanda confessed. "Remember, I told you that it's my comfort food when I'm sick?"

"I remember. I can't believe you don't put any meat on it. I can't imagine eating bread and mustard. I hope it opens up your sinuses," he yawned. "Sorry about that, but it's been a long day."

Rashanda swallowed her last bite of sandwich. "If you think mustard sandwiches are gross, Teenie eats mayonnaise and jelly sandwiches," she laughed.

"Okay, now that sounds really nasty!" he groaned. "It must be something in the Newberry East water that makes you crave weird concoctions!"

"Are you sure that you can make it back to take me to prom, Ian?" she asked cautiously. "It sounds like you're pretty busy with finals."

"Of course I'll make it back to take you to prom," Ian assured. "I have it on my calendar. The good news is that the finals for my Monday-Wednesday-Friday classes don't start until Wednesday. I have two finals on Wednesday and one on Friday," he shared. "So

I'll really only miss studying Saturday," he paused. "I won't be able to hang out with you on Sunday. I'll have to get back to campus. I feel bad about that, but I can't give up two days worth of studying, especially since I'm cutting into my own study time tutoring my students."

"I understand. I'm just glad that you'll be able to come. I wouldn't go if you couldn't take me," Rashanda confessed. "It wouldn't be the same."

"Well that's good to know," Ian said confidently. "I'm glad to hear that you haven't replaced me yet," he said softly.

Rashanda furrowed her brow. "Replaced you?" she repeated. "You're the one who's surrounded by cute college co-eds! When I couldn't reach you on the phone, I was worried that you'd replaced me," she whined. "I can hear the little she-devils now. Can you tutor me a little bit more, Ian?" she asked in a falsetto tone. "I think I need help with the periodic chart," she continued. "I bet they bat their eyelashes at you and invite you to tutor them in their dorm room," she groaned. "Ian, it's hot in my dorm room, so just wear your swimming trunks," she snickered.

Ian laughed loudly. "I do get some interesting offers," he confessed. "You'd be surprised. College girls are a bit aggressive. They do not wait for the guy to make the first move, let me tell you," he shared. "But you don't have anything to worry about. I carry your picture in my wallet and whip it out anytime I feel someone getting fresh," he assured. "I'm all yours!"

"You should pin my photo to your chest," she laughed.

"I love it when you act jealous," Ian offered. "I love you, Rashanda."

"I love you too, Ian," Rashanda exhaled, his voice and words calming her insecurities.

"Hold on for a second, Rashanda. What's up AM!" Ian said animatedly. "Where you been, dude?" he asked. "I almost called campus security to put out an All Points Bulletin on you, Roomie! You're never out this late."

Rashanda couldn't make out AM's muffled response. "Well, it's about time, dude!" Ian squealed. "I want to hear details. Let me hang up with my girl," Ian explained.

"Hey, Rashanda, AM just came in, and I need to talk to him for a few. Besides, you're sick, it's late and you need your rest," he stated. "I'll call you in a couple of days, okay? Goodnight!"

"Okay," she sighed. "Call me tomorrow or..." her words trailed away as he hung up the phone.

Rashanda reached for another tissue and wiped her nose, flinging it into the air. The tissue sailed across the room like a kite in flight, narrowly missing her waste basket. She climbed out of bed to fetch a wet cloth, casually tossing the tissue into the trash as she passed by. With a wet wash cloth in hand, she blotted the sandwich stain on her bedspread, careful not to rub the sticky mess further into the comforter. She smiled, pleased that the mustard stain had not set. Feeling a chill, she opened her closet to get her robe. Her prom dress greeted her. She caressed the soft green fabric and grinned. Ian loves me. He's coming back to take me to prom!

Chapter 6

Grace: The Telephone Game

Grace watched as her parents slowly backed the family car down the driveway, her dad's arm hugged the top of the passenger seat as he guided the car onto the street in reverse. Her mother sat frozen like a statue, careful not to let her head block his already limited vision. The car lurched as he shifted into drive, the large sedan rumbling down the street like a big cat. She guessed that they would be gone at least four hours. Factoring in travel time, plus lunch and a matinee, they might be gone as many as five hours. They always lingered over lunch at the Baker's Square pie restaurant, arguing as her dad tried to convince her mother that one small piece of pie wouldn't hurt his sugar level.

Her dad had recently been diagnosed with Type 2 diabetes, which required him to take daily shots to regulate his insulin levels. He gave himself injections in his thigh without complaint, but the restrictions placed on his diet were another matter. He had a sweet tooth, and hated to give up his daily desserts. As a compromise, her mom had started buying sugar free cookies, cakes and pies, but he complained that they didn't taste the same. He missed his regular diet. Grace got sad just thinking about it. This was yet another sign that her parents were aging. Her dad was turning seventy next year.

Grace called Maria. "The coast is clear," she said. "My folks just left for the movies. They should be gone for at least four or five hours," she explained.

She flipped through a magazine and waited for her friends. Ten minutes later, she heard a car door slam and smiled as her friends climbed out of the car. She watched as Maria manually rolled down the windows in her mom's car. She counted the days until she could take her driver's license test.

Grace met them at the door. "Hey, ladies!" she said cheerily. "That was quick!"

Maria smiled. "I couldn't wait to come over here," she said. "My mom is on the war path again!" she groaned. "Either she's on the rag, or she's experiencing early menopause!"

Tanisha swatted Maria's arm. "Maria, what did your mom do now? Let me guess. She wouldn't let you charge five hundred dollars for a new Gucci bag?" Tanisha groaned.

"No. It's worse than that," Maria whined. "She told me that I have to start using my own money for the gas that I burn in the car," she said indignantly. "She said that I can either get a job or use part of my allowance toward gas," she finished. "Have you heard of anything so foolish?"

Rashanda laughed at her friend. "We should just call the Department of Children and Family Services and have your mother claimed unfit," she laughed.

"Exactly," Tanisha agreed. "I can see the headlines now: World's Most Perfect Mother Loses Parental Rights Because Daughter Claims She's Unfit for Requiring Pampered Teen to Buy Her Own Gas," Tanisha teased. "You're tripping, Maria!"

Maria rolled her eyes at her friends. "You guys are teasing me, but this is serious. I can't believe she would make me use my own money to pay for my gas," she whined. "That's her job. She's the parent, and she's supposed to pay for everything as long as I live in her house."

"What does your dad think?" Grace asked.

Maria waved her hand across her face dismissively. "He agrees with my mother and says that if I'm paying for my own gas, I'll only drive places that I really want to go," she groaned. "He's tripping too."

"Well, you are seventeen now, Maria," Tanisha said softly. "You could get a part-time job. You could work at your favorite clothing store and get an employee discount," she encouraged. "You'd be making money and saving money at the same time."

Maria rolled her eyes into the back of her head. "Teenie, now you sound like Liz Wesley. She suggested the same thing," she groaned.

Tanisha smiled at the comparison to Mrs. Wesley, her maternal idol.

"All I know is that Liz's bank account is quite fat these days," Maria admitted. "As far as I'm concerned, I don't need to be paying for anything."

"Did you ask your mom about the bank statement that you saw?" Rashanda asked.

"Not exactly," Maria confessed. "She's going to show me how to balance her checkbook, so I'll ask her then."

Tanisha looked at her watch and tapped her wrist. "Let's not get distracted, ladies," Tanisha said. "Let's stay on task and remember why we're here. We need to call Charles Lovett!" she beamed. "Are you ready, Grace?"

Grace took a deep breath and forced a smile, her heart beat wildly in her chest. "I guess I'm as ready as I'll ever be," she admitted.

Rashanda patted Grace's back softly. "We're here for you, Grace. We're in this together," she reminded.

Maria scowled on the sofa, consumed with her own teenage drama. "Maria!" Teenie shouted. "Stop pouting! You're the one making the first call, remember? Do you have your script?" she asked.

Maria fumbled in her purse and pulled out a sheet of paper, neatly folded in quarters. "It is right here, your highness," Maria groaned.

"Place some cheerleader pep in your voice," Teenie coached. "This is a big step in Project Strong," she reminded. "Let's rehearse what you're going to say. I'll be Charles Lovett."

Maria unfolded the piece of paper and rolled her eyes at Teenie, she painted a smile on her face when she looked at Grace. "I'll put a smile in my voice for Grace," Maria said. "Although I'm really not in the mood to do this today," she admitted. "I can't believe that you chicks agree with my mother that I need to get a job!"

Rashanda tossed a pillow at Maria's head, narrowly missing her face. "Let it rest, Maria. Everything is not about you. This is about Grace," she scolded. "Let's practice."

Maria smiled again and stood up. "Brring, Brrring!" Maria imitated.

Tanisha scowled. "Maria," she said softly. "It's not necessary to mimic the ringing phone."

"If I'm going to get into character," Maria said defiantly. "I need to operate under real circumstances," she said. "Brring, Brring!" she repeated.

"Hello," Teenie said gruffly, imitating a male's voice.

Rashanda and Grace giggled in the corner.

"Hello," Maria said sweetly. "Is this the Lovett residence?" she asked.

"Don't forget to ask if it's the Charles Lovett residence," Tanisha whispered.

Maria scowled at Teenie and continued. "Is the lady of the house at home?" she asked.

"No she isn't," Teenie said.

"Is there a better time to reach Mrs. Lovett?" Maria asked.

"There is no Mrs. Lovett," Tanisha said firmly. "Who's calling?"

"What if there is a Mrs. Lovett?" Grace interrupted. "What do we say then?"

Assuming her regular tone, Tanisha stretched her arms over her head, briefly sniffing her moist armpits and frowning slightly. "If he says she's not here, Maria will ask him if there's a better time to reach her," Tanisha explained.

"My story is that I'm with a survey company and I'm conducting a survey on married couples," Maria interrupted. "I'll quickly ask him how long they've been married," she finished.

"Oh, I get it," Grace said. "This way we'll know if it's the same wife he was married to when he knew my mother or a new wife."

"Bingo!" Rashanda grinned. "If it's a new wife, she can't really get angry over something that happened before she was married to him," she explained. "But if it's the wife he was married to when he had the affair with your mom," Rashanda paused dramatically, briskly rubbing her palms together like two sticks creating friction to start a fire. "We'll have to proceed with extreme caution."

Grace shuddered when she heard the word affair. "I wish there was another word we could use," she admitted. "Saying the word "affair" sounds so sleazy. It makes my mom sound like the evil other woman who was sneaking around with someone else's husband," she said meekly.

The other girls glanced at each other and shrugged, their eyes resting on Teenie to comment. She rubbed her palms along her thighs. "I agree," she admitted. "When you put it that way, it doesn't sound very nice," she said softly. "But that's kinda what happened, Grace. He was married and your mom was his student," she continued. "Your mom knew that he was married," she reminded. "But I'm sure your mom never intended for anyone to get hurt."

"They never do," Maria groaned loudly fumbling in her purse. "My dad's secretary likes to remind me and my brother all the time that she wasn't trying to break up our family, she just fell in love with my dad," Maria mocked, plopping a mint in her mouth. "Whatever, dude. She can sugar coat it all she wants," she smacked, the mint rolling across her tongue. "But she was sneaking around with a married man, and now my parents are divorced. Period. Dot. End of story," she said coldly. "Like it or not, Grace," she paused slurping on her peppermint. "Your mom had an affair with a married man and got pregnant with you. It's not a fairy tale story, but it's your story. You were conceived from an affair. Accept it and get over it!"

Rashanda and Teenie glared at Maria. "Maria!" they shrieked simultaneously. Rashanda's words were caught in her throat.

"I can't believe that you just said that!" Tanisha barked loudly. "You don't know what was going on between Grace's mom and Charles Lovett," she continued. "For all we know he was planning to leave his wife and they were going to get married," she offered glancing softly at Grace.

"She's right," Rashanda agreed. "We shouldn't judge her without having all of the facts."

"That sounds so fairy tale. You can believe that if you want, but all I know is that Grace's mom, Lydia. That was her name right?" she asked no one in particular. "Lydia wasn't much older than we are when she got pregnant with you," Maria reminded flippantly. "If she was a freshman in college, she must have been eighteen or maybe nineteen. Or she could have been younger than that. We're seventeen, and we've already created a pact not to mess around with a boy if he already has a girlfriend. Am I right?" she reminded. "Some girls just have a higher moral compass than others," Maria shrugged. "In fact, maybe this is another area where white girls are different than black girls," she giggled. "Black girls eat. White girls don't. And white girls will mess around with someone else's man, and black girls won't." she chuckled. "It sounds like the lyrics to a song," she hummed.

Tanisha bit her lip, her thoughts drifted back to Brian Kraft for the first time in a long time. She considered sharing her secret, telling her friends that she had known that Brian Kraft had a girlfriend when they fooled around at camp, but quickly changed her mind. Her secret was buried with Lori Perkins. Maybe I'll tell them one day. Or maybe I won't.

"I don't think that's true," Tanisha offered softly. "That's another silly stereotype, Maria. Remember, I told you that my skinny white cabin mates at camp ate like black girls. So the black girls eat, white girls don't theory was disproved a couple of years ago," she paused. "Besides, I don't think that a white girl is any more or less likely to mess around with someone who is already in a relationship," she shared. "I don't think it's a racial thing at all. I really don't," Tanisha finished.

"I agree with Teenie," Grace said softly. "I think the fact that my mom was white and my dad was black didn't have anything to do with it. Or the fact that he was married for that matter. There are black women who mess around with married men too," Grace finished.

"She's right, Maria," Rashanda offered. "My mother's sister left her first husband for a guy at work. He was married too, and he was black," Rashanda shared. "Sometimes people just don't honor their marriage vows, black or white," she shrugged. "My aunt's second marriage is so tripped out too," she snickered. "Because they snuck around and had an affair to be together, neither one trusts the other," she laughed. "So now they're totally paranoid that the other one is going to cheat. It serves them right."

"Well, I disagree," Maria said boldly. "My dad's secretary is white, and she knew that my dad was married, but she went after him anyway. Grace's mom was white and messed around with a married man," she continued. "I think I'm on to something," she finished.

Grace shifted her weight and stared out the window. "I don't think that my mom went after him because he was married, just like I don't think that my dad went after her because she was white. I just think they fell in love. You can't help whom you fall in love with," she said.

"Well, if you're going to create stereotypes," Rashanda said. "Do you think it was a coincidence that the men involved in the affairs were black?"

"Welcome to the dark side," Maria beamed. "Now you're feeling me!"

"Enough of this foolishness," Tanisha said loudly. "Let's call him now before we run out of time," she said. "If he doesn't answer, we want to be able to keep calling before Grace's parents get back." She handed the phone to Maria. "Now remember, if an answering machine picks up, just hang up, Maria," she instructed. "Are you ready, Grace?"

"I think so," Grace said. "I wish Justine could be here, but she has a date tonight."

"A date? I'm so excited for her," Rashanda beamed. "I'm glad she's adjusting to her new life living in the city," she paused. "She didn't mention that she had met anyone at her new school," Rashanda finished.

Grace shrugged. "I don't think he goes to her high school. I think he's older," she explained. "I didn't get into the details because it was late, and her mom was nagging her to get off the phone," she explained.

"I'm dialing for donuts," Maria said softly.

"Dialing for donuts?" Rashanda asked. "What does that mean?"

"I have no idea," Maria giggled. "But I'm hungry, and I want a donut, so I'm dialing," she laughed.

The girls giggled loudly as she dialed the number. She waved her hand quickly in the air and pressed her finger to her lips. "Uh, hello," she said seriously. "May I speak with the lady of the house?"

The girls crowded around the receiver. "Excuse me?" the male voice said.

"Have I reached the Charles Lovett residence?" she asked sweetly, forgetting to follow the prepared script.

"Yes. This is Charles Lovett," he said. "Who's calling?"

All eyes focused on Grace. Grace held her breath.

"My name is Jessica Tanner, and I'm with the Married Couples Research Center, in New Jersey," she continued. "You and your wife have been chosen to participate in our random survey. How long have you been married, Mr. Lovett?" she asked sweetly.

There was a long pause. "I'm not married," he replied. "I'm a widower," he said softly.

Maria's eyes panned the girls' faces. They hadn't prepared for this response.

"Hello," Mr. Lovett said. "Are you still there?"

"Uh, yes," Maria continued. "I'm terribly sorry, sir. How long ago did your wife pass?" she asked softly. She shrugged her shoulders and tossed her hands into the air studying Tanisha's face for further direction. Tanisha glanced at her notes and shrugged back.

"She died four years ago," Mr. Lovett offered.

"Did you have any children together?" Maria asked quickly.

"Excuse me? I'm sorry, I'd like to help you, but I don't have time to answer any more questions, I was heading out," Mr. Lovett said politely.

"Thank you for your time, sir," Maria offered. "And I'm sorry about your wife." She gently placed the phone on the coffee table and grinned sheepishly, unsure of what to say next.

The girls stared at Grace for her reaction. Grace swallowed and remembered to breathe. "Wow! I just heard my father's voice for the first time," she said softly. Her words almost inaudible, the girls leaned in closer to listen. "I wondered how I would feel when I heard his voice," she shrugged. "He sounds nice, I guess." Staring at her intently, the girls nodded in agreement as Grace fidgeted with the tassel on her mother's favorite afghan. "He's a widower. I wasn't expecting that response," she admitted. "Now what do we do?" she exhaled loudly.

Tanisha patted Grace's knee. "We proceed with Plan A. This sounds strange, but the fact that his wife is dead is better than him being divorced. At least we don't have to worry about opening up a can of worms that was buried almost twenty years ago," she grinned before quickly covering her mouth with her hand. "I don't mean to disrespect your mother, Grace," she said quickly. "I don't mean that your mother is a buried can of worms," she explained. "I was referring to the situation," she continued. "Anyway, at this point, it doesn't matter if his wife knew about you or not," she smiled as she scribbled something on the paper in her hand.

"She's right," Rashanda agreed. "This is working out according to our plan. We confirmed that it's Charles Lovett. He's not married any longer, so we don't have to worry about a wife getting the letter and reading it. Now we can just send the letter and wait and see what happens," she finished. "Do you have the letter, Teenie?"

Tanisha reached in her purse and pulled out a long white envelope. She handed the envelope to Grace. "I type faster than I write, so I typed it, Grace," she paused.

"Thank goodness! Because no one can read your chicken scratch handwriting," Maria teased.

"You can change it if you'd like, Grace," Teenie said softly. "You might want to write the letter in your handwriting so it's more personal," she suggested. "Or if you want to send it typed," she paused. "That way you can just sign it at the bottom."

"And don't forget that you were going to include a photo of yourself with long hair so he can see the resemblance to your mother," Maria reminded.

Grace studied the envelope. She ran her finger across the name and address. Tanisha thought of everything. She addressed the envelope and even put a stamp on it. Her heart raced. She felt her hand trembling. She took a deep breath. She reached inside the unsealed envelope and pulled out the crisp sheet of paper. She studied the short paragraph. Her hands trembled. The words were blurry to her. She handed the letter to Rashanda.

"Rashanda, can you read it?" Grace asked. "I'm too nervous," she admitted.

"Do you want me to read it aloud?" Rashanda asked.

"No, genius. She wants you to read it silently to yourself so she can then read your mind!" Maria yelled. "Of course she wants you to read it aloud!"

Rashanda slanted her small almond eyes at Maria who ignored the icy stare and fumbled in her purse for another mint.

"Aagh! Where are my peppermints?" Maria groaned loudly.

Rashanda smoothed out the letter and cleared her throat.

"Now, this is only a draft," Teenie explained. "I took the comments that we all shared on the phone and pieced it together into a letter as best I could," she said, suddenly self conscious about her words being read aloud. "There's no pride in ownership," she stated. "We can always change it and start over. My feelings will not be hurt," she explained.

"Who cares about your feelings? Shut up and let her read, Teenie!" Maria barked.

"Your sniping little attitude is going to get you in trouble," Tanisha barked back. "Lose the 'tude, Her Royal Evil One!"

Maria stuck her tongue out at Teenie as Rashanda began to read:

Dear Charles Lovett,

I don't know how to begin, so I'll start from the beginning. My name is Grace Dudley. I am almost seventeen years old. My birth mother was Lydia Moore from Wilmette, Illinois. I believe that you are my biological father. My mother died when I was two years old. My adoptive parents worked for the Moore family and shared the story about my birth father. They explained that my mother was a student of yours at Northwestern University and when she became pregnant with me, her parents sent her to live with the Dudley family until the baby was born. They had arranged for her to put her baby up for adoption. When she refused, they cut off all contact with her. Sadly, I recently learned that my mother's parents were killed in a car accident shortly before my mother died. I don't want to cause any trouble in your life, but I would like to meet you or at least talk to you. My address and phone number are below. Now that I'm almost eighteen, my adoptive parents have said that they are in full support of my desire to contact you. Do you have any other children? Are you still teaching? I have so many questions that I'd like to ask you. But most importantly, I just want to see your face so that I can see what you look like. I've enclosed a recent picture of myself. Thank you. I hope to hear from you.

Rashanda laid the letter on top of the envelope on the coffee table. "That's it," she said. "Short and to the point," she finished. "Nice job, Teenie."

"What do you think, Grace?" Teenie asked nervously. "We can edit it any way that you like," she paused. "This is your letter, so you have to be comfortable with it."

Grace chewed on her lower lip. She fingered the letter in her hand.

"I didn't put a date on it, because I thought it would be better if you just date it when you sign it," Teenie continued. "You may want to read it again and show it to your parents. Or you can hand write it to make it more personal."

"I like the content of the letter," Maria commented. "But I think that it would be more personal if you hand wrote it," Maria suggested.

"No. I like it just the way it is," Grace said quickly. "I wouldn't change a thing." She signed the bottom of the letter and placed the date below her signature. She walked to a desk in the dining room and pulled out a wallet size photo of herself. "I'm glad my hair is longer in this photo," she said absentmindedly. She scrawled her name and age on the back of the photo. She folded the letter over the photo and slipped the paper into the envelope before licking and sealing her fate, and handing the envelope to Tanisha.

"Nice job, Teenie. My fate is now in your hands. Mail it!" Grace said confidently. "Let's go in the kitchen and eat some doughnuts. I'm hungry," she shared.

Chapter 7

Playing with Fire

Maria slammed the phone into the receiver. "Ugh!" she screamed. "I can't believe him!" She stared at her reflection. "I can't believe that he would do this to me! To me," she repeated meekly. "I'm a prize! Doesn't he know that? I'm a prize!" she shrieked into the mirror. "He has no idea who he's dealing with!" Maria tossed her long mane and gently stroked her fingers through it. "I can have any boy that I want," she breathed. "Any boy!" she screamed at the telephone on her nightstand. "He has no idea! I'll fix him!" She picked up the handset and slammed it into the cradle.

Plopping on her bed, she pulled open her nightstand drawer and grabbed the letters. Two in total. She clutched them to her chest and smiled mischievously, tracing her finger along the edge of the envelope. She reached inside and pulled out the tattered piece of paper and read the letter again.

Hey Maria, What's up? It was good to hear from you. Notre Dame is cool! My stats are high and the NFL is calling. Yes, I'm still dating Suzy Snowflake as you call her. I didn't know that you were interested in St. Mary's College. Call me if you come down for a campus visit and we can hook up. Gotta scoot to training table. Peace! D.

She quickly read the second letter.

Hey M! Your timing is perfect. Suzy Snowflake has melted. It's a long story. But I can take you to prom. No sweat! I'll let my publicist know so I can get some local press when I come home. D.

She tucked the letters back into her nightstand. I'll fix Todd's tail. I'll teach him to treat me like leftovers! Dante is about to be an NFL superstar!

It was the chuckle that irritated her the most. The chuckle started soft and then got louder and louder. It reminded her of a clown's laughter. She hated clowns. They frightened her. She'd been afraid of clowns since she was a small child. At first, she thought he was kidding. "Todd," she whined. "Stop kidding. It's my junior prom. You're my boyfriend. You have to take me," she finished matter of factly.

He burped. She could hear him chewing. He chuckled again. "You aren't listening, Princess Maria. I – am – not – taking- you – to – prom," he said slowly.

"Todd!" she screamed. "Stop kidding around. Prom is June thirteenth," she said casually. "And I'm wearing peach," she continued. "Wear a black tuxedo with a peach cummerbund and bow tie. I think white tuxedos are ghetto looking."

He chuckled again. "You aren't listening to me, Maria," he said lightly. "I'm serious. I am not taking you to prom," he repeated. "How would I look going to a high school prom?" Todd said flippantly, taking another bite of his sandwich. "I'm a sophomore in college," he chomped. "I don't do prom anymore. I'm an Omega man!" he barked. "Woof, Woof. Q dogs don't do prom," he chuckled again.

Maria slammed the phone into the cradle. She slammed it down several more times for effect! She waited fifteen seconds, and unplugged the phone. Just in case. She knew it wasn't really necessary, but just in case he fooled her this time. She'd hung up on him before.

The first time they had a fight, two weeks had passed and she hadn't heard from him. She didn't remember why they'd been fighting. She just remembered him chuckling loudly. He always chuckled when he didn't want to do something or when he thought she was being childish or foolish. His chuckle irritated her. She felt he was mocking her. The last time she hung up on him, she'd waited ten minutes and called him back. His dorm room phone rang and rang and rang. There was no answer. It was ten o'clock on a Friday night. He'd probably gone to his fraternity party. That irritated Maria even more. The thought of him mocking her and then casually going to his fraternity's party to step, dance and flirt. *He's supposed to be calling me back to apologize!*

He never called her back. She raced home from school every day to see if there was a message from him on their new answering machine. "You have no messages," the machine mocked. She ran her dilemma by the wise council at lunch.

"I really don't know what to tell you, Maria. I've never hung up on Ian," Rashanda admitted.

Maria exhaled loudly. "Teenie," she said. "Have you ever hung up on David?" she asked hopefully.

Teenie raised one finger to buy a few seconds as she chewed her sandwich. "No," she swallowed. "But David and I are just friends, Maria," she admitted. "We don't fight."

Maria rolled her eyes widely. "I forgot. You two are purrrrfect," she purred.

Tanisha shrugged and took a sip of her chocolate milk. "We're not perfect, psycho," Tanisha corrected. "But we're not romantically involved, remember?" she reminded. "Our conversations are fun and light," she shared. "I've also never hung up on Glen in case that's your next question."

Rashanda played with her salad and sprinkled salt and pepper in her food. "What do you two talk about, Teenie?" she asked. "Especially now that you're dating Glen, what do you and David talk about? Give up the dirt," she laughed.

Tanisha wiped her hands on her napkin and stretched her fingers, studying her long nails. She ran her thumb along the edge of her fingernails and felt a snag. She quickly reached into her purse and retrieved an emery board and began to file the jagged nail frantically.

"You are so freaking neurotic about your nails," Maria groaned. "You make me sick with that nail file, Teenie," she said. "Don't be stalling for time. Just answer the question."

"Don't be?" Tanisha mocked. "And it's an emery board, Miss Ebonics," Tanisha corrected. "A nail file is the silver pointy tool in your manicure set," she explained grabbing Maria's hand and shaking her head. "But clearly you don't use either apparatus since you are still biting your nails like a hillbilly! Tsk, tsk!"

"So what do you and David talk about, Teenie?" Grace asked softly. Upon hearing her voice, all of the girls stared at Grace curiously. They had grown so accustomed to Grace's quietness at lunch that just hearing her voice startled them. They looked from one to the other.

Tanisha smiled at Grace. "Well," she said slowly. "We talk about school, and how his classes are going. He tells me about college life," she paused, choosing her words carefully. "He pledged Alpha this semester, so he told me about that," she took a sip from her chocolate milk carton. "I tell him about my classes, and my job. Lots of stuff," she shrugged. "We talk about lots of different stuff," she repeated. Talking about David Barton made her miss him.

"Do you miss him?" Rashanda asked.

Startled, Tanisha stared at Rashanda as though looking straight through her. *How does she know?*

"Did you hear me, Teenie?" Rashanda asked. "You look like you've seen a ghost."

"I heard you," she admitted. "I guess I miss him a little," Teenie confessed, fingering the class ring that she wore on her necklace. Glen's class ring. She could see Maria pursing her lips for the next obvious question. She raised her hand to silence her friend. "I have different feelings for Glen than I do for David," she defended. "It's different."

"Do you talk to David about Glen?" Rashanda asked boldly.

"Not really," Tanisha admitted. "Glen knows about David, and David knows about Glen," she paused. "But I don't talk about either one with the other."

"Why not?" Rashanda asked.

"Because she has feelings for both of them," Maria blurted.

Tanisha rolled her eyes at Maria. "I do not!" she defended. She squirmed in her seat slightly and stretched her fingers again.

"You do!" Maria pointed. "I can always tell when you're nervous," she explained. "You stretch your fingers a lot," she observed. "Like you're doing right now."

Tanisha balled her fingers into a fist and sat on her hands. "It's different," she defended. "David's my friend, and Glen is my boyfriend. It's not the same type of feelings," she explained.

"How's it different?" Maria challenged. "As far as I know," she said. "You've still never kissed Glen," she reminded. "So technically, you and Glen are still just friends, like you and David, even though you're wearing his big class ring around your neck like a choker," she highlighted. "So how is it different?"

She chewed on her lip and ran her tongue along her new braces. "It's different because I spend more time with Glen?" Tanisha said sheepishly. Her reply came out in the form of a question.

Maria fumbled in her purse and pulled out her Vaseline tub. "If you ask me," Maria said. "If Glen was trying to be your boyfriend, he would have tried to kiss you by now. How do you know he doesn't consider you a friend?" she asked. "Have you thought about that one, Sherlock? Maybe Glen views you as a friend like you view David as a friend."

Tanisha sighed loudly. "You're right," she admitted softly, the words getting caught in her throat. "I have thought about that," she paused. "You might be right," she admitted. Her thoughts played his voice in her head. "Wait a minute," she said. "He calls me baby, and cutie. He holds my hand when we go to the movies," she shared.

"David called you pet names too, Teenie," Maria reminded.

"Have you asked him why he hasn't kissed you yet, Teenie?" Rashanda asked. "I thought you were going to just ask him."

Twelve more minutes until the bell rang. Too much time left on the clock to stall. No more time outs remaining. "I didn't," she confessed. "I didn't have the courage," she admitted weakly. "Actually, I thought about asking David if he knew why Glen hasn't tried to kiss me," she paused. "But I don't want to go there with David," she finished, her voice trailing.

"Duh! You don't want to go there with David because he'll go ballistic, and you know it, Miss Thang," Maria repeated. "David is not trying to give you tips on why another boy ain't tried to kiss you. Ain't gonna happen," Maria clucked, her neck jerking on her shoulders in an exaggerated circle, her index finger waving frantically. "Ain't no man, trying to give tips on how another man can kiss his woman. David likes your tail and you like him," she concluded. "End of freaking fairy tale!"

"Okay, thanks for that commentary, Miss Ghetto-Girl Ebonics! Stop bobbing your neck or your head will pop off," Tanisha laughed. "You must be an English major! You're so eloquent!"

"Ghetto-Girl Ebonics," she repeated. "I like that!" Maria grinned. "Just call me Ghetto-Girl for short or Miss Ebonics if you must," she bowed and adjusted her imaginary crown. "I wear my crown with pride," she laughed.

Rashanda twisted her mouth and raised her eyebrows. "I hate to admit it, Teenie," Rashanda said. "But Maria might be on to something."

"Might be on to something?" Maria asked. "I am on to something! I know boys! I could major in them and minor in advice. Boys and advice. It's what I do," Maria boasted. "I won't even charge you for my little gems!"

"If you ask me," Maria continued. "You have two men, my friend. Glen and David. You have a BF and a BU," she squealed.

Rashanda, Teenie and Grace stared at each other puzzled. Rashanda spoke first. "I'm assuming that a BF is a boyfriend, but what's a BU?" she asked.

"A boyfriend and a backup," Maria laughed. "Get it?"

Tanisha rolled her eyes and flicked her napkin across the table. "Maria," she said sternly. "David is not a backup plan. He's my friend. Period," Tanisha said flatly.

"Call it whatever you want," Maria chided. "But you are still stringing him along two years later, and he must like it or he would have cut the cord," Maria explained. "Tell the truth, Teenie. We're your girls," she leaned into the table, her eyes piercing Teenie's as though she were trying to read her soul. "You've never kissed David Barton?" Maria asked. "Not even once?"

"No. Never," Tanisha said flatly.

"Have you thought about it?" Maria asked.

Tanisha stretched her fingers again, and self consciously stopped. She looked at the clock. Six more minutes until the next period. She wouldn't be saved by the bell this time. She slanted her eyes. "Of course I've thought about it, moron," she groaned.

Rashanda slanted her almond eyes and stared at Teenie suspiciously. "You mean to tell me," she paused. "All the time you two spent together, that he never even tried to kiss you?" she asked.

Tanisha shook her head from side to side. "Nope. Not even once," she admitted.

"I don't believe that, Teenie," Maria accused. "Most guys will at least try to get a smooch," she stated confidently. "It's usually the first thing they're thinking about when they meet you," she shared. "Tanisha Denise Carlson. Do you swear on Lori's memory that fine, rich, perfect David Barton never tried to kiss you?"

Teenie took a large bite of her sandwich, chewing slowly as she watched the clock tick even slower, mocking her desire to stall for more time. She was impressed by the girls' persistence as they patiently waited in silence for her to finish chewing.

"You chicks are relentless," Tanisha groaned. "I feel like I'm being interrogated by Perry Mason!"

"I knew it!" Maria exclaimed. "You did kiss him! You lying little trampoline," she giggled.

Tanisha shook her head. "No. I didn't kiss him," she corrected. "But he did try to kiss me the night of his birthday party," she said softly.

"Which birthday party?" Rashanda asked.

Tanisha pursed her lips and tilted her head to the side. "You remember. It was right after I came back from leadership camp," she paused. "And I met Doug's friend Andre," she whispered fighting back tears.

"Who?" Maria asked. "You met whose friend?"

"She met Doug's friend, Andre," Rashanda repeated.

"Lori's Doug?" Maria asked.

Tanisha shook her head up and down and inhaled deeply as a tear trickled down her cheek. Lori's absence was felt daily. The pain in their hearts was intensified whenever someone recalled stories involving Lori. A brief period of silence ensued. Rashanda reached and patted Tanisha's hand gently. "I know," she said. "Sometimes I still get overcome with grief just thinking about her too," she admitted.

Shaking her head from side to side, Teenie continued. "Anyway, we were on his driveway, establishing the terms of our new friendship," she explained as she quickly wiped her face with her napkin. "And he asked me if he could have a birthday kiss," Tanisha finished.

"Well?" Rashanda asked. "Did you kiss him?"

Tanisha laughed quickly. "No. I wasn't lying about not kissing him. I have not kissed David Barton," she repeated. "But if I'd said yes, we would have."

Maria scowled at Tanisha. "That's it? You had me on the edge of my seat for that?" she groaned. "That's so lame. I would have given him a little taste," she teased as Tanisha tossed her napkin at

Maria's nose.

"Well, that was almost two years ago," Tanisha said. "David and I are friends, and Glen is my boyfriend," she stated flatly. "And I would like to be kissed by my boyfriend before my lips fall off," she groaned.

"Prom night is coming up," Grace said softly. "Glen will probably kiss you at prom," she whispered. "Kissing is special," Grace continued. "I don't want to just share spit with anybody."

The girls stared at her in stunned silence. Tanisha spoke first. "You're right, Grace," she said gently. "Sharing a kiss is very special," she continued. Her words were soft and delicate like the tone law enforcement uses to coax a criminal to put the weapon down and release the hostages. Don't go back into your silent cave, Grace. Keep talking. We're your friends. Join the conversation. We won't hurt you. "Any kissing is special, but a first kiss is very special," Tanisha agreed. "You'll always remember your first real kiss," she said tenderly. A picture of Brian Kraft and the poppy field flashed through her mind.

"Are you thinking about kissing someone, Grace?" Rashanda asked softly. Her tone just as delicate and gentle as Tanisha's had been. Keep talking Grace. Come on back to us.

"No," Grace said flatly. "I was just saying," she finished quickly before dropping her chin back into her chest and lowering her eyes.

She's gone again. Back into her silent cave. I wonder how she must be feeling? What was in that letter?

"Well enough about Teenie's two timing ways," Maria grunted. "I need to know what to do about Todd! Should I call him back or not?"

"Not!" Rashanda and Teenie groaned simultaneously. "Just

give it some time," Tanisha said. "You both need to calm down a little. Give it a couple of weeks," Teenie advised.

Rashanda rubbed Maria's arm. "I agree. He'll probably call you back soon, Maria," she assured. "Remember, college boys have a lot more on their plate than high school boys," she explained. "Ian is super busy and sometimes I don't hear from him for days at a time," she continued. "I know he's always thinking about me, but he has a lot going on."

ഇ)രു

Maria slumped in her chair. They'd been wrong the last time. He hadn't called her back. She waited two torturous weeks. No call from Todd. She'd had to call him. When she called him, he'd acted like nothing had happened. His tone had been flippant. "I knew you'd eventually come to your senses and call me back, kiddo!" he'd chuckled. She hated that chuckle.

"Go by yourself, Maria, or just go with a group of friends. Whatever, dude. I'm not going to buy an airline ticket to come back for a silly high school dance. It ain't happening!" Todd had said. "I don't even care if you go with one of those high school nerds from River North," he suggested. "I'm not worried about any of those high school chumps. I know you're my girl. I could care less," he'd said casually.

I can't believe that he won't take me to prom! I'll show him! Dante will escort me to prom and it'll be in the papers. I'll make sure that Todd sees the paper so he can get jealous. Once he sees that a big time Notre Dame football star took me to prom, he'll come to his senses and start treating me like the prize that I am!

Chapter 8

Pastel Pretties

The weathered swan held center court. Its chipped beak pointed due north as though searching for its missing mate. The girls smiled at the swan and at each other. The scene was exactly as they'd planned. Tanisha squeezed Rashanda's hand and stared tenderly at the lawn ornament. For as long as she'd been friends with Lori, that swan had been the undeniable marker that identified Lori's house. She only knew Lori's house by the swan. "It's the house with the swan on the lawn, Jack," she'd said countless times. "I don't know her address, Mom. It's the house with the swan in the front," she'd repeated.

Tanisha tried to remember the proper address. She couldn't. Her eyes wandered aimlessly to see if she could even see the house numbers. She squinted. She could see the faint outline of a seven, but the other three numbers were concealed behind a row of hedges that sat in desperate need of a trim. "You can't miss my house," Lori would often say. "It's the house with the swan in the front lawn." Tanisha could hear her friend's soft soprano voice in her head. She was right. Everyone knew that the house with the swan was the Perkins' family home. She sighed deeply. Tanisha missed Lori. They all did. Knowingly, Rashanda squeezed Tanisha's hand again.

Tanisha could feel tears welling in her eyes. You have spent way too much time putting on your face, girlfriend. You cannot cry and ruin your make-up! She looked up at the clear blue sky and forced the tears to pool into the back of her eye socket. She blinked several times and smiled. The girls stood side by side like a row of tulips with heads. Lavender, mint green, yellow and peach, their dresses billowed in the wind as the soft breeze blew across the lawn. Mrs. Perkins beamed proudly at the girls, as Mr. Perkins snapped photos of them with the swan.

"Now let's get you with your dates," Mrs. Perkins suggested. Glen walked up and squeezed Teenie's hand. The sun reflecting off her new braces, she self consciously ran her tongue across the metal and tilted her head to smile. She beamed proudly at him and squeezed his hand right back. He looked handsome in his black tuxedo with lavender cummerbund and bow tie. They made a nice looking couple. Out of the corner of her eye, she saw her dad's face. His brow was crinkled into a scowl as he stared intently at Glen, deliberately studying his every move. He looked sullen and forlorn. She watched as Billie chatted animatedly with Mrs. Perkins.

"Your dad looks like he wants to kill me," Glen whispered.

"He probably does," Tanisha assured. "I'm his only daughter, so you'd better watch your back. He probably has his drop gun with him."

"What's a drop gun?" Glen repeated.

"It's a gun that can't be traced to him," she explained. "He'll pop a cap in you, drop it and keep it moving," she giggled. "My dad has quite the ghetto side," she teased.

She watched as Glen gulped and slowly released his grasp on her hand.

"Glen," she said softly. "I'm kidding about the drop gun," she giggled. "He has one, but I'm sure he doesn't have it on him. It's against the law to carry a concealed weapon in Illinois," she laughed.

Teenie and Glen stood next to Maria who was being escorted by Dante one of the "double D's" from the River North football team. Maria and Dante looked like the number ten standing side by side, Maria's slender frame representing the one next to Dante's stocky frame. Tanisha smiled at how tightly the tuxedo jacket hugged Dante's bulging body.

Now a starting running back at Notre Dame, Dante was a favorite to get drafted into the NFL as an early first round draft pick. Tanisha wondered how Maria had convinced Dante to come back to attend their prom. Maria and Dante weren't even that friendly at River. Dante was dating that skinny, blonde girl. *I know Maria had study hall with him, but I didn't realize that they were chummy. Maria never talked about him.*

"At least one of the "double D's" appreciates a girl with a little junk in her trunk," Maria whispered flirtatiously, squeezing Dante's huge bicep. Tanisha smiled as a small crowd gathered in front of the Perkins' house, entranced by the news truck. *They're probably here to see the star football player and to try and get their picture in the local paper.*

The Newberry East Gazette was running a feature story highlighting how the girls had chosen to honor their friend by having their prom photos taken at her house so that her parents could participate in the joy of prom. As the editor of the River North student newspaper, Tanisha had written an editorial stressing the importance of not driving while drowsy. The guidance counselor had suggested that they try to get some local press on the story. The Gazette reporter's angle would center on the importance of prom goers not drinking and driving as well as the dangers of driving while sleepy or drowsy. He was planning to run photos of Lori and Charlotte Perkins along with the photos of Lori's Angels: Tanisha, Rashanda, Maria and Grace posing in front of the Perkins' family home. Tanisha shuddered thinking about the senseless deaths of Lori and her sister Charlotte.

Her gaze turned to Doug. He looked like he could cry at any moment. It had been over two years since Lori's death, and Doug remained deeply depressed. He continued to play basketball for his high school's team, but his heart wasn't in it. He was being recruited by Division One schools and had been chosen as a McDonald's High School All American athlete as a result of his high grade point average and basketball talent. The attention meant nothing to him. His heart had been buried with Lori.

Immediately following Lori's death, Doug's grades began to slip, and he threatened to drop out of school. His grandmother sent him to Christian counseling. Again. This time the counseling helped him process his grief, and his grades improved, but not his attitude. His anger at God returned with a vengeance.

When he was thirteen, his mother died of breast cancer, and he and his brother were sent to live with their maternal grandmother. Doug was angry with God. His mother had been his world. After her death, he retreated into a world of basketball and silence. Doug's days were consumed with basketball, eating and sleeping. He refused to go to church. Church was just a visual reminder of his loss. He spoke only when absolutely necessary. Sitting in the pew, he felt like a hypocrite, his praise a mask for the pain in his heart. Whenever he stared at the altar, all he saw was his mother lying in a coffin. He stopped attending worship services. His grandmother didn't press the issue.

Like salve on sunburned skin, meeting Lori had soothed his pain. He believed that she'd been an angel sent by God to help him heal. When he learned that her family had recently started to attend the same church where his grandmother was a founding member, he knew it was a sign from God. He gladly went to church so that he could spend time in Lori's presence. He'd described Lori to his grandmother as his soul mate.

He planned to marry Lori. And now God had called her to glory too. He stood sullenly next to Grace.

It had been Teenie's idea. "Remember, we promised to be Lori's Angels. At her funeral, we promised her parents that they would experience all of the milestones that Lori and Charlotte will miss through us," she reminded. "I know they have two sons who will go to prom one day, but it's not the same. They should experience prom through the eyes of girls," Tanisha explained. "I think they would appreciate it if we had our dates pick us up at their house on prom night," she said. "We can shower at home, but let's put on our make-up and dresses in Lori's room."

"But my mother wants to have a champagne sip at our house to watch me leave for prom," Maria shared. "She's already told my grandmother and aunts and uncles. Liz is not going to go for that."

Teenie paused. "Well, if you explained what we're trying to do, I'm sure Liz would be flexible. She knows how much this would mean to Mr. and Mrs. Perkins. Your mom could help you with your hair and make-up at home and zip you over to the Perkins' house for pictures," she continued. "We could just take thirty minutes worth of pictures over there in front of the swan and then go to our respective homes or all schlep over to your house for the champagne toast," she suggested.

"That could work," Maria agreed. "And maybe my dad could see me at the Perkins' house because my mother told him that he could not bring his girlfriend to her house," she continued. "She invited him to the champagne sip, but when he said that his girlfriend would have to come, my mother told him not to bother and slammed the phone down."

Tanisha whistled. "I don't blame her," she said. "It's too soon for all of that."

"I think having my dad see me at Lori's house is a nice compromise that my mother could live with," Maria finished.

"I think that's a great idea, Teenie," Rashanda offered. "I'm sure Lori's parents would really appreciate it. We could shower at home, but get dressed over there in Lori and Charlotte's old room," Rashanda concurred. "That would mean a lot to Mrs. Perkins."

"What about Grace? Have we found a date for her yet?" Tanisha asked.

"Not yet," Maria groaned. "As pretty as that girl is, she does not know how to work her money maker!"

"Maria!" Teenie and Rashanda groaned simultaneously.

"Well, it's true. If she weren't so timid, she could have any guy that she wants at River," she continued. "I see the guys checking her out all the time, but she acts like she's not interested so they press on."

Tanisha snapped her fingers. "Okay," she said. "This may sound crazy, but what about Doug?" she asked.

"Lori's Doug?" Rashanda asked. "What about him?"

"Hear me out," Tanisha said. "What if we have Doug escort Grace to prom? She needs a date. He misses Lori. Being around us will remind him of Lori. It might help him heal."

"Bad idea," Maria said flatly. "Have you seen him lately? He looks like a walking zombie. I ran into him at the mall a couple of months ago, and he looks like six feet six inches of bad road. He'll never go for that," she said. "Lori died almost two years ago, and he's still mourning her death like it was yesterday."

"He really loved her, Maria," Rashanda explained. "I think it's sweet that he can't forget about her that quickly."

"Me too," Tanisha agreed. "I think it's worth a shot. If we tell him that it would be a way for him to honor Lori's memory, he might go for it," she suggested. "He knows Glen from playing basketball, and he knows Ian too, so it's not like he'll be sitting with a bunch of strange people that he doesn't know," she explained.

"Do you think Grace would go for it?" Maria asked.

"She might," Rashanda said. "I think we'd be able to talk her into it."

It had been a difficult sell, but the three girls had convinced Grace that going to prom escorted by Doug would please Lori. They had enlisted the support of Mrs. Perkins and Doug's grandmother to convince Doug of the same. At his grandmother's insistence, Doug had agreed to go. He had called Grace on the phone once to ask her what color dress she was wearing so he could purchase a coordinating wrist corsage.

The day before prom, Tanisha shared with her mother that she would be doing her hair and make-up at Mrs. Perkins' house.

"You really miss your friend don't you, Tanisha?" Billie Mae asked softly.

"Of course I do," she replied tersely. "I think about her every single day."

"I never had close friends like you have," Billie admitted. "Don't get me wrong, I had friends in high school, but we weren't that close. I didn't keep in touch with any of them after graduation." Tanisha shifted her weight, unsure what to say next. She still hadn't forgiven her mother for not offering to help her pay for her prom dress. *She's doing the best that she can, Teenie. Just remember that. Your mother is doing the best that she can.* Glen's words raced through her head often.

☜☞

Her mother had finally met Glen. As agreed, Glen had pulled up to her house promptly at six o'clock. Tanisha met him on the porch.

"Remember, keep it short and sweet, Glen," Tanisha reminded.

"Please don't engage her in any lengthy discussions. I'll introduce you, and you can answer any questions that she has, but don't ask her any questions. I've told her that we're seeing a six thirty movie," she instructed. "If she invites you to sit down I'll say that we don't have time," she whispered as they walked into the house.

"It'll be fine, Teenie! Moms always love me," Glen shared confidently.

"Mom!" Tanisha called. "My friend Glen is here to meet you," she yelled. Her heart raced. Billie Mae was having a good day. She'd been having a good month. Tanisha had decided that it was finally time to stop sneaking around to date Glen. She also wanted him to meet her mother while she was being nice and taking her medication.

Tanisha exhaled as her mother walked out of the kitchen dressed in a faded pink sweatshirt and sweatpants that hung loosely on her petite frame. She'd recently started practicing yoga again. "Hello, young man," Billie Mae said. "I'm Tanisha's mother."

"Nice to meet you, Maam," Glen said politely. "Now I see where Tanisha gets her good looks," Glen offered. "What should I call you?" he asked.

Tanisha's heart fell into her stomach. Here we go! This is when Billie will show her ghetto side!

"You can just call me, Billie," Billie Mae smiled.

"I'm sorry, Maam, but my mother would peel my head if she heard me referring to you by your first name," Glen explained.

"Oh. Then just call me Mrs. Carlson," Billie said quickly. "Have a seat," Billie offered.

Tanisha stared at her mother curiously. Mrs. Carlson? Since when does she ever refer to herself as Mrs. Carlson? They're divorced now. "Mom! We're going to see a six thirty movie, so we need to be going," Tanisha explained quickly.

"You can see the seven thirty showing," Billie said casually. "Your father should be here any minute. He said he would be here at six o'clock sharp."

Tanisha's eyes opened wide. "Daddy's coming? I didn't know that Daddy was coming out today!"

Billie plopped on the sofa and crossed her legs like a pretzel. "He wasn't. But I called him so that he could meet Glen," she explained. "Your father and I discussed that we should meet your dates together to make sure that they understand what we expect."

Tanisha could feel her palms sweating. What they expect? Her mouth hung open in stunned silence.

"Close your mouth, Tanisha," Billie said casually. "A fly might buzz in there," Billie laughed.

Glen looked at Tanisha and raised his eyebrows. A car door slammed and Billie peered through the draperies. "Perfect timing," she smiled. "Here's your father now. Have a seat, young man," Billie ordered.

Obediently, Glen sat on the sofa and crossed his hands in his lap. Tanisha watched as Billie walked to the door to greet Jackie. She looked apologetically at Glen and shrugged.

Tanisha greeted her dad in the foyer with a hug. "Hi, Daddy," she said lovingly, the tender lilt of a seven year old in her voice. "This is my friend, Glen," she grinned.

She smiled when Glen stood and extended his hand to her father. "Hello, sir. It's nice to meet you," he said. The tone in his voice was deep and confident.

"Likewise, I think," Jackie said gruffly. "But don't call me, sir! Call me, Mr. Carlson," Jackie ordered.

"Okay, sir. I mean, Mr. Carlson," Glen stammered.

"Have a seat, young man," Jackie barked pointing to a chair by the window.

Jackie and Billie sat side by side on the sofa as Tanisha sat on the arm of the sofa. "How long have you known my daughter?" Jackie asked quickly. Again, Tanisha's mouth hung opened. She hadn't expected her father to interrogate Glen.

"Uh. We met at the mall," Glen said softly.

"I didn't ask you where you met, young man. I asked you how long you've known my daughter," Jackie repeated.

"We met a little over a year ago, sir," Glen said softly. The bass in his voice was gone, replaced by a soft baritone.

"So are you the young man that she sneaks out of the house to meet?" Jackie asked.

Tanisha could feel her face flush. She stared at her father in disbelief.

"Tanisha, your mouth is hanging open again," Billie smiled.

"Excuse me, sir?" Glen asked.

"Stop calling me sir!" he barked. Oh, never mind," Jackie corrected. "You're nervous. I said, are you the young man that picks her up by the pool when she tells her mother that she's going to her friend Vickie's house?" he repeated.

Pitifully, Glen looked at Tanisha for guidance. She could feel her heartbeat increasing. Her father's gaze shifted from Glen to Tanisha and back to Glen. Her dad was stalking Glen like prey. Like a lion stalking a baby antelope. She had to remind herself to breathe. Afraid to speak for fear that the lion would stalk her too, she lowered her eyes to the floor and waited for the stalker to pass.

"I don't know why you're staring at Tanisha, she can't answer the question for you, young man," Jackie snickered. "Let's move on! I'm not going to even give you the chance to lie to my face. The point is this. I was young once, and I know what young people will do to spend time together," Jackie said. "My daughter is not a liar. She's a straight A student and has always made us proud. She must really like you if she's lying to spend time with you."

Jackie glanced at Tanisha who dropped her head in shame. She braced herself for the explosion.

"Now, the good news is that I'm a man who believes in second chances," Jackie explained with a slight smile in his voice. "I can't blame you for my daughter's behavior. We'll deal with that later. Girls will lie and sneak around to spend time with boys that they like. I understand that. I have three sisters. Now, you seem like an honorable young man, even though you do have an earring in your ear," Jackie observed. "I am going to give you a second chance, Ben."

"Daddy! His name is Glen!" Tanisha groaned.

"What did I say?" Jackie asked.

"You called him, Ben," Billie explained.

"Oh! I'm sorry. But as I was saying, Glen, I'm going to let you start with a clean slate. Don't lie to me," he stated flatly. "If you are going to date my daughter, I need to believe that you are an honorable and trustworthy young man. You are to take her where you say you are taking her and have her home at the time that we say," he paused. "And if you do anything to harm her physically, I will hurt you! I know people that can do great bodily harm to you and it won't be traced back to me," he said loudly, his uni-brow furrowed into a deep scowl, like a jet black caterpillar resting on his forehead.

"Daddy! Stop it! You're embarrassing me!" Tanisha pleaded. "I didn't even know you were going to be here. That's so unfair!" she whined.

Jackie grinned, softening his face as he addressed Tanisha. "Your mother and I thought it would be better if you didn't know. The element of surprise always works best!" He patted her knee. "Tanisha,

I do not care about embarrassing you! I care about your safety. It is my job to protect you and keep you safe, especially now that you're dating," he said. He directed his eyes back to Glen. "Let me make something perfectly clear, young man," he said loudly. "Just because her mother and I are divorced, and I don't live here, it doesn't mean that I am not concerned about what happens to my daughter. She is precious cargo! You are to treat her as though I'm in the room watching your every move! Is that understood, young man?"

"Yes," Glen said quickly. "I understand you completely," he stammered. "And you don't have to worry about me lying to you, Mr. Carlson," he said. His voice had now moved into the tenor section of the Scared to Death Choir. Glen nodded his head up and down like a bobble head doll and nervously wrung his hands in his lap. Tanisha felt sorry for him.

"Can we go now, Daddy?" Tanisha pleaded.

"You are to have her home before the clock strikes midnight. Do you have any questions, young man?" Jackie asked.

"No, sir," he whispered. Tanisha stood up and walked Glen to the door.

"I'll meet you in the car, Glen," she whispered.

When she turned around, her parents were staring at her smugly.

"I can't believe that you guys just did that," she whined. "I could have at least prepared him that you were going to be here, Daddy," she pouted.

"Nope! You get information on a need to know basis, little girl," her dad grinned. "Your mother told me a few weeks ago that she saw you climbing in the car with a boy, and we agreed to confront you together," he explained. "You're seventeen now, Tanisha. You're old enough to date. Why didn't you just tell your mother about Glen so she could meet him? Why did you feel that you had to lie and sneak around to see him?"

Tanisha let out a long sigh. She'd never discussed her feelings about her mother with her dad. *How do I tell him that I was afraid that Billie might be off her medications when she met him? How can I say that I was scared that she might embarrass me?* "I don't know," she shrugged.

"Do you really like this young man?" her dad asked quickly.

"He's nice," Tanisha shrugged again. "It's not that serious."

"Is this the young man that surprised you by coming to Lori's funeral?" he asked.

Tanisha stared at her father curiously. "You remember that, Daddy?" she asked.

"Of course I remember that," he admitted. "I don't remember his name, but I remember Grace coming outside while you were talking to Aunt Helen and telling you that a boy was inside the church waiting for you."

That was over two years ago, and he still remembers that! He doesn't even live here anymore and he still remembers my friends' names!

"Well, at least he didn't lie about having known you for almost two years," Jackie observed. "He seems like an honorable young man, Tanisha. He really does. I like him," he continued. "Even though I don't normally approve of boys wearing earrings, he seems nice."

∞⊃⊂∝

Tanisha snapped out of her daydream. *What was I thinking? I forgot how petrified Glen is of my dad. I shouldn't have made that comment about the drop gun! He probably thinks my dad really has a gun on him now!*

Tanisha watched as Doug and Grace shifted their weight and

smiled nervously at each other. "Stand closer to your date, Stretch," the <u>Gazette</u> photographer instructed Doug who robotically moved closer to Grace, but his look remained somber. "Don't worry, "Mellow Yellow" won't bite you," he coached. "This is supposed to be the happiest night of your young life, Stretch," he continued. "If you play your cards right, it might be the luckiest night of your life too," he winked.

Tanisha smiled as the photographer continued to toss out the nicknames that he'd given to each of them. The girls' nicknames corresponded to their dress colors. Her nickname was lavender, Grace's was "mellow yellow," Maria's was "Georgia peach" and Rashanda's was "lime green." The crowd cheered when he recognized Dante and nicknamed him NFL! She giggled when he unknowingly nicknamed Ian, smart guy because of his glasses. She ran her tongue across her braces, still not accustomed to her newest accessory. Ian does look smart with those glasses on! I wonder what he will nickname Glen?

"Earring! Look over here, "Earring." Put your arms around lavender's waist," the photographer ordered, as if on cue. She looked at the small hoop earring in Glen's ear. She'd grown so accustomed to it that she didn't notice it any longer. I wonder how the photographer noticed his earring. He's good! But I guess if you do this for a living, you can't possibly be expected to remember the names of all of the different people that you photograph. It's much easier to come up with a personal identifier to get their attention.

With Glen's arms now resting around her small waist, she watched as the scowl on her father's face deepened. She smiled when Mr. Jordan walked over to her father, his scowl replaced by a soft smile as he greeted Rashanda's dad. Beaming proudly at Grace, the Dudleys sat in lawn chairs sipping lemonade served by Lori's brothers.

"Teenie!" Maria squealed. "There's a television news reporter who wants to interview Lori's Angels for the news tonight, and I told her that you're our spokesperson," she finished. "I didn't know that they were sending a news camera too!" Maria squealed.

"Me either," Tanisha said. "I just thought that they were sending a print journalist to write the article." She recognized the pretty features reporter from the six o'clock news. She'd often filled in as a weekend anchor.

"Tanisha, I'm Angela Weldon with Channel 7 news WLS, and I'm going to ask you a few questions," Angela explained. "The camera will be on me first and then will pan to you ladies," she continued. "We'll do a wide shot with all of you in your beautiful prom dresses, and then we'll focus on you, Tanisha. While I'm asking you the questions, the camera will be on you the entire time, and I won't be in the shot. Just look at me. Don't look at the camera at all," she finished softly. "Can you remember that?"

"Okey, dokey," Tanisha said confidently. "I've never been on television before," she shared.

"You'll be fine. We're not running this live, so if you mess up, we can tape it again," Angela explained.

"Works for me," Teenie smiled proudly.

Angela smiled. "Let's get started. Just answer my questions," she grinned. Tanisha watched as a person standing behind the camera man held up three fingers, and counted down to one, pointing at Angela to start speaking.

"Good Evening! This is Angela Weldon reporting from Newberry East, Illinois. It's prom night for River North High School and with me this afternoon are four River North High School students who are also known as Lori's Angels. Many of our viewers may remember the piece I covered two years ago where Lori and Charlotte Perkins were tragically killed in a car accident when the driver fell asleep behind the wheel," she said softly. "Lori's Angels decided to have their prom photos taken in front of the Perkins' family home so that their parents could experience prom night through them. With me tonight is Tanisha Carlson and three of her friends. Tanisha, can you tell us the names of your friends?"

Tanisha quickly ran her tongue along her wire braces and smiled boldly, pleased that her dental shame was now a thing of the past. "This is Maria Wesley, Rashanda Jordan and Grace Dudley," Tanisha introduced as the girls waved into the camera.

"Tell our viewers why you are called Lori's Angels?" Angela asked.

"At Lori's funeral, we made a promise to her family that we would somehow include Lori in our milestone events so that her memory could live on through us," Tanisha explained. "We applied our make-up and styled our hair in Lori's old bedroom," she grinned gripping her floral bouquet to ease her nerves.

"How touching and sweet," Angela said. "Tanisha, what advice do you have for teens going to prom tonight?" Angela asked.

Ignoring Angela's request to address her directly, Tanisha turned to the camera. "If you're sleepy, don't drive. It's not worth it," Tanisha pleaded into the camera. "Even if it means missing your curfew, just stay where you are and get some rest, or call your parents to pick you up," she continued. "And if you happen to indulge in alcohol and find yourself 'over served' at a prom party, definitely don't drive," she continued. "Your parents may punish you, but they won't kill you. Driving while sleepy or drunk will kill you. Falling asleep at the wheel killed our friend, Lori Perkins and her sister Charlotte," Tanisha finished.

"Well said, Tanisha," Angela smiled. "Well that about sums it up folks. To all you prom goers that will be hitting the roads tonight, don't drive if you're sleepy or if you've been drinking," Angela finished.

"I'm Angela Weldon signing off with Lori's Angels for ABC Channel 7, WLS in Chicago."

"Cut!" a voice yelled from behind the camera.

"That was great, Tanisha!" Angela beamed. She hugged her tightly. "I thought you'd be nervous and we might have to do a few takes," she said. "But we got it in one! And I love how you looked right into the camera for the last part," she said. "That was awesome!"

Tanisha noticed her reach into her blouse to display a gold charm hanging from a necklace that had been tucked into her shirt. She recognized the Greek symbols for Delta Sigma Theta. "Are you a Delta?" she asked. "My aunts are Deltas!"

"I am," Angela beamed proudly. "My mother is a Delta also, and she gave this to me when I pledged," she explained. "I wear it everywhere, for luck, but I can't display it when I'm on air," she finished.

"Do you think our piece will make the news tonight?" Rashanda asked.

"It definitely should unless there's a bigger news story," Angela explained.

"If it bleeds, it leads," Tanisha laughed.

"Exactly!" Angela smiled. "Spoken like a budding journalist! You know how it works, Tanisha. This story might get bumped by more breaking news. But we generally like to run appropriate feature stories on nights when we know a lot of kids are going to prom," she said. "My producer and I are really cool, so I'll push to make sure that we keep this piece in," she winked.

Angela reached into her pocket and handed Tanisha a business card. "Keep my card," she instructed. "If you're serious about becoming a journalist, I can probably introduce you to some people that can help you land an internship," she smiled. "It's tough breaking into the business," she winked.

"Thanks, Angela," Tanisha studied the business card and slipped it into her small lavender clutch purse as Maria gently tugged her arm.

"Teenie!" she said firmly, glancing disapprovingly at her watch. "It's time to head out of here so we can get to my house! Liz will be tapping her feet if I'm late for her big shindig!" she said. "Besides, the limousine is picking us up in an hour," she reminded.

"I'm going to go say goodbye to my parents," she whispered to Glen. He winked and continued chatting with Ian. Grasping the hem of her dress and hoisting it above her ankles, she tiptoed through the grass and crossed the street to where her parents stood with Rashanda's parents. She crossed paths with Mr. and Mrs. Jordan in the middle of the street as they walked toward Rashanda.

"You look so pretty, Teenie!" Mrs. Jordan gushed. "Doesn't she look pretty, Thomas?" Tanisha smiled that Mrs. Jordan used her nickname.

"She does. All of the girls look beautiful," Mr. Jordan said quickly. "Let's get out of the street before we all get hit by a car," he cautioned tenderly grabbing his wife by the elbow.

Mrs. Jordan patted Tanisha's arm gently. "Be careful, Teenie," Mrs. Jordan reminded. "You don't want to trip on your dress in those heels," she smiled. "You might tear your hem. Hold your dress a little higher when you walk. They don't make seams like they used to."

"I'll be careful," Teenie assured. Her father grinned as she approached.

"Here's the belle of the ball!" Jackie boasted. "You looked so confident talking to the reporter, Booger," Jackie said absentmindedly. "I hope that piece makes the news tonight!"

"Daddy!" Tanisha groaned. "Don't call me that in public, please!" Tanisha pleaded.

"I'm sorry, I forgot," he said softly. "No one heard me," he defended.

"But still," she whined. "Someone could have heard you," her voice that of a defiant nine year old once again.

"I'll try to stop calling you that, I promise," he said. "But you'll always be my little booger," he winked. Tanisha scrunched her face at her father, secretly enjoying the pet name that only he used.

"Where are you going for dinner after the prom again?" Billie asked.

Tanisha rolled her eyes to the sky before turning to address her mother. She stared at her mother curiously. For the first time that evening, Tanisha noticed that her mother also had on make-up.

"We're going to Ron of Japan downtown on Ohio Street," she said quickly. *Why does she have on make-up?* "And please don't lecture Glen today," she whispered. "I'm not in the mood."

Billie had been disappointed when she offered to help her apply her make-up for the prom, and Tanisha politely declined. "I'm seventeen, Mom," Tanisha groaned. "I know how to apply my own make-up."

She looks pretty. Maybe she decided to paint her own face and pretend that it was my face she was painting.

"I won't lecture him," Jackie explained. "But I want him to know what time I expect you home," he said sternly. "Tell him to come over here."

"Daddy!" Tanisha groaned.

She watched as her father slowly raised his left eyebrow. She knew that he only did that when the discussion was over. Without another word, she sulked across the street, stepping on the front of her dress, barely catching her balance. She paused and hiked up her dress before continuing.

Glen, Ian and Doug were now laughing animatedly. Tanisha

smiled when she saw Doug laughing. "Glen," she said. "My dad wants to talk to you."

She watched as Glen's pupils danced and he swallowed hard. "Okay," he said. "I'll be right back, fellas," he mumbled. "He's not going to threaten me again is he?" Glen asked nervously.

"I have no idea," she said, remembering to grab her dress as she led Glen to her parents. "Let's just get it over with," she groaned. "And by the way, my dad really doesn't have a gun. I was just kidding." She waved her hand across her face. "Ugh! These little teensy flies and gnats are so annoying." She swatted into the air and shook her freshly coiffed hair. "They give me the heebie jeebies!"

She found herself skip walking as Glen quickened his pace. His long legs taking one stride to her two, her gait further compromised by the lavender heels that she wore.

"Hello, Mr. Carlson. Mrs. Carlson," Glen greeted. "How are you this evening?"

Billie smiled warmly at Glen. "Glen, let's just cut to the chase," Jackie said tersely staring intensely into Glen's eyes. "I want you to have our daughter home at a reasonable hour," he finished flatly. His familiar scowl covered his face like a ski mask.

"I will have her home at whatever time you say, Mr. Carlson," Glen stammered. Tanisha watched him swallow hard again.

"Good. Have fun," Jackie finished. He hugged Tanisha tightly. "Have fun, baby girl," he whispered, gently grabbing Tanisha's hands and pressing something firmly into her hand. She opened her fingers and stared at a neatly folded twenty dollar bill. "If you need to take a taxi to Grandma Bootsy's," he winked.

"Daddy!" Tanisha whispered. "I won't need this," she insisted.

"Just in case. You never know. I'll feel better knowing that you have car fare," he said. "Hug your mother," he ordered, steering

Tanisha toward Billie who hugged her tightly too.

Glen stared at Tanisha curiously. "Excuse me, Mr. Carlson. What time did you say to have her home?" he asked. "I didn't catch the time."

"A reasonable hour," Jackie repeated without looking at Glen.

Glen stared at Tanisha. Tanisha shrugged. "What does that mean, Daddy?" Tanisha asked.

"I'm sure the two of you will figure out a time that is acceptable," Jackie grinned. "And by the way, I'll be at the house waiting for you when you get home," he finished. "Let's go Billie. I'm starving," Jackie stated as he walked toward his car.

Tanisha looked from her mother to her father and back at Glen. "Mom! What time do I need to be home tonight?" she pleaded. "Is this some kind of riddle?"

Billie smiled. "You heard your father, Tanisha. He said a reasonable hour," her mother shrugged dismissively. "Have fun!" Tanisha slanted her eyes and scowled.

Tanisha stared curiously at her parents as her father held the car door open for Billie. Her eyes bulged and her jaw hung open when she saw Billie smile tenderly at Jackie and rub her hand along his cheek.

"Gross!" she squealed.

"What's the matter?" Glen asked, his voice exuding bass and confidence once again. "I think it's sweet that your old man is such a gentleman. He looks like he was probably quite the ladies man back in the day," Glen teased.

"I think a gnat just flew in my mouth!" she groaned fanning at a swarm of gnats. Bending low at the waist, she grabbed the hem of her dress and lifted it above her ankles and carefully spit several times onto the pavement.

"Aren't you the ladylike princess," Glen laughed. "Did Cinderella spit before she went to the big ball?" he teased.

"Bite me!" Tanisha mocked. "I have a toothbrush in my purse. I'm going to go inside for a minute and brush the bug particles out of my braces and reapply my lipstick. I'll be right back, Glen," she explained.

"Good! Because I don't want to taste bug juice," Glen said softly, as he gently placed his arm around her waist and guided her across the street.

Tanisha paused. Once again, her jaw hung slack. Her spine tingled as Glen used his finger to gently raise her chin to close her mouth. Grace was right! *He's finally going to kiss me tonight!*

Not sure how to respond, she smiled sweetly and let her eyes roam over his shoulder as her dad slowly careened down the street. Squinting, she watched as Jackie casually draped his arm over the passenger seat, and rested it gently on Billie's shoulder. This time Tanisha's eyes and jaw widened simultaneously as her mouth served as a cave to another gnat.

Chapter 9

The Last Dance

The bus was late. She checked her watch. 11:37. She would miss her curfew. Again. *What will my excuse be this time? I lost my wallet? Too lame. Besides, I love this wallet. I don't want to pretend to lose it. I'll tell her that my new friend Kyle wasn't feeling well so I waited with her for her parents to return from their black tie event. Not plausible. She'll probably be looking out the window and if she doesn't see me get out of their car, she won't believe it. Andrea is already getting suspicious. Well, it won't matter anyway. It's over. I can't believe that he would do that to me!* She felt the tears pooling in her eyes. *No time for a pity party. You've got too much to deal with as it is. Get it together, girlfriend.*

In the distance, she heard the L train rambling down the tracks. If she ran she could catch it and make it home in time for her curfew. The L was only three blocks from their apartment. Three dark, scary blocks, made scarier because it was almost midnight. She weighed her options. She'd only taken the L once, and it had been quite a harrowing experience in broad daylight.

"I got extension cords!" he bellowed. "Who needs a extension cord? I also got tube socks, incense and rubber gloves," he added. He strode slowly through the car, pulling a tattered, wheeled duffle bag and studying each passenger intently as they stared idly out the window. She watched curiously as they raised their newspapers to shield their eyes from his penetrating gaze. A sample of the products that he hawked draped across his arm. "Y'all know you always need a extra extension cord," he continued. "I'm sure some of y'all have some bad kids that need whoopins, and it's nice to have a extra one on hand," he laughed. "Give it up!" he chided. "Y'all know that was funny," he insisted. He posed in the aisle like a carnival barker. "Y'all a tough crowd. Y'all could at least laugh at a brotha's jokes," he scowled. He stood stoically, never losing his balance as the L lurched to a stop at the next platform. She noticed a deep scar on his right cheek. The scar was raised like a speed bump and appeared leathery against his dark brown skin. She studied the small skull cap that was pulled over his ears, admiring the red, black and green stitching that formed the continent of Africa on the front of his cap. As he walked toward her row, she smiled and quickly diverted her gaze. Too late. She'd made eye contact with him. He quickly walked over to her seat.

"How about you, little lady," he said softly. "You need a extension cord or some tube socks?" he asked. She shook her head. "What about some incense? You look like you might like some incense," he purred. "What's your name cutie?" he continued. Justine held her breath.

"We don't need anything today, young man, now go on about your business and stop bothering my granddaughter," the woman admonished, her voice loud and firm.

"Oh, I'm sorry, Maam," he coughed. "No disrespect. I was just trying to talk to Miss Lady," he said. "Your granddaughter show is pretty," he winked. "I'm gonna go ahead and make this money right quick," he finished. Justine watched as he expertly guided the duffel bag to the next car. She exhaled slowly.

"You can't make eye contact with them, sweetie," the woman said softly. "You must not be from the city are you?" she observed.

Justine shook her head from side to side and stiffened as a standing passenger accidentally lurched into her shoulder when the train pulled into the next platform. "I'm not. I just moved here a couple of months ago," Justine replied. "This is my first time riding the Howard Street L," she said proudly.

"I thought so. These hustlers can smell new money a mile away," she continued. "You have to ride this L like you're invisible, baby. Don't talk to nobody and don't look at nobody," she whispered. "And whatever you do, don't pull out money on the L, honey. Always keep your money and your house keys in your pocket in case they steal your purse," she instructed. "Strap your purse across your body diagonally, and keep one hand on it at all times, sweetie pie. If someone bumps you on the L, check your purse, baby!" she cautioned. "There are some professional pickpockets that work this L like a full time job. I've been riding this L for fifteen years, so I know who they are and they leave me alone," she boasted proudly.

Justine listened intently like a student studies a brilliant instructor, the answers to the final exam, hidden in her every word. "I've seen them pick off so many people on this L that I could write a book about it. But I never say anything," she admitted. "The conductors that work this L know who the pickpockets are too. They don't say nothing neither. I think the pickpockets give them a little hush money to look the other way is what I think," she whispered. "I have to ride this L every day, so I just turn my head and act like I don't see nothing. They know that I see them coming. I've seen them take a wallet or a purse right in front of me, but I've never turned them in. I'm not trying to have them slit my throat because some L riding rookie was too stupid to keep his hand on his wallet. Not my problem, sugar," she shrugged. "But I could tell that you were a rookie, so I thought I'd help you out, baby doll," she continued, shifting her weight in her seat. "I keep my license in my pocket too so if they get my purse they won't have my address," she whispered. "Heck, if they steal my purse all they're going to get is some tissue, my mini Bible and some mints. I only keep a few dollars in my pocket book, everything else is right here," she chuckled patting her large bosom.

Justine held on as the L swerved slowly around a curve, pulling away from the Merchandise Mart stop.

"You have to keep a few dollars in your purse, honey, because if they rob you and you don't have any money on you, then they'll know that you're lying and hiding it somewhere," she said pointedly. "Who comes out of the house with no money, baby doll?" she asked not expecting a response. "Always have a few dollars to turn over, so they won't hurt you, but keep most of your money hidden somewhere on your body," she repeated. She studied Justine's expression, her eyes roaming up and down Justine's body. "You're such a tiny little thing, sugar. Your money might fall out of your little training bra," she laughed. "But try to remember to keep it tucked somewhere where they can't find it, baby. Don't put it in your shoe either, 'cause I've seen these thugs make people take off their shoes knowing that a lot of people keep their money in their shoe when they ride the L. "This is my stop, sugar," she said. "I'm gonna squeeze on by you and get off. Take care of yourself, sweetie," she advised. "Be safe."

Justine watched as Honey-Sugar-Sweetie Pie-Baby maneuvered her massive frame off the train. She immediately strapped her small purse diagonally across her body as the woman advised.

∽◌◡

That was the last time she'd ridden the L. After her bicycle mugging on Lake Shore Drive, her mother would not allow her to ride the L and only allowed her to take the bus to get to school.

Her father had replaced her pink bicycle with a yellow one,

and now she only rode along the lake with her brothers. "Safety in numbers," her neighbors had said. "You can't be too careful. This is a major city, and crime knows no boundaries."

The L train rumbling became louder. Her heart raced. It was decision time. The bus was the safer option. She could sit in front with the driver, and the bus stop was directly in front of her building. *I don't know how often the buses run late at night. Is it every twenty minutes like during the day or is it every hour? What will my mother do if I'm an hour late for my curfew?* She paced and clenched her fists. *If the L is a scary ride in the middle of the day, I can't imagine what it's like at night. Plus, I'll have to walk three blocks through the neighborhood to get home. But if I'm late for curfew one more time, I'll be grounded! I'll run the three blocks to my apartment. It's harder to attack a moving target, right?* She knew that if she sprinted up the stairs, she could get to the platform as the train pulled in. She turned to run, but stopped when she heard her name.

"Justine!" the voice yelled. "Justine!" he screamed louder.

She turned her head and squinted into the darkness. Her heart leaped, when she saw his face under a streetlight. He slowed his pace to a trot when he realized that she recognized him. He stopped at her feet and bent at the waist, grabbing his knees to catch his breath like a point guard during a twenty second time out.

"I've been looking all over for you," he gasped. He stood up and bent over again to breathe deeply. She felt sorry for him as he gently placed his hand on her shoulder to steady himself. The angry part of her wanted to smack his hand from her shoulder, and sprint for the train, but the compassionate part of her pitied him. He wasn't supposed to run at night. She allowed him to take several deep breaths before speaking.

"Do you have your inhaler?" she asked softly. "You know you're not supposed to run at night," she scolded.

She watched as his lips sucked at the night air, like a goldfish. "I'm okay," he said. "I can breathe better now," he paused. "I've been looking all over for you," he panted slowly. "Why'd you leave like that?"

His breaths remained small and deliberate. His asthma was activated when he ran at night. He'd explained that the mucus build up was worse at night, describing his labored breaths as being forced to sip through a tiny straw when you really want to take a big gulp. His breathing emergency under control, Justine's anger returned full throttle. "I have to be home by midnight," she said curtly.

"I know you do," he said, still gripping his knees. "I was planning to take you home. You shouldn't be out here at night by yourself," he admonished. "It's way too dangerous. Anything could happen to you."

She glared at him and studied her watch. "I missed my train," she groaned. "Now I'm going to be late for curfew again."

He stood up straight and stared into her face. "Justine, why'd you walk off like that?" he asked. "I came back from the dance floor and you were gone," he stated. "I asked Ian if he'd seen you and he told me that you said you were taking the bus home," he continued. "I ran to the bus stop and didn't see you, and I was about to turn around when I heard the L coming and something told me to check the L platform," he continued. "Please tell me you weren't going to ride the L by yourself at this time of night," he said.

"It's only five stops," she shrugged. "I'm not scared," she huffed folding her arms across her chest.

He grabbed her hands in his. "What did I do? Why'd you run off like that?" he pleaded.

She stared at her watch. "I'm going to stand here until you tell me what I did," he stated, folding his arms across his chest.

Justine raised her eyes to his. "You know what you did," Justine muttered.

"No. Actually, I don't," he admitted. "I wish I did."

"I can't believe that you would dance with her," Justine barked. "You know that I'm not feeling well and I have to be home for curfew, and you let some girl drag you onto the dance floor?" she screamed. "That was so disrespectful!" she yelled, punching him in his chest.

He took a step back and raised his eyebrow. "Is that what this is about?" he asked. "You storm off and put your safety in danger because I danced with someone else?"

She glared at him with daggers in her eyes. "I'm standing there saying my goodbyes to your friends and all of a sudden I see you getting dragged onto the dance floor," Justine shared. "And you wouldn't dance with me once. You told me that you hate to dance. How do you think that made me feel?" she asked. "I felt stupid, that's how I felt!" she screamed. "Why didn't you dance with me, AM?" Justine asked suspiciously. "Are you afraid that your snooty Northwestern friends might see you dancing with your black, high school girlfriend?"

His face became intensely serious. "I can't believe that you would say that, Justine," he said softly, his voice barely audible. "I brought you to the party," he reminded. "I introduced you to all of my friends as my girlfriend. We walked around holding hands all night. Why would you say that?" he asked.

She didn't have a response. He was right. He'd made a point of parading her around and introducing her to all of his friends at the party. No one had even looked at her oddly. She studied her watch. 12:03. Justine had turned into a pumpkin and was officially late for curfew.

"You're already late for curfew, and I'll get you home, but we need to finish this because I'm confused," he said. "You danced with

Ian, but you storm off because I danced with someone else and didn't dance with you tonight?"

"It's totally different. Totally!" she screeched.

"How's it different, Justine?" AM asked. "I'm confused. Please enlighten me," he said.

Justine rolled her eyes at him. "No, I'm serious," he continued. "I don't see the difference."

"Ian is your roommate. You know him, and I know him. And remember," she paused. "Before he asked me to dance he asked you if it was okay. I don't even know that girl's name, and you dance with her without so much as a glance at me," Justine explained, her hands flailing in the air. "I would never dance with someone right in front of your face," she continued. "That's disrespectful."

AM stared at Justine thoughtfully. "I hadn't thought of that," he admitted.

"I danced with Ian on a fast song, and he's dating one of my best friends," she continued. "Plus, he's your roommate," Justine repeated, her tone remarkably calmer. "I don't know who this girl is," she said. "For all I know she could be your campus girlfriend," she continued. "Plus, she's really cute," she added softly.

He raised his head and chuckled at that suggestion.

"What's so funny?" Justine asked. "Is this funny to you?" she whined. "Now I'm a big joke?" Her anger was returning.

"No, sweetie," AM explained. "I was chuckling that you would think that she could be my girlfriend," he laughed. "She has a boyfriend at Princeton. Her boyfriend is from my home town. We went to high school together. Her name is Kelly, and she always asks me to dance because she knows that I'm safe," he continued. "She likes to dance," he shrugged. "I should have introduced you to her. It never occurred to me that you would get upset about me dancing with her," he admitted. "Never occurred to me," he repeated. "I always dance with her when I see her at the fraternity parties, so it was like second nature for me to let her drag me out there," he explained. "I hate to dance. Hateithateithateit!" he said, the words running together quickly. "I never dance. I only dance with her because she won't take no for an answer," he continued. "So when she pulled me onto the dance floor, it was second nature for me," he admitted. "I'm really sorry, baby," he said.

Justine's face softened. Honey-Sugar-Sweetie Pie. She loved it when he called her pet names. Embarrassed, she smiled at him cautiously.

"I should have introduced you to her," he continued, his arms resting gently around her waist. "But help me understand why it made a difference that it was a slow song," he stated. "Would it have mattered if it was a fast song? Would you have stormed off?"

"You're so clueless," she laughed, staring at him oddly. She wrapped her arms around his waist. "Because when you dance to a slow song, you're inside the person's personal space like this," she explained. She pulled him into her body. "It's a lot more personal than dancing with someone to a fast song," Justine finished. "It's more intimate."

"But we weren't dancing as close as you and I are standing right now," AM shared. "There was at least a foot of space between us," he admitted. He pulled away from Justine's frame to demonstrate the gap.

"But you could have been," she explained, pulling herself back into his body. "You could have grabbed her butt and meshed your body into hers like this," Justine demonstrated.

"Hey there!" AM squealed. "I had no idea I was missing all of this action on the dance floor. Maybe I should become a dancer," he chuckled. Justine smacked him on his butt.

"Are you still mad at me?" he asked softly, taking a deep breath and squeezing her waist.

She could feel his warm breath on her eye lids. She inhaled his scent. He smelled like Prell shampoo. She ran her hands through his thick hair and shook her head. She could feel his nose on her earlobe. She relaxed in his arms as he nibbled her earlobe and ran his lips along her cheek and softly brushed his lips against hers like a butterfly kiss. Her legs felt like noodles.

∞∞∞

Justine never quite understood what had tripped his memory, but on his way to take her to the hospital to see her mother after the bicycle mugging, Ian had suddenly remembered that his roommate had misplaced his dorm key before heading to the library. "Don't worry, roomie," he'd said. I'm just going to be here studying all day and if I leave I'll leave the door unlocked for you," he'd explained.

It wasn't until they were nearing the Northwestern campus that he remembered that he'd locked their dorm room door out of habit.

"It'll just take a minute, Justine," Ian explained as he shifted the car into park. "I'm just going to run up and unlock my dorm room for my roommate. Too late," he groaned. "There's my roommate right there." Justine noticed a boy sitting against the building. "But he doesn't look too pissed. He must not have been waiting for me for too long," he observed. "Come out and meet him. He won't kill me with you as my cover."

The Tylenol that Ian had insisted that she take was making her feel a little better. Her neck didn't feel as stiff. She squinted into the sunlight and stepped out of the car.

"Whas' up AM!" Ian said loudly. "I'm so sorry, dude," he offered. "At the last second, I remembered that I locked the door, so here I am," he grinned. AM stared at Ian without speaking. "This is Justine," Ian continued. "She's one of Rashanda's best friends. She got mugged on her bike this afternoon, and I'm taking her to the hospital where her mother works so they can run some tests," he explained. "She blacked out and hit her head when she fell off her bike," he continued. "Her mother is a nurse so I figured that she may as well meet her mother at the hospital because when she finds out that she blacked out, she'll want to make sure that she doesn't have a concussion," he finished.

AM's gaze softened when he looked at Justine. He smiled. "Nice to meet you, Justine," he introduced, extending his hand to her. "I'm AM. Did you throw up?" he asked.

Justine was taken aback by the question. "Did I throw up?" she repeated.

"Yes. Did you throw up after you hit your head?" he asked again.

"No. I didn't," she replied, staring at Ian for support, her eyes wandering from AM to Ian.

"Do you feel like you need to throw up now?" he continued.

"No," she shrugged.

"Yo, dude," Ian groaned. "Enough of the vomit talk," he finished. "She's my patient. I've been with her for over an hour, and I've done a thorough assessment. I've been subtly watching her for signs of a concussion. She's good. I'm just taking her to the hospital as a precaution so that her mother can rule it out herself," he explained. "I'm pre-med too, dog, so of course I screened my patient thoroughly!"

AM laughed heartily. "My apologies, Doctor," AM teased. "It's a force of habit."

"Are you pre-med too, AM?" Justine asked.

"Yes, he is," Ian replied for AM. "I'm the chemistry whiz, but he's the biology genius. I helped him get through organic and inorganic chemistry, and he's helping me with my advanced biology course this quarter," he explained. "We're quite the science dynamic duo," he gleamed.

Ian watched as AM studied Justine. He observed how Justine smoothed out her shorts and twirled her hair. His gaze moved from Justine to AM. He noticed AM's smile as he reached into his backpack and offered Justine a mint and how she smiled demurely when she accepted it, her eyelashes batting in rapid succession.

"What does AM stand for," Justine asked curiously. "Are those your initials?"

AM looked at Ian who waved his hands across his face and backed away. "It's your name, you explain it, dude," Ian laughed.

"No. My name is Jacob Wahlberg," AM shared. "But my roomie here decided to nickname me AM because I'm an early riser," he explained. "I go to bed by eleven o'clock most nights, but I wake up at about five o'clock in the morning to get a work out in and study before classes," he continued. "Now the whole campus calls me AM," he shrugged. "No one knows me by my real name."

Ian laughed heartily. "That's because your real name is AM," Ian chuckled. "Hey roommate," Ian blurted. "Why don't you ride to the hospital with us?" he suggested. "Justine will ride home with her mother, and this way I don't have to ride back by myself."

AM looked hopefully at Justine. "I'm done studying for the afternoon," he said casually. "I was going to take a break before dinner. I don't mind going for the ride if it's okay with Justine," he said.

Justine smiled widely. "That's fine. I'll need all of the moral support I can get once my mother finds out that I was riding my bike along the lake by myself," she groaned. "The more the merrier!"

❧☙

His lips were soft and sweet. She was glad that he didn't drink. His kiss tasted like root beer. Lost in his embrace, she heard the chimes of a church clock off in the distance. She opened her eyes and peered at her watch. 12:15. By the time they walked back to campus to get in his car, she wouldn't make it home before 12:30 even if they sped the entire way. *What am I going to tell my mother?*

He slowly pulled his lips away from hers and stared into her eyes. "Do you forgive me now?" he asked.

Blinking her eyes several times, she awakened from her dreamlike state. Smiling demurely, she slowly shook her head and inhaled.

"We'd better go," AM suggested. "If we hurry, I can have you home by 12:30," he said. "Have you thought about what you're going to tell your mother?" he asked.

"You sure do know how to kill a mood," she groaned. "I haven't a clue what I'm going to tell Andrea this time," she confessed. "I'm running out of stories."

"Let's run back to my car," he said. "We'll think of something on the way."

"You're not supposed to run at night, AM," Justine reminded. "I don't want you to have an asthma attack. Besides, I'm already late," she shrugged. "What's fifteen more minutes? Plus, my leg is starting to throb."

"My breathing is cool now," he shared. "It really only gets out of control at night if I run or I'm feeling anxious, and I was so scared that you were out here by yourself, that I got all worked up," he explained.

Justine bit her lip and squeezed his hand. "I'm sorry I made you anxious and I had you running at night," she said softly. "I just couldn't watch you slow dancing with that girl."

"That's behind us now," AM reminded. "Let's not talk about it anymore. We were both at fault. Case closed," he ordered. "What was I saying? Oh, I remember now," he brightened. "We were talking about my asthma. I work out every day, and my asthma doesn't flare up at all when I run in the morning," he continued. "The doctor said that running along the lake in the morning and getting fresh air is good for me," he finished as he slowed his pace. "I sometimes forget that you have a bad leg," he said. "We can walk. I just don't want you to get in any more trouble than you probably already are," he shared, as he gently kissed her hand before lacing his fingers in hers. "Is this slow enough?" he asked tenderly. Sugar – Baby- Honey-Sweetie

"This is fine. It only aches when I've been standing for too long, and then my limp comes back," she explained.

"What's the worst that could happen when you get home?" he asked.

Justine leaned her head into his shoulder. "Who knows?" Justine groaned. "She'll try to suspend my phone privileges, but I'll use the phone to call you when she's at work," she shared. "She can't ground me from the car because we only have one car anyway, and she uses it to go to work," she sighed as AM wrapped his arm around her shoulders. "And if she says I can't leave the house at night, I'll take the bus to campus to see you on the weekend during the day while she's at work," Justine offered. "My brothers will cover for me," she grinned as AM rubbed his chin stubble across her cheek. "The only real leverage that she has is to not allow me to go to prom," Justine mocked. "But she wouldn't do that. She's not a monster."

"Looks like you have it all figured out," AM observed. "Why don't you just go for broke and spend the night in my dorm room?" he yawned. "You can sleep on Ian's bed."

"Now you've lost your mind," Justine stated. "Andrea would peel off a layer of skin if I was that bold," she said. She loved how he always opened the car door for her. She climbed into her seat and fastened her seatbelt.

AM started the car. "Fasten your seat belt, sleepy head," she insisted.

"I forgot. You're a seat belt addict," he teased.

Justine smiled at him and closed her eyes, trying to fight the memory, but the brief flashback returned in full force every time she rode in a car, like a nightmare waiting to taunt her. The therapist had suggested that Justine try to replace the terror with another, happier thought, but it never worked. Since the car accident, she suffered from post traumatic stress disorder or PTSD where traumatic events replay themselves in the person's mind. The doctor told her that with time, the realness of the accident wouldn't feel as vivid. Sadly, the memory would always be there, but time would begin to dull the intensity of the image, as Justine's mind replaced that image with others. He also told her that she suffered from survivor's guilt, a common emotion shared by survivors of a tragedy.

Daily Justine asked herself the question, "Why was I spared, God? Why did you let me live and take Lori and Charlotte?" When she asked the doctor these questions, he couldn't provide an answer, but told her that she shouldn't trouble herself trying to source one. "Don't blame yourself for surviving the crash, Justine. It won't bring your friends back. Just live your life with purpose every day," he coached. "There is a purpose in life, and a purpose in death. You are alive to fulfill some purpose that God has only for you," he encouraged.

She'd learned to live with the image and guilt. Sometimes, she could hear her voice telling Lori not to do it, but other times she couldn't remember if her words had been audible or just in her head.

The words lodged in Justine's throat. The image returned as Justine watched Lori unfasten her seatbelt and reach for the steering wheel. If she had just stayed in her seatbelt, she'd be alive today. But Lori knew that Charlotte didn't have on her seatbelt. She died trying to save her sister.

"Justine, baby, wake up," he nudged gently. "You're the only person that I know who can fall asleep on a seven minute car ride," AM laughed. "Be careful crossing the street," he insisted. He leaned over and kissed her on the lips.

"I'll flash the hall light so you know I made it inside," Justine said.

"Don't forget," AM yawned. "The last time I dropped you off, you forgot to flash the light, and I had to call you and wake up your mother," he reminded.

"I won't forget," Justine smiled, leaning over and giving him another kiss and a hug.

He gripped her hand softly. "Justine, when are you going to tell your mother about us?" he asked.

Justine lowered her head and looked at him tenderly. "AM, I'm going to tell her soon. I promise," she said.

She watched as AM put the car in park. "When?" he asked. "We've been sneaking around for almost a year, and your mother still doesn't know about me," he teased. "Are you ashamed of me?" he asked as he playfully tickled her side.

"It's complicated," she giggled. "It's just very complicated."

"Your mother was nice to me when I met her at the hospital after you got mugged," he reminded. "She was super nice, and you said yourself that your mother won't mind that I'm white," he finished.

She squeezed his fingers softly. "You're right, she won't care that you're white, but she'll care that your family is Jewish, remember?" she said softly.

AM's eyes looked at her intensely. "Oh, that's right," he sighed. "But I haven't been to synagogue since my bar mitzvah," AM pleaded. "So technically, I'm not anything," he explained. "I'm Jewish, but I'm not a practicing Jew," he finished. His soft hands rubbed her fingers gently as he stared into her face. "So we just won't tell her that I'm

Jewish. Problem solved."

Justine smiled at AM softly. "It's not that simple and you know it," she replied. "Andrea will assume that you're Jewish because of your name, and then she'll start asking you a lot of questions. And then she'll lecture me that your family wouldn't accept me if we got serious because I'm not Jewish, so why bother getting involved with a boy when you know how it's going to end, blah, blah, blah," she groaned. "I'm just not ready for her to give me the Christian lecture," Justine explained.

AM pulled her into a tight embrace, his biceps squeezing around her shoulders, she could feel his breath on her face as he slowly pulled away. His fingertips grazed the top of her shoulders as he spoke. "I understand," he admitted. "I really do, but I'm not going to keep sneaking around Justine. It's not right," he continued, his tone serious and bland. "I don't like watching you tell lies to your mother so we can spend time together," he paused. "I believe in truth and honesty, and you should too," he shared. "So the next talk we have, I want to work on our script to tell your mother about our relationship," he finished, gently tilting her chin up to his face as he kissed her goodbye.

She quickly glanced up to her apartment window and remembered to limp softly just in case her mother was peeking through the window. When he dropped her off, he always parked just out of the line of vision from her apartment windows. Justine had scoped out the perfect spot from every window in their unit, and knew that her mother could not see his car. He drove slowly down the street watching for her safety until she walked into the vestibule. She watched as AM pulled the car into the gas station across the street from her building to wait for her to flicker the light in the hallway. Justine quietly climbed the stairs and quickly flicked the hall light three times before keying into her family's unit. They'd worked out a signal. If she flicked the light once, that meant that she was in distress. Three flicks meant that she was safely in the apartment.

The house was eerily quiet. Justine tiptoed into the sun room and watched from the window as AM's car sped down Sheridan Road. Exhausted, she didn't have a solid cover story, and knew that she was not adequately prepared for an interrogation. She took a long, slow breath, and sighed as she carefully tiptoed down the long hallway into the kitchen. She braced herself, expecting to see her mother tapping her foot in the small dining room that they used as a family room. As she passed their bedrooms, she heard her brothers snoring softly. Fudge purred softly on the sofa. She walked back to the front of the apartment and peered in her mother's room. Andrea wasn't in her bed. Justine's heart raced.

She must have gone out looking for me! I wonder what time she left. Shoot! I'll tell her that my leg was throbbing, so I laid down at Kyle's to rest it and fell asleep, and when I woke up I realized it was past my curfew. She knows that my leg sometimes gives me trouble at night. I'll have to call Kyle at the crack of dawn so she can cover for me.

Justine quickly smacked herself across her forehead. If she's in the streets looking for you, she's probably already called Kyle's house, genius! She knows you weren't there tonight, stupid! She's probably called the police station by now. I'm so busted. Justine raced into her room and slipped into her pajamas. She grabbed a magazine and settled into the sofa in the living room. I need a story. Quick! She covered her face with her hands. Maybe AM is right. Maybe I should just tell her the truth tonight.

Justine settled into the sofa and dozed. Thirty minutes later, she heard voices in the hallway. Brace yourself, girlfriend. She's been out looking for you for at least an hour. You're in big trouble!

"I'll be fine, Bob," her mother's voice assured softly. Justine leaned in to listen closer. "You're such a gentleman for walking me to my door. Thank you so much for dinner. I had a really nice time, Sweetie," Mrs. Wellington giggled.

She stared at the door suspiciously. Sweetie? Since when do the police let you call them by their first name and take you to dinner?

"I did too, honey," a deep voice bellowed. "Lock this door as soon as you get inside," the male voice ordered.

"Aye, aye, Captain," Mrs. Wellington giggled. "I'll talk to you tomorrow," she whispered as the key turned slowly in the lock. Justine watched as her mother glided through the doorway, gingerly closing and locking the door before leaning her frame against the wall. She closed her eyes and sighed longingly, her lips squeezed tightly into a dream like smile.

Entranced by her mother's odd behavior, Justine felt like a voyeur. She stared curiously as her mother hugged herself and twirled in the foyer, apparently still oblivious to the glow of light from the small reading lamp nestled near the fireplace and Justine snuggled on the sofa. Andrea twirled again.

Oh my God! Is she twirling? She clearly wasn't scouring the streets looking for me. That's for sure!

Justine coughed loudly. "Hi, Mom," she said suspiciously. "Where've you been?"

"Oh, my goodness!" her mother exclaimed clutching her chest. "I didn't see you sitting over there, Justine. You scared me half to death," she stammered. What in the world are you doing still awake?"

"I couldn't sleep," Justine shared, eyeing her mom curiously. "My leg was hurting, so I wanted to elevate it on some pillows," she explained.

The mere mention of an ailment in the air shifted Mrs.

Wellington's tone from the giddy high school voice that Justine heard fluttering in the hallway to her Nurse Wellington voice. She walked over to Justine and pecked her on the forehead. "How long has it been hurting, sweetie? Have you iced it? Did you take any pain relievers?" she continued. "Do you want me to rub some ointment on your joints?" Mrs. Wellington finished, the questions spilling from her mouth in rapid fire succession.

Justine was familiar with her mother's nurse routine. Every sniffle, fever or cough was met with the same rapid fire stream of questions. She was glad that the room was dark, save the small reading lamp, and that her mother couldn't see her face very well. She hated to lie to her mother. Justine knew that her mother could look at her face and tell when she was lying. "I took a Tylenol," Justine fibbed. "It's feeling a lot better since I have it propped on these pillows."

Her mother gently patted Justine's thigh. "Good. I'm glad you're feeling better. Sometimes your hip socket will flare up when the weather is a little damp like it was today," she explained. "How was Kyle's party, sugar?" her mother stammered.

"Just fine," Justine lied. Dodged that bullet! "We had a nice time. Who's Bob, Mom?" My mom has someone calling her Sugar, Baby, Honey, Sweetie?

Chapter 10

The Jazzy Truth

Liz signed her name to the last check and inhaled deeply, her eyes casually studying the small office for a sign. She felt violated, like someone who returns home to learn that they've been robbed. She imagined the sense of loss that the homeowners must feel knowing that a stranger handled their private possessions. She'd heard stories of people moving because they couldn't recover from the sense of violation. But she couldn't move. This was her home, and the intruder was someone that she loved more than life itself. The robber had taken something more valuable than money or jewelry; the thief had stolen her trust.

The office had become her sanctuary, the place where she could retreat with a good magazine and a hot cup of coffee to escape from the pressures of her new life. Only now, the sacredness of her sanctuary had been disturbed. She loved her new job, but it carried with it a certain amount of performance stress. Recently promoted to Assistant Vice President of Personnel at her bank, Liz Wesley was on a career fast track. When she received her promotion, her boss complimented her on how effortlessly she seemed to balance her work responsibilities with her duties as a single parent. She was quick to give God the credit for the balance in her new life, sharing that her faith, coupled with her commitment to take time out for herself by exercising regularly, getting weekly manicures and monthly massages strengthened her body, mind and spirit. The blank stare that he gave her told her that he didn't understand. She stopped short of sharing that part of her secret weapon for living well and getting on with her life involved spending time alone, reading her Bible, meditating and sometimes just napping in her newly decorated home sanctuary.

Liz studied the small room carefully. She'd planned to pay the monthly bills and settle into her chair to read the Sunday paper before starting dinner, but as she reached for the checkbook, she knew instantly that something was awry. The expensive pen, a college graduation gift from her father, had tipped her off. She rubbed the shiny black pen lovingly, caressing the gold pocket clip with her thumb.

The gift had not been a surprise. John Willard was a gentleman of tradition, and believed that the proper graduation gift was a fancy pen. He'd given her a Cross silver pen and pencil set when she graduated from high school. Her brother Emmett had also received a pen and pencil set upon graduation from high school, and a Mont Blanc pen when he graduated from Stanford University. The contrast made her smile. Liz graduated from the local state college and Emmett graduated from the prestigious Stanford University. But to their dad, a college degree was a college degree. John Willard was equally proud of both of his children and celebrated their accomplishment by giving them the same fancy Mont Blanc pen after graduating from college.

She didn't have the heart to tell her dad that she'd lost her high school gift when she and Neal moved to their home in Newberry East. Riddled with guilt, she'd replaced it with an identical set, just in case her father ever asked to see it. But it wasn't the same, the replacement set was an imposter, and she knew it. Liz treasured her college graduation gift. She cleaved to it. Her Mont Blanc pen was kept in her special off limits drawer. She only used it when writing checks from the checking account that her father's extreme generosity had helped inflate.

The account was now quite "flush" as her son would say. She'd heard Neal use this word when his grandfather gave him two hundred dollars for his sixteenth birthday gift. "My account is flush, Grandpa!" Neal exclaimed. Mrs. Wesley pondered why having a lot of money in your account meant that it was flush. "Flush, Neal?" she asked. "What does that mean?" Her handsome son grinned widely. "It's a poker reference," Neal and her father replied simultaneously. "In poker, a flush is a good thing, Moms," Neal continued. She wondered how he knew how to play poker and why he added an "s" to mom, and considered asking him to explain, but thought better of it.

Initially, she'd protested against her dad giving Neal such a large sum of money for his birthday, but her father had insisted. "It's my money, Liz Wesley, and I'll do what I damn well please with it!" he'd barked. She'd acquiesced. She knew that when her father used profanity, he was not in a negotiating mood. The only thing that she had insisted is that Neal tithe ten percent of his birthday gift to church and place half of the balance in his savings account as was their family practice with gifts. Neal gladly handed his mother a twenty dollar bill to add to the family's weekly tithe. She remembered smiling as her father gently patted Neal on the back, glad that their bond had grown closer since her dad's move to Newberry East.

After her divorce, she'd insisted that her father come over for Sunday dinners, a request that he gladly obliged. She enjoyed cooking again now that her dad was a regular Sunday evening guest in their home. Neal and Maria didn't appreciate her new interest in French cuisine, part of her 'look forward and start fresh campaign,' a campaign she'd started after her divorce became final. She poured through cookbooks and whipped up interesting menu items that Neal and Maria barely noticed. The beef burgundy was devoured by

Neal in the same manner that he devoured a Big Mac and was pushed around on Maria's plate like it was tuna casserole. The honey glazed Cornish hens were consumed like chicken, with no mention of the rosemary, basil and thyme that she'd lovingly rubbed on the petite birds as they marinated in an expensive oak aged merlot that she'd bought just for the recipe. But her dad was different. Although a meat and potatoes guy, her dad always complimented her meals and took home a Tupperware container of leftovers for dinner the next day. On his next visit to their home, he would return with the Tupperware container, placing it on the counter to be filled with more leftovers. As best she could tell, she'd not prepared a meal that he didn't enjoy. Liz smiled at the newly created normalcy that their lives had taken on?

Her dad enjoyed living in the senior building, and was keeping regular company with three of the widowed female residents who were competing for his affection. All three gladly invited him to join them for dinner at least once a week. Her dad never had to cook dinner. Between the Sunday meal that she cooked, and the leftovers that he carted home after his meals, his dinners (and some lunches) were prepared for him by the women in his life.

"I'm never going to remarry, Liz," he'd joked. "Your mother can never be replaced. I've told all three of them that," he explained, his right index finger waving gently, in its customary semicircle pose. As a young teen, he'd worked in his father's butcher shop, and had severed the tendon in that finger chopping meat with a cleaver. He called this finger his trigger finger because it saved him from being drafted during World War II. He couldn't pass the basic training physical because he couldn't bend that finger, the finger that is customarily used to pull the trigger on a weapon. "But I don't mind sharing a good meal with an interesting lady. It keeps me young," he'd chuckled. "I usually see Barbara on Tuesday, Carolyn on Wednesday and Amelia on Thursday.

They know what day of the week belongs to them," he paused. "They know that I bowl with the fellas on Friday night, and play poker on Saturday night," he continued. "If they want to cook for me, then I'll eat it," he winked. "All three of them can cook, and lucky for them they're all easy on the eyes," he boasted. "I think they think it's a competition. Like I'm going to settle down with the one who cooks the best," he laughed. "Let them think that. It keeps them on their toes."

Neal had called him a player. Liz didn't need a translation for this piece of slang and shuddered imagining her dad on a date. "Grandpa, you should call them by the day of the week that you go over for dinner," Neal laughed. "Instead of calling them Barbara, Carolyn and Amelia, just call them Tuesday, Wednesday and Thursday," he giggled.

Liz was grateful that he reserved Sunday dinners for her family. Her mother always made extra special meals for Sunday dinner. No matter what the main course was: pot roast, chicken, ham, turkey or neck bones, her mother cooked collard greens on Sunday, and Liz always helped her mother pick the greens. She washed them by hand in a sink full of soapy water to remove any dirt or bug particles and then triple rinsed them before she could play outside after church. The process was laborious, but she enjoyed having her mother to herself while her brother Emmett watched television with their dad. She loved to walk into the house and inhale the smell from a large pot of collard greens simmering on the stove, a piece of fatback or salt pork floating in the pot. She and Emmett often fought over who got the largest piece of fatback, savoring the sweet taste as the fat melted in their mouth. She chuckled. Neal and Maria didn't eat pork, and the thought of eating a piece of fat was as revolting to them as eating squirrel.

"Why do you call it 'pick' the greens, Mom?" an eleven year old

125

Liz had asked. "Why don't you just say clean the greens?" she stated. "That's what we're doing. We're cleaning the greens. We're not picking them from the garden."

"Because we're picking all of the dirt and bugs off of them, Lizzy-Busy," her mother had replied. "We're 'picking' the greens," she shrugged. "That's what all of the black folks say, 'picking' the greens. I remember helping my mother pick the greens on Sunday when I was a lot younger than you," she explained. "I guess we could just say we're cleaning the greens," she paused. "But that doesn't even sound right. Cleaning the greens," she tested. "It just doesn't sound right. We're picking the greens," she shrugged. "Some things are just tradition, and you just continue it because it's in your blood, baby," she'd finished.

ৼৢঌ

Liz smiled at the sweet memory of her mother, memories that would sweep into her mind daily. The day of her mom's funeral, as her dad consoled a weeping, grieving Liz in the barn, he'd assured her that her mother's memory would live on, and he'd been right. John Willard was usually right.

This Sunday, Liz had decided to surprise her dad and prepare a traditional soul food meal of chicken (fried for her dad and Neal and baked for Maria), macaroni and cheese, collard greens, fresh green beans with Durkee fried onions, hot water cornbread and peach cobbler. She tied one of her mother's old aprons around her waist and hit play on the stereo system to begin her cooking music, her thoughts still searching for an answer. *Why were they in my drawer? Was it Neal or Maria? What were they looking for?* She smiled as her favorite jazz tape hummed. It was the perfect jazz tape.

Her ex-husband, Big Neal had made the tape for her during happier times. There were no two songs from the same artist that appeared back to back on the tape: Ella Fitzgerald, Herbie Hancock, Ramsey Lewis, Nina Simone, George Benson, Billie Holiday, Dizzy Gillespie, Ahmad Jamal, John Coltrane, Wynton Marsalis, Al Jarreau and Diane Schurr. Newer artists blended with the jazz legends. Her ex-husband hated jazz, but he dutifully accompanied her to the Chicago Jazz Festival at the Petrillo Music Shell in Grant Park on opening day as a sense of obligation, usually falling asleep on the blanket spread on the lawn as she enjoyed the free concert.

Liz had studied the piano for twelve years and loved everything about the art form of jazz, often catching the train to the outdoor Ravinia Festival to sit on a blanket and picnic by herself just to hear her favorite performers and get a glimpse of them in the pavilion. She'd wanted a tape of her favorite songs to play in the car, but didn't have the patience to create one from her beloved records. Shortly after Neal, Jr. was born, her husband had surprised her with the tape. She imagined him watching the counter to pause the tape at the end of each song as he lovingly labeled the cassette case with the song title and artist. He'd left the tape on the dining room table wrapped in a red bow. "Enjoy! Liz, my love!" Love, N.

She still had the note and the ribbon. When he'd moved out, she'd painstakingly destroyed most of the memorabilia of their failed marriage. Her wedding band and small diamond ring were unceremoniously taken to a jeweler and traded in for a gold bracelet. She'd considered destroying her wedding photos, but had been advised that Neal and Maria's future offspring might like to see the photos when they got older, so she'd placed the photos in a safety deposit box in Maria and Neal's name. As she walked through the house on her purging rampage, she grabbed the tape, prepared to unravel it with a pencil. But she couldn't bring herself to do it. She knew that it must have taken him over three hours to prepare it, and it had truly been the best gift that he'd ever given her. She loved all of the artists and had memorized the playlist that he'd carefully created. It touched her to think that he'd remembered hearing her exclaim which songs were her personal favorites from the albums in her collection. Her husband had managed to select the perfect song from each of the different albums and put them in the exact same order that she would have had she made the tape herself.

It was the jazz tape that had snapped her out of her rampage. She remembered dropping to her knees and sobbing as she clutched the tape, grateful that her children were with their father for the weekend and wouldn't walk in on her mental meltdown. Standing on her tiptoes, Liz placed the tape on the top of the stereo cabinet. Months later, as she dusted the top shelf, the tape fell at her feet. She bent and studied it, carefully placing it in the cassette player as she cleaned.

She smiled as the jazz sounds danced through the speakers, grateful that she hadn't destroyed her treasured tape. She knew that her father would be arriving in a couple of hours to play chess with Neal, their before dinner Sunday ritual. She loved that her new family structure had a sense of tradition. If only she could convince Maria to help her in the kitchen the way that she'd always helped her mother on Sunday afternoons.

After handling her checkbook, she habitually tucked the pen into the checkbook the same way each time. The Mont Blanc symbol always faced the outside binder of the checkbook, greeting her like a happy pet greets its owner at the end of a long day. The Mont Blanc symbol was like a smile from her dad. But this time when she reached for her checkbook, the pen did not smile at her, the Mont Blanc insignia was upside down. Someone had gone through her things. Which one has been snooping? Probably Maria. I knew it was too much to ask for them to respect my drawer and not go through my things. She's my daughter. I would have snooped too. No wonder she was asking me to show her how to balance a checkbook. She's too afraid to come right out and let me know that she's seen the high balance in my account. She turned on the faucet and filled one side of the double sink with warm soapy water, the other with cold water.

She was singing along with Diane Schurr as Maria walked through the garage door. "Hey Mom, sorry I'm a little late, but the car was dirty so I got it washed when I filled up the tank," Maria said casually. "I hate driving around in a dirty car."

"Thanks, baby!" her mother replied. "I always try to run it through the car wash when I fill up the tank too," she agreed. "I can't stand driving around in a dirty car. It's my pet peeve too," Liz shared. "My mother was the same way," she continued. Some things are just in your blood. "Of course, things were different when your grandmother was alive," she paused. "Grandpa had to wash the car back in those days. They didn't have car washes at the gas stations," she explained. "In fact, all of the gas stations were full service stations and you got your oil checked every time you got gas," she explained. "My mother never took the car to get gas. That was Daddy's job," she laughed. "Portia was old fashioned about a lot of things," she shared.

Maria rustled the shopping bags in her hand. "You've told me that before," Maria groaned. "You repeat yourself a lot, Mom," she finished.

Liz tossed the collard greens into the soapy water and rubbed them together. "I'm sorry, baby," she said. "Your mother is getting old, and I can't remember when I'm repeating myself. Forgive me," she said.

"You're not old yet, Mom," Maria groaned. "You're not even forty. You won't be old until you turn forty. Forty is old," Maria shared.

"Since when is forty old?" Mrs. Wesley asked. "Never mind. Don't answer that. Just hearing your logic will make me feel old," she groaned. "So I'm knocking on the door of old," she mumbled under her breath. "What'd you buy at the mall, sweetie?"

"I bought those jeans that I wanted, and a new pair of sandals to match this adorable sun dress that was on sale," Maria gushed. "I only spent fifty dollars more than you told me to spend," she said quickly. "I have homework to do so I'll be in my room," Maria finished.

Hearing Maria mention money hit a nerve with Liz. "Maria, help me pick these greens," Liz ordered. "We need to talk. You can do your homework a little later. It's only one o'clock." Her tone was serious and stern.

She watched as Maria eyed her suspiciously. Bingo! It was Maria. She was snooping in my drawer. "And don't put on those rubber gloves," she continued. "You need to be able to feel the greens to make sure that you're picking all of the dirt off of them," she finished. "If we do this together, we can finish it quicker," she explained, her tone still firm yet softer. "I'll give you a manicure tonight after dinner. I'll tear the stems."

Maria placed the shopping bags at the bottom of the stairs and walked into the kitchen. Mrs. Wesley was surprised that Maria immediately walked into the small powder room in the laundry room and washed her hands without being told before expertly submerging her hands into the soapy water, gently scrubbing a handful of greens and dunking them in and out of the soapy water. She watched as Maria rinsed the greens in the cold water and placed them in the colander to be rinsed again.

Liz tore the stems and dropped a batch of greens into the water, her hand brushing gently against her daughter's hand as they picked the greens together. Her father's voice rang in her head. Liz, when you have something weighing heavy on your heart, just cut to the chase and get it off your chest, quick, fast and in a hurry. Strike before the person knows what hit them. The element of surprise is the best combat weapon.

"Maria, why were you looking through my checkbook?" she asked. She watched as Maria's face turned red.

She could see Maria searching for a reply. "I, I wasn't looking through your checkbook, Mom," she stammered. "I don't know what you're talking about."

Mrs. Wesley gently placed her hand over her daughter's and stared her directly in the eye. "I don't want to give you the opportunity to lie to me, Maria," she shared. "I know for a fact that you were looking through my private drawer, and that you've been looking at my checkbook. Why?" she repeated sternly.

Maria could feel her heart pounding in her chest. How does she do this? How can she always tell when I'm lying? Is it in the mothering handbook that you don't get until you give birth? Did she have a camera installed in the office? Did she see my fingerprints on the checkbook? Come clean, Maria. "I know you asked us not to open that drawer, Mom, but I was just curious to see what you kept in there," she said softly, her voice that of a six year old. "And when I saw the checkbook I just peeked."

That little girl voice brought back a flood of memories. Maria's first steps, her first day of kindergarten, the first time she tied her shoe by herself.

"Maria, sometimes I need privacy," Liz said softly. "Even though this is my house, and I have the right to rummage through you and your brother's drawers anytime I want, believe it or not, I don't. I respect your privacy," she paused. "I will continue to respect your privacy until I suspect that there is a reason for me not to," she said.

"As I've explained to you and your brother before, this is my house, and everything in this house belongs to me, including what's in your rooms because I'm the parent. However, you and your brother are to respect my privacy at all times. Is that clear?" she finished.

"Yes. I'm sorry, Mom," Maria said. Her hands working slowly as she dunked the greens in the soapy water.

"That batch is clean enough now, sweetie," Mrs. Wesley instructed. "Rinse them off and then rinse the ones in the colander again so I can season them and get them in the pot. They need to simmer slowly for a couple of hours to get the right texture."

"But where did you get so much money, Mom?" Maria asked. "Since you can tell that I looked through your checkbook, I know you can tell that I looked at the bank statements too," she admitted.

Actually, I didn't know that, but thanks for telling on yourself. "Is that why you wanted me to show you how to balance my checkbook?" Mrs. Wesley asked.

Maria smiled sheepishly. "I figured I could play it off and ask you about all of that money then," she confessed. "That's a lot of money, Mom," Maria repeated. "Where did you get so much money?"

Liz inhaled deeply, wishing that the phone would ring to buy her a few minutes to think. You expect your children to tell you the truth, Liz. She's a young lady now. Tell her the truth.

"Your grandfather gave it to me," she explained. "Your grandfather is a very generous man, and when he sold his house, he decided to give your Uncle Emmett and me a part of our inheritance early," she said. "I told him that I was fine, and that I didn't need the money, but he insisted," she shrugged. "You know how your grandfather is."

Maria whistled. "I didn't realize that Grandpa was loaded!" she said loudly. "He doesn't drive a big fancy car, and he doesn't wear expensive clothes or jewelry," she paused. "Who knew?"

Mrs. Wesley shrugged again. "Your grandfather was always that way," she shared. "He hoarded his money like a squirrel saves nuts for the winter," she continued, grateful for the light banter with her daughter. "When we were growing up, I thought we were poor," she offered. "We never had expensive clothes like you and Neal wear. Your uncle and I went to Catholic school and wore a uniform everyday, and we only got new school shoes if the old ones wore out or didn't fit. I didn't have a closet full of designer clothes like you do," she paused. "Even when my mother was alive, we didn't do extravagant things. Don't get me wrong, we had just enough. We weren't drinking out of tin cans, but we didn't have a lot of material things either," she explained. "I always thought we didn't have those things because we couldn't afford them. I remember my mother always clipped coupons from the Sunday paper, and she did her hair and nails herself," she shared. "She loved fashion and sewed most of her own clothes, and I think she may have gotten a new dress once or twice a year from Marshall Field's, which was her favorite store," she paused as she put on rubber gloves to rinse the chicken under the faucet.

"Then one day when I was helping your grandfather get ready to sell the house, he wanted to review his financial records with me in case something happened to him," she stammered. "Anyway, as we were reviewing all of his paperwork and investment data, I learned what his net worth is," Liz paused careful to make sure that the raw chicken didn't touch the produce. "Move those greens out of the way, sweetie. I don't want this raw meat to touch those greens or we will have to throw them out," she cautioned.

"Net worth? You know what Grandpa's net worth is?" Maria asked animatedly. "What is it, Mom? Tell me, pleeeeaaaase," she pleaded.

Mrs. Wesley bit her bottom lip and studied her daughter

curiously. "That's personal information, Maria," she admonished. "I don't feel comfortable sharing this information with you."

Maria's eyes widened. She loved secrets. "But I'm your daughter, Mom. I'm family," she pleaded.

Liz bit her bottom lip. "I'll tell you under one condition," she teased.

"Under what condition?" Maria asked suspiciously.

"If you agree to help me cook Sunday dinners so we can chat like this once a week," Mrs. Wesley blurted.

Maria slanted her eyes at her mother. "Mom, you know cooking isn't my thing! It messes up my nails," she whined.

"Fine. Then I won't answer your question," Liz sighed.

Maria playfully splashed water into her mother's face. "Fine," she groaned. "I'll do it."

Mrs. Wesley shook her head from side to side, rubbing her hand on her apron. "Pinky swear," she demanded.

"Mother!" Maria groaned. "I'm seventeen years old!"

"Pinky swear!" Liz repeated.

"I'll pinky swear to help you cook on Sundays, but only if I don't have a major test on Monday," she offered.

Mrs. Wesley laughed heartily. "Nope. Not good enough. Even when you have big tests, you always manage to chat with Teenie or Rashanda on the phone the night before," she reminded. "You have to pinky swear that you'll help me in the kitchen for at least an hour on Sunday," she offered. "Every Sunday."

"Fine," Maria laughed. "Now tell me what his net worth is."

"Maria, this is family business," Mrs. Wesley cautioned. "Do not share this information with your friends, or even your brother. And definitely do not let your grandfather know that I've told you this," she explained. "I'm very serious."

"I won't, Mom!" Maria groaned. "Spill the beans!"

Mrs. Wesley leaned into Maria and whispered.

"You're kidding! No way!" Maria squealed. "Are you serious?"

Mrs. Wesley shrugged her shoulders. "It's probably more than that now, because his investments continue to do well," she paused. "When I was growing up, your grandfather used to always say that a lot of people on our street wore big hats but didn't have any cattle, and that he'd rather wear a small hat and have lots of cattle," she laughed. "He would say to me, 'Lizzy-Busy, you don't want to wear a big hat and then not have any cattle in your field. You can't make money off of a big hat. A big hat only keeps your big head warm, but cattle can work for you. A lot of people like to wear a big hat to pretend that they have money, but it's all an act. I'd rather have cattle and wear a small hat. The key is that you want to make money while you're sleeping. Remember that, Lizzy-Busy,' she said, her voice a few octaves deeper to imitate her father. "I didn't understand that saying either," she paused.

"How do you make money while you're sleeping?" Maria asked

"While you're sleeping, your money is working for you," Mrs. Wesley explained. "Your money can only work for you if you invest it," she continued. "It doesn't work for you if you're wearing it on your back or driving it around," she explained. "Daddy always said that rich people didn't work for their money. Their money works for them."

"Whew!" Maria whistled. "It sounds like Grandpa is rich now! He must have a lot of cattle," Maria said.

"He wouldn't say that," Mrs. Wesley shrugged. "He would say that he's blessed. But he does have a very high net worth," she paused. "But he doesn't consider himself rich, and neither should you," she cautioned. "When we were reviewing his financial material, he shared that he and my mother worked hard for their money, while his money was working part-time for him. He would always tease that he was working harder than his money. Anyway, now after all of these years, he's finally ready to let his money do all of the hard work," she paused. "He's just living off of the interest, and he's sharing his estate with your Uncle Emmett and me now, to 'lighten our load a little bit' as he says," she smiled. "Your grandfather is a very smart man, Maria," Liz finished. "Do you want me to show you how to season the greens?" she asked.

"Sure," Maria said casually. "If Grandpa is so smart, why didn't he go to college, Mom?"

"Back when your grandfather was a young man, things were different, sweetie," Liz shared as she sprinkled Lawry's seasoning salt in the pan of greens. "It wasn't that easy for a black man to go to college, or get a good job like some of the white men could get," she paused. "He was accepted to a major university in Chicago, and when he showed up on the first day, they wouldn't enroll him because he was black," Mrs. Wesley shared. "Now, don't add too much salt, just three or four shakes of your wrist," she explained.

"I didn't know that," Maria said, her wrist gently shaking the seasoning can.

"It's true," Liz continued. "I thought I told you that. Well, anyway, your grandfather didn't let that discourage him. He always told us that just because you don't go to college it doesn't mean that you're not smart, and just because you do go to college it doesn't make you smarter than anyone. Life makes you smart. College is just another tool that you can use in your toolbox," she continued. "Some people have college in their toolbox, and some people don't and do just fine," she finished. "Your grandfather is quite wise."

"Why don't you just measure the salt with a measuring spoon, Mother?" Maria asked.

Liz shrugged her shoulders. "This is the way my mother taught me to sprinkle in seasonings. It's a feel. When you cook enough, you get a feel for it," she explained.

"Oh. Do you think Grandpa can teach me how to invest so that I can learn how to make my money work for me while I'm sleeping?" Maria asked.

Mrs. Wesley looked tenderly at her daughter. "Of course, sweetie! He'd love that," she paused. "But the first thing he is going to do is lecture you about your spending habits, so be prepared. He's going to give you the big hat, no cattle speech and ask you how many pair of shoes you can wear at one time and ask you to explain how much interest those expensive jeans are earning hanging in your closet," she cautioned. "Are you ready for a lecture like that?" she asked.

Maria groaned loudly. "Not really," she confessed. "But I'll tough it out because I want to learn from him," she paused. "But technically, it's your fault that I'm a shopping addict. Why do you let me buy all of these clothes, Mom?" Maria whined.

"Oh, so it's my fault?" Mrs. Wesley laughed. "Your shopping addiction is my fault?"

"You give me the money," Maria chided. "So you're a co-conspirator," she laughed.

"That's a fancy shmancy word," she giggled. "But I guess you're right," Liz admitted. "But I just want you and your brother to have the things that I never had as a child. And you seem to enjoy shopping so much," she said. "I just wanted you to be happy, especially with the divorce and everything," she finished softly.

"I like clothes, Mom," Maria offered. "But believe it or not, I'm not addicted to them. Going to the mall every chance I got just gave me something to do so that I wasn't here watching you and daddy argue or ignore each other," she shared. "Shopping doesn't really make me happy, but it gave me a purpose," she finished. "But I'm ready for a new more meaningful purpose."

Liz smiled warmly at her daughter. "A new more meaningful purpose," she repeated. "I like that. That's my new goal for you and Neal. I want you to find your meaningful purpose in life," she finished. "I think if you find your purpose, happiness will happen as a by product of living your life with purpose."

"Okay, now you're getting all psychological and philosophical on me," Maria groaned. She picked up a wooden spoon and slowly stirred the pot of greens, sprinkling in a few shakes of pepper. "Mom, show me how to season and coat the chicken," Maria stated. "And after that, teach me how to make salt water cornbread. I know how to make Jiffy mix, but not the salt water cornbread that you make," she said. "I like that better."

Liz Wesley stood frozen in her tracks, not sure if she should react to her daughter's admission regarding trouble in paradise or hug her that she appeared to show a genuine interest in learning to cook.

Maria stared at her mother curiously. "Are you okay, Mom?" she asked. "Did you hear me? Do you want to show me how to season the chicken first or make the cornbread?" she repeated.

Shaking her head up and down, Liz spoke. "I'll show you how to make the cornbread first," she said. "I prefer the taste of salt water cornbread too," she continued. "But sometimes it's easier to just grab a box of Jiffy. Get the box of white cornmeal and an egg, Maria. The cornmeal is in the pantry next to the grits," Liz said. "Don't get the yellow cornmeal, the white cornmeal is better for cornbread," she explained.

George Benson's 'Mr. Magic' played in the background, as the greens simmered slowly in the large pot, the same pot that her mother used to simmer her greens. A smoked turkey drumstick played understudy for the salt pork.

Chapter 11

Closet Therapy

The sunlight created a thin line beneath the door, a pinstripe against the darkness that she sought. Fumbling with her fingers, she patted until she felt the weaving of a basket. She reached inside and gripped the first item that her fingers touched. Feeling the dampness from her morning shower in the towel, she held it up to her face and breathed in her scent. She inhaled again as her nostrils picked up the fragrance of her favorite body wash mixed with laundry fabric softener. *This towel doesn't smell dirty. I could use it at least one more time. No. You know Mom's rule of three. Towels should be washed after you've used them three times.* She laid the towel neatly against the door frame, masking the thin ray of light and embracing the darkness. She closed her eyes and leaned her back against the wall, clutching the shoebox to her chest. Grace was running out of excuses.

Her first set of excuses had been plausible. *Get through midterms.* She passed her midterms with her usual B + average. *Get through Maria and Rashanda's birthday parties. Don't ruin their birthday celebrations because of your brooding.* The celebrations had been low key and fun. *Get through your dad's prostate cancer surgery. If it's not good news, then you don't want to be distracted. Your parents have enough on their plate without you adding your self* inflicted tale of woe. Six weeks post surgery, her dad was back to his regular activities, and but for an occasional incontinence problem, he was doing great. Her secret had lived in the box for over nine weeks.

Her life was now in a steady state period. She was well prepared for her upcoming final exams. And there were no pending celebrations or health challenges looming on the near horizon. Now she was just paralyzed by fear. Good old fashioned fear.

What does fear stand for? Failure to execute a response. Is that what fear stands for? Or is it: failure to energize a reaction? I'll come up with twenty different definitions for the word fear using its letters. I'll open the box once I come up with the twentieth definition. You're an idiot! You're stalling. You're scared. You're damn right I'm scared.

The second letter had arrived one month after the first. She'd placed it in the box unopened and written the word: FEAR across the box. She'd nicknamed the box "Gracie's Box of Fears." The third letter had arrived the day before and had her sitting on her closet floor, grateful that her parents had an unlisted number. Fear. She knew that he couldn't call her. She wanted to open the letters. She needed to open the letters.

Her arm brushed against the short plastic dress bag holding her prom gown. She couldn't believe that she was going to prom with Lori's boyfriend, Doug. She knew that it was a publicity stunt crafted in Teenie's mind, an attempt to include Grace in the Lori's Angels' prom tribute. Teenie had even given the project a name, Project Swan. She gave everything a name. Tanisha had been the mastermind behind their last project, Project Strong, which now had Grace crouching in her closet like a coward. I should call it Project Fear.

Reaching her arm inside the garment bag, she gently caressed the gown's fabric, wondering what it would be like to go on a date with a boy. In her angst over the letters received from Charles Lovett, Grace hadn't had time to enjoy the anticipation of the big dance. She was going to prom with a boy! But not just any boy, Doug was Lori's boyfriend.

I wonder if my friends realize that prom will be my first date, ever. Doubt it. They're so self absorbed in their own lives with their own boyfriends that they haven't given my sad, pathetic life any thought. But how could they not remember that I've never been on a date? That's easy, simpleton. They don't remember it because you never talk about anything, so it's not unusual for you not to talk about a date. You're the mute friend, remember? They've grown accustomed to politely ignoring you and your sad little life.

Grace clenched her hands into fists and lowered her head to the floor. She stretched her lanky frame as far as she could in the tiny closet, knocking over the shoe boxes stacked in the back. She lengthened her body and stretched her arms over her head until her toes touched one end of the small closet and her fingertips touched the other. This was her personal torture position. She liked to elongate her body to help stimulate blood flow to her brain. She rested her cheek against the carpet and closed her eyes as her thoughts continued to wage war in her head.

How can I remind them now that I've never been on a date? They'll think I'm a charity case. No they won't. They know that you're a year younger than they are, so they won't think you're weird. They're turning seventeen now, but you're only sixteen.

Her sixteenth birthday had fallen on a Saturday, and her parents were prepared to host a party for her, but Grace had declined, telling her parents that she wanted to celebrate it quietly. Happy to oblige, they'd taken her to the Golden Bear Restaurant for an early lunch. Maria, Teenie and Rashanda had surprised her by coming to the restaurant wearing small cardboard birthday hats with the plastic strings under their chins and bearing a wrapped gift.

They'd each declined even a small bite of the complimentary birthday cupcake that the restaurant had provided. Maria and Teenie insisted that cake was not allowed on their new dessert free prom diets, and Rashanda didn't want the cake to smudge her lipstick since she wouldn't be able to reapply it because she'd left the tube on her dresser at home. They pressured Grace to open their gift at the restaurant. Grace carefully untied the blue ribbon and could tell that Rashanda had been in charge of wrapping the gift. Maria had probably purchased the gift on one of her regular mall visits. The gift selection idea had probably been Teenie's.

"Do you like it?" Maria squealed. "The theme was Teenie's idea, but I picked out the make-up," she shared. "And of course I dropped it off with Suzy Homemaker a.k.a. Rashanda to wrap it," Maria finished.

Bingo! I know my friends. Grace smiled widely. "It's perfect," she said softly.

"We thought that a lighted make-up mirror and new makeup would be the perfect gift," Teenie paused. "So you can practice applying your make-up like a professional," she added. "When you plug it in and move this lever, the lights get bright to mimic the daylight, and then you can dim it for evening," she demonstrated. "Many people don't understand that you are supposed to apply lighter make-up during the day, and heavier make-up at night when the lighting is dimmer," she finished. "I love my make-up mirror," she shared. "I have the same one."

"What are you talking about?" Maria interrupted. "You barely wear make-up, Teenie. I didn't even know that you had a make-up mirror!"

"I wear make-up," Teenie defended. "I always wear eye liner and lipstick."

"But you don't need a lighted make-up mirror to apply eye liner and lipstick, genius," Maria teased. "I wear foundation, pressed powder, mascara, blush, and eye liner," she boasted. "That's make-up! I can't believe you wasted good money on a lighted make-up mirror to apply eye liner and lipstick!"

"Sometimes I wear foundation and blush," Teenie offered. "Besides, I got my make-up mirror from Save Mart. It was on clearance, and I love it," she finished, eyeing Maria suspiciously. "Since when do you care about how much anything costs?" Teenie asked.

Maria cracked her knuckles and stretched her fingers. "I'm turning over a new leaf," she shared. "I've decided to start saving money instead of spending it like it's going out of style," she continued.

Rashanda and Teenie made eye contact and scrunched up their faces.

"What brought this on, Maria?" Grace asked. "Shopping is your passion."

"Not anymore," Maria stated. "I'm now into investing. Shopping is still my favorite past time, but I'm going to only buy stuff that I absolutely must have," she paused. "My grandfather opened a stock fund for me and Neal. He's giving us money every month to invest. At the end of six months whoever has the most in their stock fund will get double that from my grandfather," she finished.

"Wow!" Teenie whistled. "Are you serious?"

"I'm dead serious," Maria said. "That's enough motivation to keep me out of the stores for awhile. My grandfather helped us pick out two stocks, and he's teaching me how to find the stock symbols in the newspaper to track how they're doing. I bought stock in McDonald's and Coca Cola," she finished proudly. "My grandfather said that it's more important to have wealth in your portfolio and not wear it on your back. I plan to use some of the proceeds from my stock windfall to buy myself a new outfit as a reward. Gotta have a goal," she smiled. "Now let's go so the Dudley family can enjoy the rest of their meal in peace," she smiled warmly at Mr. and Mrs. Dudley.

"We should make a side bet to see if Maria can go six months without buying a new outfit," Rashanda whispered.

"Count me in," Teenie laughed. "I give her three weeks, tops!"

"What are you two hens whispering about?" Maria asked.

"Oh, nothing. Nothing at all," Teenie smiled. "We'd better head out."

"You ladies can take your time," Mrs. Dudley smiled. "We don't have anywhere to go. Today is Grace's special day."

"Thanks for the make-up and mirror, you guys," Grace smiled. "I don't really know how to apply make-up, but I guess I better practice so I can wear some for prom," she said softly.

"Exactly," Maria explained. "We'll make sure you're adequately glammed up for prom night, birthday girl!" Maria gushed. "We'll come over and show you how to apply it," she paused and reached for a compact case. "Since you don't wear any make-up now, and your skin is so fair, I thought you should start by wearing Clinique foundation and blush," Maria continued as she held up the products. "It's hypo-allergenic and good for people with sensitive skin," she explained. "I prefer Fashion Fair products now, especially during the summer when I have a nice tan, but sometimes I go back to Clinique," she continued. "I switch up. Clinique has a nice three step cleansing process too, if you want to get the whole line," Maria continued.

"I've heard about Clinique's cleansing line, but it's kind of pricey so I just use Cetaphyl cleanser on my skin," Tanisha shared.

"I use Cetaphyl soap too, Teenie," Rashanda offered. "I was starting to get acne on my forehead, and my parents took me to a dermatologist who suggested that I switch cleansing products," she continued. "It's working."

"It is," Teenie noticed. "Your skin looks great now. Believe it or not, my mother suggested that I use Cetaphyl soap on my face," Teenie shrugged. "I've used it since I was ten, and I haven't had a problem with acne."

Maria waved her hand in the girls' face to silence them. "Anyhoo. If I may continue with my beauty consultation, I got you a lipstick in a soft pink shimmer to blend with your natural lip color," she paused. "You don't want your lipstick to be too drastic or you'll look like a clown," she laughed. "Hi. I'm Grace the Clown," she mocked.

Rashanda rolled her eyes and tapped her watch. "We've got to head out girls, or we're all going to be late."

"Oh, that's right," Grace said. "Todd and Ian are in town for the weekend. What are you guys going to do?" she asked.

Maria looked at Grace's parents and grinned. "Todd and I are going to the Lincoln Park Zoo today," she said loudly. "I told him that I was tired of just hanging out at his house and playing, uh, chess, if you know what I mean," Maria winked.

Grace played along. "That's right. You and Todd like to play chess," she smiled and winked. "What about you, Rashanda?"

Rashanda shook her head from side to side as she used Grace's fork to sample a bite of the birthday cupcake. "Ian and I are going to his friend's bar-b-que in the city. It's in Beverly," she said between bites. "So it's not far."

Tanisha stood up and stretched her long arms into the air. "And Glen and I are going to a White Sox game," she shared as she smoothed out her shorts. "Rashanda, put that fork down! You're going to eat off your lipstick, girlfriend," she chided. "And I don't have that shade. My lipstick is too pink for you to wear. Now I've lost my train of thought. What was I saying?" she paused. "Oh I remember. Glen knows that I was raised a Cubs fan, and that I prefer to go to the friendly confines of Wrigley Field, but he's trying to convert me. He thinks that I'm the only black girl raised on the South side of Chicago who's a Cubs fan," she giggled.

"You probably are! Black people don't go to Wrigley Field. Why are you a Cubs fan, Teenie? Most black people in Chicago are Sox fans," Maria asked.

Teenie waved her finger in Maria's face and clucked her tongue. "Tsk, tsk, tsk! You people and your small minds! Can't a black girl like the Chicago Cubs?" she laughed. "And by the way, I've been to Wrigley Field and I wasn't the only black person rooting for the Cubbies," she groaned. "Haven't you learned that I am too complex to fit into your narrow minded racial stereotypes?" she quipped.

"You can call it a stereotype if you want, but Maria's right, most black folks are Sox fans. So why are you a Cubs fan, Teenie?" Rashanda asked. "Answer the question, chick!"

Grace watched curiously. Tanisha carefully removed the sunglasses perched on her head and ran her fingers through her hair while she spoke, fanning out her soft curls as though primping in front of a mirror. "My Grandma Bootsy is a Cubs fan," she shrugged. "As far back as I can remember, she always has a Cubs game on whenever I visit her, so I just started following the Cubs," she explained. "I like the Sox. My dad is a Cubs fan and a Sox fan. I've just never been to Comiskey Field, so Glen says that I need to get in touch with my inner black girl and hang with the homies," she laughed. Teenie glanced at her watch and stood up. "You're right, Rashanda. We'd better scoot. I told Glen that I'd be at his house in five minutes because it's a one fifteen start," she finished, gently perching the sunglasses back on her head.

"It's Comiskey Park, not Comiskey Field, little Miss Cubs fan," Maria grinned. "Get it right! If you call it Comiskey Field, the Sox fans will skin you alive, dingbat. It's Comiskey Park," she shrieked.

Narrowing her eyes into tiny slits, Teenie quickly stuck her tongue at her friend, stood up and gathered her purse. Following suit, Rashanda and Maria also stood and bid farewell to Mr. and Mrs. Dudley as Grace excused herself to walk her friends to the parking lot. Once outside, the sun's rays danced on the searing hot asphalt. Grace watched in awe as each of the girls casually placed sunglasses on their noses as though shielding their expressions from lurking paparazzi. She clumsily raised her hand to her brow in a futile attempt to block the punch of the bright sunlight that slapped her face like a right hook.

I've never owned a pair of sunglasses. When did they start wearing sunglasses and how did I miss the buy sunglasses memo?

"Did you hear me, Grace?" Teenie repeated. "Are you sure you don't want us to hang out with you tonight?" Teenie asked. "It's your birthday. I can have Glen drop me off right after the game if you want to hang out," she offered.

"Me too," Rashanda agreed. "I feel bad leaving you alone on your birthday."

Maria opened the car door and turned the ignition, manually rolling down the window as she turned on the air conditioning in the hot car. "We've got to cool off the car a little bit or our thighs are going to sweat and stick to the leather seats like pigs in a blanket," she exclaimed. "I can't believe that it's this hot already in May."

"I'll be fine," Grace shared waving her hand dismissively

across her face. "Don't worry about me. I always like to spend my birthdays quietly," she admitted. "This is exactly what I want to do. I'll probably go to an early matinee with my parents and go to the mall to pick up a new pair of sunglasses," she paused. "I lost mine," she said quickly. "After that, we'll probably catch the senior citizen special at Red Lobster," she chuckled.

"Old people sure do like to eat early," Maria observed as she applied lipstick in the side mirror.

Tanisha and Rashanda shook their head at her. "Forgive her, Grace," Teenie whispered. "She's an idiot. Your parents are not that old."

Grace laughed. "Yes they are, Teenie. They're in their sixties. They're old," she agreed. "That's why we eat dinner by five thirty," she offered. "They are in bed by nine o'clock," she finished. "I'd better get back inside. I don't want you guys to be late for your dates. Thanks for my gift!" she squealed. Grace hugged each of her friends quickly and slowly walked back into the restaurant toeing a small pebble like a soccer ball.

∞⟩⟨∞

Flexing her feet in the closet and cracking her ankles, she took a deep breath. She loved her friends, but sometimes she felt invisible or like an afterthought in their midst. She wished she had more courage. Somehow the fact that she hadn't had a first date had seemed to escape them. Or maybe they were just too polite to discuss her dateless status, the looming elephant in the room.

Just as well, Grace wasn't prepared to discuss her lackluster love life. She knew that boys were showing an interest in her. She wasn't blind. As she walked through the corridor at River North High School, the high school boys eyed her with approval; their eyes roamed her body like she was a pepperoni pizza with extra cheese. She turned a blind eye to their jeers, and stoically ignored their flirtatious comments and advances, her shoulders hunched over in a futile attempt to disguise her height and appear invisible. It never worked. No girl was safe. The unattractive girls were booed, and the attractive girls were ogled like construction workers ogle the ladies on their lunch break. Grace felt like a high school misfit and dreaded the daily catcalls as she walked the hall on her way to class. I may be a circus freak, but at least I don't get booed.

As she walked through the hormone crazed group of boys, she instinctively hit play on her personal list of Grace's shortcomings to drown out their voices. I'm almost six feet tall, I just learned that I am adopted and half white. My adoptive parents are in their sixties. And if that isn't enough, my biological grandparents are dead bigots, and the father that I've never met is a black, married drama professor who conceived me while having an affair with my white mother, his student. And the cherry on top of my misfit sundae: I haven't started my period yet! Did you hear that boys? I'm sixteen, and my period hasn't started yet. If I shared even half of this stuff with you, you'd probably start booing me.

Sometimes she would have to hit replay on her Grace's faults tape. She knew that she couldn't do anything about the lineage to which she'd been born, her history was what it was. But she was becoming increasingly more disturbed that her period hadn't started. I'm a sixteen year old girl who hasn't started her period. If that doesn't qualify for freak of the year, nothing does.

Grace hadn't shared this humiliating fact with her friends. The girls had all started their periods within three months of each other with Rashanda running anchor in the get your period relay. They knew that Grace was a year younger, and they'd all assured her that her period would come a year later. By the time later arrived, her friends were all proficient tampon users and referred to their period as "the curse," or their "little friend," something to be tolerated and not discussed. Midol was passed around like tic tacs. Grace was too embarrassed to share that she still hadn't started hers yet, and no one seemed to remember. She didn't want to change the tone of their brief lunchroom chats by sharing her dismal news. The lunchroom chats were always giddy and light. The topic was usually boys or clothes. Teenie spent her lunchtime chat minutes sharing tidbits about her dates with Glen Horton or letters she received from David Barton. Maria's time was spent sharing stories about her beloved Todd, and of course Rashanda spent her time fawning about Ian. Occasionally, Grace would share something interesting about Justine, but even Justine had been less available lately now that she was dating AM.

Grace had always been the quiet one. The good listener. That's how they often described her. "You're such a good listener, Grace," Maria would beam after a marathon phone chat about Todd.

"Thanks for listening, Grace-Wacie," Rashanda would laugh. "Sometimes it's nice to just share stories with a friend without having someone try to solve it like Teenie and Maria always try to do," Rashanda finished. "It's not that I don't appreciate their advice," she'd pause. "I do, but sometimes you just want to talk about something and not have it fixed. You just want someone to listen."

"I figured you'd be home, Grace," Teenie shared one evening. "I just need you to listen to what Glen said to me and tell me what you think. And you're the captain of the listening squad!" she'd beamed.

Grace had learned to multi-task while listening to her friends. What value could she add to their whimsical boy banter? She had no experience to share or frame of reference. So she just painted her nails and straightened her room while she listened and recycled their own words back to them, validating their own opinions of the situation. She had a role to play in their friendship circle after all. She was the good listener.

ℰᴑᴄ℞

The closet darkness was so black, it appeared blue. She pulled her knees into her chest and inhaled deeply. Grace knew that her friends were curious to learn if she'd received a letter from Charles Lovett. They had as much invested in Project Strong as she did. They'd crafted and sent the letter as a team. They were in this with her. Sort of, minus one large detail; their self worth wouldn't be inextricably linked to the words written on a thin sheet of paper.

Her friends loved her and would be supportive of her no matter what happened, that much she knew, but they wouldn't feel the emotions that she would feel after finally hearing from her birth father after seventeen years. How could they? Their elation or sadness would only touch the surface of the deep, dark sea of emotion that she swam in daily, sometimes gasping for air to give a name to the feelings that clutched her heart.

The therapist had called it abandonment disorder. Acute abandonment disorder to be specific. The doctor had explained to Grace that the shock and trauma associated with learning that she was adopted had been her trigger event. Dr. Dudley had shared that her condition was new and had not been categorized in the Diagnostic Statistical Manual for Mental Disorders, the Holy Bible for psychiatrists and psychologists. The doctor had shared that Grace's self destructive behavior as demonstrated through her brief bout with bulimia, her impulsive decision to chop off her hair, and her moodiness were classic symptoms of acute abandonment disorder. Dr. Dudley recommended weekly group and private therapy sessions. Grace balked at the group session and refused to attend.

"I am not going to sit in a semi-circle and share my feelings with complete strangers, Mom," Grace whined. "I'm not going to do it!" she shrieked, crossing her arms defiantly across her chest. Her mother sat stone faced and looked at her husband for support. Mr. Dudley rubbed his chin and shrugged. "To tell you the truth, I wasn't never no big fan of group therapy no how," he shared. "But I think your mother and I would feel better if you talk to the doctor one on one for a little while, Grace," he insisted. "I think it's funny that the doctor's name is Dr. Dudley," he paused trying desperately to introduce levity into the situation. "It's almost like she's family," he smiled. His smile turned serious as he reached for Grace's hand and gently patted her slim fingers. "Grace, when Mrs. Wesley told us that Maria said that you had been making yourself throw up for over three weeks," he shared. "I almost had a heart attack," he said softly. "I was so sick with worry that I almost had a heart attack," he repeated shaking his head from side to side. "Your mother and I had no idea that you were doing that to yourself, and I just want to make sure that you don't still want to hurt yourself," he said softly. "I forget what she called it," he said.

"Bulimia, Dad," Grace said irritated. "It's called bulimia," she repeated softly.

"That's right. Boo-lemia," he said. "You're not doing boo-lemia to yourself no more are you, sugar?" he asked.

She opened her mouth to correct his pronunciation, but thought better of it. Grace sighed loudly. "No, Dad. I'm not making myself throw up anymore," she admitted. "I haven't made myself throw up in several months," she groaned. "I just can't believe that Maria's mom called you," she whined slouching in her chair. "Maria had no business telling her mother. It wasn't her place to share my business with her mother," Grace mumbled under her breath.

"Maria had every right to tell her mother," Mrs. Dudley replied. "I would have done the same exact thing if you'd told me that Maria was making herself throw up," she stated. "That's what's wrong with the world today. People don't spend enough time minding other folks' business. When I was coming up, everybody was in everybody else's business," she shared. "Whether you liked it or not, children were being watched by the neighborhood. If you spit gum on the street in front of another adult, you could rest assured that your mother was going to know about it, and you would be outside with a scraper, scraping that gum off the sidewalk the next day, and that's the truth," she finished.

Grace stared at her mother curiously, surprised that her mother's failing hearing had heard the softly mumbled comment.

The tissue box teetered on the edge of the table as Mr. Dudley strained to reach the box. Grace leaned over and nudged the box toward her dad who wiped his nose as a scowl clouded over his face. "My allergies are really acting up today," he complained. "I know these paper tissues are convenient," he stated. "But I sure do miss my old handkerchief," he lamented. "Nothing like the feel of a soft, crisp handkerchief across your nose," he said longingly.

"You're an old fool!" Mrs. Dudley said loudly. "You miss those handkerchiefs because you weren't the one handling them and all their mess. I bet if you were the one scrubbing those nasty things you wouldn't miss them. Hmmph!" she snorted. "I sure as heck don't miss scrubbing and ironing those cotton snot rags, that's for sure," she continued. "I used to curse your name and wonder what you had growing in your nose for all of the stains that would show up on those things," she said, matching Mr. Dudley's scowl with a look of disdain.

Mr. Dudley blew his nose loudly into the tissue and stuffed it in his pocket. "Woman!" he shouted. "You know I used to chew snuff, and the snuff would sometimes get into my sinuses. That's what those stains were, Ethel!" he grunted. "Now I done forgot what I was going to say," he mumbled.

"Well, snuff, snot, whatever it was, it was nasty," Mrs. Dudley replied, her hand waving dismissively. "And take those nasty tissues out of your pocket before you put those trousers in the laundry basket," she scolded. "I don't have time to be checking your pockets before I wash, and when you leave tissue in there they get lint all over the clothes in the dryer."

Grace watched as her dad scratched his head, trying to recollect his thoughts. "I remember now," he said quickly. "I agree with your mother, Grace," he shared. "I'm glad Mrs. Wesley told us what was going on. That's what grown folks do. She's not your friend. She's an adult, and adults don't sit on information like that," he explained. "Maria did the right thing in telling her mother, and her mother did the right thing in telling us," he concluded. Grace watched as he carefully reached in his pocket and discarded a handful of tissues. "I'm really glad that she gave us the name of a good black psychiatrist for you to talk to," he continued. "To tell you the truth, I've never seen a black lady psychiatrist in my life," he continued. "I'm glad women have an opportunity to do whatever they want nowadays. But that's beside the point. I want you to keep talking to Dr. Dudley, okay?" he ordered. "It couldn't hurt 'cha and it just might help you, honey."

Grace dropped her head into her hands and allowed her hair to cascade across her face. *Now I can add head case to my "Grace is a Misfit" list.* She rolled her eyes into the top of her head. *At least my hair is growing back. What was I thinking getting my hair cut in that Dorothy Hamill style? My head is too big to wear my hair*

"I'm so glad you're letting your hair grow back, Grace," her dad offered. "I liked it short, it showed off your cheekbones, but I think women look better with long hair. Makes them look more feminine," he finished.

ഇരു

The closet door slipped off the track. Gripping the door with one hand, and bracing herself against the wall of the closet with the other hand, she stood up slowly and leaned the door against the wall, squinting as the bright sunlight filtered into her room, slapping her from her trance like state. Grace stared into her now messy closet. I'll deal with that later. She clutched the unopened letters to her chest and sat on her bed, her slim fingers tracing the numbers on the telephone. You're not strong enough to do this by yourself. Call for backup! She tucked the letters beneath her pillow. Standing, Grace exhaled loudly and ran her fingers through her now shoulder length hair.

With her bedroom door closed, she could hear the muffled, yet undeniable sound of the doorbell chime. "Grace," her mother's voice rang. "Teenie, Maria and Rashanda are here," she said. "They're coming up."

Her heart raced.

"Surprise!" Rashanda squealed. "We thought we'd surprise you and come over to help you practice putting on your make-up for prom," she said. "I knew you'd be home. You're always home on Sunday afternoons."

Maria flopped on Grace's bed and cracked her knuckles.

"Maria!" Teenie scolded. "That is so disgusting! Your knuckles are going to swell into little bowling balls if you keep that up! Stop it! Stop it! Stop it!" Teenie shrieked.

155

Cracking her knuckles again, Maria smiled. "I'll stop it when I'm good and ready," she laughed. Grace followed Maria's eyes as she stared at the closet door propped against the wall. "What happened to your closet, Grace?" Maria asked.

Grace walked over to the closet door quickly. "It, uh, it fell off the track," she stammered. "It does that sometimes."

"So does mine," Teenie agreed. "I'll help you put it back up," she offered walking toward Grace. "Once mine fell off in the middle of the night," she said. "It scared me half to death." The girls lifted the door panel and slipped it back on the track.

"That almost defies one of the laws of physics, Teenie," Rashanda doubted. "An object at rest will stay at rest until placed into motion, or something like that," she explained. "Maybe your dog bumped it in the middle of the night."

Tanisha's eyes grew wide. "I know. That's what I thought at first too," she explained. "But my bedroom door was closed, and the windows were closed, so it's not like a breeze made it fall," she shuddered. "It freaked me out."

Maria stretched her hands over her head.

"Were you taking a nap, Grace?" Rashanda asked. "You seem like you're kind of out of it," she noticed.

Grace smiled softly at Rashanda. "No, I wasn't napping. In fact, I was just about to call you guys and start the phone tree," she stammered. "Close the door, Teenie," she instructed. "I, I need to talk to you guys about something," she paused.

Tanisha closed Grace's bedroom door and leaned on her dresser. "Grace, if this is about prom," she started. "If you really don't want to go to prom with Doug, I completely understand," she offered, her right hand covering her heart. "I just wanted to make you feel included. I know that you haven't even been on a date yet, so if you're uncomfortable about prom being your first date, I'll call Doug myself and explain," she rambled. "Or if you want to go on a double date with Glen and me and you and Doug before prom, I can work that out," she continued. "I admit that I can be kind of pushy at times. We didn't want to make you feel uncomfortable about not having any dating experience," she continued. "But if you're nervous…"

"Teenie," Grace interrupted, shaking her head rapidly from side to side. "That's not it at all," she paused. "It's not about Doug and prom," she finished.

"Is it about Charles Lovett?" Maria asked.

Grace shook her head. "Maria, lift up that pillow and pull out what's underneath," she said softly

Maria quickly obliged and fanned the three envelopes in her hand. She studied the postmarks. "Grace, you have three letters from Charles Lovett!"

Grace slumped in the chair next to her bed. Tanisha and Rashanda stared at each other and walked over to Grace's bed and sat next to Maria. The silence was as thick as pea soup.

Maria turned the letters over in her hand. "They're not open," she said. "Why haven't you opened them, Grace?" she asked softly.

The walls of the small room seemed to tighten around her shoulders like a vice grip. The cat's out of the bag, scaredy cat. Answer her. Why haven't you opened them, huh? Say something. Grace wanted to speak. She wanted to explain, but fear gripped her tongue, paralyzing her vocal cords. Forcing herself to breath, she felt a hand rubbing small circles on her back.

"Were you afraid, Grace?" a voice asked. Her head nodded up and down, not sure which of her friends had spoken.

"Of course she was afraid, knucklehead," another voice

scolded. That's Maria's voice. Only Maria would go off on a friend while another friend is having a moment. Grace began to sob softly. Her gaze focused on the shag carpet, she could feel their eyes boring through her. Judging her.

Teenie's voice was loud and confident. "Grace," she said loudly. "You need to snap out of it. Now!" she barked. "You knew this was inevitable. This was the point of Project Strong. To make contact with your biological father," she continued.

Rashanda's eyes bulged at Teenie's tone. "Tanisha!" she said. "Why are you yelling at her? Can't you see how upset she is?"

Tanisha continued unfazed. "Of course I see how upset she is," Teenie continued. "But someone needs to reason with her, and I'm just the person to do it," she stated. "Grace. Get over it. He has written you three letters, so clearly he wants to get in touch with you," she reasoned. "If he were trying to dismiss you or not acknowledge you, he wouldn't have written you three times. There must be good news in one of those letters."

Maria sat upright on the bed and casually tossed her long hair over her shoulder. "I hate to agree with General Teenie," Maria offered. "But she's right, Grace. The three of us have been wondering if you'd received a letter, but we didn't want to make you feel bad if you hadn't," she paused. "We figured that you'd let us know as soon as you got a letter. Why didn't you tell us when you got the first letter, Grace?"

Time seemed to stand still as Grace slowly raised her gaze. Her eyes panned the top of the dresser and slowly she could see her friends' feet dangling off the side of her bed. She inhaled.

"You don't have to answer that," Rashanda said firmly. "The important thing is that you have three letters, and we're here. Remember, we're in this together, Grace," Rashanda coached. "Look

Dancing with God's Grace

at how God worked it out for us to be here today," she observed. "We haven't all been available to hang out on a Sunday afternoon in God knows how long," she finished, her hand covered her mouth. "My fault," she said. "I know I just used the Lord's name in vain," she smiled and glanced at the ceiling. "Tell God I'm sorry about that one, Lori," she winked.

Maria's slender arm hung loosely in the air, a long white envelope at her fingertips. "This is the one that's postmarked the earliest. Open this one first," she ordered.

Feeling more courageous, Grace's gaze now rested on her friends' faces. She watched as Teenie took the envelope from Maria and held it within three inches from Grace's face. "Grace." Tanisha said. "It's time to face the rest of your life," she said firmly. "I could open the envelope for you, but I think you should do it."

A force greater than Grace willed her arm to take the letter. Tanisha handed Grace a small plastic letter opener that she'd received as a gift from Justine when she moved.

Fingering the letter opening, she ran her tongue along her lips. "Maybe we should wait and open it when Justine can be with us," Grace offered. "She was part of Project Strong too," she finished.

"No. Justine will understand. Open the letter, Grace," Tanisha said firmly. "If you don't want to share the letter with us, that is your choice, but you need to stop being controlled by the fear of the unknown. It's not healthy," she said. "You've had these letters long enough. It's time to open them," she finished. "It's time."

Grace held Teenie's gaze. It's time. It's time. She repeated silently as she sliced into the envelope. She pulled out the white piece of paper and read. Her eyes welled with tears again. Grace crumpled to the floor and squeezed the piece of paper in her hand before thrusting it at Teenie.

Without waiting for permission, Tanisha read the letter aloud.

Dear Miss Dudley,

You must have me confused with another

Charles Lovett. I never knew a Lydia Moore.

Signed,

C. Lovett

"It's not even him!" Grace shrieked. "All of this anxiety, and it isn't even him!" she moaned.

Unfazed, Tanisha snatched the next letter from Maria and thrust it in Grace's hands. "Open this one!" she ordered.

"What does it matter, Teenie?" Grace sobbed. "It's not him. There must be a different Charles Lovett," she reasoned. "Just rip up the other letters!" she pleaded. "I don't even want to know what else he has to say," Grace whined. She pulled the letter from Tanisha's hand and tossed it on the bed.

"No!" Maria stated. "We will do no such thing! He wrote you two more times for a reason. We're going to read what else he has to say. Open the letter, Teenie!" she ordered thrusting the second letter into Tanisha's chest.

Tanisha grabbed the letter opener from Grace and sliced into the envelope. "This letter was written just two days after the first letter," she observed. She flipped the letter over in her hand. "It's a page long, with a sentence on the back," she said excitedly.

Grace's pale hands covered her face as she sat motionless on the floor. Tanisha read.

Dear Grace,

Where do I begin? I am the Charles Lovett of whom you spoke. To say that your letter stunned me would be an understatement. I nearly fainted. I read the letter at least twenty times, fearful that someone from my past was playing a cruel joke on me. I have behaved as though the

Northwestern University chapter in my life doesn't exist for so long, that receiving your letter was like being visited by a ghost from a past long dead and buried. When I saw the photograph that you sent me, all I could see was Lydia Moore's beautiful face staring back at me.

Please forgive me for my first letter. I was afraid to acknowledge who I was for fear that somehow my troubled past would be resurrected and serve to damage the new life that I was forced to create for myself. I tossed and turned for two nights wondering what to do. And I knew that I had to contact you again and tell you the truth.

I taught and loved a student named Lydia Moore. If she was your mother, then I am your father. When I was sent into professional exile by the Moore family, I tried desperately to reach your mother, but to no avail. I still remember what she was wearing the last time I saw her. I believe that God sent you to me. I would love to meet you. I have to meet you. I will fly to wherever you are. Please call me or write me again.

C. Lovett

Tanisha paused and smiled widely. Grace rocked on the floor, her hands covering her face. "Grace, it's him," Tanisha stated. "It's him, and he wants to meet you!" she squealed. "Isn't that great? It worked. Project Strong worked!"

Grace wiped her eyes with the back of her trembling hand. "Open the last letter, Maria," she said softly.

Maria tore into the letter with her fingers. "It's a short one," she shared breathlessly. "Just two sentences."

Dear Grace,

If you would prefer to exchange letters or talk on the phone to get to know each other before we meet face to face, I'll understand. Please contact me.

C. Lovett

"Wow!" Rashanda exclaimed. "Wow! That's all I can say. This has been one crazy afternoon. So much for our make-up lesson," she giggled.

"Teenie, what do you think I should do next?" Grace asked.

Tanisha smiled at her friend and shrugged. "I think you should share the letters with your parents first," Tanisha suggested. "Do they know that you wrote him?" she asked.

Grace shook her head. "No. I didn't want to worry them with this, especially after my dad's prostate cancer surgery," she shared. "But he's doing fine now."

"Share the letters with your parents," she repeated. "And then I think the safest thing to do would be to talk to him on the phone," she paused. "Since your mom raised Lydia Moore, she can tell you things about her that only someone who knew her really well would know," she said.

"Good point, Teenie," Maria offered. "Find out if she had an unusual birthmark anyplace," she continued. "For all we know, this guy could be some psycho killer."

"She's right," Rashanda agreed. "You need to be absolutely certain that this Charles Lovett is your father."

"I'm not sure if she had any birthmarks, but my mother told me that she had a burn on her right wrist from touching a radiator pipe when she was two," Grace shared. "The scar was at the base of her right wrist and about two inches long. After I talk to my parents about the letters, I'll find out if there were any other unique things that only someone who knows her really well would know," she brightened.

"Precisely," Teenie commented. "If he knew her as well as we think he knew her, then he should be able to tell you about that scar. We just want to make sure that he is who he says he is," she finished.

"There's no time like the present, so we'll leave shortly so you can talk to your parents today," she paused. Grace squirmed and bit her lip.

"Grace," Teenie encouraged. "You've sat on this information long enough. You're telling your parents today," she ordered. She reached out and patted Grace's hand gently. "But I think we'd be remiss if we didn't pause and thank God for this praise report," Teenie suggested softly.

Maria scowled. "Praise report? Since when did you assume Lori's church girl duties?" she questioned. "None of us can pray like Lori could," she frowned.

Teenie opened her mouth to speak, but Rashanda's soft alto voice filled the room. "Let's hold hands and bow our heads," she said softly, her arms outstretched. "Maria, stand up," Rashanda ordered. The girls stood in a small circle at the foot of Grace's bed as Rashanda prayed. "God, thank you for leading us to Charles Lovett, and thank you for keeping Grace strong during this journey," she stammered. "Protect her as she continues to find out more about Charles Lovett. Thank you," she finished.

"That's it?" Maria questioned. "That's the shortest prayer that I've ever heard," she teased.

Tanisha grinned. "Short and sweet. Like Project Strong!" She glanced at her watch. "We still have time to do a quick make-up lesson," she observed. "Grace, plug in your make-up mirror so we can glam you up! Prom is only a couple of weeks away!"

Chapter 12

Faking a Smile

Teenie tensed at the deafening noise, clutching Glen's hand as the limousine drove toward the offensive sound. Peering through the sunroof, she watched the elevated train rumble over their heads. Sensing her fear, Glen softly patted her hand. His tenderness made her smile.

"It's just the L, babe," he comforted. "When you're not used to that sound, it sounds like an earthquake overhead," he paused leaning to speak over his shoulder. "Sir, you're going to turn left at State Street and then turn right at Balboa," he instructed the driver. Glen nestled into his seat and reached for Teenie's hand. "We could have just taken the Dan Ryan to Lake Shore Drive, to get to Buckingham Fountain, but I wanted to show you where I used to live, Teenie," Glen explained.

"I thought you moved to Homer from the Beverly area?" she asked, glad that the noise from the elevated train trailed away in the distance.

Glen peered out the window and spoke over his shoulder. "We did," he explained. "But before we moved to Beverly, we lived in these apartments," he pointed. Teenie peered over his shoulder at the graffiti covered cinder block buildings shaped hexagonally. "We lived here until I was in second grade, and my old man got a better job," he continued.

Teenie stared at the dirt covered ground where grass should have been. Her jaw dropped at the people lounging in front of the buildings, many sipping beverages wrapped in brown paper bags. Glen lived in the projects?

Her thoughts were interrupted by Glen's voice. "My parents never let us play outside alone," he explained. "One of my parents walked us to school, and picked us up every day," he said. "Looking back on it now, I'm glad that they did," he sighed. "My brother and I probably would have been beaten up if they hadn't," he observed. "One thing that I miss about living here is that my family used to walk to Chinatown every Friday for dinner," he sighed. "Chinatown is only two blocks west of here, just on the other side of the train tracks that we just drove under. One day I'll take you to my family's favorite restaurant in Chinatown," he finished.

"That would be nice," Tanisha smiled sweetly as she surveyed her surroundings. A park in the center of the buildings was devoid of children. Adult men sat on the jungle gym and smoked, passing the lit cigarette after two puffs. Where are the children? The playground was cluttered with litter, not a blade of grass in sight. The swing set chains hung limply, the rubber swing seats missing. The lone swing seat that was not missing was wrapped tightly atop the swing pole. She stared at the broken glass that glistened under the bright sky. This looks like Good Times! No wonder he didn't react when he came to Cedar Grove Apartments to pick me up. At least we have grass!

"Teenie!" Maria shouted. "Snap out of it, chick!" she giggled. "Pass me a mint from your purse!" her friend ordered. Tanisha made a silly face and tossed her the mints. Teenie noticed that Dante's large hand rested casually on Maria's thigh. She glanced at Rashanda and Ian who sat snuggled as one. Rashanda's petite frame rested comfortably on Ian's lap like a child sits atop Santa. Ian whispered something into her ear, making Rashanda giggle.

The girls' purses and shawls occupied the space where Rashanda should have been sitting. Teenie noticed two shoulder belts in the back where Ian and Doug sat. Her back to the driver, she looked around for seatbelts for the other passengers and didn't see any. No one has on a seatbelt! I don't remember if the limousine that took us to Lori's funeral even had seatbelts. How ironic. A seatbelt would have saved my friend's life, and we rode to her funeral without buckling up. Maybe I should make everybody buckle up. What if we have an accident? Chill, Teenie. Think positive thoughts!

Doug sat next to the purses, his hand cupping his chin as he stared silently out the window. Teenie's eyes panned over to Grace who shrugged. Teenie motioned with her finger for Grace to come here. Grace squinted and shrugged again.

"Come here for a minute so I can fix your hair, Grace," Teenie said loudly. "Some of the strands are sticking out in back. You look like Kizzy from Roots," she teased. "Dante, scoot over so Grace can sit next to me," Teenie ordered. Grace instinctively patted her perfectly coiffed hair as Maria and Dante slid down on the long bench seat.

Gripping the hem of her dress, Grace hunched over and carefully moved next to Teenie.

She plopped down on the seat. "This would make me dizzy," Grace shared. "I couldn't ride backwards for too long in a car. I'd get motion sickness and want to throw up," she shared.

"You better not get sick in this limo," Maria ordered. "And if you get sick, don't throw up near me, or you're reimbursing me for this designer gown," Maria stated. Teenie looked for something to toss at Maria to silence her, but reconsidered. She could hear Glen discussing Malcolm X with the driver.

"Malcolm X was really not the monster that the media made him out to be," Glen explained. "You should really read the Autobiography of Malcolm X by Alex Haley," he suggested. "It's eye opening. He believed in social and economic justice too. He was no different than Rev. Dr. Martin Luther King, Jr.," Glen paused. "Malcolm just believed that we had to fight for it, and not wait for the majority culture to give it to us," he continued. Teenie remembered the Malcolm X tee shirt that Glen wore the day she met him at the arcade. Glen is always trying to educate people about his beloved Malcolm X.

"Hurry up and fix my hair, Teenie," Grace ordered. "I don't like riding backwards."

Teenie gently smoothed Grace's silky hair. "Is everything okay with Doug?" she asked. "He's barely said two words since we left Maria's house," Teenie whispered grateful that Dante's deep voice now filled the stretch limousine, his stocky body serving as a human barrier between Doug and Grace as he leaned forward to join the Malcolm X discussion.

Once again, Grace shrugged. "I guess he's fine," she sighed. "He just seems so sad. He smiled a few times for the pictures at Maria's house, but he's not much of a talker," she paused. "You double dated with him and Lori before. Was he talkative then?"

Teenie ran her tongue along her braces. "Not really," she lied. "He's generally a pretty quiet guy," she paused. "But he's a basketball fanatic," Teenie shared quickly. "Talk to him about basketball," she coached. "That should get him going. Boys like to talk about their sport."

"I don't know that much about basketball," Grace whispered.

"You don't have to," Teenie coached. "Just ask him questions about it. Ask him what position he plays, and how long he's been playing. Ask him about his teammates and how his team did this season," she rattled quickly. "You know. Just make conversation," she finished. As the words seeped from her lips, Teenie watched in slow motion as Grace's expression grew somber. Teenie's palm covered her mouth, as she slowly lowered her eyes and turned her friend's face toward her. "Grace, I'm so sorry. I forgot that this is your first date," she whispered into her ear. "I'm such an idiot. Have you ever had a one on one conversation with a boy?" she asked softly.

Grace shook her head. "Not really. I've talked to boys in school about school stuff, but not anything personal," she admitted. "I should have had you guys coach me on how to talk to him," she said softly. "He's clearly still mourning Lori," Grace sighed. "Maybe this wasn't such a good idea, Teenie."

Tanisha shook her head from side to side. "Don't say that!" she said. "You look beautiful. The night's still young. We'll get him talking," she assured. "I'll make sure Glen sits next to him at the hotel. Glen can talk anybody's head off," she laughed.

"Did you need me for something, Teenie?" Glen asked. "I heard my name."

"Nope. I was just telling Grace how much you like to discuss Malcolm X," she smiled. Tanisha glanced out the window as the limousine drove past a statue in the middle of the street with an Indian atop a horse. She remembered that this statue was on Michigan Avenue. Her view obstructed, Maria stood to peer through the sunroof, Dante's large hands wrapped around her small waist to steady her in the moving vehicle. Tanisha opened her mouth to scold Maria and make her take her seat reminding her that they were in a moving vehicle, but she bit her tongue when she realized that they had reached their destination. She could see Buckingham Fountain through the window. Maria quickly ran her fingers through her long, wavy hair which obeyed and snapped back into place. *My hair would be standing on end if I stuck my head out of the window in a moving car.*

The limousine pulled parallel to the curb and parked behind another long, stretch limousine which was parked behind yet another limousine. Prom goers swarmed the fountain like flies. Ian helped Rashanda out of the car and stood by the door, extending an arm to the ladies as one by one, the River North prom goers climbed out of the limo. Tanisha smiled as Dante motioned for her and Grace to go ahead of him. *Is he being chivalrous or is he just trying to sneak a peek at our butts as we climb over him?*

"Smile," a girl giggled. "Now let's take one with just the guys," the girl stated. "And then we'll take one with just the girls," she continued.

Buckingham Fountain was one of Chicago's most famous prom and wedding photo backdrops. The stone fountain sat in the heart of Grant Park along Chicago's famed Lake Shore Drive. Couples strolled through the park and admired the beauty of the large flowing fountain with its water spouting twenty feet into the air, creating a foam mist that doused visitors on windy days. Tanisha took a deep breath and thought of the last time she'd visited Buckingham Fountain. She'd been with David Barton.

☙◊❧

One week before David was scheduled to leave for Georgetown, he'd picked her up after the early shift at Save Mart. "I'm kidnapping you," he'd said. "Before I head off to college, I have to say farewell to an old friend, and I'm taking you with me," he paused. "And don't ask me where we're going. It's a surprise. Just buckle up and enjoy the ride. I know you were going to go home and take a nap after work, so just lean back and doze," he suggested.

Tanisha had grown accustomed to David's whimsical ways and was happy to oblige. Tired from a late movie with her girlfriends the night before, and her early wake up call to work her nine am shift, she snuggled into her seat and took a nap. Not long after, she felt something wet along her chin. "Wake up, Teenie. We're here!" David said excitedly. "You must have been really tired. Your head was bobbing back and forth the whole ride, and you're drooling," he laughed.

Wiping her mouth with the back of her hand, Teenie squinted and peered out the window. "We're at Buckingham Fountain," she yawned. "We're meeting your friend at Buckingham Fountain?" she asked flipping down the passenger mirror and combing her hair. "I look a mess David," she whined nervously. "Let me touch up my eye liner and put on some lipstick. I don't want to have bed head when I meet your friend," she groaned. "Do you have a mint or some gum?" she asked.

He laughed loudly. "You look fine, Teenie. My friend won't notice the drool on your chin," he teased. "But he might notice that bat in the cave," he pointed. "I'm just kidding. You don't have a bat in the cave," he grinned. "Hop out," he said cheerily.

Ignoring him, Teenie checked her nose in the mirror just in case, quickly applied lipstick and smoothed out her hair as David tapped his foot holding the passenger door open for her. "I can't believe you have me meeting one of your friends without any warning, David," she whispered. "I could have at least worn something cuter to work today or brought a change of clothes," she whined.

"You look fine. I love that little sailor outfit that you have on," he complimented as he helped her out of the car. "Teenie, meet Buck. Buck meet Teenie," he smiled.

Tanisha looked around and stared at David curiously. "There's no one there, David," she said.

"My friend is Buckingham Fountain," David said. "I'm going to miss him while I'm at Georgetown," he laughed. "And I wanted to say goodbye to him. We go way back, so I call him Buck."

"Your friend is a fountain?" she asked. "Have you been drinking early again, David? It's only two o'clock in the afternoon. Please tell me that you weren't intoxicated while you drove me from the suburbs into the city in that little death trap that you call a car," she screamed. "You could have killed us both. I can't believe you!" she squealed, her arms flailing overhead.

David reached for her hands and inhaled deeply. "Calm down, Teenie," he laughed. "I haven't been drinking," he shared. "Honestly, I haven't. In fact, I haven't had a beer in several months because every time I reach for one I have your voice in my head telling me that I shouldn't be drinking," he admitted. "And in case you haven't noticed, I also fasten my seatbelt every time I get in the car," he boasted.

"I noticed that. I'm glad that I'm having a good influence on you and your wicked ways," she laughed softly. "Sorry about that little moment just now, but you know how worked up I get about things that are important to me," she finished.

"Do I ever," he mocked. "You get worked up about so many things that it's hard to keep track of them," he laughed.

Tanisha scowled at David. "I get worked up about things that are common sense. Things that people should get worked up about," she ranted. "Like you shouldn't be drinking when you're in high school, you should wear your seatbelt in the car. You shouldn't litter," she paused.

David placed his index finger near her lips. "I get it. Trust me, I'm familiar with your long list of things that get you worked up," he paused. "You're like a goody two shoe ghost who's haunting me and preventing me from having any fun," he whined. His gaze turned to the fountain. "I love Buckingham Fountain. It's a Chicago landmark," he continued. "It's one of the things that I'm really going to miss about Chicago," David admitted softly. "I'm going to miss seeing Buckingham Fountain, and you, Tanisha Denise Carlson. I'm going to miss you when I leave," he said confidently, his eyes staring directly into hers.

Embarrassed about her recent tirade, her face grew soft. The emotions that gripped her heart tangled in her throat like a puzzle. "I'm going to miss you too, David," she said softly.

His large hand rubbed her arm and wrapped around her thin wrist, his thumb caressing the dial of her watch. A gust of wind blew a soft fountain mist over their faces. She could feel her heart beating wildly. Tanisha held her breath as David used his thumb to casually wipe a bead of moisture from the tip of her nose. He's going to kiss me. If he tries to kiss me, I'm going to let him.

Casual and comfortable were the two words that best described their friendship. David and Tanisha shared a casual, comfortable closeness. Yet, at Tanisha's insistence, they still had not met each others' parents.

One evening, on their nightly phone marathon, she opened up to him and shared the shame that she felt about where she lived and her fear that her family couldn't afford to pay for college. He'd listened and assured her that her family's current economic status was not programmed into her DNA, reminding her that she was a straight A student and would get a scholarship to a good school and create a new economic reality for herself like his parents had done for themselves. His advice had been delivered very matter-of-factly, without prejudice or judgment. "I'm glad that you opened up to me about that. I feel like you're finally beginning to trust me, Teenie."

She wanted to tell him about Billie's mental illness, but whenever the topic of her parents arose, she spoke confidently about Jackie and their closeness, but limited any discussion about her mother, always giving the same terse reply, 'we're just not that close.'

After a year of serving as her mother's pharmaceutical technician, Tanisha noticed a positive change in Billie. She dutifully reported for work at the cable company, her mood swings were less frequent, and the manic phase of her bipolar condition was being managed effectively by her medication. As they'd agreed, Tanisha brought her mother a small glass of cold water with the two tablets every morning. If Tanisha spent the night at Maria's house, she would place the tablets next to a glass of water on her mother's dresser inside a napkin with a note for her mother to have a good day. She always remembered to paint a smiley face in the napkin. Tanisha wanted to share this part of her life with David, but feared that this level of disclosure might tarnish their friendship. Billie's behavior was still too new and too unproven for Tanisha to trust.

Whenever she felt herself softening up to the idea of telling David about Billie's mental illness, she would talk herself out of it just as quickly. She didn't want to disturb the comfortable closeness that they shared. Tanisha liked things just the way they were. Although David continued to date Patty, Tanisha and David talked on the phone every day, and had lunch on her lunch breaks from Save Mart frequently. Patty had adopted Tanisha as her little sister. Teenie and David shared a bond that she couldn't frame into words, not even for her closest friends. It was casual, comfortable, and it worked.

A parade of pigeons marched behind them, pecking at the gravel. Tanisha nervously ran her tongue along her lips. Taking a step away from her, David reached into his pocket and pulled out a small camera. "I kidnapped you because I want to take a picture of you in front of Buckingham Fountain," he explained. "And I knew if I told you ahead of time, you'd make a big fuss about what to wear, and your hair not looking right," he teased, rustling her hair with his free hand.

The tender moment passed like Buckingham Fountain's mist. Tanisha forced herself to breathe. "And I won't take no for an answer," he continued. "I don't have any pictures of you," he stated. "Not one. I don't even have your school picture," he shared. "So stand over there, and let me take a picture of you in front of my friend Buck," he ordered. Tanisha willingly obliged.

As Buckingham Fountain's mist sailed overhead, Teenie prayed that the disappointment in her heart wasn't as obvious as it felt. She feared that her emotions were the size of a drive-in movie projection screen and the sub titles beneath her face read, "I really like you, David. I want to be your girlfriend!" Taking an exaggerated breath, she snapped into the moment. "Fine," her voice said. " I'll let you take a photo of me, but hurry up because this mist is getting my hair wet, and you know black women do not like to get their hair wet!" she giggled, masking her emotions with humor like she'd done so many times before. Her energy quickly transferred to the task of concealing her cavity when she smiled.

෯ාൽ

Pigeons co-mingled with tourists, couples and the homeless people who panhandled for money. "Earth calling, Teenie," Glen whispered. "Are you okay?" he asked. "You seemed like you were in another world. You daydream a lot," he noticed.

"I'm fine," she said. "I was just thinking about the last time I was at Buckingham Fountain," she offered quickly. "And I was thinking about my friend," she sighed.

Glen rubbed her back. "Grace and Doug seem to be getting along fine," he said. "Lori is up in heaven smiling down on us. Let's try to have fun tonight," he smiled widely thru his large gap.

"Lori?" Tanisha asked. "You're right. I was thinking about Lori," she stammered. "But I'm fine now. Let's get these photos taken before the fountain mist messes up my hair and make-up," she laughed.

The four couples posed in front of the fountain, shifting their positions to dodge the mist that chased after them, threatening to assault their prom finery. Tanisha noticed that their group was the only group of African American students taking prom photos at Buckingham Fountain.

"Glen," she said. "Why aren't there more black couples out here taking prom pictures?" she asked.

"My girl!" Glen squealed. "I was wondering when you were going to notice that," he admitted. "I would have been disappointed if you hadn't said anything."

"Noticed what?" she asked. "I just thought that more black people would be coming later. You know how we're always on 'CP' colored people's time," she laughed. "But now the sun is about to go behind the skyline, it's almost six thirty, and most proms are about to start so it's really late to be trying to get pictures at Buckingham Fountain," she noted. "What's going on?"

Glen reached for her hand and escorted her toward the limousine. Tanisha carefully tiptoed across the gravel, hoisting her gown above her ankles. "The inner city schools have their proms late in June," he explained. "Several years ago, a white high school from Glenview had their prom at the same hotel as Ghorliss High School on the south side of Chicago, and a huge fight broke out," he continued. "Now it could have just been students being students, but since all of the students from the Glenview school were white, and all of the students from Ghorliss were black, it became this huge race thing," he paused. "So since then, the superintendents get together and schedule the suburban school proms for May, and the black, inner city school proms for late June. In fact, some of the south suburban towns that are mostly black hold their proms in late June too like the inner city schools," he highlighted. "Just another example of how quickly the world will segregate the races," Glen sighed. "All it took was one altercation and an edict was passed to make sure that the black kids didn't have prom on the same day as the white kids," he groaned. "And they don't know for sure if it was race based or not," he continued.

Tanisha laughed. "Calm down, little Malcolm X," she laughed. "It's all good."

"We are a bunch of lazy lima beans," Dante said. "I can't believe that we're taking the limousine. The Conrad Hilton Hotel is on Balboa which is just a couple of blocks down Michigan Avenue," he groaned. "I'm an athlete. I prefer to walk every chance I get," he boasted.

"I am not walking two blocks in these heels," Maria squealed. "Get in the car, and shush up, Mr. Football," she laughed.

The girls giggled as the limousine pulled in front of the hotel, a black doorman scurried swiftly to the curb, a wide grin across his face as he reached for the door. His smile seemed to fade slightly as the students piled out. Tanisha watched as Glen quickly reached into his pocket and folded three dollars into a small square.

"What are you doing, Glen?" she asked.

"I'll tell you in a minute," he explained. Glen exited the limousine ahead of Tanisha, and reached inside to gently lift her by her elbow as she held the hem of her dress above her ankles, feeling like Cinderella in her lavender gown.

"Thank you, sir," Glen said politely, shaking the doorman's hand firmly with both of his hands. Tanisha watched as the doorman's wide grin returned. Glen casually placed his arm over Tanisha's shoulder and escorted her toward the hotel doors.

"My old man worked as a doorman to put himself through college," Glen whispered. "He taught me the proper way to tip," he explained. "He told me that you shouldn't wave the money in the doorman's face, it's demeaning. The proper way to give a tip is to fold the money in your hand," he paused. "You then press the bills into his palm when you shake his hand to thank him for the service that he's provided," he explained. "It's more discreet, and it helps him maintain dignity about his position," Glen finished. "He also taught me to honor the black doormen by calling them sir," he whispered as they walked. "My dad told me that when he worked as a doorman, a lot of the white customers would call him 'boy', just because they could," he continued. "Even the customers that were younger than he was, would refer to him as 'boy', or they would deliberately toss his tip at him so they could watch him chase it down the street," he frowned. "My dad knew that they were doing it just to degrade him," he said. "But he needed the money so he chased after it."

Teenie stopped walking and tilted her head to the side. She could feel her eyes filling with tears as she stared at Glen, admiring his tall, muscular frame in his tuxedo. "That is so touching," she cooed. "You are the most thoughtful boy in the world," Tanisha beamed. "The other guys just jumped out of the limousine and didn't even think to tip the doorman," she observed. She blinked several times to keep the pool of tears in her eye socket.

Glen turned to face her. Teenie's body tensed as he leaned his tall frame down and rubbed his nose against hers. "I am just doing me, Teenie," he said softly. "Their fathers probably never worked as a doorman and never explained doorman etiquette to them," he whispered. "When you know better, you do better," he said. "I learned that saying from my dad too," he finished, his face inches from hers. "My dad is full of wisdom," he grinned.

Teenie's heart wanted to leap out of her chest as his hazel eyes stared into her eyes, his peppermint breath blowing like a cool breeze across her cheeks. Why hasn't he kissed me yet?

"Let's go inside so we can get this party started," he sang. She smiled as the same doorman raced to hold the lobby door open for them.

Her arm rested comfortably inside Glen's as they floated through the crowded lobby in search of her friends. She pointed when she saw Ian standing above the crowd, waiting to have their prom photos taken.

"Maria and I reserved a table inside," Rashanda shared. "But we thought we'd better get the prom photos taken while our make-up is still fresh," she finished.

Tanisha smiled and chatted animatedly with some of her River North classmates as they waited in line outside of the ballroom. Her eyes panned the crowd, and as best she could tell, no one else from her high school wore the same lavender gown as she.

"Let's leave the guys to hold our place in line while we freshen up our hair and make-up," Maria suggested tugging Teenie's arm before waiting for a response, and leading her down the stairs. Grace and Rashanda skip walked to keep pace as Maria led the group through a narrow corridor that led to a small ladies room.

Rashanda and Teenie stared curiously at each other. "How in the world did you know that there was a bathroom in this little alcove, Maria?" Rashanda asked.

Maria laughed loudly. "I've been here for the jazz brunch a few times with my mother," she explained. "You know how Liz loves her jazz. Frankly, I just come for the food. Anyway, brunch is in the same banquet room where our prom is being held," she continued. "One day the restroom that's closest to the ballroom had a really long line and a person in housekeeping waved me over and brought me to this little bathroom," she explained. "She told me that I reminded her of her granddaughter, so she was willing to share this secret bathroom with me," Maria said. "Watch your step," she cautioned as she held the door ajar. Following Maria's lead, the girls hoisted their prom dresses above their ankles and carefully stepped down to enter the tiny bathroom.

The bathroom could be accessed only by walking down one tile covered step. Two small stalls and two sinks filled the tiny space. The sinks were adorned with two large mirrors. A small chair sat against the wall beneath the paper towel dispenser.

Immediately positioning herself in front of one of the mirrors, Maria pulled out her mascara wand and began expertly swabbing her already thickly coated eyelashes. Rashanda followed suit and reapplied her lipstick in front of the other mirror. "The housekeeper explained that there are some meeting rooms down the hall so this bathroom gets used occasionally when people are using those conference rooms," she continued. "But most people don't even know that this bathroom is here," she finished. "Plus, because of that step to get down here, it would be hard for an old person to maneuver," she chuckled.

"You're right, Maria," Grace agreed. "That step down is at least six inches, maybe eight. An older person could trip trying to get in here," she commented, plopping down in the small upholstered chair.

Pulling out a tiny compact hair brush, Maria brushed her long hair. "I always laugh at how people will wait in line like cattle to use the bathroom instead of wandering around and trying to find a restroom that doesn't have a long wait," she observed. Her brush strokes were long and methodical. "And don't tell anyone about it. This bathroom will be our little secret in case we have to use it during prom," Maria ordered. "Don't tell a soul, or I will torture you," she laughed.

"Good call, Maria," Teenie chirped. "The bathroom near our ballroom had a line full of wannabe prom queens snaking out of it, and you know I have to pee like a racehorse," she shared as she rushed into the stall.

"Just don't do number two in there," Maria laughed. "It's way too small in here to be stinking up the joint."

Gripping the hem of her dress, Teenie slipped into the narrow stall, her knees bumping into the toilet as she turned to close the stall door. "This is the smallest public bathroom that I've ever seen," she whined. "Help! What am I supposed to do with my dress while I'm using the bathroom?" she asked. "Should I hoist it up to my chest and squat or just step out of it and hang it on the back of the door?"

"Just line the toilet seat with toilet paper, hoist the dress up with both hands and sit on the toilet, drama queen," Maria groaned. "If you try to squat, you might pee on your shoes. Just sit on the toilet," she ordered. "You are not going to catch butt cooties tonight!" she laughed.

Teenie shrugged and obeyed. Grace and Rashanda moved aside as Teenie approached the sink to wash her hands. "No one else has to go to the bathroom?" she asked.

"You're the only one in the group with a child size bladder, Teenie," Rashanda teased. "This bathroom is much too small for all of us to be in here together. Grace and I will wait for you guys in the hallway to give you more space," she finished.

David used to always tease me about having a tiny bladder. He would call me Teenie with the teensy, tiny bladder. No more David wanderings, Teenie! You're here with Glen tonight!

"Hello! Anybody home? Teenie, I asked you if I could borrow your blush," Maria repeated. "My blush wouldn't fit in my tiny evening bag," she explained.

"Sure," Teenie replied, handing her the small compact. Carefully adjusting the bobby pins holding her swept up hair in place, she turned sideways and smiled approvingly at her reflection. "I'm glad that you told me to consider wearing my hair up, Maria. I like it. It looks more sophisticated," she admitted.

"Duh! You know I am up on all things fashionable and sophisticated," Maria boasted. "You have a nice, long neck, Teenie," she complimented. "And with your hair swept up, it highlights your neck and cheekbones. I actually thought about wearing mine up too," she shared. "But Dante likes to run his fingers through my hair," she purred.

Carefully wiping off her lipstick to apply a fresh coating, Teenie spoke through her teeth. "Truth, Maria," Teenie said seriously. "I'm your girl, and you know you can tell me anything," she continued, staring at her friend's reflection in the mirror. "When did you get so chummy with Dante? What's up with that?" she asked. "And don't lie to me, chick. Spill it!" Tanisha ordered.

The grin gave her away. Maria's eyes met Tanisha's, and she put her finger to her lips. "Hold on for a second," Maria said. She turned and opened the bathroom door. "Rashanda and Grace," she said softly. "Why don't you go back and get in line with the guys. I need to do some magic on Teenie's hair. She has wispy ends flying all over her face," she explained. "We just need about five more minutes."

"Works for me," Rashanda shared. Tanisha could hear their footsteps padding down the carpeted hallway.

Leaning against the bathroom door, Maria exhaled. "We're not that close, Teenie," she shared. Her look was sad and serious. "I didn't want Rashanda and Grace to hear this," she explained. "Dante is really nice. He's not the dumb jock that I thought he was in high school," she admitted. "He's smart and has already worked out a plan for his life after he's done playing in the NFL," she shared. "He's planning to get a business degree so he can run the franchises that he plans to buy with his NFL money," she continued.

Tanisha stared at Maria, wondering where her comments were leading. She plopped on the chair and placed her chin in her hands, staring intently at her friend.

"At first I was just flirting with Dante to make Todd jealous about not taking me to prom," Maria confessed. "I led Dante on so he'd agree to take me," she whispered. "But now I think that he really likes me," she whined.

Tanisha laughed loudly. "Maria, you think that the clerk at the McDonald's drive thru wants to marry you because he smiles when he takes your money at the window," she teased. "In your self absorbed, princess world, everyone likes you," she chuckled.

"Dante asked me to be his girlfriend last week," Maria blurted.

Teenie felt her mouth opening wider and wider. "He asked

you to be his girlfriend?" she repeated. "I knew something was going on by the way he was looking at you while we were taking pictures in front of Lori's house," she paused. "And the way that he was cozying up to you in the limo. What did you say? What about Todd? What are you going to do?" she whispered.

"That's where you're supposed to give me some advice," Maria pleaded. "I don't know what to do," she admitted. "I told him that I would tell him my answer tonight. He's really nice, Teenie, but I don't want to be his girlfriend. I'm Todd's girlfriend," Maria stated pointedly.

The chuckle was accidental, like a burp that escapes after eating a greasy Polish sausage. The laugh just slipped from her lips.

"What's so funny?" Maria shrieked. "Just because Todd didn't want to take me to prom, doesn't mean that I'm not his girlfriend," she said defensively.

Her hands in the surrender pose, Tanisha leaned back in her chair. "I'm sorry about that, Maria. Calm down. I didn't mean to laugh. I really didn't," Teenie confessed. "And I didn't say that you weren't still Todd's girlfriend," she explained. Careful, Teenie. This is a slippery slope that you're skiing on. If you say the wrong thing, she'll blow like dynamite. "But since Todd is away at college," she said slowly. "Maybe it would be good for you to date Dante for awhile so that you can be sure about your feelings for Todd," she said cautiously. That was a safe, soft, friendly suggestion. I don't think that should set her off.

"Now you sound like my mother," Maria groaned. "She said the same thing."

Teenie raised her eyebrows curiously. "You told your mother that Dante asked you to be his girlfriend?" she asked.

"Of course I did. I tell my mother almost everything, Teenie,"

Maria confessed. "I thought you knew that," she paused. "Liz gets on my nerves a lot, but she gives great advice. Most of the time. Sometimes her advice is old fashioned, but most of the time, what she tells me makes sense," she finished. "I usually talk to her about stuff before I talk to you guys about it, just to compare your advice against hers."

I can't even imagine talking to Billie about a boy. Liz Wesley is my hero.

"But when I told her what Dante said, Liz had the nerve to tell me that I should put things on hold with Todd and date Dante," she continued. "She said that she's certain that Todd is dating other people, so I should too," Maria rambled. "Liz called me Todd's hometown honey. His h.t.h.," she explained. "She said that college guys always have a hometown honey, and most of them have at least one or two girls on campus that keep company with them," she finished. "Can you believe my mother said that?" Maria shrieked. "I was so mad at her!" Maria growled, exhaling slowly and walking toward the mirror, grabbing her small hairbrush from the counter, she brushed her long tresses violently.

Maria's flailing arm and hairbrush waved inches from Tanisha's nose. Teenie slid out of her chair and stood with her back against the door.

She watched as Maria slammed the small brush against the counter, and it slid into the sink. "I think Liz is still bitter about my dad and his affair with his secretary," she pouted staring at her reflection. "So she doesn't believe that anyone is capable of being faithful in a relationship. That's what her problem is," she concluded.

Unsure what to say or do, Teenie watched as Maria unceremoniously wiped her hairbrush with a paper towel and slipped it into her purse.

"I'm not Todd's hometown honey," she said softly. "I'm his girlfriend," she whispered, plopping in the chair to stair directly at Teenie. "What do you think about what my mother said, Teenie?"

This is a black diamond ski run here, Teenie. You're only a blue level skier. Be careful, girl. Teenie took a deep breath and stared at her friend. "I think that what you and Todd have is special between you and Todd," she said confidently. "I may not understand it. Your mother may not understand it, but it works for you and Todd," she continued. "And I guess that's all that matters," she shrugged. "If Todd hasn't openly talked to you about what he's doing on campus, and you don't have any confirmation that he's dating anyone else, then maybe he isn't," Tanisha offered meekly.

"I'm glad that you agree with me for a change instead of my mother," Maria grinned. She stood up and smoothed out her prom gown. "To tell you the truth," she paused. "I don't even feel comfortable kissing Dante. I don't want to feel like I'm cheating on Todd," she confessed.

This time the laugh was guttural and uncontained. Teenie could feel the tears welling in her eyes. I wonder why your tear ducts are triggered by so many different emotions: laughter, awe, fear, sadness?

"What's so funny this time, Teenie?" Maria demanded.

With her right hand she gripped her convulsing chest, while her left hand cupped her mouth, careful not to smudge her freshly applied lipstick. "Maria, please," Teenie said. "Do you honestly believe that Todd isn't kissing someone else at college? Of course he is," Teenie blurted loudly.

"Shh!" Maria cautioned. "Keep your voice down! I knew that you'd get loud if I shared what was going on," she confirmed.

"That's why I sent Rashanda and Grace away," she pouted. "Now you sound like my mother again," she whined. "I can't believe that you said that."

The giggles under control, the honesty flowed like a raging river, raw and unapologetic. "Maria. You know that I love you like a sister," Teenie admitted. "I really do, but enough is enough. Your mother is right. Todd is definitely seeing other people. Just believe me. Don't ask me for specifics, I don't have any. But just trust me on this," she said confidently as though sipping another swig of truth serum. "That's why I think that if you like Dante, then you should try to get to know him," she suggested softly. "There's no crime in getting to know someone," Teenie explained. "You don't have to call yourself Dante's girlfriend. Just spend some time with him and see what happens," she encouraged.

"Like you're doing with David and Glen?" Maria asked. "You still have feelings for David, but you're getting to know Glen?"

Teenie stared at Maria in the mirror. "We've covered this ground before, Maria. David isn't my boyfriend. He's my friend," she said. "It's not the same as your relationship with Todd. End of discussion," she said firmly.

"Whatever, chick," Maria laughed.

Teenie rolled her eyes at her friend and inspected her braces for food. She'd brushed her braces after eating hors d'oeuvres at Mrs. Wesley's champagne toast, but didn't want food dangling from her mouth in her prom pictures. She quickly powdered her nose one last time.

"Should I show my braces when I smile or not?" she asked Maria.

"Let me see you smile with your braces," Maria instructed. Tanisha beamed into the mirror.

"Hmmm," Maria murmured. "Now let's see your smile without showing your braces," she ordered.

Teenie pursed her lips together and smiled into the mirror again.

"You look too sinister with your lips stuck together," Maria noted. "Try to smile softer so that some of your braces are showing, but not your whole mouth," she suggested.

"Sinister? How do I look sinister?" Teenie asked smiling again.

"Maybe sinister isn't the right word," she corrected. "But it doesn't look right." Maria stood next to Tanisha in the mirror. "Just smile with your lips stuck together and then open them slightly so that some of your teeth show," Maria explained. "Like this," she demonstrated.

Tanisha watched and mimicked Maria's smile example.

"Perfect!" Maria pointed. "That's the look we're after. Just let your top lip rest on top of your upper braces," she finished.

Teenie repeated the smile again. Maria's right. This is the look we're after.

"I practice smiling in the mirror all the time," Maria shared. "I practice my pouty girl look," she demonstrated. "My surprise look. My disappointed look. My sad face," she laughed. "You have to be ready to use all of your tricks in a flash," she coached.

Her hand gently resting on Teenie's shoulder, she pleaded, "By the way, don't mention any of this to the other girls. I haven't decided what I'm going to do about Dante," she paused. "And tell Glen not to show his gap when he smiles. You don't want your pictures to be messed up," Maria continued.

Tanisha pinched Maria's arm lightly. "I will do no such thing," she shrieked. "Glen's gap doesn't bother me at all. I hope he smiles widely," Teenie finished.

"Suit yourself. If you want to mess up perfectly good prom pictures by showing your railroad track braces, and his football field goal post gap, have at it," Maria shrugged. "The two of you together look like a dental "before" picture," she laughed quickly scooting thru the narrow door frame before Teenie could pinch her again.

Laughing, Maria speed walked away from Tanisha and hid behind Dante in the prom photo line.

"Just in time, beautiful," Glen beamed. "There are only two more couples ahead of us," he shared. "You didn't really need to freshen up. You always look great," he complimented.

Teenie allowed her fingers to caress his jawbone softly, tracing the stubble from his shaven face. "Sorry we took so long," Teenie purred. "Maria had to fix my hair," she lied. "How are you planning to smile for our photo shoot?" she asked quickly. "I don't think I'm going to show my braces," she admitted. "Maybe you shouldn't show your gap," she whispered.

Glen covered her fingers with his large hand. "I wasn't planning to, Teenie," he said stunned. "But I didn't realize that my gap bothered you," he mumbled.

"It doesn't," she confessed. "It doesn't bother me at all," she continued. "But I don't want our prom pictures to be focused on our teeth," she explained. "Especially with me having enough metal in my mouth to wire a telephone pole," she continued. "I plan to smile softly without showing my braces, and I think the picture would look better if our smiles matched," she explained. "It'll look weird if you have this huge, wide grin, and I have this soft, demure smile," she finished.

"Good point," he said. "I'll tone down my smile to match yours. Is that what you were doing in the bathroom, practicing your smiles?" he asked.

Blushing, Tanisha nodded her head up and down. "Yup! You know how girls are," she grinned. "We try to coordinate everything."

"Next couple step on up," the photographer bellowed. Like robots, Teenie and Glen scurried to the backdrop and stood on the small tape lines marked with the symbol for male and female. Tanisha smiled and inhaled deeply as Glen wrapped his arms around her waist, playfully rubbing his chin against her cheek, his beard stubble tickling her face.

"Nice try, stretch," the photographer laughed. "But we're going to shoot the profile shot first, and then the cuddle shot," he teased. "So don't kiss the pretty girl now and muss her make-up," he ordered. "I still have at least ten more couples waiting for their photos to be taken, and I don't have time for her to primp in the mirror and reapply the lipstick that you'll kiss off," he rattled. "These kids will mutiny if they have to wait five extra minutes before they can go inside and enjoy their lukewarm, rubber chicken dinner. You have all night to kiss," he joked. "So turn the lady around so her back is facing you."

"We have a lifetime to kiss," Glen whispered softly as he guided Teenie around and repositioned his arms around her waist, his right hand cupping the base of her prom bouquet. The photographer adjusted their pose so that Glen's chin rested snugly on Teenie's hair. His breath danced on the back of her neck. "Your hair smells so good, Teenie," Glen complimented. Teenie felt her face flushing.

We have a lifetime to kiss? What does that mean? Does a lifetime begin tonight? Is he planning to kiss me tonight or what? Ask him Teenie. After you take the picture, just ask him. Enough is enough.

"Pretty, girl," the photographer sang. "I don't think you want to scrunch up your forehead like that, it looks like you're ready to charge a bull," he teased. "Don't look so serious. It's prom night. Soften your face and think happy thoughts," he smiled. "Happy thoughts make for happy photos, and happy photos make for happy customers, and happy customers make for a happy photographer," he sang.

Tanisha gently shook her head and smiled softly, trying desperately to duplicate the smile that she'd practiced in the mirror with Maria.

Her thoughts in a daze, Glen led Tanisha from the photographer's backdrop to stand near Rashanda and Ian.

"Hey, Teenie," Glen purred. "I'm going to run to the bathroom with Ian right quick," he said excitedly. "Why don't you and Rashanda go to the table and have a seat," he suggested.

Rashanda and Teenie stared curiously at each other as Ian and Glen whispered and walked away. "Since when do guys go to the bathroom in pairs?" Rashanda asked. "What's that about?"

"Who cares," Tanisha groaned. "I can't even worry about that right now. Go get Maria and Grace," she ordered. "I need a girl conference."

Rashanda eyed Teenie suspiciously. "What's the matter, Teenie? Are you okay?"

Her eyes were icy and cold as she stared at Glen and Ian walking down the hotel lobby toward the restrooms. "I don't think Glen is planning to kiss me tonight," she whispered. "The photographer made a joke that we had all night to kiss, and Glen's response was, 'we have a lifetime to kiss,'" Teenie repeated. "What the heck does that mean?"

Rashanda's eyes were soft, her look one of confusion. "I haven't a clue what he could have meant by that," she confessed. "But you're right, we need a conference. Ian is acting weird, and keeps going to the bathroom," she whispered. "I'm scared he's going to break up with me, Teenie!   I'll go get Maria and Grace," she finished before Teenie could offer.   Rashanda's prom gown made a swooshing sound as she walked swiftly into the ballroom.

The lines on her forehead felt heavy and thick.   Stop scowling, Teenie or you're going to get premature wrinkles like that wrinkly dog that looks like an eighty year old.   What's that dog called?   It's on the tip of my tongue.   A sharpei!   What kind of dumb name is that for a dog?   A sharpie is a pen and a sharpei is a dog!   She could feel her forehead creasing tighter and tighter.

"Teenie?" the voice asked tentatively, her name bouncing off the back of her head.

I don't feel like chatting with any more of these River North prom geeks tonight. We barely chat at school, and now all of a sudden, everyone wants to pretend like we're best buddies just because it's prom night.

"Is that you, Teenie?" the voice repeated.

Rolling her eyes into the top of her head, Teenie sighed softly, making only a small effort to erase the scowl on her face as she turned toward the faintly recognized voice.

Gasping, she felt like someone had jumped out of a closet and frightened her out of her wits.   Forcing herself to breathe, Teenie squinted to be sure that her eyes weren't deceiving her.   They weren't.

Like the rays of sunlight that fight their way through a partly cloudy sky, illuminating the terrain with bright light, her lips parted and a soft smile lit up her face.

"I thought that was you," he said softly, his eyes staring directly into hers.

Chapter 13

Two for Tea

The small window air conditioning unit hummed softly, dripping condensation onto the thin tray in a rhythmic pattern. Even with the air conditioning unit working overtime, the air stood still, thick and motionless, like a street mime holding a pose. The silence of anticipation broken only by the mahogany mantel clock that chimed on the quarter hour. The clock had been his housewarming gift when they moved into their new apartment. Justine smiled at the clock. That should have been her first clue.

Taking a deep breath, she gripped AM's hand and led him to the porch. Sunlight flowed into the brightly decorated space. The whir of a ceiling fan moved the thick air around the room creating the illusion of a breeze with the view of the calm, blue waters of Lake Michigan providing a cooling optical illusion to the sun's hot rays. A white wicker and glass table was covered with a crisp yellow and white tablecloth and matching napkins adorned with sunflower holders. Her grandmother's silver tea set rested on a small side table, next to a glass pitcher of lemonade, lemon slices floating amidst the melting ice cubes. A small crystal vase of daisies served as the centerpiece, next to a short, three tiered buffet stand that held small white luncheon-sized plates filled with crust-free, finger sandwiches: cucumber, dill and egg salad on wheat, white and rye bread. A basket of scones, mini muffins and raspberry tarts completed the centerpiece trio. Her mother's wedding china framed the table, completing the formal place setting.

"You're not nervous are you?" Justine whispered. "Your palms are sweating."

AM quickly wiped his hands along his khaki shorts and looked over his shoulder. "Of course I'm a little nervous," he confessed. "I've not done the meet the mom thing that many times," he shared quickly. "Remember, I've only had one other girlfriend before you," he whispered. "And she wasn't really my girlfriend. We attended Hebrew school together, and she was my first dance at my bar mitzvah," he stammered. "She was also my prom escort, but she had a boyfriend in college at the time, and I think she only went with me because my mom and her mom were in the same bridge group and her mom told her to go with me," he rattled.

Justine laughed quickly. "Don't tell that story, babe. It makes you sound like a loser. Like a dateless geek," she teased. "And remember. You've already met my mom," she reminded, pecking him on the cheek quickly.

"But I wasn't your boyfriend at the time," AM corrected. "This is so different," he groaned, wiping his palms along his shorts again.

"This was your idea, Mr. Wahlberg. You wanted to meet my mom, so here you are," she giggled. "And it's too late to turn around now. Here she comes," Justine whispered as small footsteps echoed down the hall.

"Hey Mom," Justine beamed. "This is AM. AM this is my mother, Andrea Wellington," she finished.

"How do you do, ma'am," AM stammered, extending his hand to shake hers.

"Hello. Nice to meet you," Andrea smiled. "And please don't call me ma'am. It makes me feel so old. Please call me Andrea, or Mrs. Wellington," she insisted. "On second thought, just call me Andrea. You're a young man. You're old enough to call me Andrea," she concluded.

AM stared at Justine who shrugged and smiled.

"What's your real name, young man?" Mrs. Wellington asked. "I know Justine told me, but I don't recall what it is."

"It's Jacob. Jacob Wahlberg," AM replied.

"What would you like for me to call you?" Mrs. Wellington asked.

Again, AM looked at Justine for approval and support. "I hadn't thought about that," AM confessed. "You can call me whatever you like."

"Justine calls you AM, so I'll call you AM to keep it simple," she smiled. "Have a seat, AM," she ordered. She stared at Justine oddly. "Justine, I can't believe that you have your guest standing in this heat," she groaned. "You could have at least offered the young man a cold beverage. Where are your manners?" she admonished. "AM, I really did raise her better than that," she winked.

Playfully, Justine rolled her eyes at her mom and stuck out her tongue. "Would you like lemonade, big head?" Justine teased.

"That would be fine, babe. I mean, Justine," AM corrected quickly.

Mrs. Wellington laughed at the pet name slip of tongue. "So you're the reason that Justine has been missing curfew so often," she smiled. "I should have known she wasn't spending that much time with her new friend Kyle from high school."

Not sure if her comment warranted a response, AM watched nervously as Mrs. Wellington placed one of each type of sandwich on his plate along with each type of pastry. He smiled when Justine handed him the sweaty glass of lemonade and sipped it quickly, glad to have a task for his nervous tongue.

"I know it's too hot to have tea," Mrs. Wellington shared. "But high tea is my favorite time of the day," she smiled. "And you certainly can't have someone over for tea, and not serve tea," she laughed. "Tea time is such a nice time of day to meet people. This way you can chat without having to consume a big meal over lunch or dinner," she concluded, pouring herself a steaming hot cup of tea.

"Justine seems to be very fond of you, AM," Mrs. Wellington continued. "And I know that she's told you that I'm concerned that you're Jewish and she's not," she said quickly avoiding eye contact with Justine who glared at her mother. "But I've assured Justine that we're not going to worry about any of that now since the two of you are just getting to know each other. But for the record," Mrs. Wellington stated. "It's hard for two people to get serious who aren't evenly yoked. I'm sure you realize that, AM," she blurted.

"Mom! What are you doing? You promised that you would stay away from religious talk with him!" Justine groaned.

"That's all I'm going to say, sweetie," Mrs. Wellington said quickly. "Calm down. I just had to get that out there for the record. I didn't offend you, did I, AM?" she asked.

"No. You didn't offend me at all," AM replied. "And for the record, I've not practiced my faith since after my bar mitzvah. My mother is Jewish, but my father is Catholic," he shared.

Justine stared at AM curiously. "You've never told me that," she said. "I thought both of your parents were Jewish."

AM shook his head from side to side. "Nope. Just my mom.

It was important to my mom that her children go to Hebrew school and have a bar mitzvah," he shared. "Of course, my sister had a bat mitzvah," he corrected. "My mom still goes to temple regularly," he finished. "When I was growing up, we celebrated Hanukkah and Christmas, although my mother called the small Christmas tree that we had a Hanukkah bush," he laughed.

A look of contentment on her face, Mrs. Wellington grinned knowingly. "See Justine, if I hadn't made that comment, you wouldn't have learned that about AM," she said smugly. "Even though your father is Catholic, which I have a problem with, you're Jewish since you were born of a Jewish mother."

"Why do you have a problem with Catholics?" AM asked.

"I saw a special on one of the news shows about this priest who molested boys in his church. And to make matters worse, the church just moved him to another parish. They didn't involve the police or press any criminal charges or anything, they just moved him along. That man should be in jail," she blurted quickly.

"Did you see that special, AM?" she asked. "Frankly, I think it's just unnatural for a man not to fulfill his natural sexual urge," she continued without waiting for his reply. "I know there are monks who take a vow of celibacy, but I think that's just a bunch of hogwash. Some of the other nurses at the hospital saw that program too, and a few of them had personal stories involving priests. One girl said that her brother committed suicide after their priest molested him. He told his parents, but they didn't believe him and still invited the priest over for dinner. Can you imagine being forced to have dinner with someone who was molesting you? If you ask me, I think the Catholic Church is a safe house for men who are really just closeted homosexuals. If you're gay, just be gay, who cares? But don't prey on children and hide behind religion. And another thing," she rambled.

"Mom!" Justine shrieked, choking on her egg salad sandwich, food sputtering from her mouth. "Stop it!" Justine screamed. "I can't believe that you just said that! That's enough. Not every Catholic priest is a pedophile or gay, and you know it," she chastised. "That's so judgmental and stereotypical of you. Just stop it! Your views are offensive and wrong, and you're embarrassing me!"

Mrs. Wellington rolled her eyes at her daughter and handed her a cloth napkin. "Wipe your mouth, dear," she ordered. "I really did teach her not to talk with food in her mouth, AM," Mrs. Wellington said casually.

Justine snatched the napkin and glared at her mother intensely. Inhaling one of the finger sandwiches, AM grinned comfortably and took a swig of his lemonade. "I think it's healthy when people ask questions and state their honest feelings," he smiled. "Everyone is entitled to her own opinion. I think the world would be a better place if people had honest dialogue," he shared, popping another tiny finger sandwich in his mouth, and swallowing after four quick chews. "And I'm glad that I'm finally meeting you, Andrea. I didn't like having to sneak around to spend time with Justine," he shared.

Mrs. Wellington smiled at AM. "You have morals. I like that AM," she grinned. "Are you worried about your parents meeting Justine?" she blurted.

"Why are you grilling him?" Justine whined. "His parents live in Bethesda, Maryland, Mom. It's not like I can just show up at their house for tea," she groaned.

AM leaned into his chair and patted Justine's hand. "It's alright, babe," he said confidently. "Your mother isn't grilling me. These are fair questions to ask, and I don't mind answering them," he shrugged. "I'm not worried about my parents meeting Justine," he shared. "My parents already know that she's black. I told them over the phone."

Justine stared at AM curiously. "You did?" she asked. "You didn't tell me that. When did you tell them about me?" she asked.

"Last month," he said in between bites. "You know I talk to my parents every Sunday at six thirty," he reminded reaching for another sandwich. "Andrea, my folks are creatures of habit and have a standing, seven o'clock dinner reservation at their country club every Sunday," he shared. "They call my brother and sister and me at six o'clock, six fifteen and six thirty, every Sunday," he explained. We each get fifteen minutes which gives them fifteen minutes to drive to the club for dinner," he laughed. "And if I'm not there to take that call or my roommate Ian is on the phone, and the line is busy, they will have the operator interrupt the line," he laughed. "My sister is married with two kids now, and she still knows to expect a call from our parents every Sunday at six fifteen," he explained. "Even if she's talked to them the day before," he paused. "My folks will still call her at six fifteen on Sunday to check in. And if she's busy with her family and can only chat for five minutes," AM continued. "They still won't call me until six thirty. It's hysterical," he finished.

"What did your parents say when you told them that I was black, AM?" Justine asked.

"Oh, right," he said. "They didn't say anything. They don't care about that," he shrugged. "My sister is married to a Japanese guy," AM shrugged. "My parents are just glad that their children are making a positive contribution to society," he finished. "Or at least two of their children are making a positive contribution to society. My sister is a lawyer now, and my brother graduated from Harvard Law School, but he's now living in Vermont working on a dairy farm," he shrugged. "Not that my parents have anything against dairy farmers," he explained. "But my father is very concerned about my brother getting a return on his law school investment, and can't believe that he helped send my brother to Harvard Law School, and now he's milking cows," he finished.

"It sounds like your family is very accepting of diversity. I like that. It's the way the world should be," Mrs. Wellington sighed. "I'm sure that your brother is just going through a phase, and he will put his law degree to good use soon," Mrs. Wellington shared. She watched Justine's surprise reaction. "Something else that you didn't know, Justine?" she laughed. "I can only wonder what you and AM talk about during your time together since you're learning so many new things about him at tea today, sweetie," she laughed. "By the way, are you planning to have sex with my daughter, AM?" Mrs. Wellington blurted.

This time, AM choked on his egg salad sandwich, coughing several times to catch his breath.

"That's enough, Mom!" Justine whined. "You are really out of bounds now, she groaned. "Don't answer that question, AM! I am so embarrassed. Bringing him here to meet you was such a bad idea. What was I thinking?" she shrieked.

Ignoring her daughter's pleas, Mrs. Wellington continued. "AM, I don't know if Justine has told you, but she and her friends from Newberry East have this pact that they're not going to have sex until they get married," she chuckled. "Which I think is very noble. I respect that immensely, but now that she's dating a college boy, that high school pledge may get tossed out the window," she sang. "Pat him on the back, Justine. Your boyfriend is choking," she observed.

His face flushed, AM coughed several times to catch his breath as Justine gently patted him on the back. Waving her away with his hand, Justine slumped in her chair. Clearing his throat,

AM took another swig of lemonade, his eyes darting from Justine to her mother. Her hands covering her face, Justine looked like she could strangle her mother. "We haven't talked about that," AM stammered nervously.

"Good. I'm glad to hear that. That talk always complicates things. You're both young. But if you decide to have that talk, remember, I am a nurse," she winked. "I really like you, AM," she smiled. "Justine, freshen up AM's lemonade, sweetie," she ordered. "I have really enjoyed getting to know you, and would love to keep chatting and learning new things about you, AM, but I have a date," she beamed. "And I need to freshen up before he gets here," she shared, scooting back her chair. She grinned when AM stood quickly and walked behind her chair to pull it away from the table.

"Thank you for having me over," AM said politely. "I really enjoyed meeting you. And your egg salad is the best I've had since I've been home."

"He has manners too, Justine," Mrs. Wellington observed. "You passed AM. You have my permission to date my daughter," she smiled, embracing AM in a quick hug. "I'm sure at some point her father will also want to meet you," she offered glumly. "And meeting her dad will be another thing altogether, but as far as I'm concerned, you are a nice young man, and I approve," she smiled. "There's a Tupperware bowl of egg salad in the refrigerator that you're welcome to take back to your dorm with you if you'd like," she offered. "As long as you return my container," she ordered. "Make sure AM takes home the egg salad, Justine. You know that your brothers don't like it, and I'm watching my diet these days," she said. "You'll have to come back again sometime and meet my boyfriend, AM. It's too difficult to park around here on a Saturday afternoon, so Bob's going to double park and ring the buzzer for me to come downstairs when he arrives," she explained. "We're going to have a picnic at the Ravinia Festival in Highland Park to hear Ramsey Lewis and Nancy Wilson," she said. "He's white too by the way," she shared. "My boyfriend is white," she explained. "Not Ramsey Lewis."

An imaginary white flag waved above Justine's head, as she surrendered to her mother's antics, the look of defeat plastered across her face. Her look suggested that she had fought nine rounds with the verbal heavy weight champion and lost. Justine bristled slightly as her mother pecked her on the cheek and tossed her hair.

"Thanks for bringing AM over to meet me, Justine," she smiled. "We'll have to double date sometime," she said walking through the doorway, her fingers tracing the top of AM's shoulders lightly as she exited. "Justine, if Bob hits the buzzer, just hit talk and tell him that I'm freshening up and will be down in five minutes," she ordered over her shoulder.

"Will do," Justine mumbled. Her shoulders slumped over the table, AM stared at Justine for a reaction.

"Your mom is really nice," he said. "She made me feel really comfortable," AM continued. "It's probably her patient care training. Good nurses always have a way of making people feel comfortable and at ease," he explained. "She's probably a very good nurse." He filled his plate with the remaining egg salad finger sandwiches.

Justine leaned into the table. "She has super, duper, mother hearing," she whispered. "So let's not talk about anything until she leaves," she cautioned.

"Where are your brothers?" AM asked.

"They're at a baseball game with my dad," she explained. "And then they're going to visit my grandmother," she continued. "My dad knows that I'm not a baseball fan, so he didn't sweat me about going. I may take the train and meet them at my grandmother's for dinner later," she said.

Moments later, the smell of Chanel No. 5 wafted into the sun porch. "My mother wears the same perfume," AM observed.

Andrea Wellington fumbled in her purse. "How do I look?" she asked loudly. AM and Justine walked into the foyer to admire her ensemble. She wore a white cotton eyelet blouse over a brightly colored, flowered skirt. Her freshly painted toes danced in brown leather thong sandals that matched the purse whose contents were spilled on the foyer table.

"I know I dropped them in here," Andrea announced. "I can never remember which pocket I've placed my keys in whenever I carry this purse," she giggled. "Oh, there they are."

The buzzer sound lasted five seconds, followed by a short two second blast in syncopation with the mantel clock chime.

"That's Bob," Andrea giggled. "He's so punctual!" Andrea quickly hit the talk button on the intercom system. "I'll be right down, sweetie," she sang. "What are you kids doing tonight?" she asked, checking her reflection in the hall mirror and casually running her fingers through her hair.

AM and Justine stared at each other curiously, their shoulders shrugging in unison. "We might catch a matinee," AM offered halfheartedly.

"Justine, don't leave that food on the sun porch too long or it'll spoil," Andrea ordered.

"There's not much left. AM's eaten almost all of the sandwiches," Justine teased.

"Bye, kids," Andrea chirped out the door. "Lock this door, Justine."

After double locking the door, Justine ran into the sun room and kneeled on the window seat cushion. Peering through the window, she could see the rear of Bob's car double parked on the busy street, his tall frame towering over the hedges as he leaned against the vehicle. She watched as her mother sashayed down the path, her smile widening when Bob walked toward her and greeted her with a kiss on the lips.

AM leaned over her shoulder and peered through the window too. "Do you always spy on your mother, Agent 99?" he teased. His arms wrapped around her waist in a comfortable embrace, she leaned her head into his chest and wrapped her arms around his, squeezing his muscular biceps.

"I've never seen my mother so happy," she announced. "She's like a giddy school girl."

AM sat on the window seat and grabbed the plate of tuna sandwiches from the buffet stand, popping one in his mouth before reaching for his sweaty glass of lemonade.

"When my parents were together," Justine continued. "My mother never seemed as happy as she seems right now," she shared. "I almost feel like the divorce was good for her. Like she was dead before, and now she's come alive," she said. "I don't know if that makes any sense."

The ceiling fan whirred softly as AM chewed and swallowed quickly. "It makes sense to me," he comforted. "Sometimes people stay in relationships that are dead because the relationship is all they know, and they're too afraid to bury it," he said. "I think that some couples have been in a dead relationship for so long that they forget what it feels like to be in a happy, healthy relationship. They just don't remember," he explained. "My parents have friends like that. Some of their friends have been married for thirty plus years, but they sleep in separate bedrooms, they don't do anything together, they take separate vacations, they barely talk," he paused. "But every year, they celebrate their wedding anniversary and boast to the outside world about how long they've been married. Even my parents think it's sad," he continued. "They've been married forever, but are they happy?" he asked. "I don't think so," he answered.

Justine sat sideways on the narrow window seat and studied AM's profile as he spoke. His sturdy jaw line moved quickly as he devoured the finger sandwiches. Her gaze drifted to Lake Michigan as a sailboat drifted by the window.

AM said, "My parents aren't big fans of divorce, but after spending time with some of these dead marriage couples, I've overheard them telling each other that if their marriage came down to a peaceful co-existence, that they'd just end it civilly and go their separate ways," he said. "It's almost like they've made a pact."

Justine tucked her feet beneath her on the cushion and reached for her plate of half eaten finger sandwiches. "Do your parents seem happy?" she asked.

"As best as I can tell. My dad refers to my mom as his best friend, and so does my mom," AM shared. "He describes my mother as his best buddy, and my mom says that my dad is her hero," he smiled. "When I was younger, I thought their pet names were goofy, and annoying, but now I think it's cute," he shared. "They took up golf together when I was in high school, and now that they're retired, they play golf a lot," he paused. "They each have other friends, and don't do everything together, but you can tell that they enjoy spending time with each other," AM shared. "My mom still goes on an annual pilgrimage with her college girlfriends. Last year, she and her friends went skiing in Colorado," he laughed. "They've been getting together once a year for the past fifteen years. No husbands or children are allowed," he explained. "And they really don't like it if you bring a new friend along either. My mom says that it's their way of staying connected as a group while they're still healthy enough to travel," he said. "My dad goes on an annual golf trip with his golf buddies. And my parents take couples' trips now too," he paused. "They have a group of happily married friends that have been married about as long as they have, and they hang out with them regularly. My parents call them their accountability couples," he explained. "These are the couples that hold them accountable to do the right thing by their marriage. 'If you lie with dogs, you'll wake up with fleas' is one of my dad's favorite sayings," he explained, his index fingers marking quotation marks in the air. "I think it's cool that they hang out with couples who seem to be committed to their marriages," he finished casually.

Justine furrowed her brow. "Why did you say they 'seem' to be committed to their marriages, AM?" she asked.

AM shrugged his shoulders. "Things are usually never what they appear," he said. "People will seem happy, and then, blam-0! They're filing for divorce and you find out that the wife has been having an affair for the past ten years," he offered. "That's what happened with one of the families in our neighborhood. They appeared to be living an idyllic life, and the next thing we knew they were splitting up. It happens all the time," he shrugged.

Justine's thoughts shifted to her parents and the demise of their marriage. "I don't think that my mom was surprised when she learned that my dad was having an affair," she blurted. The words slipped from her tongue before she realized what she was saying.

His head tilted to the side, AM creased his brows and frowned. "I didn't know that your dad had an affair," he said softly. "Is that why your parents divorced?"

"Well, that's one of the reasons," she offered. "I guess it was the straw that broke the camel's back," Justine shrugged. "But my mother doesn't like us to talk about it, so let's not," she diverted.

"Whatever you want, princess," AM smiled. "My mother says that my father is the only person who can spend over eighteen hours in her space for days on end, and not get on her nerves," he laughed. "Beryl Wahlberg is a piece of work. She still keeps in touch with friends that she's had since she was a little girl," he explained. "My mother is really cool, but if you cross Beryl, she will bite you like a King Cobra and not look back," he laughed. "As much as she loves my dad, I know that she loves herself more. She always manages to factor some Beryl quiet time into their vacations, and she always says, 'I'm my biggest fan. If I don't celebrate me, who will?'" he finished.

"I'm my biggest fan," Justine repeated. "I love that motto. And I agree with your parents, I think it's important for two people to be happy in a marriage. Life's too short," she finished, extending her legs into a ballet point before standing to clear the table. She smiled when AM jumped up to assist. "AM?" she paused. "Do you think that your parents will like me?" she asked nervously.

"Of course. What's not to like?" he asked rhetorically. "They are going to adore you, because you're adorable, and I adore you," he continued tickling her side.

Smiling, she carefully stacked the three china luncheon plates and empty buffet plates as AM popped the last finger sandwich into his mouth and gathered the utensils and glasses. "AM?" she paused. "What's going to happen to us if I wind up getting accepted to a college far away?" she asked quickly. "My grades and test scores aren't good enough for me to be accepted to Northwestern," she whined. "And even if they were, my parents couldn't afford the tuition."

AM set his dishes on the table, gently took the plates from her hand and pulled her into his arms. "Let's cross that bridge when we get to it, okay?" he suggested quickly.

Staring into his eyes, Justine could feel tears welling in hers. "I want to talk about it now," she pouted. "We need to have a plan before we get too serious."

Inhaling deeply, her small hands cupped in his, he spoke with confidence. "I've been giving this a lot of thought too, babe," he confessed. "And there are a lot of other good schools in the city that could work for you. You could get accepted to Mundelein College or Loyola University which are right down the street," he offered.

"I don't want to go to college three blocks from where I live," she whined. "I want to move away and live on campus in a dorm," she said.

"Well, there's also DePaul or the University of Illinois at Chicago," he said. "And a lot of local students live in the dorms so that it's easier for them to get to their early morning classes. Besides, I'll be applying for medical school early admissions at the end of this year, so depending upon where I get accepted, you can apply to schools near my med school choice," he suggested tentatively.

"I thought you only wanted to go to Harvard Medical School?" she asked. "Are there schools in Massachusetts that you think I should consider?"

"Harvard is still my first choice, but it's not the only good medical school in the United States. And yes, there are a ton of good schools in Massachusetts that I think you could get into,"

AM brightened. "In fact, I've been having brochures sent to me on colleges near Boston," he said cautiously. "But I didn't want you to think that I was being presumptuous to assume that we would still be dating," he said softly. "Or that even if we were that you'd want to go to college near where I would be," he paused. "Assuming Harvard accepts me."

"Of course they'll accept you, doofus. You're brilliant," Justine teased. "And of course I want us to still be dating," she said softly. "I think it's so sweet that you were thinking about college choices near Harvard for me to consider," she said.

"But I'm also willing to apply to a medical school near a college that you're interested in," he offered quickly.

"You'd give up your dream of going to Harvard Medical School to be near me?" Justine asked. "I couldn't let you do that," she blurted.

AM cupped her chin in his hand and tilted her head up slightly. "I know we haven't been dating for that long," he stammered. "But I really like you, Justine. I enjoy spending time with you," he continued nervously. "I've never felt like this about anyone, and I don't want to be separated from you," he shared. "I want to be wherever you are, and see where this goes," he confessed. "I've been toting the college brochures around in the trunk of my car, waiting for the right time to have the college choice chat," he said excitedly. "Looks like this could be the right time!" he grinned. "I'll run out and get them so we can look them over."

The words stuck in her throat, she squeezed tighter as AM tried to pull out of her embrace. She buried her head in his chest, inhaled his scent and squeezed tightly. Justine smiled as his strong arms enveloped hers. Beaming with pride, she smiled as two sailboats floated along Lake Michigan past the sunroom window.

Chapter 14

The Dark Truth

She'd never been inside of the Newberry East police station. The décor was sparse. Sterile gray walls and three metal folding chairs faced a small counter, where a uniformed officer completed paperwork. A picture of the Newberry East Chief of Police hung crooked on the wall. The whirr of a police scanner could be heard in the background, barely audible over Jackie's booming voice. Tanisha shifted her weight from her left foot to her right and stared at the carpet, as her father's angry words bounced off the cinder block walls. Exhibit A, the royal blue bicycle, was leaned against the wall behind the desk.

"It's called driving while black, Tanisha," her dad explained loudly. "Or I guess in this case it's called, pedaling while black," he corrected, directing his words toward the desk officer. "My son has not broken any real law, and you know it," he shouted. "He was less than two blocks from home, and it was only five minutes past this bogus curfew that the town just implemented," he grumbled. "If he'd been a white boy, you would have brought him home and scolded him in front of his parents and that would have been the end of it," he ranted. "But since he's a black boy, you haul him into jail and lock him up like a common criminal," he barked. "You probably handcuffed him," Jackie barked. "The justice system in this country makes me sick!" Jackie spit the words angrily.

Tanisha gently grabbed her dad's arm and whispered. "Daddy, maybe you should calm down," she suggested. "You don't want them to arrest you for disorderly conduct."

"I don't give a damn!" he barked. "My conduct is not disorderly! I am merely expressing my first amendment rights to free speech in a loud voice!" he shouted. "Let them arrest me! Jesse Jackson is a friend of the family! I'll have the NAACP down here so fast that their little racist heads will spin," he ranted.

"Sir," the officer said softly. "Your son is being released now. And under the circumstances, since this is his first run-in with the law, we won't require you to pay the curfew violation fee this time," he offered. "But make sure that he understands that he is under age and cannot be out past curfew."

Jackie burped rudely in the officer's direction. The smell of beer mixed with a polish sausage permeated the stale air. Tanisha closed her eyes and held her breath. Like a glacier ready to explode, Jackie continued, "And another thing. Tell me why you took the girl home to her parents, but my son gets dragged into the police station? Huh? Riddle me that, Batman?" Jackie screamed. "I'll tell you why you took her home," he continued. "You took her home because she's WHITE!" he emphasized loudly. "The little white girl who breaks curfew gets taken home, but the little black boy who breaks curfew gets hauled down to the police station!" he screamed. "Justice is always different for black people!" he finished.

Embarrassed, Tanisha raised her eyebrow and studied the police officer awaiting his response. The officer lowered his eyes and rearranged the paperwork on his desk.

"He can't even offer an answer for that one, Booger," Jackie said. "Because he knows that it's racial. This whole thing is racial.

Byron was trying to ride that girl home on his bike. They weren't committing a crime," he continued. "And she gets escorted home to her parents, and we're in the police station. This is a racist world!" he barked. "I'll be right back. I have to piss," he shared, walking toward the restroom sign.

Her eyes turned toward the sound of a buzzer. Seconds later a large door opened behind the registration desk. Tanisha watched as her brother Byron walked toward the front of the police station, and wheeled his bicycle through the door as another buzzer sounded. His head hung low, his eyes panned the lobby. Confused, he stared at Tanisha. "Hey, Tanisha," he said softly. "Where's Daddy? I thought they said that Daddy was here to pick me up," he stammered.

"He is. He's just in the bathroom. Are you okay, Byron?" Tanisha asked, hugging her brother's shoulders.

"I'm fine," he offered, patting her back in a quick embrace. "Is Daddy pissed?" he asked quickly gripping his handlebars tightly.

"He's pissed," she replied. "But he's more pissed at the police for bringing you down here," she whispered. "He was yelling at them and telling them that the only reason they brought you to the station was because you're black," she said. "And that if you were white, they would have taken you home to your parents."

Byron shook his head in agreement. "That's how I felt too," he whispered. "They took Sarah home, and took me to the police station," he shared.

"Here comes, Daddy," Tanisha announced.

"Why did you come with him?" Byron asked quickly.

"Because when I got home from my date, he had just hung up the phone from you and he said that he'd had a couple of drinks and was in no condition to drive," she explained quickly. "And

211

mom had already taken her evening pill which makes her sleepy, plus, she was so upset that she wasn't in any condition to drive," she paused. "So he told me to drive him here. Good thing I came home when I did," she finished.

"There's my boy!" Jackie bellowed. "Did they hurt you, son?" he asked. "You let me know if they hurt you because Jessie Jackson is a personal friend of the family," he said loudly. "He's Aunt Helen's neighbor, and one phone call and we'll have the NAACP down here picketing," he stated.

"Dad, Jessie Jackson runs the Rainbow Push Coalition," Tanisha corrected softly.

"I know that, Booger," Jackie replied. "But these white folks only get scared when they hear the NAACP," he chuckled. "Let's get out of here," he ordered.

Byron and Tanisha stared at each other curiously and obediently followed their father to the car. Jackie paused to light a cigarette. Tanisha glanced toward the Village Hall clock which chimed midnight.

She keyed open the trunk and watched as Byron lifted the bike and maneuvered the wheels to fit snugly inside the large trunk. Tanisha settled into the driver's seat and fastened her seatbelt as Byron slumped in the backseat. "Fasten your seatbelt, Daddy," Tanisha suggested before placing the car in gear. She watched as Byron fastened his.

Lowering the window and resting his arm on the car door, Jackie inhaled his cigarette, taking long pulls from the slender stick and expertly flicking the ashes out of the open window. "You know I never wear my seatbelt, Booger. Now hush and listen up," he ordered, turning in his seat to face his son, his right arm perched on the door frame.

"Byron, you've just experienced what's called racial profiling," Jackie explained seriously. "Police officers have been accused for years of pulling over black motorists for no good reason or what they call probable cause," he paused. "They just pull you over for being black," he continued. "I've been pulled over several times, your uncles have too," he shared, inhaling his cigarette and blowing the smoke over his shoulder and out the window. "Hell, I don't know a black man who hasn't been pulled over just for driving in a nice neighborhood or driving a nice car," he said. "I used to get pulled over all the time when we moved to Newberry East until the police started to recognize me," he finished. "They know that if you become irate with them, they'll say that you were uncooperative with a police investigation which then gives them probable cause to haul you in for questioning," he said. "So I've learned that when they pull you over for a DWB or what's also known as a driving while black violation," he explained. "It's best to just be polite and treat them with respect, even when what you really want to do is spit in their face," he barked.

Staring at his profile quickly, Tanisha was surprised by the crispness of his words. His diction eloquent, peppered with only a hint of irritation. The anger, emotion and intoxication that she'd witnessed at the police station had been overshadowed by calm.

"Even though you were riding a bike and not driving a car, son," he continued. "It's the same concept. You were out less than five minutes past curfew, and you were two blocks away from home," he said. "Instead of bringing you to the police station, they could have just as easily dropped you off at home with a warning, but they didn't," he spat. "They wanted to make an example of you, son," he explained, his voice sad and distant. "When your brother Jack started driving I took him down to the Newberry East

Police station so that the officers could meet him," Jackie explained. "We went three different times so that he could meet the officers on each shift," he continued. "I wanted them to know who he was and what type of car he'd be driving so that they wouldn't harass him," he said. "Some of the officers knew me from when they used to pull me over," he chuckled. "And as far as I know, Jack never got a DWB violation," he paused. "Did he ever mention being stopped by the police to you, Tanisha?"

"No. He never mentioned it to me," Tanisha replied shaking her head.

"Me neither," Byron offered from the backseat.

"Well, that's good," Jackie mumbled. "Maybe it worked and the officers recognized him when they saw him driving around. I didn't recognize any of the officers in there today, they must be new," he said. "I plan to take you down there to meet the police officers when you start driving, Byron," he finished.

Turning around in his seat, Jackie stared out the window for a few seconds, slowly inhaling his cigarette. "I didn't take you down there when you got your license, Booger, because the police don't usually pull over black girls," he offered. "But I wanted you to come with me tonight so you could see this, Booger," he said. "I've only had one beer. I'm not drunk and could have easily driven myself to pick up your brother," he paused. "But I wanted you to see how this racist world sometimes treats people of color," he said. "We've made some improvements since the 1960's and the Civil Rights marches," he acknowledged. "But to tell you the truth, things really haven't changed all that much," he sighed. "They really haven't. Race is still a major factor in this country."

Gripping the steering wheel, Tanisha turned into the Cedar Grove complex and listened as her father sighed loudly. She glanced in the rearview mirror and saw her brother's somber expression, a combination of shame and fear.

Jackie turned in his seat to face his son again. "Now I'm not saying that what you did was right, Byron," Jackie continued. "You were out past curfew, so technically they were within the letter of the law to bring you in," he highlighted. "But at least they decided to drop the charges and not make me pay their stupid curfew violation fine," he said. "And as far as I'm concerned, you've been punished enough," he continued. "Did they handcuff you?"

"Naw," Byron mumbled. "I think they thought about it, but then they would have had to handcuff Sarah," he said. "They just threw my bike into the squad car and told us to climb in the back," he finished. "I did notice that they referred to Sarah as young lady, but they referred to me as boy," he added.

Tanisha watched as Jackie's fair complexion turned beet red. Even in the darkness, she could see his cheeks filling with heat and anger as he turned to face his son, his back leaned against the passenger door. Only a few blocks from home, Tanisha slowed her speed.

"They called you boy?" Jackie shrieked. "Those racist bastards! Where do they learn this shit? Why didn't you tell me that at the station, Byron?" he yelled.

Tanisha glanced at her brother through the rearview mirror as his eyes met hers, searching for the correct response. "I didn't think about it, Dad," he stammered.

"What else did they say to you?" Jackie shrieked. "Tell me everything!" he barked. "Everything!" he ordered.

"That's it," Byron muttered. "They just said that it's too late for a boy my age to be out and I was in violation of curfew," he paused.

His face calmer, Jackie's words softened slightly. "Tell me exactly how they said it, Byron," Jackie coached. "Word for word. Try to remember exactly what they said and how they said it. It's very important."

Tanisha pulled the car into the parking spot. Not sure if she should move or get out of the car, she turned off the engine and froze.

"When we got to Sarah's house, they let Sarah out of the car and watched her walk inside," he paused. "I thought they were going to walk her to her front door and talk to her parents, but she told them that her mom was at work and her father was asleep. So when she got out of the car the officer that was driving said 'It's too late for a boy your age to be out. You're in violation of curfew, and we're taking you to the station,'" Byron stammered.

"Go ahead," Jackie encouraged. "What else did they say?"

"So then I said. 'Sir, why are you taking me to the station when you took Sarah home?'" Byron asked. "And the other officer said, 'Don't question what we're doing. We're in charge here, boy,'" he finished. "And that was it. I didn't say another word until I got to the station and the person behind the desk asked me for my address and phone number and called home."

The redness returned to Jackie's cheeks, and he slapped his palms together. "Those racist bastards!" he repeated. "I knew it!" he screamed. "Calling a black man a boy is derogatory. It's humiliating. Back in slavery times and up until the early seventies, many whites referred to black men as 'boy' as a way of showing their authority. They knew it was demeaning, and they did it deliberately," he explained. "Even if the black man was older than the white person, the white person would call them 'boy,'" he spat. "They probably still do it in the South," he continued. "Another term they use with older black people is Auntie or Uncle," he continued. "That's why to this day I won't buy Uncle Ben's rice or Aunt Jemima pancake mix. Those titles are carryovers from the slavery times," he explained. "It's not flattering that they have pictures of black servants on the box. Uncle Ben and Aunt Jemima were the house servants, cooks and slaves of white people," he continued. "And somebody in those companies needs to change it, but they won't because those are popular brands. It's a subtle reminder to racist folks of the good old days. Their good old days," he corrected. "Sometimes I feel like things haven't really changed at all," Jackie mumbled. "Not at all."

Tanisha stared at her father curiously. "But dad," she paused. "Byron is a boy. All they said was 'boy.' It's not like they used the N word," she said softly. "I don't get it."

Jackie stared at his daughter in disbelief. "Those cops wanted him to feel demeaned, Tanisha Denise. Trust me. They knew exactly what they were doing. I wasn't there and I didn't hear the tone, but I can imagine it," he grimaced, his thick brows creasing sharply. "I am so glad that I was here tonight to go up to that damn police station. If I hadn't been here ranting and raving and threatening to sue their racist behinds. Those cops probably would have made you spend the night in jail or at least held you longer. They probably would have succeeded in intimidating your mother," he coughed. "But I wanted them to know that I wasn't afraid of their tactics. I know how they treat us. You've just been initiated into the double standard of being a black man in America, son. Welcome to the club," their father groaned.

Tanisha watched as Byron squirmed in his seat.

"But you did the right thing, son," Jackie continued. "The less you say to them the better. When you get stopped by the police again, just cooperate," he sighed. "Notice I didn't say 'if' you get pulled over by the police again, I said 'when' you get pulled over," he continued. "Because once you start driving, you will be pulled over again and again and again. Especially if you have a white girl in the car," he paused. "Is Sarah your girlfriend?" Jackie asked quickly.

Slouching in his seat, a sly grin came over Byron's face. "Not really," Byron offered. "She's cool, but I wouldn't call her my girlfriend," he stammered. "She's just a friend," he chuckled slightly.

"I hate that you had to get hauled down to the jailhouse, but I think this was a good experience for you, son. I really do," Jackie explained. "Look what happened tonight. For the same offense, they took Sarah home, and they took you to the police station," he paused. "And don't think for a moment that they treated her differently because she's a girl and you're a boy. Their actions were racially motivated, not gender based," he continued. "As a black man, you have to be very careful, Byron. If you do start dating a white girl, some of these white cops will pull you over just because they don't like the fact that you have a white girl in the car with you," he sighed. "So just get prepared for it. In fact, some black cops will pull you over for the same reason," he said. "A lot of blacks don't like the idea of interracial dating either."

"What do you think about interracial dating?" Tanisha asked quickly.

Jackie arched his thick eyebrows and took a long pull from his cigarette. "It really doesn't bother me one way or the other," he shrugged. "It really doesn't. Some of the women in our family are so fair that they almost look white. Uncle Curtis' wife Lorraine and Uncle Tony's wife Miriam could pass for white, so I'm used to having different types of people around the family," he continued.

"I thought they were white for a long time," Tanisha agreed.

"Me too," Byron offered. "They still look white to me," he said.

"Both of their parents were just very fair, but they're black," Jackie explained. "Interracial dating doesn't bother me, but what bothers me is how people are treated. That's what bothers me," he repeated. "I'm not a racist. I don't have anything against white people or Asian people, Indians, Native Americans or Latinos for that matter. There are good white people, just like there are bad black people. People are people. I just hate that blacks get treated differently time and time again for no reason other than being black," he sighed. "And then when you call them on it, folks want to act like racism doesn't exist. They want to pretend that with the passage of the Civil Rights Act everything became equal. It's not equal," he bellowed. "You can make laws, but you can't change people's attitudes with legislation. And as long as you have to deal with people, you are going to have to deal with their messed up attitudes," he finished, inhaling quickly as they climbed out of the car.

"Do you have any gum, Tanisha?" Jackie asked. "I promised your mother that I would cut down on my smoking, and I don't want her to smell the cigarette on my breath," he chuckled, sucking one last pull from the cigarette butt before carelessly flicking it to the ground and smashing it with the toe of his shoe.

Staring at her father curiously, Tanisha fumbled in her purse and handed him a stick of gum. Wide as saucers, Byron's eyes met hers, the same confusion plastered on his face as they silently followed their father to the front door, a thousand questions dangling from her tongue.

Chapter 15

Breathless

With her left hand, she drummed her nails on her nightstand, smiling at her fingers and forcing herself to breathe. Her joy had lasted only a night. What would Lori do? What was that scripture she sometimes quoted when we were sad? 'Trouble don't last always. Joy cometh in the morning?' I think that's how it goes. I wish I knew how to find that scripture in the Bible. I bet Mrs. Perkins could tell me how to find it. I'll call her. How can this be happening? God, why are you doing this to our family?

୫୦୯୫

Ian had been acting goofy all evening, slipping off to the restroom three or four times during prom, once leaving her at the table alone as her friends danced with their dates. Rashanda feared that he wasn't enjoying himself, that as a college student, he felt out of place at the high school dance.

"The music that they're playing sucks," Ian groaned. "I'm going to make a request," he boasted walking toward the disc jockey's table. By this time, Rashanda wanted the night to end. Ian had complained all night. 'The food was too bland. The music was too loud or too boring.' Nothing was right. Even Doug seemed to be having a better time than Ian. Doug and Grace danced together several times, and Doug was smiling. Rashanda just wanted to go home.

Ian appeared to be sweating as he walked back to the table. The speakers blared 'You're The Biggest Part of Me' by Ambrosia.

"Let's dance, Rashanda," Ian asked nervously.

Glumly, Rashanda allowed him to pull her out of her seat and lead her to the dance floor. His palms were uncharacteristically sweaty as he walked her toward the stage, the same stage where the prom court had been photographed.

Bypassing the dance floor, Ian guided Rashanda up the stairs. "Ian, what are you doing?" she asked. "We can't dance on the stage," she protested, almost tripping on the hem of her prom gown as he quickly led her up the stairs without replying.

As he pulled her to the center of the stage, the disc jockey turned down the volume, the music a faint whisper in the background. As if on cue, the dancers stopped swaying and faced the deejay table. Many students yelled for the deejay to turn up the volume while others silenced the crowd and pointed to the stage. Trembling slightly, Ian turned Rashanda toward the crowd and grabbed the microphone.

"What's going on, Ian?" Rashanda whispered.

Dropping to one knee, he held both of her hands in his.

"Oh, my God," she gasped. The girls in the crowd gasped too as a chorus of 'Oh, my God, he's proposing' spread through the ballroom.

"Rashanda, I wanted this prom to be special for you, and I know I've been acting strange all night because I was nervous," he confessed. "But you're the biggest part of me and I want you to know that I want to be with you forever," he stammered. "I'm not asking you to marry me yet, because I don't want your father to shoot me since I haven't asked his permission, but I know if I asked him now he'd say that you were too young, so for the record everybody, I'm not proposing to her," he said loudly facing the crowd. "Did you hear that teachers? This is not a marriage proposal!" he repeated as he turned to face Rashanda again. "But I wanted everyone to know that I love you, and I wanted to make a public commitment to you," he smiled. "This is a promise ring," he explained placing the microphone on the stage and slipping the small ring that dangled on the tip of his pinky finger onto the ring finger of her right hand.

The tears burst forth like a glacier. It was the prettiest thing she'd ever seen, the stone was her birthstone. She buried her head against his chest.

Ian gently wrapped his arms around Rashanda's waist and tilted her chin with his hand. "You know I want to marry you, Rashanda Rochelle Jordan," Ian whispered. "But since you're still in high school, your father would say that we're too young and we should wait until we're older," he whispered as the prom goers cheered loudly. "My grandmother told me that when she was young, boys would give their girls promise rings before they went off to war," he finished. "I don't plan on enlisting in the armed services," he chuckled. "But my pre-med classes at Northwestern are getting more intense, so it feels like war now," he laughed. "But you have my promise that I'm your guy," he finished. "Does that work for you?"

Speechless, she nodded her head up and down as Ian kissed her on the lips. Beaming widely, Rashanda gasped when she turned and saw a swarm of prom goers crowding the stage to get a glimpse of her ring. She felt like the prom queen.

ഇൻ

Inhaling deeply, Rashanda smiled at her hand again, the small green stone glistened against the thin, gold band. God never gives you more than you can handle. God never closes a door without first opening a window.

Her mother's voice was barely audible from behind the door. Rashanda forced herself to sit up. "Come in," she said.

Smiling softly, her mother walked toward Rashanda's bed. "Were you napping, sweetie?" Mrs. Jordan asked. "I didn't mean to wake you."

"No. I wasn't napping," Rashanda replied.

Mrs. Jordan sat at the foot of the bed and smoothed the comforter with her hands. "I'm so sorry that we had to tell you this today," she paused. "But we couldn't avoid it, since I go to the hospital tomorrow," Mrs. Perkins explained. "I've known for a couple of weeks, but I didn't want to ruin your prom with this news," she sighed.

Rashanda stared at her mother's profile. "But you don't even look sick, Mom. You look perfectly normal."

"I feel fine too," Mrs. Perkins agreed. "That's what makes this whole thing so surreal. It's almost hard for me to believe it myself since I'm not in any pain," she paused. "But I have a lump in my breast, and the biopsy revealed that it's malignant," she sighed. "And hopefully the cancer hasn't spread into my lymphoid area."

Rashanda watched as her mother reached under her armpits and rubbed.

"What if it has, Mom?" Rashanda asked. She'd already called Ian for an explanation that she could understand. She knew the answer, but she wanted to hear her mother say it.

Mrs. Jordan took a deep breath and feigned a smile. "Well, if it's spread to my lymphoid area then we'll do chemotherapy and radiation," she said quickly. "But let's not think about that. Let's stay positive and pray that it hasn't spread."

"Mom, what stage is your cancer?" Rashanda asked.

Her mother stared at her, as though surprised by the sophisticated question. "It's at stage two, sweetie," she replied softly.

Rashanda closed her eyes to fight the tears. Ian had explained that stage IV cancer was the most advanced, difficult to treat stage and the likelihood that it had spread to other parts of her body was increased in stage IV.

But let's think positive, healing thoughts," Mrs. Jordan chirped. "I'm prepared to fight this with everything that I have," she stated. "And I need you to be strong, Rashanda. I'm going to need you to help run the house while I'm in the hospital and recovering," she explained. "Remember, God never closes a door without first opening a window."

She forced herself to smile at her mother.

Chapter 16

Bitter Sweet Sixteen

His eyes bore into hers. The intensity of his gaze made her insides feel like a batch of gooey, chocolate brownies just removed from the oven. She forced herself to breathe and stared at him in disbelief. "I'm surprised that you remember my name," Teenie stammered meekly. "I never thought I'd see you again," she offered coarsely, or as coarsely as her mixed emotions would allow.

"I always hoped that I'd see you again, Tanisha Denise Carlson," Brian Kraft confessed softly. His teeth seemed whiter against his tan skin. Teenie quickly diverted her eyes to the floor, not sure what to say or do next. She studied the geometric pattern in the carpet. The seconds ticked on like hours. She glanced at his face again, forcing herself to conceal the delight that she felt in just seeing his face.

Brian's grin widened. "You look beautiful," he stated. "No, you look stunning. And you have braces now," he noticed. "How long do you have to wear them?" he asked.

Her shoulder shrugged casually. "I should get them off at the end of next year," she offered, her thoughts waging war in her head. *I can't believe he's making small talk about my braces. I haven't heard from him in over two years! But he remembered your full name, Teenie. That says something. But he never tried to call me or write me like he said he would. Ask him why he never called* you, Teenie.

"I know you probably hate my guts," he offered quickly. "I don't even know what to say to you," he whispered. "I'm not even going to lie and tell you that I lost your number, because I didn't. I memorized your number. It's 555-5589," he paused, staring at Tanisha for effect.

An intense scowl eclipsed her face. "Am I supposed to be impressed by that?" she shrieked, the words spilling out angrily. "So what if you have my number memorized, you never bothered to call me!" Teenie barked.

She watched as Brian shifted his weight, noticing for the first time that he wore jeans and Converse Chuck Taylor sneakers with a tuxedo jacket and bow tie. The sneaker laces had red hearts on them. She stared at his feet curiously. His eyes followed her gaze.

"You're probably wondering why I'm dressed like this," he laughed. "We're having our prom here too," he explained. "But one of my classmates is also celebrating her sweet sixteen tonight, so she asked the guys who were invited to her party to wear jeans with their tuxedo jackets, and she bought Chuck Taylors for all of her guests. Her party invitations were tucked into the Chuck Taylor boxes," he paused. "She got all of our shoe sizes about two months ago," he shared. "Even the girls have on sneakers with their prom gowns. She wanted to do a wacky theme for her party, but she knew everyone had to dress up for prom. After prom we're going to a party on her parents' boat. It's docked at Monroe Harbor, and we needed to have on rubber soled shoes so we don't slip on the deck," he stammered. "So she thought it would be cute to have everyone wear sneakers to prom," he finished.

"Where's your girlfriend? Susan's her name, right?" Teenie asked coldly.

"Wow! I can't believe that you remembered her name," Brian admitted. "Susan's not here. She goes to boarding school in Indiana now. She was being rebellious and giving her parents a lot of drama last year," he explained. "She died her hair fuchsia, went through a drug phase and was failing a couple of her classes, so her parents shipped her off to boarding school. She gets to come home on the weekend if she's completed all of her weekend homework and assignments by three o'clock on Friday afternoon," he paused. "But who does that? Who completes all of their weekend assignments before the weekend?" he chuckled nervously. "So she rarely gets to come home. By the way, she's not my girlfriend. We broke up last year. The fuchsia hair and drug scene did it for me. I'm not here with a date. I came to prom with a group of friends," he finished.

Teenie stared at him oddly. Is he a couple inches taller or is it my imagination? She wanted to walk away. No, she wanted Glen to walk up so that Brian could see that she'd moved on.

"Where's your prom date?" Brian asked. "Is the guy that you were taking the prom picture with your boyfriend?"

Caught off guard by his observation, she blinked her eyes rapidly searching for a reply. "Yeah, he's my boyfriend," Teenie offered quickly. "He's a senior at Morgan Park Academy."

"Did he say something to piss you off?" Brian asked boldly. "You seemed distracted when you were taking your picture, you were frowning," he observed.

Teenie stared at him curiously.

"I've been watching you for about thirty minutes," he confessed.

Teenie's scowl intensified at this revelation. "You've been watching me for thirty minutes?" she repeated.

"I saw you walk down the hallway with your friends. I wasn't sure that it was you at first, because your hair is pinned up, but when I saw your profile, I knew it was you. I wanted to come over and say something to you, but I didn't know what to say, so I've just been sitting by that window watching you, hoping I'd catch you coming out of the ballroom to go to the bathroom by yourself," he continued. "But then I remembered that girls always go to the bathroom in pairs or packs," he laughed. Teenie's stare softened a bit. "When your boyfriend walked away with that other guy, you seemed pissed when you were talking to your friend, so I thought I'd strike while the iron was hot," he finished.

"Strike while the iron was hot?" Teenie repeated. "What's that supposed to mean?"

"I figured that if you were mad at him, you would be so shocked to see me that the element of surprise might work in my favor, and you wouldn't be mad at me," he laughed nervously. "Did it work?" he asked.

"I am shocked to see you," Teenie admitted.

"So why are you mad at your boyfriend?" Brian asked. "What's boyfriend's name by the way?"

Teenie waved her index finger in Brian's face. "His name is Glen, and who said I was mad at him?" she whispered. "And don't try to change the subject! You haven't told me why you didn't bother to call me in two years. Why should I share anything with you? Nice try!" she giggled.

"Finally! A smile! The iceberg is melting!" he cheered. "I told you I've been watching you for over thirty minutes. Even Stevie Wonder could see that Glen said or did something to piss you off."

"Why didn't you ever call me?"

Tilting her head to the side, she slanted her eyes and watched as Brian shifted his weight, digging his hands into his pockets. "I'm sorry that I never called you, but I was scared," he blurted quickly.

"Scared of what?" Teenie asked.

Brian fidgeted nervously. "I'm just going to say this. I didn't call you because I was scared of where it might lead." He offered softly. Teenie stared at him, the sarcasm and doubt battling for position in her expression. Brian batted his eyes several times, as though searching for the words in his eyelids. "I'm embarrassed to admit this, but I was afraid that my parents might not approve of me dating a black girl so I didn't see any reason to call you," he said softly. "But now after seeing you again, my feelings for you flooded back like a waterfall. I really missed you, Teenie. I don't care what my parents will think," he stated boldly.

Her lower jaw ajar, Teenie's eyebrows creased into a deep frown, like an intense letter M, her mother's voice echoing in her head, 'Close your mouth, Tanisha or a bug is going to land on your tongue.'

"Sorry it took us so long, Teenie," Rashanda blurted. "Grace and Maria were on opposite sides of the room dancing and prancing. And Doug was actually having a good time so I didn't want to interrupt that vibe by pulling Grace away," she finished. "We can go and conference now."

"Doug seems to be having fun after all," Grace beamed proudly. "I'm glad we came. Where are we going after prom?"

"Are Glen and Ian still in the bathroom together?" Maria interrupted. "I actually have to pee. That punch they're serving is so good, I've had four cups already," she announced, shifting her gaze to Brian and studying him curiously. "Who are you?" she asked bluntly. "I don't recognize you. You don't go to River do you? And why do you have on jeans and sneakers with a tuxedo jacket?"

Brian stared at Teenie for direction. Her face flushed, Teenie took a deep breath. "This is Brian Kraft. I met him at leadership camp two years ago," she explained. "He goes to Old Trier High School, and their prom is here tonight too. How funny is that?" she stammered nervously. Do they know about Brian? Did I tell them about him? I remember telling Lori about him, but did I tell them? Of course I did! He was my first real kiss. I told them that part, but I didn't tell them that he had a girlfriend. That's the detail that I omitted in my Brian Kraft story. Will they remember him?

"Kids at Old Trier wear sneakers and jeans to prom? Is that some north shore preppy thing?" Maria teased.

Brian smiled warmly at Maria. "A group of us are going to a sweet sixteen party after prom tonight," he explained. "It's a theme party on a boat, and we have to wear soft, rubber soled shoes on deck, so the birthday girl ordered Chuck Taylors for all of her guests to wear to prom," Brian explained. "The invitations were tucked inside the sneakers."

"She ordered sneakers for all of her guests? How many people are going to this party?" Maria asked.

"Yup, she did. I think there are about forty of us going on the boat," Brian nodded.

"It must be a pretty big boat," Maria whistled. "And she bought forty pair of sneakers as invitations? That must have cost a pretty penny," Maria said. "What do the birthday girl's parents do?" she asked curiously.

The look of irritation apparent, Teenie intervened. "That's enough, Maria. That's enough of the third degree! Give him a break! And what do you care anyway?"

Brian smiled and shrugged. "I don't mind her questions, Teenie. Her dad owns a steel company in Hammond, Indiana," Brian shared casually.

"No wonder," Maria mumbled staring at Brian suspiciously,

her eyes slanting slightly. "How do you know Teenie again? I wasn't paying attention to what Teenie said when she introduced you. I usually tune her out," Maria laughed.

Teenie playfully pushed Maria's shoulder.

"Did you say that his name was Brian, Teenie?" Rashanda asked. Teenie's eyes diverted to Rashanda, the flicker of recognition registering across her friend's face. She closed her eyes. Here it comes.

"It's Brian Kraft," he said. Rashanda stared knowingly at Brian. The glow from the large iridescent light bulb of recognition illuminated over Rashanda's head, her mouth pursed as though the words were trying to squeeze through her gated lips, but it was Grace who won the recognition foot race.

"Brian Kraft," Grace repeated quickly. "I remember your name now. You're the boy that Teenie really liked at camp," she blurted.

Crossing his arms confidently across his chest, Brian blushed and smiled at Teenie. Her face flushed. She closed her eyes, wishing she could disappear into the geometric pattern of the carpet.

"Oh! You're that Brian," Maria laughed. "Good kisser, hickey giver Brian," she continued. "Teenie was right, you are a hottie!"

"Maria!" Teenie screeched, her eyes bulging from her head. "That's enough!"

Now Brian's face flushed crimson. "That's me. Guilty as charged," he blushed.

Teenie covered her face with her hand and shook her head from side to side.

"Maria, there's no line at the main bathroom," Rashanda observed. "Why don't you and Grace go to the restroom and Teenie and I will be right there," she suggested.

"Good idea," Maria agreed. "I have to pee like a racehorse!" she shared loudly as she scurried to the main restroom with Grace on her heels. "Don't move!" Maria yelled over her shoulder. "I want to see the fireworks fly when Teenie's militant boyfriend gets back," she cackled, her heels making a click clack rhythm on the tile floor.

Rashanda placed her arm on Teenie's back and gently led her a few steps away. "Brian, if you'll excuse us for two seconds," Rashanda stated smiling at Brian. "We'll be right back," her voice sang as she led Teenie away, whispering as they walked. "I don't know what you and Brian were talking about, but it looked pretty intense," Rashanda admitted. "Actually, I think Maria is right, if Glen saw what I saw, there will be fireworks," she advised. "How are you going to explain who Brian is to Glen?" she asked.

"Good point!" Teenie agreed. "I don't think I could take any more drama tonight," Teenie moaned. "Let me tell you what just happened, Rashanda! You're not going to believe what Brian just said to me," Teenie whispered.

Smiling over her friend's shoulder and waving at Brian, Rashanda placed a finger up to Tanisha's lips to silence her. "By the way he was looking at you, I have an idea," Rashanda shared. "But you know you can't whisper, so just tell me later."

"Hey cutie," Glen cooed. "What are you two whispering about?"

Gasping, Tanisha and Rashanda looked like the cat that swallowed the canary. "Glen! Where'd you come from?" Teenie stammered.

"I walked right down the main hallway," Glen laughed. "I was whistling trying to get your attention, but you two looked like you were planning a coup d'etat!" he laughed.

"We were just trying to figure out where you and Ian were,"

Rashanda offered quickly. "Where is Ian by the way?" she asked seriously. Out of the corner of her eye, Teenie noticed Brian quietly walk over to the window sill and sit down.

"Ian stepped outside to get some fresh air. He's fine. He just needed some air," Glen said. "You know he's stressing about his final exams. He'll be back in ten minutes. He asked me to come and dance with you until he got back," Glen continued. "You don't mind if I dance with Rashanda do you, Teenie?" Glen asked.

"Of course not," Teenie smiled. "I have to go to the bathroom anyway," she said.

"Let's go, Rashanda," Glen beamed. "I'll twirl you around the dance floor a few times," he laughed as he led Rashanda into the ballroom. Glancing over her shoulder, Rashanda's eyes diverted to Brian and back to Teenie as dance music bellowed loudly through the open door of the ballroom.

As the door closed behind Glen and Rashanda, Teenie took two steps toward Brian, spun on her heels, hiked up the hem of her dress like Cinderella and walked briskly down the corridor.

"Teenie, where are you going?" Brian asked jumping from his perch in the window. Without turning around, she dropped half her hem and finger motioned for Brian to follow her. She could hear his feet walking faster on the carpet as she turned down the small corridor leading to the private bathroom that Maria had discovered. She peered inside. It was empty.

"Let's talk in here," Teenie suggested. "I don't want to have to explain to Glen who you are."

"This is the ladies' bathroom," Brian protested. "What if someone comes in here?"

"No one knows about this bathroom," Teenie said. "It's too far off the beaten path. And if someone comes in here we'll leave. It's not like we're in high school, we're not going to get a detention for talking in the girls' bathroom," she said plopping on the upholstered chair as Brian leaned against the sink.

They stared at each other for a few seconds. "I can't believe that you dropped all of this on me tonight," Teenie said. "On my prom night of all nights," she groaned. "That is so arrogant of you, Brian!"

"I wanted to call you, but I was afraid you'd hang up on me. I actually wrote you a letter, but I never mailed it. Teenie, I never thought in a hundred years that I'd see you tonight," Brian confessed. "But when I saw you standing there by yourself I had to say something. I miss you, Teenie."

"You miss me?" Teenie repeated standing to her feet, tilting her head slightly to stare at Brian. "You have a lot of nerve! I don't hear from you for over two years, and now you say you miss me?" she repeated sarcastically. "Let me explain something to you. The world does not rotate on the Brian Kraft axle," she spouted. "The sun does not rise just because you wake up in the morning," she continued.

And then it happened. Pursing his lips to speak, he kissed her instead. Boldly yet softly, he kissed her on the lips, his arms embracing her small waist. Without thinking, she found herself kissing him back as her hands involuntarily floated up to encircle his neck. She felt like an ice cream cone melting on a hot pavement. Teenie found herself lost in the familiar rhythm of Brian's breathing pattern. Placing her fingers on his shoulders, she pulled out of his embrace, and remembered Glen. She gently pushed herself away from him and took a step backwards.

Like small lake ponds, his eyes bore into hers. She felt hypnotized. She wanted to look away from his gaze, but couldn't. Her tongue felt tangled in a thousand knots. "I can't believe that we just did that," Teenie managed to say, wanting to say something else, but that was all she could muster.

"What? We just kissed. We've kissed before."

"But I have a boyfriend," Teenie reminded, rubbing her hands along her prom gown and stretching her long fingers.

Brian leaned against the sink, crossing his legs at the ankle and his arms across his waist. "I know. I saw him," he paused. "But something is obviously not right with this guy or you wouldn't have brought me to this private bathroom to be alone with me," he offered playfully.

"I brought you here so we could talk in private," she clarified.

"Well, you must still have feelings for me too or you wouldn't have kissed me back," Brian stammered, tracing his fingers along her collarbone and fingering the ruffle on her dress. Teenie swatted his hand away. "Either that or your boyfriend is just a horrible kisser. Either one is a win for me," he laughed. It was a nervous laugh.

Teenie stared at him blankly. He'd said it. She hadn't been kissed by a boy since she'd kissed Brian Kraft over two years ago. Do I still have feelings for Brian or did I just want to be kissed? With all of her might, Teenie pushed her hands into his chest forcing him to almost sit inside the sink bowl.

"You are such an arrogant jerk!" she shrieked as she reached for the bathroom door handle.

Jumping from the counter, Brian held out his forearm and effortlessly held the door shut with one hand. "What did I do, Teenie?" Brian pleaded. "I kissed you. We've kissed before. Why does that make me a jerk?"

Teenie turned around slowly to face him, "It makes you a jerk, because I have a boyfriend, Brian," Teenie stated slowly, her voice the pace of someone speaking carefully as if a translator were capturing her every word. "And my boyfriend is here with me tonight as my prom date," she said even slower, emphasizing every syllable. "Don't you have any morals?" she asked. "What am I saying? Of course you don't," she chuckled with a smack to her forehead. "At camp two years ago, you made out with me while you were Susan's boyfriend. How could I overlook that little detail? So in the immoral universe where you exist, it's perfectly okay for you to kiss me knowing that my prom date is down the hall. How silly of me," she laughed.

His eyes bore into hers again. And again, she felt hypnotized under his gaze, angry with her heart for betraying her face. "I'm sorry, but I couldn't help myself. I can't stop thinking about you, Teenie," Brian blurted. "I'm crazy about you."

Teenie stared at him blankly. "Yeah, right! I don't hear from you for two years, when you promised me that we'd keep in touch. 'I will write you and call you, Teenie. I promise.' That's what you said, Brian." Teenie jabbed her index finger into his chest. "And now I'm supposed to believe that you're crazy about me? You're a liar!"

"I love you, Teenie."

"You're a liar and an idiot!"

Brian kissed her again on the lips. Teenie pushed him away and kicked him in the shin.

Brian darted out of her reach as she prepared to kick him again. He grabbed both of her hands in his. "I guess I deserved that. But you're not getting rid of me that easily. After seeing you tonight, I can't hide it any longer. I love you," he repeated. "I didn't mean to hurt you, but please give me another chance. If you want me to go into your prom and tell Glen that I love you and I kissed you, I will," he said quickly. "He'll probably want to kick my butt," he paused. "He's a big guy, but I'm not scared," he laughed nervously. "That's how crazy I am about you. I think it is fate that you're here, and I'm here."

Teenie rolled her eyes at him, jerked her hand from his grasp, spun around and reached for the door handle. Again, Brian gently pushed it shut and whispered in her ear. "Please let me finish, Teenie. Just hear me out. I kissed you because I am in love with you," he said seriously. "I've tortured myself for two years afraid of what my parents would think if I told them that the girl that I can't get out of my mind is black," he stammered, his breath dancing on her earlobe. "Admitting that to you now makes me so angry with them. I thought it was puppy love and that I'd forget about you eventually. But I can't. I've thought about you almost every day. And then seeing you tonight, I'm at a loss for words." She felt him inhale the scent of her hair and felt his warm breath race down her neck as he exhaled slowly. "I don't care what my parents think anymore. I want you to be my girlfriend, Teenie." Brian gently pulled her away from the door and held it open for her.

"I know that my timing is awful, and you have every right to be mad at me, but I just wanted you to know how I feel. Please give me another chance."

She forced herself to look at him. Using her hand like a visor, she shielded her eyes and shook her head from side to side. She stared at her lavender shoes and noticed a scuff mark on the toe.

"Tell me what you want to do, Teenie. Look me in my eyes, and tell me what you want me to do. If you tell me that you never want to see me again, it will break my heart, but I'll leave you alone," he whispered. "Just say something."

Removing her hand visor, her eyes were drawn to his like a magnetic force. This time, she felt like she was treading water.

"Say something, Teenie."

"I have to pee, please step outside and give me some privacy."

Chapter 17

The Scene of the Crime

The trees lined the street on both sides, creating a forest green canopy that shaded the pavement from the bright sun. The traffic inched along slowly. Grace shifted in her seat, for once glad that her father insisted on driving the posted speed limit which was twenty-five miles per hour on this particular stretch of Sheridan Road. It felt like her heart was beating at least ninety miles an hour.

From her backseat perch, she watched as her mother gazed out the window like a school girl visiting Disney World for the second time.

"Ooh, I remember this area like it was yesterday," Mrs. Dudley cooed. "It hasn't changed a bit," she beamed. "Some of the trees are taller, but the houses are just as beautiful as I remember."

"It sure is," Mr. Dudley admired. "I've always loved this stretch of Evingston," he smiled, adding an 'ing' sound to Evanston's pronunciation. "I wonder if any colored people live on this street now," he said.

Grace smiled and didn't correct her father's pronunciation of Evanston or scold him for his refusal to say black or African American. His gaffes no longer angered Grace the way they once had. Now when he spoke, her mother's voice rang through her head. 'He's just used to saying 'colored' Grace. That's what we were called back in the day, and your daddy ain't one to change his ways easily. Sometimes you just have to accept people the way they are, faults and all, love 'em anyhow and move on, Gracie.'

Grace studied her father's round head, playfully pinching the fold of skin encircling the back of his neck. She smiled at the sight of her parents holding hands in the front seat like sixteen year olds on a date.

A breeze blew through the partially cracked window, bringing with it a small ladybug that settled on her hand. She watched as the ladybug slowly crawled across her fingers, quieting herself to see if she could feel the ladybug's movements. Inhaling deeply, she slowed her breathing, almost holding her breath to focus her energy on her hand. She closed her eyes to increase her sense of touch in an attempt to discern if she could feel the ladybug on her skin. She couldn't. With her eyes closed, she was startled as her body jolted up and down, the car rumbling over a pothole in the pavement. The ladybug fell from her hand, its wings engaged in flight as it settled on the back of her seat. She extended her hand to coax the ladybug back into her grasp and sighed as it flew out the open window. Grace crossed her hands in her lap, self consciously smoothing out the folds in her summer sundress.

"Today's a very important day, Grace," her mother stated. "You should always dress up for important occasions," she continued. "You only have one chance to make a first impression, so you always want to put your best foot forward," she advised. "Not that you have to worry about making an impression on him," she paused. "He's your blood father, but in general, you always want to be dressed appropriately for occasions, and I think meeting your blood father for the first time is reason enough to wear a dress," she finished.

Grace hadn't protested. She'd planned to wear a dress. Teenie and Rashanda had suggested it too. Maria thought that wearing a dress would make her look like she was trying too hard to impress him. "Be yourself," she'd coached. "Just wear a nice pair of jeans with a cute top and some cute sandals," she advised. Grace was glad she'd listened to her mother and worn a dress.

ℰ⫷⫸ℛ

She'd written Charles Lovett a letter the same day that she'd mustered the courage to read his letters. She read it aloud and then read it to Teenie on the phone. Teenie had been pleased, insisting that she share the letter with her parents before mailing it.

Grace had tucked the letters under her thigh at the dinner table, unsure how to properly transition to this topic. Teenie's voice rang in her head. "You're going to be nervous," she reminded. "So just blurt it out. Don't wait for trumpets to sound, just say it." Teenie had offered to come with her when she told her parents, but Grace assured her that she could handle it.

Her hands trembling, she pulled the letters from beneath her thigh and waved them in the air. "I received letters from Charles Lovett," she smiled. Her mother's gaze one of confusion.

"Charles who?" Mrs. Dudley asked. "Who is that?"

Mr. Dudley coughed into his hand and scowled at his wife. "You know who that is, Ethel. Charles Lovett!" he said loudly. "Lydia's professor from Northwestern," he stammered. "You know who it is," he finished, the words choking in his throat as he realized how difficult it was to describe him as Grace's father.

"Oh, my!" Mrs. Dudley exclaimed. "I completely forgot that you wrote him!" she squealed. "What did he say?" she asked.

"He didn't say anything," Mr. Dudley corrected. "He wrote

240

her a letter. Letters can't speak," he continued. "You should ask her 'what does the letter read?'" he finished.

Mrs. Dudley narrowed her eyes at her husband. "That sounds stupid. You know what I meant," she barked.

"Well you sound stupid when you ask her what the letter said," he retorted. "Get it right. Letters can't talk. I've told you this before," he sighed. "I don't know why you can't remember it."

"You're an old fool," Mrs. Dudley barked. "If I went around correcting you for every mistake you made, we'd never have a conversation," she growled.

"I'll read the letters to you," Grace interrupted, shocked at her father's surprisingly sophisticated grammar knowledge, but grateful that her parents' casual bickering had calmed her nerves. She quickly read all three of the letters to them.

When she finished, they were staring at her, their eyes soft and warm. Mr. Dudley gently grabbed Mrs. Dudley's hand with one of his, reaching across the table and patting Grace's hand with his other.

"What do you want to do now, Gracie?" he asked.

Exhaling slowly, Grace pulled out the letter that she'd written. "I wrote him a letter," she offered. "Do you want me to read it to you?" she asked.

"Only if you feel comfortable sharing it," Mrs. Dudley replied quickly. "We'll leave that up to you," she said looking at her husband for approval.

"I agree with your mother, Grace. That's up to you," Mr. Dudley echoed.

"I don't mind," she offered. "I want to read it to you. I want you to be involved. You're my parents," she paused. "My letter to him is really short, but here goes," she continued. "Tell me what you think."

Smiling, Mr. Dudley gently patted Grace's hand and beamed proudly at his wife as Grace read.

Dear Mr. Lovett,

Thank you for writing me back. I received all three of your letters and just read them. I think I would like to meet you eventually. I don't know what I'm supposed to write, so I'll start by asking you some get to know you questions. Are you married? Do you have any children? Are you a professor now? Can you send me a picture of yourself? You mentioned that you would come to Chicago to meet me.

Do you have a trip coming up or would you just be coming to meet me? Please write back.

Grace Dudley

"Well, what do you think?" Grace exhaled timidly. "I told you it wasn't very long."

Her parents were grinning softly at her. "I think it's perfect, Gracie," Mrs. Dudley offered.

"Me too," her dad echoed. "Short and right to the point," he finished.

ഔരു

Grace studied the small photo in her hand. She flipped the photo over, wondering when it had been taken. He hadn't written any information on the back. A handsome man, posed in a wicker back chair, his right leg crossed over his knee. His feet were wide and flat. He'd described himself as six foot four. Some of the basketball players at River North High School were six foot four, and Grace struggled to remember how tall that looked. Her mother had been five feet six inches tall, so she knew that she got her stature from her father. She wished that he'd been standing in the photo.

She received her next letter from him less than a week after mailing hers. Grace learned that his wife died of ovarian cancer when she was thirty. They had been trying to have a baby and the doctor suggested that she stop smoking, but it was too late. When they went to the doctor for a check up, they learned that she already had cancer. She died six months later. He never remarried and didn't have any children. He'd sent the photo in his next letter.

Like a game of ping pong, they wrote each other back and forth for three months, always waiting to receive a letter from the other before sending the next letter. Always filled with questions, the letters were brief and general. After receiving his photo, Grace sent him a more recent photo of herself.

Following her friends' advice to confirm that he was who he claimed to be, she'd asked her mother if there were any identifiers that she could share about Lydia Moore that only someone who knew her really well would know. 'Is there anything that you can tell me about Lydia/my mother that only someone who knew her really well would know?' she wrote. 'I don't want to offend you, but I need to make sure that you're not some psycho maniac.' She inserted a smiley face after this sentence.

In her next letter from him, he included a small, yellowed envelope. The envelope was addressed: 'To my Beloved Charles.' Grace opened the envelope to reveal a photo of Lydia Moore, a string of pearls around her slender, bare neck, her gaze distant and her expression serious. She flipped over the photo and read: 'To my beloved Charles, with all my love, Lyddie'

Showing the photo to her mother, she knew from her mother's reaction that it was authentic. "I taught that child how to write," Mrs. Dudley shared, her eyes misting. "And I would recognize her handwriting anywhere. This was her senior class picture," she explained fingering the edge of the photograph gently. "Back in those days, the girls took a cap and gown shot and also took a formal portrait shot wearing a tube top dickey that showed just their collarbone and pearls," she continued. "I have this same picture of her in one of my photo albums," she said.

Mr. and Mrs. Dudley called Charles Lovett to arrange the meeting details. They agreed to meet at Northwestern University. Grace craned her neck as her father slowly turned the sedan into a parking lot that appeared to be suspended on the water.

"I told him that we'd meet him at the student union," her father explained. "This way there will be lots of people around in case something happens," he continued.

"Nothing is going to happen, Mr. Dudley," Ethel groaned. "You are such a paranoid old fool! You're scaring the child," she finished.

"Ethel, you never know," Mr. Dudley said. "I've never done anything like this before, and I want to make sure there are witnesses in case anything goes down."

Grace's heart rate increased again. She forced herself to breathe. Her dad parked the car and walked to the passenger side to open his wife's door. "I bet you're surprised that I still know my way around campus," he chuckled. "I have a chip in my head that helps me remember directions. Hurry up now, ladies, I have to go to the bathroom," he shared reaching for his wife's hand and guiding her out of her seat.

"Do you have on your Depends?" Mrs. Dudley asked. "I just bought you a new box."

"Ethel! Why are you talking about my business in front of Grace?" he barked. "I don't need my business all in the street!"

"What? Grace knows you have to wear Depends since your

prostate cancer surgery," Mrs. Dudley shrugged. "She helps me put the groceries away. She's seen them and knows they're not for me," she finished.

Grace pretended to fumble in her purse. "Did you say something, Mom?" she asked.

"Lucky for you she wasn't paying attention, Ethel," Mr. Dudley exhaled. "Nothing, baby. I'm going to walk ahead. I'll meet you in there," he finished, scurrying off.

"What are you looking for, sweetie?" Mrs. Dudley asked. Let's go on in so we don't lose your daddy in there," she paused. "I know you follow this path to get inside, but I don't remember my way around places like he does," she said.

Grace smiled and reached for her mother's arm. "Mom, remember Justine is meeting us here, so she may already be inside," Grace reminded.

"That's right," Mrs. Dudley said. "You did tell me that she was going to meet you here. I think that's so nice of her to want to be with you to hold your hand," she smiled. "I miss Justine. How does she like living in Chicago now?" she asked as they walked, her mother's gait slower than Grace remembered.

"She likes it," Grace shared. "But of course she misses her friends in Newberry East," she paused. "Her boyfriend goes to Northwestern so this works out nicely. I'll finally get to meet AM," she finished.

"What did you say? You wished we'd met Mr. Lovett in the a.m.?" she asked. "I wanted to leave this morning, but Mr. Lovett's flight didn't land until noon."

Grace smiled sweetly. "Nothing, Mom. It's not important," she shrugged.

Mr. Dudley was waiting for them at the door when they

approached. "I swear woman, you walk as slow as molasses," he chuckled. "I could have peed twice for as long as it takes you to walk from the car," he moaned. "Justine is here, Gracie," he announced. "She was coming out of the ladies' restroom as I was rushing in to the men's bathroom to piss. I felt like I was going to piss my pants so I didn't give her a proper greeting."

"Don't say piss, Mr. Dudley! You know I don't like that kind of talk. Just say relieve yourself."

"I can say whatever I damn well please, woman! Now you done made me lose my thought," he paused. "Oh, yeah, Justine told me that she reserved a table in an alcove near the Cone Zone ice cream parlor," he finished with a smile, clearly pleased that he'd remembered the ice cream parlor's proper name. "The Cone Zone," he repeated. "I hope it's not too secluded or Mr. Lovett won't find us," he added.

Grace's eyes panned the crowded student union. Book absorbed college students (most in Northwestern University sweatshirts) filled every table. Cardboard boats filled with French fries and onion rings served as centerpieces, cans of Mountain Dew, Coke and Pepsi products stood guard like soldiers. A television suspended from the ceiling broadcast a football game, the volume down, no one appeared to be watching. Soft music played through the ceiling speakers. An arm waved frantically by the Cone Zone sign near the window as Justine motioned them to her table. Excited to see her friend's face, Grace quickened her pace, leaving her parents to fend for themselves through the maze of students.

Justine bolted from her seat and met Grace in a warm embrace, both squealing loudly, the studying students briefly glancing at the reunion distraction before returning to their books.

"Grace!" Justine squealed. "It's so good to see you!" she

beamed as she hugged her friend tightly.

"Me too, Justine," Grace exhaled. "I'm so glad you came."

"I'm so glad you wanted me to come," Justine stated. "I know how important this is to you and I feel honored that you want me to meet your father with you," she blushed.

Grace turned and watched as her parents slowly navigated through the tables, making their way over to the girls. "Justine, we've been referring to Charles Lovett as my 'blood' father," Grace whispered. "I don't want my dad's feelings to be hurt if we call him my father," she added quickly.

"Got it," Justine smiled. "I completely understand," she finished. "You look different. Did you lose weight?" Justine observed.

"Nope. I haven't lost any weight," Grace paused.

"I know what it is," Justine said. "Your posture is better," she paused. "You've stopped walking with your shoulders hunched. I noticed it when I was watching you walk over here," she finished.

Laughing, Grace smiled widely. "You can tell?" she asked. "Teenie, Rashanda and Maria have been making me walk with books on my head so that I could learn to walk straighter," Grace giggled. "I feel so dumb doing it, but I guess if you noticed it, then it must be working," she shrugged.

Justine shook her head. "I should have known that those chicks had something to do with it," she laughed. "They are all about self improvement."

"When will I get to meet AM?" Grace whispered.

"Shhh! Your parents are within earshot," Justine grinned. "We'll talk about that later," she paused. "Hi, Mr. and Mrs. Dudley," Justine smiled embracing them in a warm, joint hug.

"Justine, you look pretty as ever," Mrs. Dudley observed.

"Let's go ahead and order some lunch," Mr. Dudley barked. "I'm

247

starving. I think I burned off my breakfast walking to this table. You picked the table farthest away didn't you, Justine?" he chuckled.

"I thought it would be nice to sit at a table where you could have some privacy," she stammered. "It's not every day that Grace will meet her father, I mean her blood father for the first time," she corrected.

Grace smiled at her friend.

"I'm just giving you a hard time, Justine," Mr. Dudley teased. "This table is perfect. I always liked looking out on Lake Michigan," he reminisced, his gaze focused out the window transfixed on the water. "That's what I miss most about working at the Moore estate," he paused. "That view that they had was to die for," he shared. "And of course you don't appreciate nothing until you ain't got it to enjoy no more," he finished. "What does everybody want for lunch? I'm buying," he beamed.

"Will the waitress come here to take our order?" Mrs. Dudley asked.

"Woman! This ain't Denny's! There's no waitress walking around taking orders. You have to go up to that counter and order your food," he barked. "Act like you been somewhere before," he finished.

"You act like you been somewhere before and stop barking at me like an old dog, you old fool," Mrs. Dudley barked right back.

"Dad, I'd like a hot dog, fries with ketchup and a pink-lemonade," Grace interrupted. "What do you want, Justine?"

"I'll just have some fries and a pink-lemonade too," Justine said.

"I'm not sure what I want," Mrs. Dudley shared. "I'll go with Mr. Dudley to get the food so I can look at the menu," she said.

"Ethel! I told you that they don't have no menu," Mr. Dudley barked again.

"Well, they have something posted up there by the register that shows what they have to eat," she replied. "That's a menu. You know what I meant," she finished, reaching for Mr. Dudley's hand and walking with him to the counter.

"Your parents are so cute," Justine offered. "They remind me of George and Louise Jefferson the way they're always barking at each other," she laughed.

"Gotta love'm," Grace grinned. "But enough about them, when do I get to meet AM?" she ordered. "I can't believe that you're dating Ian's roommate," she finished.

A radiant smile lit up Justine's face. "Isn't that the oddest thing?" she agreed. "Grace, AM is so awesome! You'll meet him today," she paused. "Where's your overnight bag?" she asked.

"It's in the car," Grace replied. "I told my parents that your mom would be picking us up on campus tonight," she finished.

"Perfect!" Justine said. "AM is in the library studying until five o'clock and then we'll join him for dinner," she explained. "And then he'll take us to my house."

"He eats dinner at five o'clock?" Grace frowned. "I thought that only senior citizens like my parents ate dinner that early," she said.

"In college, the students eat early so they can study. Plus, the dorm cafeterias close at six thirty," Justine shrugged. "Some of the students eat as early as four thirty, but AM is a creature of habit, and he always eats at five," she paused. "I'm getting used to it now. Every Saturday he studies until five o'clock and then he takes a break from studying until Sunday morning. He normally goes to bed every night at eleven o'clock and wakes up super early to run and study," she explained. "But on Saturday nights he'll sometimes stay up until midnight or one o'clock," she giggled. "But no matter how late he stays up, he wakes up no later than seven to get his run in and hit the library before breakfast. He says that he likes to wake up his heart and feed his brain before he feeds his stomach," she shrugged. "It must be working for him because his grades are awesome. I told him that you wanted to see the campus, so he'll take us on a quick tour after dinner."

"Is the dorm food gross?" Grace asked.

"It's actually not bad," Justine replied. "I've eaten with him a few times and lived to tell about it."

"Some of the dorms have better food than others. When I was here, Allison had the best food on campus," a deep male voice said.

Startled, Grace stared in the direction of the voice. Her features staring back at her from the face of a tall, middle aged man.

Chapter 18

Dinner for Four

Pacing on the deck, her steps slow and methodical, she counted to twenty, filling her lungs with fresh air. At twenty, she reached for the door handle before changing her mind and walking through the grass, narrowly dodging the garden hose sprinkler that danced in the early June heat, cooling the grass beneath her bare feet.

The garage door in its permanent up position, she considered entering the house through the garage but remembered that she'd left the front door unlocked when she picked up the mail at the end of the driveway. Maria wanted to experience the ambience in its truest state. Wiping her damp feet on the door mat, she walked inside and inhaled deeply. She closed her eyes and inhaled again, this time savoring the inhale to discern the different spices in the aroma. She breathed in the rosemary and thyme mixed with lemon. Julia Child had been right, walking into a house where food was cooking felt comforting, like a food hug.

Watching the French Chef had become one of Maria's favorite pastimes. It relaxed her. She watched the show with intense passion now, frantically taking notes on the recipes and cooking instructions. She'd even purchased a Julia Child cookbook. Her Sunday afternoon cooking sessions with her mother had morphed into a love for cooking. She'd adopted Tuesday and Wednesday nights as her nights to cook dinner for the family, a practice that her mom appreciated and cherished. But today was different. Today was a special occasion. It was Saturday night, and she was making dinner for four. She wanted everything to be just perfect.

Her eyes panned the room from the doorway. She smiled at the flower arrangement on the dining room table, her mother's best china and crystal perfectly positioned. She'd even ironed the linen tablecloth herself. The family room adjacent to the dining room still tidy, Nina Simone beamed softly through the speakers. Maria walked over to the stereo system and turned up the volume, her mother's insistence that jazz be playing while they cooked on Sundays had given her a neophyte appreciation for jazz. "Nice pitch, Nina," she said aloud. Months before, she hadn't known what pitch was, but thanks to her mother's sophisticated jazz ear, she was learning.

Satisfied that the ambience was warm and inviting, Maria returned to the kitchen to check on her guests of honor: four Cornish game hens swimming in a broth of rosemary, thyme and lemon butter. Once complete, they would sit atop a throne of wild rice and honey glazed carrots. She'd never cooked Cornish hen before and wanted to ensure that she didn't overcook the delicate fowl. She opened the oven and grinned at the browning birds, resisting the urge to baste them.

The carrots were resting in the new stainless steel colander that she'd begged her mother to purchase, insisting that the aluminum colander that the family had used for as long as she could remember was no longer adequate. Besides, Julia Child advised that a stainless steel colander was the best. Her fingers gently played with the rice, measured and ready to be cooked once the timer rang. She decided not to attempt to make home baked rolls for the first time and had prepared crescent rolls instead. Even the rolls were already positioned on the cookie sheet, covered in foil, and poised to be placed in the oven ten minutes before dinner would be served. Lori made the best homemade rolls. I wish I'd gotten her recipe or watched her make them before she died. But I wasn't into cooking then.

Glancing at the clock, she added five more minutes to the kitchen timer and skipped up the stairs to her room to lay out her clothes. She opened her closet and admired its new sparseness. The clothes were no longer smooshed together barely able to breathe. Now her jeans didn't fight for space with her nice blouses, dresses and shirts. The task hadn't been as difficult as she'd imagined it to be. Maria had been relieved by the exercise, describing it as therapeutic to Teenie.

The former military man inspected her closet like a drill sergeant. Maria braced herself for part two of the lecture.

"Just as I expected," he observed with a click of his tongue. "This clutter is unacceptable. Every time you buy something new, Maria, you should discard something," he explained. "If you buy a new pair of shoes, then you must give an old pair of shoes away," he paused. "I want you to get rid of half of the clothes in your closet," he ordered. "If you haven't worn it or touched it in one year, then give it to charity or toss it. And do the same for your shoes," he ordered. "I will be doing an inspection next Sunday," her grandfather said. "If you pass this test, then I will teach you something else about fiscal responsibility and discipline," he finished.

"But Paw Paw, what does cleaning out my closet have to do with learning how to make money?" Maria whined. "I don't get it."

"It has everything to do with discipline and prioritizing, young lady," he explained. "If you can discipline yourself to do this, then I'll know that you're serious. Making money requires discipline and prioritizing. Get busy!"

ℬᑐᏋ

Embarking on the project that night, the task had made her slightly ashamed of herself. She felt like a glutton. Is this how obese people feel when they look at themselves naked in the mirror? They hate what they see but feel powerless to do anything about it so instead they feed the glutton with a donut, biscuit or dessert? Am I a shopping glutton?

She counted fifteen pairs of jeans. Why do I need fifteen pairs of jeans? Many of them were the same designer in the same size, their differences subtle, discernible only to Maria: a twirl in the pocket stitching or a smaller belt loop. She decided that she only needed seven pairs of jeans, one for each day of the week. She tossed the oldest jeans into a heap on her bed. She followed the same process for the other clothes in her closet and her shoes. Next, she moved to her bureau. The drawers stuffed with clothes, some items were two sizes too small. When she was finished, she'd filled four Hefty garbage bags for Goodwill. The sense of accomplishment was gratifying.

Now, when she opened her closet, instead of prying the clothing loose to study the item and get a better look, her hand easily fanned the hanging garments. Maria casually traced her fingers along the clothes, stopping on a white halter sundress with a soft eyelet fabric. She laid the dress across her bed and grabbed her tan thong sandals. Liz Wesley's advice echoing in her head, she prepared to take a quick shower. 'Maria, now that you're a woman, when you change clothes, you should freshen up. Why drape fresh clothes over a body that isn't fresh? Just take a quick freshen up shower. You'll feel like a new woman.' Maria smiled. Her mother had been right.

She turned on the shower and pinned her hair into her shower cap. She peed in the toilet and hopped in the shower, the warm water tingling over her body. Glad that she'd shaved her legs and armpits that morning, she closed her eyes and enjoyed the soothing water massage, lathering quickly so she wouldn't miss the kitchen timer. Her pick me up showers never lasted more than two minutes, but she felt rejuvenated just as her mother said that she would. Maria applied her favorite moisturizer and pulled on sweats and a tank top to finish cooking.

Bouncing into the kitchen, she glanced at the timer. With eight minutes to spare before she needed to prepare the rice, Maria decided to apply her make-up. She grabbed her purse from its perch on the dryer and walked into the small powder room adjacent to the laundry room. Fumbling through her crowded cosmetics bag, she pulled out her eyeliner and lined her lower lashes. Searching for her mascara wand, her finger rubbed across the small eye liner pencil sharpener that she carried in her cosmetics bag. A small trickle of blood ran down her finger. She quickly stuck it in her mouth and then ran her finger under cold water, applying pressure and watching the blood trickle in small droplets in the sink. The phone rang. She stepped into the hall and grabbed the wall phone that hung above the dryer.

"Hello," she said, annoyed by the minor cut. "Hello!" she repeated. "I can't hear you," she said loudly, wrapping her finger in toilet paper. "You need to turn down your music." Instead, the volume was turned up louder. She creased her eyebrows and closed the bathroom door so that she could listen closer. "Who is this?" Maria asked. "Helloooooooo," she sang. "Is anybody there?" She heard muffled giggles in the background. "Is this Teenie or Rashanda?" Maria asked. "Turn down your music!" she barked cradling the phone against her chin and shoulder. She reached for the small first aid box from the laundry room shelf and wrapped a band aid around her finger.

"She doesn't have a clue," the female voice said. "Maria, this song's for you," the voice said. The phone had been placed directly in front of the speaker now. The lyrics were loud and crisp, the voice that of James Ingram. "Who is this? Is this some weird joke?" Maria asked. The music coming through the phone receiver was turned down, the giggles resumed. The next sound she heard was the toilet flushing, hysterical laughter and the phone being slammed down.

She stared at the phone in her hand. The kitchen timer beeped. Maria hung up the phone and basted her Cornish hens, pouring the rice into the waiting sauce pan to simmer. She pulled on her mother's rubber gloves and began to peel the cucumber for the salad. The doorbell rang. Maria instinctively glanced at the clock. Who could that be? She peeked through the window and saw a white van with FTD and the gold logo emblazoned across the side.

Maria opened the door and smiled at the delivery man. "I have a delivery for a Liz Wesley," he said.

"I can take them," Maria grinned. "I'm her daughter."

"Sign right here, young lady," he instructed. Maria scribbled her name and closed the door. More flowers from Richard. He's trying way too hard. You're just jealous because Todd never sends you flowers.

As Maria walked into the kitchen balancing the large vase and bouquet, her mother rushed in through the garage door, fresh from her tennis lesson.

"Hey Sweetie," her mother panted. "Don't worry. I won't be late for dinner. You know I can be ready in ten minutes. I've already ironed my clothes, and you know my shower never lasts more than three minutes," she panted. "I'm just going to grab a cold glass of ice water and run upstairs to shower and change," she paused. "It smells so good in here," she said. "I love that you've taken an interest in cooking," Liz beamed. "I'm starving. Who sent you flowers?" she asked.

"They're not for me," Maria said. "They're for you," she corrected.

Her mom walked towards her and removed the card. "For me?" she repeated.

"Didn't Richard just send you the ones that are on the table?" Maria asked. "Did you guys have a fight or something? Why does he keep sending you flowers?" she asked. "These are bigger than the ones on the table. Do you want to use these as the centerpiece, Mom?" Maria finished.

Ignoring her daughter, Mrs. Wesley tore the card and tossed it in the trash.

"Did you hear me, Mom?" Maria repeated. "Should we use these flowers as the centerpiece instead?" she asked.

"No. In fact, you can put them in your room if you'd like," she said.

"Put them in my room? Won't Richard want to see them?" Maria asked.

"Just put them in your room, Maria," her mother ordered walking up the stairs. "They're not from Richard."

Maria stared at the flowers and looked on the counter for the card that her mom had been reading. She glanced into the trash and picked up the four, torn pieces of paper resting on top of the cucumber shavings. Maria heard the shower running. She placed the small bits of paper in her hand, pieced them back together like a puzzle and read.

"Liz, Please forgive me. Love Neal"

Maria's jaw hung open. The doorbell rang again. She crumpled the paper into her hand and peered out the window. She could make out the tail end of Richard's convertible Porsche parked on the driveway.

"Hi Richard," she smiled. "Come on in."

"Hi Maria," he returned. His smile was wide and sincere. He cradled a bottle of wine under his arm and a bakery pie in his hands. "Thank you so much for inviting me to dinner," he offered. "Your mom tells me that you're quite a cook. It smells delicious in here," he complimented. "I love the smell of rosemary and thyme. And there's nothing like being invited over for a home cooked meal," he finished.

Maria beamed proudly, pleased that he appreciated the smell of her spices.

"I told your mom that I wanted to bring something," he continued. "And she told me that key lime pie was your favorite dessert, so I picked one up," he paused. "I hope you didn't already have a dessert plan," he finished.

"This is perfect, Richard," Maria smiled. "Mom told me that you were bringing dessert. Thank you," she said.

Richard walked into the dining room and admired the table setting. "I see your mom got the flowers that I sent," he noticed. Glancing quickly over her shoulder into the kitchen he spotted the larger bouquet on the counter. "Those are pretty," he said.

"These are from my boyfriend," Maria offered quickly. "I was just taking them upstairs to my room," she stammered. Opening the refrigerator, Maria pulled out a small tray of vegetables and dip and set it on the breakfast bar. "Here's something for you to snack on," Maria offered. "Everything is almost ready. I wasn't expecting you for another twenty minutes," Maria announced. "Mom is in the shower, so she should be down any minute," she continued. Maria stirred the rice and covered it with the lid, turning off the oven to allow the Cornish hens to marinate in their juices.

"I wanted to get here a tad early so that I could open this bottle of wine and allow it to breathe," Richard explained. "But I won't be in your way. I'll just open the wine and then I'll be out of your hair," he assured. He reached into the utensil drawer and pulled out the wine opener. "Unless there's something that you'd like me to do," he offered. "I don't mind helping out."

He sure knows his way around our kitchen. I guess when my brother and I are at Dad's for the weekend, he and Mom play house.

Maria stared at the half peeled cucumber on the counter. She glanced at the clock.

"Do you mind peeling that cucumber and slicing it for the salad?" she asked. "I just need to race upstairs and finish getting dressed."

"I'd love to," he offered. "Do you want me to toss the salad for you?"

"No. Just peeling and slicing the cucumber would be fine," Maria said.

"Consider it done," Richard smiled.

Maria picked up the vase of flowers and walked upstairs.

At the top of the stairs she knocked on her mom's door. "Entréz vous!" Liz sang.

Maria walked into her mother's room. Liz sat at her make-up table brushing her hair. "Mom," Maria whispered. "Richard is here. He rang the bell while you were in the shower, and he saw these flowers," Maria shared. She could tell by the way her mother stared at her that Liz knew that she'd read the tattered card and knew the flowers were from her dad. "But don't worry, I told him that the flowers were from my boyfriend," she finished.

Her mother smiled softly. "Thanks, sweetie."

Returning her mother's smile, Maria walked into her room, rearranging the items on her bureau to find a spot for the large vase. She tossed her father's flower card in her trash can. Glancing at her reflection, she remembered that she hadn't finished applying her make-up so she bounced down the stairs and raced through the kitchen into the powder room. Hunched over the counter, Richard obediently peeled the large cucumber and hummed along to the music, ignoring the brief distraction created by her presence. Maria quickly scooped the make-up that was scattered on the sink and tossed everything into her purse before scurrying through the kitchen like a thief. One hand on the banister, she paused and turned slowly, her fingers tapping quickly. Inhaling deeply, she walked back into the kitchen and casually turned her rice pot to simmer, stirring the steaming rice with a wooden spoon that rested on a ceramic spoon rest that Maria had made in Girl Scouts.

"Richard," she said quietly. "My friend Dante is coming over for dinner," she paused. "But Dante is not the one who sent me the flowers that you saw," she said softly. "My friend Todd sent me the flowers," she continued.

"Got it," Richard winked. "Say no more. I have two older

sisters," he laughed. "I know how girls are at seventeen. I won't say a word about the flowers," he said. "What flowers?" he laughed.

Maria heard her mother's bedroom door open and could smell her signature scent wafting down the stairs. "Hurry and get changed, Maria," her mom ordered. "You don't want to keep your date waiting or he'll think that I prepared this wonderful smelling meal," she laughed. "I can't believe that we're on a double date," she giggled, pinching Maria's butt playfully as she walked past her daughter. "Hello there, handsome! Has Maria put you to work?" Liz beamed as Maria scooted up the stairs two at a time.

Maria slipped on her sundress and finished applying her make-up. She brushed her hair and decided to wear it in a high ponytail. She scooped her long tresses into a pink ponytail scrunchie. Frowning at the result, she quickly wrapped a pink ribbon around the scrunchie. Satisfied, she returned downstairs to check on her meal. Maria was glad that her mother and Richard had vacated the kitchen and were relaxing in the family room. She tied on an apron and tossed the salad, carefully studying her mother's body language in the other room. Liz wore a long denim skirt and a sleeveless white blouse tied in a knot at the waist, her feet tucked under her body, her knees touched Richard's thigh, as she sat sideways on the sofa.

Glancing at her recipe instructions, Maria carefully removed the Cornish hens from the oven. She filled the water glasses on the dining room table and was placing the heavy crystal water pitcher back in the refrigerator when the doorbell rang. She smiled. She knew without glancing at the clock that it was six thirty. Dante was always punctual.

"Are you always on time?" Maria groaned on their first date after prom. "Girls take longer than boys to get ready," she whined. "I have to shower, do my hair, apply make-up," she continued. "You could give me a fifteen minute window," she groaned.

Dante laughed. "And then you would be complaining to your friends that I'm always fifteen minutes late," he teased. "I've been playing football competitively since I was ten years old, and once I started playing at the high school level, the coach would make us do extra laps if we were late, so I just learned to always be on time," he shrugged. "But I don't mind waiting for you to finish getting ready," he shared. "It's always worth the wait." She smiled at him.

After prom, she'd heeded Teenie's advice and gone on a 'get to know you' date with Dante. He'd taken her to a batting cage. It was the most unconventional date she'd ever been on. He'd worked with her on her hand eye coordination, trying to help her improve her timing so that she could hit the ball. She'd groaned that the hard helmet was mussing her freshly washed hair, but after an hour of batting practice, she'd made contact a few times and was having fun.

As a star Notre Dame football player, Dante was routinely recognized whenever they went out in public. As a student at River North High School, Dante always had a swarm of students surrounding him, especially a flock of girls, who seemed poised to cater to his every whim. He marched through the hallways like royalty, and the students were his royal subjects. Naturally, Maria assumed that he was an arrogant jock. But the first time she saw a fan recognize him and ask for an autograph, she was surprised by his humility and the sense of grace with which he greeted the fan and smiled warmly at the praise being offered. She would witness this sincerity and humility each time he was approached by a fan.

"Don't you get tired of people bothering you?" Maria asked on their third date.

"Nope," he shrugged. "It comes with the territory. I feel blessed that they appreciate my God given talent. If they're not trying to get my autograph, then I'm not doing my job on the field," he said. "That's when I'll know that it's time for me to do something else," he finished.

Maria's dates with Dante were always varied and unconventional. One weekend, Dante picked her up and they took the train downtown to tour the museums. They spent one hour in The Field Museum, John G. Shedd Aquarium, and Adler Planetarium before grabbing a cab to Michigan Avenue and touring the Art Institute of Chicago for exactly one hour.

"Dante, we're whizzing through these museums like it's a race," Maria complained. "What's the rush?" she asked as he checked his watch and motioned that it was time for their next visit.

"I just like walking around the museums," he laughed. "It's fun to see how much you can cram into one afternoon," he continued. "Like a tourist. If you're focused, you can squeeze a lot of stuff into a four hour tour," he paused. "Plus, when I become a big football star, I won't be able to do some of this stuff for awhile," he said casually.

"My, my, aren't we arrogant?" Maria teased.

"I'm not arrogant. I'm just confident. I'm good, and I believe in myself. And if I don't believe in my ability, no one else will. Besides, only art history majors, archaeologists, astronomers, or marine biologists really need to spend more than one hour in each of the museums. Plus, after four hours, I have to eat or I get cranky," he explained. "By the way, I'm glad to see that you've gained an ounce or two on my watch," he noticed. "You were way too skinny before," he said.

"I was not," Maria defended. "But eating with you every time we hang out is making me chubby," she groaned. "I'm not a star athlete, so my metabolism isn't as fast as yours.

Before she could finish, Dante grabbed her purse, tossed it at his feet and picked her up at the waist. Like a professional wrestler, he turned her sideways, squatted and hoisted her above his head as she squealed in shock, her feet flailing wildly.

"What are you doing?" she screamed. "Put me down, Dante!" Maria screeched.

He lifted her over his head again before standing her to her feet. "You probably weigh about one hundred and ten pounds," he laughed. "I can squat lift over two hundred pounds with no problem, and lifting you was easy as pie," he laughed. "I could probably lift you over my head with one hand," he teased.

"Don't even think about it!" she said.

"You know you liked it," he teased. "So for the record, you're not getting chubby. When I can't lift you like that, that's when you need to push back from the table," he laughed. "Now let's eat. I'm starved."

&)(&

She had been spending a lot of time with Dante. But now he was preparing to head off to Notre Dame for preseason football camp, and she wanted to do something special for him. The double date had been her mother's idea.

"I'll get it," Maria said as she scurried to the door. Dante grinned widely when she opened the door.

"Hey, good looking!" Dante crooned. "You look like a

domestic goddess," he teased waving a large bouquet of flowers in her face. "Whatever you're cooking smells delicious!"

"It's a surprise," Maria grinned. "I hope you like it. Oh, you brought me flowers," Maria noticed. "How sweet of you."

"Actually, one is for you," Dante corrected, separating the identical bouquets. "And the other is for your mom," he explained. "I can't take credit for the idea though," he whispered. "My parents told me that you always bring something for the hostess," he finished, walking into the house as Mrs. Wesley approached.

"Hi, Dante," Mrs. Wesley beamed. "It's always good to see you."

"The same here, Mrs. Wesley," Dante replied. "And of course, you look lovely as usual. Maria has good genes in her future," he offered. "And these flowers are for you," he grinned thrusting the bouquet at Maria's mother.

Blushing like a school girl, Liz smiled. "That's awfully nice of you, young man." She handed the flowers to Maria. "Sweetie, put these in water while I introduce Dante to Richard," she instructed.

Maria watched as her mom glided into the family room. Richard stood and extended his hand to Dante.

"Dante, this is my boyfriend, Richard Dawson," she introduced.

"Hello, young man," Richard bellowed. "Everyone knows the star running back for the Notre Dame Fighting Irish," he smiled. "I'm pleased to meet you. Have a seat, big fella," Richard suggested.

Mrs. Wesley walked into the kitchen and squeezed Maria at the waist. "Our boyfriends seem to be getting along," she grinned. "I'm so glad you are dating other people, Maria," her mother whispered. "I really like Dante. He's a very nice young man. He has manners, and he really likes you. He's a keeper," she finished softly. "What can I do to help?" she asked as she poured herself a glass of white wine.

Maria forced herself to smile as she placed the crescent rolls in the oven. "I like him too, Mom," she whispered, untying the apron and slipping it in the kitchen drawer. "There's nothing left to do. Everything's all taken care of," Maria shrugged. "We can eat as soon as the rolls brown. They should be ready in about ten minutes." The smell of food warming the small kitchen, Maria watched as her mother sang along with Diane Schur, a look of obvious contentment plastered on her pretty face. Liz seemed to glide back into the family room before snuggling comfortably next to Richard. I like Dante, I really do, but I love Todd. And I think that Dad still loves you, Mom.

Chapter 19

Because You're Worth It

"I wish I could go with you, Grace," Rashanda offered. "But my mom has her last chemotherapy treatment on Saturday, and I need to be home to help her. The chemo treatments take a lot out of her the first few days," she finished.

"Girl, I completely understand," Grace said. "I just wanted you to know that you were invited," she paused. "Justine is going to meet me on campus. Teenie can't take off work, and Maria is cooking dinner for Dante since it's his last weekend in town for awhile," Grace said. "I can't believe how much Maria likes to cook now," she observed. "And I think she's really into Dante now too."

"I don't know about that one," Rashanda sighed. "I think she likes Dante, but I think she's still holding a candle for Todd," she groaned. "When I talked to her last night, all she could talk about was Todd and what would happen if he found out that she was dating Dante. She kept scripting these imaginary scenarios in case someone who knows Todd saw her in public with Dante," she paused. "That boy has a grip on her heart like you wouldn't believe."

Grace brushed her hair. "She must really be in love with him," she offered.

"Either that or she's been hypnotized," Rashanda giggled.

"Do you really believe in hypnosis, Rashanda?" Grace asked. "Whenever I see someone being hypnotized on television, it always looks so phony."

"I was just kidding. I think hypnosis is fake too, but I saw on television once that these people swore that hypnosis helped them quit smoking," Rashanda observed. "Maybe one day I'll try it. It might change my opinion. Who knows?" she paused. "Ian actually suggested that my mother try alternative health treatments for her pain relief," she offered. "He said that we should look into acupuncture."

"Acupuncture?" Grace repeated. "Are you serious?"

"Yeah. He said that the Asian cultures are thousands of years older than Western Civilization, and that even though Western medicine is more advanced in some treatments, there are many Asian healing practices that have been around for centuries that work," she continued. "But the Federal Drug Administration (FDA) doesn't subscribe to some of the practices," she finished. "It's a little unorthodox, but I think it's worth a shot," she trailed. "It couldn't hurt."

"Good point," Grace agreed. "Do you think your mother will try acupuncture?" she asked. "I can't imagine my parents agreeing to something as new age as acupuncture. Even though it's an ancient Chinese healing practice," she paused. "They would consider it new age, hocus pocus. Is acupuncture only practiced by the Chinese or all Asian cultures?" she asked.

"I have no idea," Rashanda admitted. "But I know there are several acupuncture places in Chinatown on 22nd and Cermak Road," she shared. "I looked it up in the phone book."

"That's another thing," Grace paused. "Why is it called Chinatown? Do only Chinese people live in Chinatown? Aren't there any Japanese, Korean or Vietnamese residents there or do they have their own part of town?" she asked. "Or is this just another stereotypical name assigned by the majority culture to label a neighborhood that has a heavy Asian population? I wonder if they have a name for parts of town with lots of black people."

Rashanda laughed heartily. "Aren't we feisty? Now that we're entering our senior year, are you going to turn militant and challenge the mainstream establishment?" she asked. "If that's your plan, you will have a hard time convincing people of your militant ways because that long, silky, strawberry blonde hair of yours will not kink up enough to wear an afro," she teased. "I don't care how much Pink Oil moisturizer you run through your locks," she laughed.

"I've thought about it," Grace said. "Speaking of locks, not to change the subject, but have you heard about locks of love?" she asked.

"Locks of love?" Rashanda repeated. "What's that?"

"It's a charity where people have their hair cut short and the hair is donated to someone to make a human hair wig," she explained. "A lot of chemotherapy patients benefit from the wigs."

Rashanda chewed on her lip as Grace talked. "You can designate that your hair be donated to a specific person," she paused. "I could donate my hair to your mother if she'd like," Grace continued. "I was thinking about getting my hair cut short again anyway," she said quickly. "And you know how quickly my hair grows back," she laughed nervously. "You know I have this white girl hair," she teased. "My hair will be long again before graduation. What do you think?"

Forcing herself to smile, Rashanda could feel her eyes filling with tears. "That's so thoughtful," she stammered. "I don't know what to say."

"Don't say anything," Grace said. "I'd be happy to do it," she exhaled. "I would be honored. Just ask your mother."

"My mom's hair was coming out in clumps whenever she combed it, so my dad used his clippers and shaved it off," Rashanda explained. "She also lost her eyebrows too. But she pencils those in," she said, her voice cracking slightly. "She's been wearing a scarf around the house and whenever she leaves the house she wears a wig. She looks so different now," she sighed. "Her hair stylist knows a Korean man who makes human hair wigs, and he said he would make her one for half price if she brought him the hair," she groaned. "I just want this to be over."

"Do the doctors think they got all of the cancer?" Grace asked.

"They're not sure," Rashanda shared. "For the next year, she'll have to go in for tests every two weeks so they can check," she offered. "And the doctor explained that sometimes cancer will go into remission and may flare up again years later," she paused. "It's just hard to tell," she sobbed quietly.

"How's her attitude?" Grace asked. "And if you don't want to talk about this, we can change the subject," she suggested.

"I don't mind talking about it," Rashanda sighed. "My mom is really handling this well," she offered. "But my sister is having a hard time with it," she offered. "Sometimes Tiffany crawls into bed with my mother and sleeps under her like a baby."

As if on cue, Tiffany walked into Rashanda's room and sat on her bed.

"Speak of the devil," Rashanda said. "Tiffany just walked in my room without knocking again," she groaned. "So I need to let you go, Grace, so I can peel Tiffany's peanut head," she shared. "Call me when you get back from Evanston. I want to hear all about your meeting with Charles Lovett! And I'll talk to my mom about the other thing," she finished.

Rashanda placed the phone in its cradle and smiled at her younger sister, carefully studying the serious look in her eyes. "What's the matter, Pooh?" Rashanda asked casually using her sister's nickname, their fight from the night before a distant memory.

Tiffany plopped on the bed, gently placing her head in Rashanda's lap and curling her feet beneath her body. At fourteen, Tiffany was short for her age. Stroking her hair lovingly, Rashanda listened to her sister's rhythmic breathing pattern. "Are you okay, Tiff?" Rashanda asked.

"I'm just worried about Mom," Tiffany shared. "Last night I overheard her telling Dad that she's ready to die," she sobbed softly. "She said that she's in so much pain that sometimes she thinks that it would be easier for her if she would just die," she sniffled. "Do you think Mom wants to die, Rashanda? I don't want Mom to die. What if she dies? What are we going to do without her?" Tiffany asked quickly.

Rashanda's gaze was intense and serious. She'd overheard a similar discussion through the paper thin walls separating the small bedrooms in the narrow hallway. Her mother's pain, and the suffering that she watched her endure, fueled Rashanda's desire to research pain remedies and alternative treatments. She steadied herself and stared at her sister softly, forgetting that if she could hear the whisperings of her mother, of course Tiffany could hear them too.

"I don't think Mom really wants to die, Tiff. It's just really hard for her right now," she explained. "Dad is getting the best possible treatment that medicine can offer for Mom," she explained. "He said that if the cancer comes back, they'll fly to the Mayo Clinic in Minnesota for a second opinion and treatment. Mayo is the best cancer clinic in the world. Even Ian said so," she explained. "Mom is strong. We can't give up hope," Rashanda insisted. "This is her last chemo treatment and then they'll run some more tests and see what's what. We're not going to talk about death," she said firmly, trying hard to mask her own fear and calm her frightened sister.

"But she could die, couldn't she, Shanda? Mom could die," Tiffany repeated weakly, using the nickname that she'd given her older sister when she first learned to talk and couldn't pronounce her name properly. Tiffany had scolded anyone who tried to call Rashanda 'Shanda.' She would scream, "She's my Shanda, not your Shanda!" The nickname had been reserved for Tiffany's private use. Rashanda hadn't heard her sister shorten her name in several years, not since Rashanda had chastised her and asked her never to use her nickname in public for fear that others might call her by the nickname. Now, hearing the precious term of endearment roll casually from her sister's tongue was like a walk down memory lane.

"Of course there's always a risk that she could die," Rashanda stammered. "But Mom is prepared to fight this cancer with everything that she has," she continued. "She's fighting for her life. She's fighting for us and for Dad," she shared. "And we have to fight for her too," Rashanda ordered. "We have to pray to God for Mom. We can pray that he heals her and gives her strength. And we also need to pray for strength to be able to handle whatever God's will is through this whole process," she continued, afraid of the hidden intent behind her words. "Because no matter what happens, Tiffany, we have to believe that it's God's will," Rashanda finished.

"God's will?" Tiffany asked. "Do you think it could be God's will to take my mother from me when I'm only fourteen? I haven't even started my period yet," Tiffany said. Rashanda could feel the tears slipping from her sister's eyes. "Why would it be God's will to take our mother from us and we're so young? That makes no sense to me," she admitted.

"I'm not saying that's going to happen," Rashanda corrected. "But I was talking to Maria's mom, and she shared that she lost her mother to cancer when she was in high school," she paused, searching carefully for words that wouldn't serve to further frighten her sister and fuel her fear. "And she told me that we need to pray and believe that God's will is sovereign," Rashanda paused. "Do you know what sovereign means?"

"Of course I know what sovereign means," Tiffany chided. "I'm a straight A student too, dingbat," she groaned.

Rashanda playfully smacked her sister on the back. "Anyhow, as I was saying, Mrs. Wesley told me that she knows exactly how we're feeling. She said that we should be encouraged because cancer research has come a long away since her mom was diagnosed twenty years ago," she paused. "She also suggested that we pray and convince Mom to try different treatments," she paused. "For instance, switching Mom to an organic diet," Rashanda explained.

"What's organic?" Tiffany asked.

"Oh, I finally found something that the straight A student doesn't know," Rashanda teased. "Organic means that the food is grown pesticide free. And if it's an animal product, the animal isn't injected with any growth hormones and only eats things that are pesticide free," she explained. "Apparently, some farmers inject hormones in animals to make them produce more eggs or to make them grow larger. Mrs. Wesley has switched to an organic diet because she read somewhere that it's better for you and that some doctors are suggesting that some of the pesticides, hormones and chemicals used to preserve foods could be carcinogens," she paused. "I'm going to talk to Mom about that tonight," she paused, not sure if her sister was listening as her eyes were closed shut.

Nonetheless, she continued talking. "I really believe that everything is part of God's divine plan, and we have to help Mom through this," she paused. "Not that Mom is going to die," Rashanda whispered. "I'm not trying to put negative energy into the atmosphere, but Mrs. Wesley lost her mother young, and she turned out fine," she stammered, fighting back the tears that wanted to flood her cheeks. "But we're not going to lose Mom without a fight," Rashanda declared. "We're going to fight this cancer with everything that we have as a family. Ian even suggested that we look into acupuncture," Rashanda finished.

"You mentioned that to me the other day," Tiffany said. "Were you crying on the phone with Grace?" Tiffany asked. Her eyes still shut. "I heard you sniffling when I walked in," she admitted.

"Was Mom still sleeping, Tiff?" Rashanda asked.

"Uh huh," Tiffany replied. "Her room was quiet and her door was closed when I walked by," she said.

The tissue box was just out of reach. Rashanda lifted her sister's head slightly to stretch for a tissue. "Guilty as charged," Rashanda smiled blowing her nose loudly. "Grace offered to get her hair cut off and donate it to Mom so she could have a human hair wig made," she explained. "I thought that was so sweet that it made me cry," she said, tears rolling down her cheeks now. "Can you believe that? It makes me cry just thinking about it."

"Grace would chop off that long, beautiful hair just to help Mom?" Tiffany asked. "I can't even imagine Mom as a blonde," she stated.

Rashanda laughed through the tears. "Me either, silly. Mom would probably dye the hair brunette and have it cut into her regular hairstyle, or maybe not. They say that blondes have more fun," she laughed.

"Mom uses that L'Oreal hair color on her hair now to hide the gray," Tiffany shared. "I saw it under the sink. I love their commercials. 'Because you're worth it!'" she sang. "When I start to gray, I'm going to use their hair dye, because I'm worth it," Tiffany declared.

"You are worth it, but by the time your hair starts graying, they'll probably invent a pill you can swallow to stop the gray before it sprouts on your peanut head," Rashanda groaned.

"Will Mom have to wear a wig for the rest of her life, Shanda?" Tiffany asked.

"No. The doctor said that her hair will start to grow back eventually," Rashanda explained.

Tiffany sat up and stared at her sister's tear stained face. "Rashanda, do you really think Mom would try acupuncture?" she asked.

Rashanda shrugged casually. "I don't know, Tiff," she paused. "But I'm going to try my best to get her to do it," she continued. "By the way, Tiff, I miss hearing my nickname. Why'd you stop calling me Shanda?" she asked.

"Why'd I stop?" she repeated incredulously. "Because you yelled at me at the mall one day and told me to never call you Shanda in public, don't you remember? That's why I stopped," Tiffany reminded.

"I did, didn't I?" Rashanda remembered. "Well, I'm sorry. You can call me Shanda at home. It'll be our special thing," she encouraged. "I feel like I need something to soften our home experience these days, and hearing my nickname just might be what the doctor ordered."

"We'll see," Tiffany said. "I'm so used to calling you Rashanda now that it might be hard to switch back. Maybe I'll call you monkey breath, instead," she teased. "What does your honey, Ian, call you? Snookums or Honey? I know," she paused. "He probably calls you Honeycomb as in 'Honey, comb your hair,'" she laughed loudly, scrambling to the floor to avoid the pillow that Rashanda tossed at her.

Tears flowing freely down her cheeks, her hand covering her mouth, Mrs. Jordan listened in the hallway before tightening her robe and walking slowly back into her bedroom. The glass of water that beckoned her out of bed was now a distant memory. *Acupuncture, prayer, organic diet, new wig! Bring it on! I'm not going to give up without a fight, because they're worth it.*

Chapter 20

The Man in the Mirror

The tan corduroy trousers matched the subtle stripe in his wool blazer. A black turtleneck completed his look. She glanced quickly at his feet and smiled at his black loafers. He looked like a professorial mannequin, the only thing missing were the suede elbow patches on his blazer. The resemblance was undeniable. From his cheekbones to his height and square chin, he was a tanned, male version of Grace. She stared from Grace to Charles Lovett and back. His gaze was locked on Grace like radar, as though seeing a ghost. Grace appeared glued to her chair, unsure what to do or say next, her eyes shifting nervously from the table to the floor. It was Justine who spoke first.

"You must be Charles Lovett?" Justine stammered, her statement phrased in the form of a question, she stumbled to her feet and extended her hand.

Awakening out of his trance like state, the man nodded in agreement and squeezed Justine's palm gently. "I am," he offered. His voice was deep and confident. Their eyes shifted nervously back to Grace.

Sweaty palms. Her palms felt like a waterfall oozing moisture. She wanted to leave. Should I stand up and shake his hand? Where are my parents? They are supposed to be here for the introduction, to make the situation less awkward. *What is taking them so long? Say something, Grace. He's staring at you.*

"And you must be, Grace," he suggested softly.

"I am," she mumbled to the table. "Nice to meet you," she stammered, wiping her palms on her dress, forcing herself to look at him.

"I'm Justine," she said. "Grace's trusty sidekick," Justine laughed. "Her parents are here too. They're just at the deli counter getting lunch," she explained. "I mean, Mr. and Mrs. Dudley are here," she corrected awkwardly. "Well technically, they are her parents too," she rambled. "You know what I mean, Mr. Lovett," she exhaled. "They should be back any minute. Maybe I should find them and see if they need help with the tray," she finished, standing up to leave.

"I'm sure they'll be fine!" Grace offered quickly, her voice loud and firm.

Looking over his shoulder, Charles Lovett pulled up a chair from a nearby table. "Do you mind if I join you?" he asked.

"Of course," Justine answered. "Of course not," she corrected. "I mean we don't mind if you join us," she stammered. "I never know if you should agree with the question or negate the question in your response," she giggled nervously. "Not that anyone cares to have an English lesson today," she mumbled. "We literally just got here ourselves, and I was just about to pull up a fifth chair," she explained. "But you sneaked up on us."

As Justine rambled, Grace stole quick glances at him, studying his profile and hands suspiciously. His hands were large, and his nail beds were deep. She glanced at her own slim, graceful fingers and admired her long nail beds. She noticed that his complexion was almost as fair as hers, a yellowish pink with hints of bronze. She had expected him to be more olive toned. In the photo that he'd sent, his skin appeared more olive tone. And then she remembered that he had been wearing a fedora that shaded his face somewhat. Grateful for Justine's idle chatter, Grace allowed her gaze to shift upwards to his face. His hair was jet black and curly with hints of gray at the temple and forehead. She could see the beginning of a receding hairline. She decided that he was handsome. I'm sure he was even more handsome seventeen years ago. No wonder my mother was attracted to him. She could feel her heart rate increasing again.

"Grace mentioned you in one of her letters to me, Justine," Charles Lovett shared. "I think it's great that she has such good friends in her life," he offered, his gaze now fixated on Grace. "I'm so glad to finally meet you, Grace," he said softly. "I can't believe that I'm sitting across from you," he choked.

Is he going to cry? His exhale was audible, and the moisture on his pupils was unmistakable. He was fighting back tears. He's nervous too!

"You must forgive me," he explained. "I'm a drama teacher, but no amount of training can prepare you for seeing your daughter for the first time after seventeen years," he exhaled. "Whew! I don't even know what to say." Now it was his turn to rant. "I am just so filled with joy at the sight of you," he paused. "I'm speechless," he laughed nervously. "Me. The drama professor who can usually never shut up is rendered speechless," he continued.

"They didn't have pink lemonade, girls, so we got you water instead," Mr. Dudley explained as he rested the tray on the table, which now seemed much too small. "I'm Mr. Dudley, and who might you be?" he asked. His question directed to the back of Charles Lovett's head.

Mrs. Dudley smacked her husband gently on the back. "Who do you think he is?" she criticized. "You must be Charles Lovett," Mrs. Dudley interrupted. "I'm Ethel Dudley and this is my husband, Greg Dudley," she introduced. "Pardon him, Mr. Lovett. His memory is fading. He knows we came here to meet you."

Charles Lovett stood to his feet and shook their hands. "I'm pleased to meet both of you," he smiled softly.

"Woman! I saw the man from behind," he barked. "And why are you telling the man that my memory is fading? There you go spreading my business in the street," he groaned. "From behind, he could have been Justine's boyfriend."

"Well, I'll take that as a compliment," Charles Lovett grinned. "I haven't been mistaken for a college student since I was a young professor on campus," he offered. "In fact, when I first started teaching, I wasn't much older than many of my students, so when I wore jeans, I blended in too much," he continued. "So I started wearing a tweed blazer so I could look the part of a professor," he finished.

Like the ball on a roulette table, their eyes shifted from one to the other in a counter clockwise motion, waiting with baited breath for someone to speak. Their roulette eyeballs settled on Grace.

"I hope you don't mind, but we haven't had lunch yet," Mrs. Dudley explained. "We weren't expecting you for another hour," she continued. "Eat your food, girls," she ordered gently, nudging their orders toward them. "We don't want it to get cold. No one wants to eat a cold hot dog and fries," she finished. "Will you join us for lunch, Mr. Lovett?"

"Please call me, Charles," he corrected. "I'm so sorry to intrude upon your lunch, but I arrived early, and when I saw Grace sitting by the window, I had to come over and introduce myself. I'm sure you understand," he explained as he stared intently at Grace, his gaze was tender and soft. "By all means, please eat," he encouraged. "In fact, I'm hungry myself so I think I'll go up to the counter and order some food," he decided. "But don't let me hold you up. I inhale my food, so I'll probably finish my food before all of you anyway," he chuckled. "If you'll excuse me for just a moment," he said as he walked toward the grill.

The click clack of his loafers could be heard on the tile floor, barely out of earshot when Mrs. Dudley placed her boney fingers over Grace's hand. "Gracie, are you okay, honey?" her mother asked.

"Does she look okay?" Mr. Dudley groaned. "She looks like she's seen a ghost," he said. "I'm so sorry that we weren't here when he came up. The food took longer than we expected."

"And he is an hour early," Mrs. Dudley reminded.

"He just walked up two minutes before you got back," Justine explained, studying her friend for a clue as to how to behave.

"Say something, Grace," her mother encouraged. "If you don't want to stay, we can leave right now."

"That's right, Grace," Mr. Dudley explained. "We can just get the hell out of here right now, if you want."

"Greg Dudley!" Mrs. Dudley shrieked. "Don't cuss in front of the child!" she ordered.

"She's almost seventeen, Ethel! She's not a child," Mr. Dudley reminded. "But if you want to leave right now you just say the word and we're out of here. What do you wanna do, baby?"

"Let her eat her hotdog at least," Mrs. Dudley suggested. "She said she was starving."

Grace watched as Justine ripped open a packet of ketchup and mustard and squeezed them into a squiggly design on her plate, trailing her fries through the red and yellow pattern like a paintbrush before shoving three greasy fries into her mouth. Grace picked up her hotdog, grateful that her mother had spread mustard and relish across the top just like she liked it. Although her appetite had disappeared, the chewing provided a nice distraction and gave her time to think.

What do you want to do, Grace? You've seen him and you've barely said two words to him. What am I supposed to say to him? I should have had Teenie give me a list of questions to ask him. Why didn't I think of that? Teenie could have scripted me on what to do and say just like she did at prom with Doug. Wait a minute. I can just make small talk with him. Keep him talking about himself.

She quickly took another large bite of her hotdog and managed to squeeze a French fry into her mouth. Grace was glad that Justine had been available to come. Justine's gift of gab kept her parents distracted.

"Depending upon what he's ordering he may not take as long at the counter as we did," Mr. Dudley explained. "So do you want to stay, Grace?" he asked. "It's your call, sweetie. Just tell me what you want to do."

Inhaling deeply, Grace nodded her head in the affirmative, her confidence bolstered by the large hotdog in her hand. She pretended that the hotdog was her courage food. With every bite, she became more powerful and courageous. Like a super hero. She took another bite. "I want to stay and talk to him," Grace offered confidently.

The fly never stood a chance. Mr. Dudley squeezed his hand into a tight fist.

"Daddy!" Grace shrieked. "Don't kill flies while we're eating. That's so gross!" she groaned.

Reaching for a napkin, Mr. Dudley laughed and wiped the dead fly from his palm.

"Wow! Did you just catch and kill that fly in your palm?" Justine asked.

"Yup. And I caught him with my left hand too," Mr. Dudley boasted. "And I'm a righty."

"Well at least go and wash your hands," Grace whined. "You have fly juice on your hands now."

Mr. Dudley smirked and ignored her, grabbing his sandwich with his thick hands. "Fly juice ain't never killed nobody," he laughed. "I wiped the little feller into the napkin. You've probably eaten more fly parts than you realize, Gracie," he finished.

"Is that your nickname?" he asked. "Do you go by Gracie?" Charles asked.

Startled, Grace smiled softly. "No, not really," she replied. She gently fingered her courage hot dog. "My parents call me Gracie, but none of my friends call me that. They just call me Grace," she finished. "You sneaked up on us again," she laughed softly. "You walk very quietly."

He placed his plate and bottled water on the table. The yellow mustard formed a zig zag pattern, stopping at the tip of the wooden stick protruding from the end of his corndog. "Not really. I must just be catching you engrossed in conversation," he grinned before taking a large bite.

I like mustard on my corndogs too. Ask him a question, Grace. Ask him if he thinks that you look like your mother.

"What should I call you?" Grace asked, surprised by her hotdog fueled boldness.

At least one third of the large corndog rattled around in his mouth. Hearing her question, he raised his eyebrows and chewed quickly.

"What would you like to call me?" he asked between chews.

"I haven't a clue," she replied quickly. "That's why I asked you," she shot back. Justine and her parents stared at Grace curiously, as though they didn't recognize her. Take another bite of your courage filled hotdog, Grace. This feels good. Maybe hotdogs have special powers that give courage when needed.

His fingers traced the shape of the water bottle. "I've been thinking about that one too," he confessed. "My family calls me Chip," he shared. "There are about ten people in my family named Charles," he explained. "So we came up with nicknames so that we could tell everyone apart. My grandfather is Charles and my father was Charles the third, so his nickname was Trey," he paused.

"We have a Trey in our family too," Justine shared.

"I haven't met a black family yet who doesn't assign the nickname Trey to anyone named the third," he laughed. He took another quick bite and spoke between chews, careful to hide the food behind his moving jaws. Grace took another bite of her hotdog.

"We already had a Charles, a Charlie, a Chuckie, a big Chuck and a little Chuck," he continued. "So when I was born and became Charles the fourth, my parents nicknamed me Chip because I looked just like my grandfather and father and they said that I was a chip off the old block," he laughed. "And the nickname just stuck. No one in my family calls me Charles unless they're mad at me," he finished.

"Oh," Grace stated. "Do you want me to call you Chip?"

"That would be fine. If that's okay with you," he replied.

"What did my mother call you?" Grace asked boldly. She took another bite of her hotdog and realized that she couldn't taste the food rolling around in her mouth. It didn't matter. She was chewing as a distraction. She chewed slower, trying to savor the food in her mouth.

Justine stared at Grace curiously. Mr. and Mrs. Dudley

munched on their lunch, silently observing the conversation unfolding right before their eyes.

Chip finished the last of his corndog. He'd consumed it in three quick bites. He swallowed quickly, staring at Mr. and Mrs. Dudley for permission to speak. They stared at him blankly.

"Well," he paused. "She called me Professor Lovett in class, but once we became friends," he offered slowly. "She called me Chip."

"Then I'll call you Chip," Grace stated flatly.

Amazed, Justine finished her fries and watched as Grace's shyness shield seemed to disintegrate one layer at a time.

"Did you ever meet my grandparents?" Grace asked.

"I met them once," he confessed. "I met them during parent's week. It was very brief. Your mother had decided that she wanted to decline her admission to Wellesley College and remain enrolled at Northwestern to pursue a theater major," he explained.

"Oh, I remember that like it was yesterday," Mrs. Dudley chimed in. "That was quite the firestorm. Mr. and Mrs. Moore about peeled that child's head when she told them that she didn't want to transfer to Wellesley and she wanted to act," she paused. "I don't know if they were madder that she didn't want to go to the east coast or that she wanted to be an actress instead of an art history major," Mrs. Dudley reminisced. "I thought they were going to disinherit her on the spot. They sure threatened to," she finished.

"That's right," he smiled. "Lydia was terrified to talk to her parents about her decision. She thought that if I talked to them that I might be able to persuade them to allow her to stay at NU. She really was a talented actress. She had a lot of potential," Chip explained. "She was quiet in person, but she lit up the stage when she was in character. She was a natural talent." He stared out the window momentarily, his thoughts on an obvious trip back down memory lane. "Anyway," he continued. "The Moores were huge contributors to the university, so I knew who they were, but to meet them in person was quite an experience," he chuckled. "It was quite an honor. For as much money as they had, they were quite regular. They gave millions to the university, so I think I expected Mr. Moore to be draped in a chinchilla cape and Mrs. Moore a diamond studded tiara," he chuckled. "But they looked like regular folks. They didn't look like they were worth hundreds of millions or whatever their estimated net worth was at the time."

"Were they racist, Chip?" Grace asked boldly, using his name for the first time.

"Grace!" Mr. Dudley exclaimed. "What kind of question is that to ask the man? I've told you before that they were lovely people. The times were different back then. The races didn't mix up the way they do now. Let's not go looking for dead bones," he ordered.

"I don't mind answering her, Mr. Dudley," he smiled. "They weren't racists, Grace," Chip offered. "They were very kind to me," he paused. "At first."

"Yeah, I bet they were kind until they found out that you were involved with their daughter," Justine blurted. Her jaw hung slack when she noticed everyone staring at her. "Oops! Did I say that out loud?"

Grace giggled softly, following her lead, the others smiled in support.

"Actually, Justine is right," Chip agreed. "They were very kind to me until they found out that I was in love with Lydia. Like Mr. Dudley said, the times were very different back then. Plus, I was married. It was a very complicated situation. I can't say that I blame them really. I never met them again, but I know that they orchestrated my removal from the university," he sighed.

Wasting no time, Grace continued her battery of questions. "Did you know that my mom was pregnant?" she asked.

Chip stared at Grace softly. "I did not," he said. "If I had known, I would have gone to the ends of the earth to find her," he paused, the scar tissue over his broken heart now visible.

"Did you try to contact Lydia?" Mrs. Dudley blurted, her frail fingers covered her mouth in embarrassment. "Look at me, now I'm acting like a nosy teenager. I need to mind my own business. This is about Grace," she recanted.

"This is your business too, Mom, and that's a fair question. I'm glad you asked," Grace assured. She turned her gaze back to Chip. "Well, did you?" she asked. "What did you do to try to contact my mother?" she asked.

Like an eclipse, the scar tissue now covered his face like a veil of shame. "I, uh, I, I called her several times," he stammered. "But they moved her out of the dorms almost overnight," he recollected. "Her roommate wouldn't give out any information. And I lost my job almost as quickly," he explained. "She was a student and I was her professor, so our relationship violated the university's code of conduct policy," he sighed. "And I was married. Lydia was white and I was black," he continued. "It was wrong on so many levels and I knew it," he paused. "But I loved her deeply. I really did," he repeated. "I was told by the university that if I tried to contact her, they would make sure that I never taught again. They threatened to blackball me as a professor. They told me that if I left quietly they'd write me a letter of recommendation so that I could teach somewhere else," he explained sarcastically. "I was thinking about my future and trying to avoid a scandal," he sighed. "But I should have tried to find her. I thought she would try to find me until I realized that she didn't know where I was from," he said, his fingers tracing the water bottle.

Grace took another bite of her now cold hot dog. She watched as her father rhythmically ate his meal, her mother picked at her salad, her eyes glued to Chip's face.

"Years later, I ran into some of my former colleagues at a conference and I found out that the university had destroyed any record of me having ever been there. The president of Northwestern had told the faculty that they were all under strict orders not to give out any personal contact information on me," he continued. "At the time, the Moore family was the university's largest donor family. I think they still are. Northwestern is one of the finest universities in the country, I was a new professor, and I'd violated their rules," he paused. "The school didn't want a scandal, and I don't blame them. If I were an administrator, I would have done the same thing," he continued. "Anyway, the young faculty that knew me feared that they'd lose their jobs," he explained. "And to tell you the truth, many of my colleagues believed that it was wrong of me to become involved with a student, especially a student of a different race. The few friends that I'd made as a young professor evaporated like a mist once the rumor mill churned out our affair. I was toxic," Chip trailed. The scab now removed, the wound over his heart was blistery, red and raw.

Her arthritic fingers gripped his hand tightly. "For what it's worth, she did try to contact you, young man," Mrs. Dudley comforted. "Lydia wrote letters to the university and tried to hire a private detective to find you so she could tell you about her pregnancy," she continued. "I saw it with my own eyes. But her parents found out about it and cut off her access to her trust fund. And then once she started showing in her pregnancy, they sent her to live with us expecting that she'd have the baby and place it up for adoption," she blurted. "Well, clearly she couldn't do that," she smiled. "She loved the baby in her womb too much to do that. And I'm glad she did because we were able to raise Grace as our own," she smiled, patting Grace's hand with her free one. She released their hands and waved hers in the air. "The good Lord does not make mistakes," she exclaimed. "No siree! He never closes a door without first opening a window. I don't care what nobody says. I will go to my grave believing that," she declared, smacking her bony hand on the table. "I was never blessed with my own birth child, and I felt that God was punishing me and had closed the door on my dream of motherhood, but I raised Grace from the time she was two, and for the record, I raised her Mama too," she chuckled. "So God opened two windows for the one door that he closed because I done raised and mothered two babies," she grinned proudly.

"You remind me of my mother, Mrs. Dudley. My mother always says the same thing, 'God always opens a window before he closes a door,'" he explained. "She also used to say that 'you should make your pain your platform,'" Chip offered. "Use your pain to be a blessing to somebody. She'd say. Don't be scared. Share your story to help somebody. Give your testimony," he uttered, his index finger waving boldly as though in the pulpit. "God is putting you through something so you can be a blessing to somebody. Your trash might be someone else's treasure," he finished. "She was right," he chuckled softly. "As always, mama knows best."

"How do you plan to make the pain in your heart your platform in this case?" Grace asked. Teenie would be so proud of me. These are the types of questions that she would have asked.

Chip stared at Grace and fingered his water bottle. "Well, now that I know about you, the years of pain that I endured about losing your mother will fuel me to be a part of your life in whatever way you'll allow me to participate. I'm prepared to be there for you no matter what, Grace," he offered sincerely. "For years I felt ashamed of myself and believed that the painful hole in my heart was God's punishment for committing adultery and falling in love with your mother. But now looking at your face, I know that my pain was not in vain," he declared. "Who knows? Maybe I'll be a spokesperson to champion interracial dating and marriage so people can see that love is colorblind. Love is love and can't be contained in society's narrow boxes. I loved your mother, and your mother loved me," he explained boldly. "I know that's difficult for some people to understand," he paused. "And to many, it seemed like a hot mess, but now with hindsight, the only mess was the fact that the world was too narrow minded to see the beauty in our love," he shared. His eyes bore directly into Grace's, willing her to believe him. "She was my student, but she was eighteen, so she was an adult. Our love was not against the law," he clarified. "I betrayed my marriage vows by becoming involved with your mother, and that was wrong, but that's a sin in the eyes of God. It's not illegal," he defended.

"In some states it's illegal," Mr. Dudley interrupted. "I think adultery is still illegal in the state of Utah," he offered, shoving another forkful of food into his mouth.

Justine and Grace stared at each other curiously thinking the same thought. How does he know this stuff? Bewildered, Grace shrugged and shook her head.

"You're right, Mr. Dudley. I stand corrected," Chip said. "I believe adultery is against the law in the state of Utah. But our love was consummated in Illinois," he clarified. His eyes shifted back to Grace. "All of these years, I wondered why God allowed my heart to be hurt the way it was. Losing your mother the way I lost her was like a death. It was like losing someone in a car crash where you don't have a chance to say goodbye. When you lose someone suddenly, there are so many emotions, so much unfinished business," he continued. "There's no closure."

"You got that right," Mrs. Dudley agreed. "We lost Grace's mama that way. She complained of a headache one night and the next thing we knew she had fallen out on the floor. A brain aneurysm. She was dead before we knew what happened. Doctors said she was dead before her head hit the ground so she didn't suffer none," she finished.

Chip shook his head. "You lost her as suddenly as I lost her. You don't get to say farewell or make peace with the person. They're just gone."

Justine and Grace exchanged knowing glances. "I know," Grace offered. "We lost a friend and her sister in a car crash two years ago," she choked. "I'll tell you about that later. Please continue," she encouraged.

"I'm so terribly sorry," he comforted. "But you know exactly what I mean then too. All these years I always wondered what happened to her. So many times I thought about trying to find her, but then I thought it would be best to just leave the past in the past," he paused. "I called Wellesley once to see if she was enrolled, but they wouldn't give out student enrollment information. So I buried my feelings for her. I buried the past. So when I got your letter," he choked. "I thought it was a cruel joke. I really did. But now I know that you were the window that was open when the door to my life with Lydia was closed."

Grace twirled her water bottle and pondered her next question. What would Teenie ask him now? He continued before she could formulate one.

"I told my wife about my relationship with Lydia Moore," he confessed. "When I got fired, I planned to lie to her and tell her that my job had been cut because they were downsizing the drama department," he rambled. "But I didn't want the threat of blackmail to follow me forever, so I told her myself," he shared. "She asked me if I loved Lydia and I told her that I did and always would," he said. "I know that was painful for her to hear, but it was God's honest truth. I wanted her to know that I had feelings for Lydia that were different than the feelings that I had for her," he continued. "I loved my wife, but not the way that I loved Lydia."

Both hands cupped her chin, her eyes hung on Chip's every word. "You told your wife about your affair with Lydia Moore? And you admitted that you loved Lydia more than you loved her?" Justine blurted loudly. "And you lived to tell about it? What did she say to you?"

The table erupted in laughter. Even Grace chuckled at her friend's brazenness.

"I sure did," he replied. "Don't get me wrong, I'm not particularly proud of this time in my life. What I did wasn't honorable, but I did tell my wife the truth," he sighed. "Of course she wasn't happy. She left me. That was a really rough time. She moved home with her parents for a few months and started seeing someone," he paused. "And of course that hurt me deeply. I was prepared to give her a divorce, but then she and I decided to try again. We'd been friends since high school," he added. "We started over and stayed married until she died. We tried to have children and when it wasn't working we learned that she had ovarian cancer. I was with her when she died," he choked. "That was another dark period in my life, let me tell you," he shared. "But now I feel like the sun is finally shining on my dismal, imperfect life after all these years," he smiled.

Taking a sip of her water, Grace returned his smile. "Mom, how far away is the house where my mother grew up? I want to see it," she stated.

"It's just ten minutes up Sheridan Road," Mr. Dudley replied. "I could probably drive there with my eyes closed."

"She asked me, old man," Mrs. Dudley barked playfully, waving her arthritic fist in her husband's face. "I don't need you speaking for me. I'm not mute," she said. "Next time you do that I'm going to clobber you! Hmmph! And drive there with your eyes closed," she mocked. "You can barely drive straight with your eyes wide open, you old fool," Mrs. Dudley teased.

Mr. Dudley slanted his eyes into a playful grin. "Woman, don't be out in public acting up," he growled playfully. "You know I know Ka-Ka-razy!" he stuttered. "I may have to show you some of my new moves when we get home," he winked.

Justine giggled and Chip smiled at the playful banter, while a very embarrassed Grace rolled her eyes. "Justine, you'll come with us," Grace insisted. "Do you want to see it, Chip?" Grace asked.

"Well, I uh," he stammered. "I hadn't thought about that. But if you'd like for me to join you, Grace, I'd love to go," he beamed. "I rented a car, so I'll just follow you," he offered.

"Nonsense," Mr. Dudley stated. "I have a big Cadillac out there that has plenty of room. You'll ride with us," he ordered.

"I'd love to see where your birth mother was raised," Justine admitted. "In my mind I pictured this big, old, spooky mansion covered in cobwebs," she gestured with her hands. "Almost like the spooky witch's castle in The Wizard of Oz. I need a visual," she confessed as she noticed Mrs. Dudley slowly pushing her chair back. "You sit, Mrs. Dudley," Justine insisted. "I'll take care of this." Hopping from her seat, Justine stacked the lunch debris onto one tray and quickly wiped the table crumbs with her napkin. "Thanks for lunch, folks," she smiled as she walked toward the trash can.

"You're welcome," Mrs. Dudley returned. "I haven't seen that house in years myself," she shared.

"What does it look like, Mom?" Grace asked.

"Well, it's a big house, but it's not as big as you'd think for as much money as they had," she cautioned. "Don't get me wrong, it's a grand old house, but compared to some of the other estates surrounding it, it's rather modest," she finished. "But that's how the Moore family was," she sighed. "They didn't flaunt their wealth like some of their neighbors."

The scowl was deep and intense. "What are you talking about they didn't flaunt their wealth? They got a brand new Cadillac every year. Only rich people trade in their car for a new one every year, Ethel," he stated. "If you ask me that's flaunting your wealth."

"They drove a big, new Cadillac every year, but their neighbors on either side of them drove that big silver car with that naked lady on the hood," Mrs. Dudley stammered. "What do you call that kind of car, Mr. Dudley?" she asked. "I forget what it's called."

"It's a Rolls Royce. I don't know why you can't remember that. Rolls Royce," he repeated. "And they didn't drive the car themselves," he corrected. "They had a driver too, just like the Moores had," he paused directing his gaze to Chip. "I was the Moore's chauffeur," he explained.

"I remember when the neighbor folks on the left of the house got that Rolls Royce," she paused. "It seems like the folks on the right got one the very next day," she chuckled. "They were sure trying to keep up with the Joneses."

Justine and Grace giggled at the familiar exchange.

"Mr. and Mrs. Moore had a driver and a private plane like the rest of the neighbors, but at least they weren't being driven around in a Rolls Royce," Mrs. Dudley continued. "One day I heard Mr. and Mrs. Moore say that they thought their neighbors were showy for being driven around in such an expensive car," she shared. "Mrs. Moore said that people with real money don't make it obvious to the world that they have money," she said. "Ethel," Mrs. Dudley imitated in a falsetto. "The truly wealthy don't flaunt their wealth. It's gauche. People hate people who have more than they do," she continued, her voice an octave higher. "You don't want to give people a reason to hate you. And you don't want people to know how much you're really worth. Keep 'em guessing. Make them wonder where your money is. Don't drive it around the neighborhood," Mrs. Dudley finished. "That's what she'd say to me. And I know they had the money to be driven around in whatever they wanted. Believe you me," she whistled. "They were loaded."

"Hmph! I don't know why she was giving you tips like that," Mr. Dudley said. "They were barely paying us a living wage back then and Lord knows we didn't have a pot to piss in," he shared. "She may as well have been giving that advice to some squirrels," he laughed.

"Greg Dudley!" Mrs. Dudley admonished. "Watch your tongue. You know I don't like to hear that kind of talk," she chided.

Mr. Dudley laughed. "Woman! You're just showing out in front of company, now stop talking about stuff you know nothing about and let's get to walking. You know I want to be home before dark so I can watch my house," Mr. Dudley shared. "I'll go drive the car up to the front steps of the building. Justine and Grace, walk with Mrs. Dudley and make sure she uses the restroom," he ordered. "You know she crawls like a snail so if we don't get a move on it, it'll be this time next Tuesday before she shuffles to the car."

Mrs. Dudley balled her small fist and waved it in her husband's face. "If I didn't have to pee like a racehorse right now, I'd knock the taste out of your mouth, old man!" she laughed. "Come on ladies, let's go to the powder room to freshen up and let the men folk bring our chariot around."

Smiling, Grace reached for her mother's arm to help her from her seat. Her grin disappeared when she glanced at Chip's face. His gaze far off and distant, he opened his mouth to speak, his index finger poised to ask a question or make a point and then just as quickly, he pursed his lips together and shook his head.

"Are you sure you have time to visit the Moore house?" Grace asked. "You seem distracted. You don't have to go if you don't want to," she said defensively.

"Huh?" Chip stammered. "No, no, I want to go. I want to spend as much time with you as possible," he smiled, the tenderness in his face returning. "It's just that. Never mind," he stammered. "A wild thought just crossed my mind, but it's too absurd to share," he laughed waving his hand in front of his face dismissively. "Don't mind me," he smiled warmly. "As a drama professor, sometimes I'm just prone to the dramatics," he explained. "We'll meet you ladies in the front," he said. I need to tweak this idea a bit, but I think I'm on to something.

Chapter 21

Beer for Bullets

The first rejection letter stung like the flu shot. By the time she received the second and third letters, the inoculation still hadn't kicked in, the rejection strain of the flu making her sick once again. The mere anticipation of more disappointment caused her stomach to knot and her fragile heart to race. Inhaling deeply, she braced herself for the next slap in the face. "Don't take the rejection personally," people said. "The programs are very competitive," others warned. "If you don't get accepted to your first or second choice, maybe the third or fourth choice will be the charm," they encouraged. The letters had come in rapid fire succession, one every day for a week.

Like a sad, cruel joke, each new letter made her more numb than the last. Daily, she sorted through the stack of mail, praying that this would be the day for some good news. But she hadn't received any news in two weeks. Jack and his friends had warned her that a small envelope usually wasn't a good sign. The small envelope represented a rejection, or a "bullet" as it was affectionately known. The large envelope meant that you were accepted and your registration paperwork was enclosed. She gripped the small envelope in her hand, resisting the urge to squeeze her clenched fingers into a tight fist.

Look on the bright side. You're holding a beer in your hand. The bar in the student union on Jack's college campus gave out a free beer for every bullet you brought in. The rejection letters were prominently displayed on the bar's cork wall like a community wall of shame. The seals from graduate programs bordered some of the letters while the recognizable letterhead from top corporations framed others. The students didn't bother to white out their name, unashamed to have their rejection plastered like wallpaper for the campus to see. "Rejection is inevitable and nothing to be ashamed about," Jack explained. "Just brace yourself and expect it," he coached. "The seniors proudly bring in their bullets. Some of them get rejected for jobs, and others get rejected for graduate study programs. Either way, they bring'em in, tack them to the wall of shame and have a beer to toast their sorrows," he grinned. She fingered the small, letter size envelope in her hand. Bullet number four. She sighed loudly.

"Here we go again," she groaned. Tempted to rip the small envelope in half, and spare herself the agony, she robotically inserted her index finger and tore open the flap. Her eyes bulged as she read in a sarcastic tone. "We are pleased to inform you that your application for admission has been accepted." She stopped and stared at the letter in her hand. "I got in?" she asked. "I got in?" she repeated. She read the letter in its entirety. "I got in!" she screamed. "Hallelujah! I got in!"

Her trembling hand reached for the telephone. The doctor had told her to breathe deeply when she felt anxious. She hung up the phone and took several deep, cleansing breaths. "Breathe, Billie, breathe!" she coached.

Billie closed her eyes and took several long inhales, slowly allowing the air to escape from her nostrils like her yoga instructor had encouraged. After five breaths, she could feel her hands relaxing and her heart rate slowing. Opening her eyes, she held her hand in front of her face. The trembling had subsided enough for her to dial the telephone. She dialed the number from memory.

"Dr. Dudley speaking," the voice sang.

"Dr. Dudley, this is Billie Mae Peterson," she panted. "I got in to Chicago State University," she stammered breathlessly. "I just got my acceptance letter today," she beamed, forcing herself to take a deep inhale.

Elle removed her glasses and smiled wildly. "That's wonderful! Congratulations, Billie! I'm so proud of you," she shared. "I knew you could do it!" she beamed.

"I can't believe it! I'm going back to college," Billie stated. "After all these years, I'm going to get my degree."

Dr. Dudley cleaned her glasses and smiled. "You deserve it, Billie," she encouraged. "You worked really hard on those applications, and Chicago State is a good school."

"Before I forget, thank you for your help, Dr. Dudley," Billie admitted. "I'm sure the letter of recommendation that you wrote helped a lot."

"You're very welcome, but I certainly can't take too much credit. You had to write the essays," she reminded. "All I did was edit them for you, and I didn't recommend that many changes," she explained. "But I'm glad that I was able to help you with this step in your life," she paused taking a sip from her now room temperature coffee. "I think you're going to do really well as a student, Billie," Dr. Dudley continued. "When I teach my psychiatry course at the University of Chicago, I find that the older students usually outperform most of my younger students," she shared as she removed her glasses and rubbed the bridge of her nose with her thumb. "Obviously, they're more mature and they work hard, but they also just seem to want it more. They just seem more focused than many of the students who enter medical school right from undergrad," she continued. "It's as though they feel that they've been given a second chance and they want to get it right this time," she explained, using the tip of her cardigan to wipe her smudged lens.

"From your mouth to God's ears," Billie beamed proudly. "God willing, I think I'm going to get it right this time," she stated. "I mean it," she paused momentarily searching for her words carefully. "I believe that I've been given a new lease on life," she smiled. "Everything is really falling into place for me these days. First my marriage and now this," she shared.

"Since you raised the subject, how's that going, Billie? How are things going with you and Jackie now if you don't mind my asking?" Dr. Dudley probed.

"I don't mind at all," Billie offered. "Things are going well. The kids were surprised at first when we told them that we were getting back together, especially my daughter," she paused. "I think she thought that it was a joke," Billie laughed. "But now that her dad has moved back in, she realizes that it's for real."

Elle shifted the phone in her hand. "Are you planning to get remarried right away?" she asked. "I don't remember what you told me about that."

"I think we're going to give it six months," Billie shared. "We're seeing a marriage counselor and taking part in the couples' counseling with a deacon at our new church," she continued. "But so far, my children are settling into a different routine nicely. We have a new family rhythm that feels good."

"Well, I'm happy that things are falling into place for you,

Billie," Elle offered. "Are your medications working out okay?" she asked.

Billie placed the letter back into its envelope before answering. "They are," she replied. "I take them every day like clock work," Billie said. "The medicine has caused me to gain about ten pounds, which I don't like," she groaned patting her thicker mid section. "But I'm still able to fit into my clothes," she sighed. "Thank goodness Jackie likes the thicker me," she giggled. "But I don't like it so I've started exercising more to counteract the weight gain side effect. I'm taking a yoga class, and I also walk two or three miles about four times a week," she explained.

Tossing the car keys on the coffee table, Tanisha plopped next to her mom on the sofa, dropping her book bag at her feet. Billie smiled warmly at Tanisha and held up one finger.

"Weight gain is a common side effect of the prescription that you are taking," Dr. Dudley said. "But you were underweight for your height, Billie, so ten pounds probably looks really good on you," Dr. Dudley comforted, straightening the folders on her desk. "And don't worry, with the dosage that I prescribed for you, the medication shouldn't cause you to gain any more weight. Ten pounds is usually all the patients gain," she explained. "So don't overdo it on the exercise. I'm sure you look fine," she encouraged. "I'm so glad that you called, and I was available to chat for a bit, but my next patient is due to arrive any minute, so I better scoot, but thanks for sharing your good news with me, Billie. It made my day, and I'm very proud of you," she said. "I'd love to stay in touch, so feel free to call me anytime," she stated. "I mean it."

"Thanks again, doctor," Billie finished, her grin returning as she placed the phone in the cradle.

"You smell good, Mom," Tanisha shared. "Is that a new

perfume?" she asked.

"It is and it isn't," Billie shared. "It's Chanel No. 5. I used to wear this all the time, and then I stopped," she explained sniffing her thin wrist.

"Keep wearing it. It smells nice on you. Very crisp and light," Tanisha encouraged.

"Your father gave it to me on our one month reunited anniversary," Billie smiled.

Tanisha rolled her eyes into the top of her head in a mock scowl. "Gag me," she teased. "I'm just kidding, Mother. That's really sweet," she offered sincerely.

"Guess what?" Billie asked, her eyes wide as saucers. "I got into Chicago State!" she shared before Tanisha could guess. "I got my acceptance letter today," she beamed waving the envelope toward Tanisha.

"Get out, Mom!" Tanisha smiled. "That's great. Wow! You're really going back to college."

"I am," Billie laughed. "I can't believe it, but I'm going to be a student again," she sighed. "And if I work really hard, I should finish before your second year of college starts."

"What's the rush?" Tanisha asked as she read the acceptance letter.

Billie smoothed her daughters shoulder length hair. "No rush," she confessed. "It's just been so long since I've been a student that I want to set a goal for myself so I can work towards it," she explained. "I want to be done in a little over two years," she shared. "I hope I remember how to maintain good study habits and how to take notes," she sighed.

Tanisha placed the letter back in the envelope. "You'll do fine, Mom," Tanisha encouraged. "You're smart and you're pretty organized so school shouldn't be any problem for you," she finished. "Maria's mom went back to college as an adult and she did well. She works at a bank downtown now and she seems to really love it."

Billie hugged the envelope against her chest. "I know, I talked to Mrs. Wesley and she was very encouraging," Billie explained. "Liz told me that she was nervous on her first day too, but once she got over the freshman jitters, she was fine," she paused. "Technically, I'll be a second semester sophomore because they're accepting the credits that I had from the junior college that I attended before Jack was born," she corrected. Billie Mae pulled the letter from the envelope and smoothed it on the table. "I think I might get this letter framed," she stated proudly.

"You should, Mom. Go for it! That's a huge accomplishment," Tanisha smiled, her tongue playing with one of the rubber bands connecting the braces in her mouth. "I can't wait to get these things off my teeth," she groaned.

"You only have six more months to wear them, Tanisha," Billie reminded. "And then you'll have to find something else to complain about," she said, gently patting Tanisha's tan thigh. "Your legs are so muscular. Do I look fat to you?" she asked.

Tanisha scowled at her mom and shrugged. "No fatter than you always do," she laughed, quickly scooting away before her mom could pinch her thigh.

"Do I really look fat?" Billie asked seriously.

"Of course not, Mom," Tanisha said. "You're still the skinniest mom of all my friends. You're even skinnier than Liz," Tanisha laughed.

"Liz?" Billie Mae asked. "Mrs. Wesley allows you to call her Liz?" she quizzed.

Tanisha laughed loudly. "Of course not," she giggled. "But we call all of the Peez by their first name behind their back," she laughed. "But to her face I call her Mrs. Wesley."

"Peez?" Billie Mae repeated.

"Parents, Mom," Tanisha groaned. "P is short for parent," she sighed. "You are so out of touch," she mocked.

"I've gained ten pounds, can you tell?" her mother asked.

"Not really. Maybe a little. Your face looks fuller," Tanisha observed. "You can't dodge raindrops anymore, but you're still skinny," she laughed.

"I wasn't that skinny before," Billie defended. "I wasn't skinny enough to dodge raindrops."

"You were well on your way," Tanisha laughed. "You don't want to get as skinny as your sister. Aunt Shanay can definitely dodge raindrops," Tanisha groaned. "She's way too skinny. She looks sick."

The mention of her younger sister's name caused Billie's smile to fade. She reached down to pet Butch, the family dog, who'd just plopped at her feet, his snout wet from a recent drink from the toilet bowl. A water bowl filled daily with fresh water was no match for a sip from the toilet. Closing the bathroom doors to keep Butch out of the bathrooms resulted in deep scratches in the door frame as he tried to pry his way in for his daily toilet bowl drink. Lowering the lid on the toilets resulted in a toilet bowl lid covered in dog slobber as he repeatedly tried to lift the lid himself. Dropping a tidy bowl freshener in the toilet to change the water to midnight blue resulted in a trip to the vet as Butch drank the water anyway. Now the family just let him drink from the toilet.

"Is Aunt Shanay sick, mom?" Tanisha asked. "We need to brush Butch's teeth," Tanisha stated. "Or at least buy him some tooth cleaning doggie biscuits. His teeth are the color of butter."

ॐ

"I'm so sorry that she wasn't supportive, Billie," Jackie offered. "But some people are like a barrel of crabs. I'm sure you've heard that saying before," he continued. "You don't have to put a lid on a barrel of crabs because if one crab tries to escape, another crab in the barrel will pull that crab back down," Jackie explained. "My daddy told me that when I was young. Shanay is your sister, and you would think that she'd be supportive of something that will make you happy, but she's not. Shanay is only happy when you're unhappy," he offered gently. "I noticed that a long time ago about her. I just hoped that I was wrong, but it looks like I was right," he sighed. "A lot of people are like that. They don't want you to do better than they're doing. They want you to be miserable like them. So when you are trying to pull yourself out of the misery barrel, they pull you right back down with them, like a barrel of crabs," he said. "Ignore Shanay. If you want to go back to school, then you should," he encouraged.

He was right. Shanay was a crab. Billie regretted sharing her plans with her younger sister. "Why would you go back to school?" Shanay asked. "You're almost forty years old. You're too old to be a college student." Her list of reasons why Billie shouldn't go back to school was long. "Besides, you have a mental illness. You can't do well in school. You're setting yourself up to fail." This last comment had been the final straw for Billie Mae, and the words had poured forth like a gusher.

"You are a mean spirited heifer, Shanay! You can't stand for anyone to be happy because you're miserable. Well, I've had enough of your evil ways and your negativity," she shrieked. "The only thing that you encouraged me to do was to divorce Jackie.

You didn't try to encourage me to get counseling or try to work it out, you just encouraged me to end my marriage," she ranted. "You are poison! I hate that I'm related to you," she continued, her hands shaking uncontrollably, her desire for a cigarette strong.

Shanay laughed. "Look at you. How can you go back to school when you can't handle feedback from your only sister," she mocked. "You're probably having a nervous breakdown as we speak," Shanay teased. "You're just not mentally strong enough to go back to college and you know it or you wouldn't be getting so defensive."

"I am not having a nervous breakdown," Billie screamed. "I finally see you for what you are, a mean spirited, jealous heifer! Get out of my house!" Billie barked. "And don't bother contacting me until you can be supportive of my dreams!"

After her fight with her sister, Billie had contacted Dr. Dudley and scheduled a therapy session, rehashing the scene with Shanay in vivid color. As usual, Dr. Dudley had listened intently as Billie talked and cried her way through the story, speaking only when it was clear that Billie was finished.

"Sadly, Billie, some people can't handle other's success," Dr. Dudley explained. "Your sister may feel threatened that if you better yourself then the dynamics of your relationship will change," she explained. "It's very common in relationships. When one person seeks any type of self improvement, the other person in the relationship can't handle it and tries to discourage the person. They usually try to make the person feel bad about wanting to do something positive," Dr. Dudley continued. "But relationships are dynamic, not static. It's healthy for people to change in relationships. Ideally, you want to grow and evolve together so that each person can support the changes occurring in the other," she shared. "Generally, a conflict occurs when one person in the relationship is evolving and the other is not," she said. "I see it all the time in my practice. It's one of the most common reasons for the death of different types of relationships including: marriages, childhood friendships, sisterly bonds, you name it. One person matures and evolves and the other doesn't," she repeated. "It's as old as time. You can't pick your family, but I believe that people are in your life for a reason and a season and sometimes the season ends before we're ready for it to end," she coached.

"I'm not saying that you shouldn't have any more contact with your sister or try to work this out, but as your therapist, I'm giving you permission to set limits on how close you allow people to be in your life. You may choose to only invite some people into the second balcony of your life. Others may have front row seats, mezzanine level seating or first balcony," she paused. "And there are some who don't get invited into the theatre of your life at all. And that's perfectly okay," she continued. "Even if the person that you're restricting is closely related to you," she paused. Dr. Dudley inhaled deeply as Billie hung on her every word.

"I'm telling you this because it's necessary for you to preserve your own mental health. You have to give yourself permission to not allow people to make you feel bad about yourself, Billie. When you encounter people who make you feel this way, keep downgrading their seat assignment until either their behavior changes or they're in the street watching you from afar wondering why they are not invited into the theatre when at one time they had a front row seat," she offered as Billie chuckled softly. "It sounds cruel and heartless," Elle admitted. "And it's difficult at first, Billie, but the more you practice this technique, the easier it becomes," she coached. "And don't get me wrong. Receiving constructive feedback from a trusted confidante and being told something that you need to hear but may not want to hear is completely different than someone making you feel bad about yourself because of their own fears and insecurities," she finished.

Billie hadn't spoken to her sister Shanay in over six months. They'd had fights before, but had never gone this long without communicating. Billie made the first move and called her after three weeks of no contact. As each day ticked by without a return phone call, Billie was beginning to believe more and more that her sister was envious of her new goals. It had been so long since she'd heard from her sister that Billie hadn't shared that she and Jackie were now cohabitating once again. Although she missed her sister, she didn't miss the emotional baggage that Shanay carried with her like a backpack filled with rocks.

"Did you hear me, Mom?" Tanisha repeated. "Is Aunt Shanay sick? I haven't seen her in awhile, but the last time I saw her she looked sick she was so thin."

"I don't think so," Billie shrugged. "She's always been thin, but I think that she's started drinking again, and whenever she starts drinking heavily, she loses a lot of weight."

"Did you guys have a fight?" Tanisha asked as she rubbed Butch's head.

Billie stared at her daughter briefly, her hesitation spoke volumes.

"What did you have a fight about?" Tanisha asked knowingly.

"I didn't say that we had a fight, Tanisha," Billie defended.

"You didn't need to," Tanisha laughed. "I could tell by the way you hesitated. What happened? Dish?" Tanisha coaxed.

Her relationship with her daughter had improved tremendously. Every time Tanisha sat near her on the sofa,

Billie's heart melted and she knew that progress was being made. A gesture as simple as smoothing her daughter's hair without a grimace and scowl in return had seemed unattainable just two years before, when the wall between them was fortified in layers of solid granite. Looking back, she knew that her confession about her mental illness and plea for Tanisha's help with her medication had been the trigger event that slowly began to melt the Titanic sized ice glacier. Billie also learned to ask open ended questions that couldn't be answered with a simple yes or no response. At first, her attempts were scorned by Tanisha, the eye rolling increased and the stares were blank and discouraging. Not thwarted by her teenage daughter's disinterest, Billie forged ahead like a miner searching for gold, cataloging things of importance and following up with her daughter to spark more chatter.

"Aunt Shanay was not happy when I told her that I was planning to go back to school," Billie sighed. "She said some things that I felt were hurtful and mean spirited, so I told her off," she shared.

Tanisha's mouth hung ajar. "I knew you guys must have had a knock down drag out fight because we've never gone this long without seeing Aunt Shanay," she confessed. "Not that it bothers me. I think she's a loser," she admitted. "She's a nice, funny loser, especially when she's been drinking. But she's lame," Tanisha shared.

"Tanisha!" Billie scolded. "That's not nice. Why would you say that about your aunt?"

"You know it's true, Mom. Your sister is a bona fide, class A loser. Why would she not be happy for you to go back to school?" Tanisha asked. "I'll tell you why," she continued. "She's a hater. If you go back to school, then she won't have anyone to go to bars with," she continued.

"Tanisha, your aunt and I haven't gone to a bar together since I stopped drinking a couple of years ago," Billie defended.

"Well, if you go back to school then you'll be busy studying and you won't have time to hear her whine about the parade of losers and bums that she dates," Tanisha shot back. "Face it, Mom. Dad warned me about people like her. She's like a crab in a barrel," she continued. "Frankly, I think Aunt Shanay is jealous of you and always has been," Tanisha stated. "She's jealous because her lame daughter Wanda is such an academic midget and your kids do well in school," she listed counting on her fingers. "Aunt Shanay was married to a neurotic man who belonged to a cult, and your baby sister doesn't even know how to spell college, let alone know how to apply to one as an adult," Tanisha laughed. "There isn't one good reason why she should be mad at you for returning to school. She should be happy that you're getting your life together," she finished. "If you ask me, she's just jealous of you. Good riddance."

Billie stared at her daughter in disbelief. "Tanisha, where did you hear that barrel of crabs comment?" she asked.

"Dad told me that a few years ago," she shrugged. "On one of our daddy-daughter lunches, he was asking me about my friends and warned me that as I get older I might not have the same group of friends because when your friends see you doing things that are bigger than things they have the courage or talent to accomplish, some of them might resent you and hate you for it," she paused. "He said something about you don't have to put a lid on a barrel of crabs because the other crabs will always pull down the one who's trying to get out," she explained. "I think that's what he said. Aunt Helen gave me the crabs in a barrel speech one day too. It must be a Carlson family tradition," she shrugged. "Anyway, I didn't understand it at first, but he explained that it's a metaphor for people trying to hold you back and keep you down. I certainly didn't think that it would apply to people who are related to you, but I guess it does," Tanisha said. "She's a hater, Mom. Your sister, Aunt Shanay, is a king crab. Dad also told me that you can't pick your family, so you have to choose your friends wisely and be prepared to dump friends who try to keep you down," she continued. "So far, I haven't had to give any of my friends their walking papers yet, but once my fabulousness fully manifests itself, anyone who can't handle the Tanisha Denise Carlson show will be dismissed. POOF! They'll be history," she laughed.

Speechless, Billie stared at her only daughter admiring how Tanisha gently rubbed Butch's head with one hand and scratched under his chin with her other. "Mom, what's for dinner tonight?" she asked casually.

Chapter 22

There's No Easy Way

Gripping the pillow tightly, she punched her fist into the center as hard as she could. "Did he really play that James Ingram song, There's No Easy Way?" she asked again. "I can't believe that he would do something that prosaic," Rashanda groaned tossing the pillow into the air. "But I don't know why I'm surprised. He's as simple as a penny," she continued. "I just wish that you'd dumped him first, Maria. I hate that he had the chance to hurt you again," she offered. "It's like a sport for him." Dropping the pillow and waving her hands in the air she shook her head from side to side and stared at her friend, wishing she could hug away her hurt. "Do you think he had anything to do with the girls that called you and played that song?" she asked. "What am I saying? Of course he did. He probably had them call you." The thunder shook the room, causing the lights to flicker.

Maria wiped her nose and tear stained face with the sleeve of her new shirt. "I'm sure he had something to do with it," she sniffled. "It all makes sense now," she concluded, reaching for the tissue that Teenie waved in her face. "He's probably been planning this for months. Once he saw that picture of Dante and I in the newspaper, he went ballistic," she said. "He tried to act like he didn't care, but I know he did. And that time he saw me and Dante at the mall, I could tell he was pissed."

"Dante and me," Tanisha corrected. "You wouldn't say once he saw that picture of 'I' in the paper. You'd say once he saw that picture of 'me' in the paper. So it's 'once he saw that picture of Dante and me in the paper,'" she explained neurotically. "And never say me and Dante," she continued. "The personal pronoun that references you is always last. It's Dante and me or Dante and I," she finished. Maria stared at Teenie glibly. The other girls glared at Teenie like she was an alien.

"For crying out loud, Teenie," Justine whispered. "Not now! Must we have a grammar lesson now? We're in crisis mode. Helloooooo!"

"I'm just saying," Teenie whispered back, waving her hands in the air. "You know I can't stand to hear people butcher the King's English. You know that drives me crazy. It's like nails on a chalkboard to me," she shuddered. "Maria didn't hear me anyway," she shrugged.

Out of nowhere, Rashanda erupted in a fit of giggles. "Maria," she paused between giggles. "I'm not laughing at you. I'm laughing at the situation," she explained. "The way that Todd broke up with you is absurd. It's so absurd that it's comical," she chuckled. "It's like a bad sitcom story. I can't believe that he played theme music as he broke your heart."

"Technically, his cousin was playing the music in the other room while he was dumping me," she sighed. "But the volume was up so loud that it was obvious that he was playing the song for me to hear it," Maria explained glancing around the room at the friends spread across her poster bed and bedroom floor. She could see the concern on Justine and Teenie's faces while Grace's was a look of bewilderment. Her eyes rested on Teenie's thick eyebrows, a look of sorrow and worry etched in each caterpillar size brow. Maria shifted her eyes to the window and watched as the storm slammed sheets of water against her window pane. She walked over to the window and stared aimlessly outside, placing her palm against the pain and fanning her fingers widely. Her head bowed, she turned slowly and paced back and forth like a caged lion.

"At first, I wasn't paying attention to the music, and I thought his cousin was just goofing around," she admitted. "But then Todd had this stupid grin on his face like he wanted to laugh," she demonstrated. "The music kept getting louder and louder and finally Todd yelled for his cousin to turn the volume down, but instead he kept turning it up," she explained. "When Todd finally walked into the room where the stereo was to turn down the volume himself I listened to the lyrics and it was definitely There's No Easy Way," she finished. "I thought it was a coincidence, but later I realized that it was the same song that someone played on the phone the day that I cooked Dante's farewell dinner," she reminded. "Todd probably staged the whole thing just to hurt me," she stammered. "And what's worse is I think he invited his cousin over to dee jay and witness the whole thing," she sobbed. Another lightning bolt flashed like an exclamation point, sending a fresh wave of sobs pouring from Maria's eyes.

"Don't cry, Maria. Rashanda's right. Todd's a loser," Teenie comforted. "You're so much better off with Dante," she assured.

Maria reached for another tissue and blew her nose loudly. "I'd never paid attention to how much they play that stupid song on the radio."

"I actually like that song," Rashanda stated absentmindedly.

"And of course, I've heard that song on the radio at least five times since he dumped me," she offered. "Every time I hear it, I get hysterical all over again."

"I know that song," Justine said. "But I can't think of any of the words right now. Hum a few bars," she encouraged.

"I'm not going to sing it, but the words are: There's no easy way to break somebody's heart. There's just no easy way to break somebody's heart," Rashanda said, erupting into a fit of giggles once again.

This time Maria was not amused. "I don't see what's so funny, Rashanda," Maria growled. "My boyfriend of four years dumps me while playing break up theme music in the background and you think that's funny?" she asked. "I can't believe that he did that," she cried.

Rashanda covered her mouth with her hand. "I'm so sorry, Maria," she offered. "I don't know what's wrong with me. But when you told me about it on the phone you sounded like you didn't care," she explained. "I really didn't expect you to be this upset when we got over here," she confessed. "The whole situation is so freakishly cruel that it's funny," she admitted.

"Well, it's clearly not funny to her, Rashanda," Teenie scolded. "Justine, hand her another tissue from that nightstand," she ordered.

Plopping on the bed, Maria buried her face in the pillow, her mascara and eyeliner smearing the yellow pillow sham. The girls stared at each other, unsure what to do next.

Rashanda shrugged and bit her lip, admiring her promise ring and smiling widely at thoughts of Ian. "Anybody else need a manicure?" she asked casually.

This time, Grace stared at Rashanda coldly. "How can you think about doing your nails at a time like this?" she asked. "Look at her, she's a mess," Grace pointed.

Maria carefully rolled on to her back and stared at her hands.

"Actually, I could use a manicure," she sniffled. "Do you feel like doing my nails, Teenie?" she asked.

"I'll do them for you," Rashanda offered, happy to vindicate herself from her inappropriate giggle outburst.

"Just because I'm feeling bad, that's no reason for me to walk around looking bad, right?" she mumbled sitting up in her bed and staring at her reflection. "That was my mother's mantra when my dad first moved out," Maria explained sighing. "I put on some make-up this morning, and then I stopped," she paused staring at her reflection closely, the mascara and eyeliner smudged beneath her swollen eyes making her look like a raccoon. "I look a hot mess," she admitted. "Tore up from the floor up," she said. Maria fingered her long hair which was now a tangled, matted mess. "I didn't get around to combing my hair today," she confessed. "Let's give me a makeover, ladies," she ordered. "Hair, nails, make-up – the works!" she brightened. "I am not going to let that snake, Todd, get the best of me," she sniffled. "Just because he dumped me, it doesn't mean that I should look down in the dumps!" she declared. "Right?"

"That's right, girl," Teenie said. "That's the right attitude. Life goes on! Boys are like buses! Miss one and another one will be along in twenty minutes or so," she encouraged. "Besides, your mane looks like a bird's nest. You look like the Bride of Frankenstein," she teased. "Let's piece you back together.'

"What did you say when he dumped you?" Grace asked.

This time it was Teenie who laughed loudly. "Where'd that come from, Grace?" she asked. "I'm sorry for laughing, Maria," she offered quickly. "I can't believe that I just laughed out loud, but I wasn't expecting Grace to just ask you that," she explained. "But Rashanda is right, when you think about how he staged the break-up," she snickered. "It is kinda funny in a sick, twisted way," she explained.

"And then to hear Grace ask you what you did so matter of factly," she snickered. "It pushed me over the gigglesnort edge too."

"Welcome to my world," Rashanda giggled.

Maria grinned and shook her head. "I guess you're right," she smiled. "In a way, the whole thing is comical. Maybe I'll find it amusing in a few days or weeks, but right now I'm just pissed!" she shrieked squeezing her fists tightly. "I hate his guts and wish I could scratch his face," she said loudly scooping up Sugar, the cat. "I wish I had claws like Sugar and could scratch his sneering face!"

"Meow! Calm down there, Cat Woman," Rashanda advised. "You have every right to be upset with him," she assured. "But before we plan revenge on Todd the creep, let's get started on this makeover. As Teenie would say, you look like five miles of bad road," she laughed.

"Get it right, it's ten miles of bad road. If you're going to quote me, my phrase is ten miles of bad road," Teenie corrected. "And today, Maria looks like twenty miles of bad, bumpy road. I'll brush her hair. Justine, you, and Grace can slap some make-up on her after Rashanda does her nails," she ordered.

"Should I change clothes first?" Maria asked.

"No, your snot stained shirt buttons in the front, so you can change clothes when we're done and it won't smear your make-up or mess up your hair," Teenie advised.

Maria walked over to her desk and sat in her study chair as Rashanda began to file her nails. Teenie stood behind the chair gently brushing Maria's hair. "You know what ladies, this is a first for us," Teenie stated. "We've never had to deal with a break-up scenario in our group. What **did** you say to him, Maria?" she asked seriously. "Do share. In fact, stand up so we can turn your chair around. That way Grace and Justine aren't looking at the back of your tangled nest of hair," she laughed.

Inhaling deeply, Maria's eyes wandered around the room as she resettled into her chair. "I just stared at him," Maria offered. "At first, I thought he was joking. But then, he looked at me with this serious look and I knew that he was serious this time," she remembered. "I was stunned and didn't know what to do," she explained. "I don't remember exactly what I said, but I think I asked him if he was really serious a few times," she paused. "And then I asked him why. 'Why are you breaking up with me?'" I asked. "And all he said is that he wanted to explore his options on campus guilt free," she finished softly.

"Well, that certainly proves my theory," Teenie shared. "You can't hold on to your college boyfriend when you're still in high school."

"Teenie, this is not about you being right," Rashanda groaned. "Besides, I still have Ian," she reminded. "So your stupid theory is false."

"And AM and I are still kicking it," Justine offered.

"Well, that's because you and Ian are chemistry freaks and there aren't that many chemistry freaks floating around," she blurted. "And you and AM are only fifteen minutes away from each other," she explained to Justine. "And you don't have a long distance relationship. So I just need to modify my theory and add some distance parameters," she paused waving her hands in the air like parentheses. "If your college boyfriend goes to school more than two hundred miles away it's doomed for failure," she offered.

"Well, that would doom my relationship with Dante then too," Maria sniffled.

"Nice going, Teenie," Rashanda whispered. "Way to put her in a happy place," she scowled. "Don't listen to Teenie, Maria. She doesn't know what she's talking about."

"What was I supposed to say when he broke up with me?" Maria asked. "I've been with Todd for so long that I didn't know what I was supposed to do," she admitted. "We've been dating since I was in eighth grade," she groaned. "I don't even remember how I broke up with the boy that I dated before him."

"Wow!" Teenie whistled. "I forgot that you've been with him for that long," she said. "We need some break-up etiquette rules," she shared.

"That's not a bad idea," Grace said. "I wouldn't have the first clue how to act if someone dumped me."

"Can we please stop saying 'dumped' and just say broke up with me," Maria requested. "Just hearing the word 'dumped' sounds so harsh."

"Well, it is harsh," Teenie offered. "You've been with Todd, off and on, for more than four years," she reminded. "So, for him to end it like that was harsh and cruel."

Rashanda nodded her head in agreement. "What did Liz have to say?" she asked.

Maria crossed her legs like a pretzel in the small chair. "I didn't tell her what happened," she shared. "My mom thought I broke up with Todd a few months ago. Liz thought that I ended it with Todd before I started dating Dante," she admitted. "So I couldn't tell her. She has this rule about dating more than one guy at a time, blah, blah, blah," she trailed. "I didn't want to hear the lecture."

"I know you and your mom talk about everything, but I don't blame you, Maria," Teenie offered. "And since he was away at school, why go there?"

"Exactly," Maria sighed. "My mother got married at nineteen so she doesn't understand the modern dating rules. My dad was her first real boyfriend, so I don't think she could share much wisdom about how to handle getting dumped," she said. "Now I'm saying the D word," she shrugged.

"Let's come up with a code of conduct for handling break-ups," Teenie suggested. "Let's list the things that we should do if we're being dumped and the things we should do if we're the dumper," she said. "So we know how to act in each scenario."

Teenie dropped the hairbrush on the desk and picked up a notebook and pen. She sat on Maria's desk and placed her toes under Maria's thighs in the chair.

"Let's start with the behaviors for being dumped first," she suggested. "We'll call it 'Being dumped with dignity,'" she sang. "Number one – 'Don't cry,'" she wrote.

"I like that one," Grace said. "Crying will just make you look weak."

"I cried in front of Todd," Maria confessed.

"Well, you didn't know better, and we didn't have it as a rule," Grace reminded. "But never let 'em see you cry. Cry later with your girlfriends," she agreed. "How about don't beg him not to leave you?" she suggested.

"Good one! That will be number two," Teenie said. "By the time a boy has a break-up chat with you, he's probably been planning to dump you for a while, so his mind is already made up. Just suck it up and take it," she scribbled. "Don't beg for him to change his mind while he's dumping you. Besides, if you want to plan a get him back strategy, you'll need to get advice from your girlfriend and mom before going back into battle."

"Exactly," Rashanda echoed. "You'll need to go back to the base camp and get some more ammunition to wage a different attack in the battle for his heart. Or your friends may tell you to just concede defeat in that war and move on," she finished.

"What else?" Teenie asked. "Make him give you a reason," she wrote before anyone could reply.

"I like that one," Maria said. "Make him stare you in your face and tell you why he's breaking up with you so you can learn from the break-up," she said.

"Did he say that he wants to be friends?" Rashanda asked.

"No. He didn't say that, but he said that he'll be in touch," Maria mocked. "He was so casual about the whole thing," she offered. "I think that hurt more than him breaking up with me. He didn't seem phased by it at all."

The girls exchanged curious glances. "Maybe boys just aren't as emotional as girls," Grace said. "I'm sure he felt something, Maria," she encouraged.

"Doubt it," Rashanda whispered as Teenie nudged her.

"What do you think about that?" Teenie asked. "If he'd said 'let's be friends' would you have agreed?" she asked.

"I don't know. Probably," Maria admitted.

"I don't think you can really be friends with a guy after he dumps you," Rashanda stated.

"Why not?" Justine asked.

"I think it's just too complicated. Think about it. Are you really going to want to hear about his new girlfriend and vice versa?" she asked. "I think it's just better to go your separate ways and keep it moving," Rashanda stated flatly. "You don't have to end up as arch enemies, but I wouldn't want him calling me to hang out like one of his boys."

"Me neither," Maria said. "I don't know how your heart could heal with him still in your life," she said. "It would be too confusing."

"Aren't your parents friends now, Maria?" Grace asked. "And they're divorced."

"That's different," Teenie interrupted. "Neal and Liz have children together, so they'll always be a part of each other's lives. That's the deal you make when you pro-create with someone," she explained. "The person is in your life forever because of the kids. But absent that, I don't think I'd want to be friends with someone after a break-up," she concluded. "That'll be number four. If a guy is breaking up with us and he says 'let's be friends' we say thanks but no thanks," she wrote. "Is everybody cool with that one?" she asked.

Justine and Grace nodded in agreement. Maria sat motionless, staring out the window watching the rain.

"At least for now," Rashanda amended. "There might come a time where we want to be friends with the guy that dumps us," she advised. "You never know. So let's put a footnote by that one."

"True," Teenie agreed. "We could say 'I'll think about it' and look at each situation on a case by case basis. But if pressured we can always say no and then change our minds later," she suggested. "What else should we add to the 'how to handle being dumped with dignity' column?" Teenie asked, her gaze resting on Maria. "With hindsight, is there anything you wish you'd said or done differently in the moment, Maria?" Teenie asked gently. "Anything at all?"

"Yes," Maria admitted. "I hugged him," she whispered.

"What did you say? I couldn't really hear you," Rashanda said. "Did you just say that you hugged him after he dumped you?" she asked.

Maria lowered her eyes and stared at the floor. "I also offered to do it," she whispered.

"Offered to do what?" Grace asked. Justine nudged Grace and raised both eyebrows.

"No!" Teenie shrieked. "Maria, please tell me that you did NOT offer to trade in your virginity so that creep wouldn't break up with you!" she screamed.

The tears streamed down Maria's face once again. "I did," she whimpered.

"You didn't do it, did you, Maria?" Rashanda asked.

Maria shook her head and spoke weakly. "No. We didn't do it," she confessed. "But I thought that if I did he wouldn't break up with me. I felt desperate, like I was really losing him for real this time," she shared softly. "I hugged him really tight and he didn't hug me back," she said. "He finally had to pry my hands from around his waist," she stammered. "I think he felt sorry for me," she sobbed.

"Oh, Maria," Teenie offered. "Thank God you didn't do it," she comforted. "I'm so glad that you told us that. That's definitely going on the list," she finished. "Number five will be 'don't offer to do it just to convince a boy not to break-up with you.'"

"That one should be number one," Justine suggested.

"They're not rank ordered. They all really have the same value and level of importance," Teenie said.

"Why do you think he didn't take you up on your offer?" Justine asked.

Maria shrugged dismissively. "I think he was really just ready to move on," she sniffled through a partial smile. "He's almost twenty years old now, and I think our relationship just ran its course," she yawned. "I didn't sleep well last night, so I'm really tired," she explained. "I don't think he thought I was serious," she continued.

"Were you?" Rashanda asked. "If he had called your bluff, would you have gone through with it?"

Maria stared at her friend blankly. "I don't know," she confessed. "I honestly don't know."

"We need to carry these break-up rules in our wallet so we can commit them to memory," Grace said.

"Maria, where's your Bible?" Teenie asked. "There's a scripture that Lori used to mention about our bodies being a temple," she explained. "We need to commit that scripture to memory so that when we feel temptation with a boy, we can recite it," she finished.

"There's a Bible in the study office next to my room," Maria said. "It's on the book shelf."

"I'll go get it," Grace offered.

"We need a few more break-up rules. What should the sixth one be?" Teenie asked no one in particular.

"We could thank the boy for the experience?" Justine suggested.

"I love it!" Teenie yelled. "Even if your heart feels like it was ripped out of your chest, we'll smile and be polite. Thank him for the festivities," she scribbled. "That'll throw any boy for a loop!"

Rashanda laughed again. "Some boys like drama and scenes, and if you don't give him one, it'll freak him out. I know Todd was definitely looking for a scene playing theme music when he broke up with you," she shared. "I'm glad you didn't give him one, Maria."

"I cried, but I cry all the time with him so that's nothing new," Maria admitted.

"I found it!" Grace announced. "I looked in the Concordance in the back of the Bible, and I found the scripture that Lori used to reference," she said.

"What's a Concordance?" Rashanda asked.

"It's the index in the back of a Bible that helps guide you to scripture. It's like a roadmap for the Bible, so I looked under the word body, and it lists all the scriptures that have the word body in them with a link to the phrase," she explained. "It's in 1 Corinthians chapter six, verse nineteen. I'll read it," she offered. "Do you not know that your body is a temple of the Holy Spirit, who is in you, whom you have received from God?" she read. "You are not your own; you were bought at a price. Therefore honor God with your body," she finished. "The passage before that one explains that our bodies are not meant for sexual immorality," she explained. "You guys should read the sixth chapter of 1 Corinthians. It really helps you value your body as something special."

"Since when did you become such a biblical scholar, Grace?" Maria asked.

Grace shrugged casually. "After Lori's funeral, I just started reading and studying it more and I really enjoyed it," she confessed. "Before Lori's funeral, I'd never really opened a Bible," she admitted. "But I like reading it now. It relaxes me."

"Well, I'm glad you didn't let Todd the creep destroy your temple," Rashanda stated.

"Amen to that," Teenie concurred. "And I'm glad you shared that one with us, Maria. We have to learn from each other," she reminded. "We have to talk about our experiences so we know how to handle stuff," she coached. "Since we have six tips, let's go for an even ten. Here's what we have so far," she read.

Don't cry in front of him, or try hard not to cry. Cry later.
Don't beg him not to break-up with you.
Make him explain why he's breaking up with you.
You can't be friends with a guy who dumps you. Maybe later, but not initially.
Do NOT offer to "do it" to prevent a break-up. Your body is a temple!!!! Remember our pact!
Thank him for the festivities.

"These are all great, but we can't just leave it at six," Teenie said. "We need to round it out to an even ten. The top ten things to do when being dumped," she laughed. "We only need four more," she reminded. "Think of something else, ladies."

"That's your obsessive compulsive disorder kicking in again," Rashanda laughed. "If six is all we got, six is enough," she stated.

The girls stared at each other silently. "I can't think of anything else, Teenie," Maria shrugged.

"What about don't take his calls for awhile," Justine suggested.

"Perfect!" Teenie squealed. "After he dumps you, why should you take his stupid calls? He can talk to the answering machine. Good one, Justine!" she encouraged. "We only need three more ladies, come on, think!"

"Wear something cute?" Grace suggested in the form of a question.

"But of course! And I know our girl Maria had on something cute, right?" Teenie asked Maria pointedly.

"Come on," Maria smiled. "I may have broken rule number one and cried, and I may look like ten miles of bad road today, but you know I never leave the house unless I'm looking fly," she stated, a familiar edge back in her voice. "You know my rule. 'Always leave the house looking good. No excuses,'" she recited.

Teenie scribbled frantically. "Well, let's add it to the list anyway. Number eight will be: always look cute when you're with your boyfriend in case he's planning to dump you."

"How about don't kiss him goodbye?" Rashanda asked. "Once he ends the relationship, there's no more affection exchanged," she suggested.

"Love it!" Teenie beamed.

"Won't that be hard to do?" Justine asked. "You can't just

turn off your feelings just because his feelings have changed," she suggested.

"She makes a good point, Teenie," Maria advised.

"We'll just have to fake it. Just be strong and fight the urge to show him any signs of affection. Be the Ice Princess," Teenie advised. "One more, ladies. One more gets us to ten," she urged.

"Leave first," Grace offered. "After a guy dumps you, you should leave before he asks you to leave," she finished.

"Grace, you're a genius," Teenie squealed. "Get your stuff and get outta there as quickly as you can," she scribbled.

"And if he dumps you in your house walk him to the door as fast as you can," Grace continued.

Teenie scribbled in her notebook quickly. "We did it, ladies!" she beamed. "We have a top ten list of things to do when a guy dumps us," she boasted. "I'll read the last four that I wrote:"

After a break-up, don't take his calls for awhile.

Always look cute when you're with your boyfriend in case he's planning to dump you.

Once he dumps you, don't be affectionate with him. Turn into the Ice Princess.

Leave quickly. Don't give him the satisfaction of asking you to leave or him walking away first.

"What if he dumps you in a restaurant or a public place?" Rashanda asked. "Or what if you're sitting in his car when he dumps you?" she continued. "You can't very well exit if he's driving," she reminded. "He's in control."

"Well, you just ask him to take you home," Maria coached. "Don't say another word to him until he takes you home. Just give him the silent treatment," Maria advised. "That'll drive him crazy because he won't know what you're thinking."

"Don't make a scene," Justine advised. "In fact, maybe we should make that one number eleven."

"We are not trying to send Teenie into a tizzy fit," Rashanda teased. "You know she needs balance and order. We can just add don't make a scene to number one," she suggested.

"Thanks, Rashanda. You know how I am," Teenie smiled. "I'll scribble 'don't make a scene' at the end of number one. It fits anyway," she observed. "In general, crying invites a scene so don't cry and don't make a scene are compatible."

Maria moved Teenie's feet from beneath her and stood, stretching her arms into the air and slowly bending at the waist to touch her toes. Without bending her knees, she spread her palms flat at her feet and cracked her knuckles. "Aaah, that felt good," she said. "Man, I wish we'd created this list sooner. But at least now we'll have something to reference the next time someone dumps us," she yawned. "Other than needing a nap, I'm actually feeling better," she smiled. "Talking with you guys always cheers me up. Don't get me wrong, I still want to scratch Todd's face for playing break-up theme music," she corrected. "But I feel a lot better. Maria tucked her nose under her armpit and inhaled. "Phew! I need a shower," she frowned. "Why didn't you guys tell me that I was funky?" she asked.

"I thought you knew, Bride of Frankenstein," Teenie laughed.

"Ha, ha, Teenie," Maria smirked walking to her armoire and taking out panties and a bra before fumbling in her closet and pulling out a pair of jeans and a fresh shirt. "I'm going to take a shower."

"Don't take one of your usual thirty minute steam showers, Maria!" Teenie ordered. "It stopped raining now so let's do something," she suggested.

Flicking her wrist at Teenie, Maria rolled her eyes. "I'll be quick. I'm not going to wash my hair, so I won't be in there all day," she said. "Plus, I really need some fresh air. Just paint your nails to kill some time. It looks like you've been clawing your way out of a grave with those jagged cuticles, Tanisha Denise," she laughed walking through the door.

"By the way," she leaned in from the hallway twirling a strand of her hair. "We've been so busy with my Todd drama, that I haven't heard the latest update on your relationships, guys," she said. "I know Rashanda and Ian are still on cloud nine because I see her staring at that damn promise ring every chance she gets," she laughed. "But when I get out of the shower I want to hear the updates on Justine and AM first," she paused. "And then I want to hear what's going on with your David Barton, Glen Horton, Brian Kraft love triangle, little miss, Teenie the two timer," Maria mocked. "Or should I say three timer?" she laughed walking out of the room with her clothes before peeking her head around the corner once more. "I'm starving. Let's go out for pizza," she suggested. "When your girlfriend gets dumped by her boyfriend, her friends should treat her to pizza to eat away her sorrows," Maria advised. "Maybe we should add that to the list too," she finished. "By the way, since you're loaded now, little miss trust fund, you can treat, Grace," Maria winked.

Chapter 23

A Spoonful of Sugar

The dimly lit restaurant still smelled of beer and cigarettes. The red leather booths displayed the initials of love struck teenagers, their relationships now a bad dream. Missing ceiling tiles revealed the exposed wiring. Orange cone barricades encircled a large, gray bucket that once carried salt pellets. The occasional drip of rain fell into the bucket in a helter skelter pattern. The red carpet was stained a dark maroon beneath the bucket. The restaurant was empty save a young family who munched on their food, a toddler trying desperately to escape from the confines of the wooden high chair. The handsome waiter smiled as he jotted down their order, the flush moving through his cheeks like a wave as he glanced at her repeatedly. The other girls giggled knowingly.

"She's so clueless," Rashanda whispered.

"If I gave her a quarter, she wouldn't know how to buy a clue," Justine replied.

"So that's one extra large pizza with half sausage and mushroom, and the other half is pepperoni and green pepper," he replied. "And a pitcher of root beer," he added staring at Grace. "Does that complete your order?" he asked.

"That should do us," Maria answered. "So, how do you like River North?" Maria asked. "I'm Maria Wesley by the way. We have third period study hall together, Dell," she smiled as she read his nametag.

"Oh, hi. I thought you looked familiar," Dell replied nervously, dropping his pencil to the floor. Bending to retrieve it, he bumped his head on the table.

"Are you okay?" Maria laughed.

"I'm fine, it's cool. I mean River North is cool," he corrected. "My family just moved here from Sugarland, Texas, so it's different than Texas," Dell offered, his southern drawl heavy and slow. "But it's been cool so far," he finished.

"Your dad played for the Dallas Cowboys, right?" Maria asked. "My mom's boyfriend mentioned that your family moved to the area."

"Yeah. My old man just retired from the Cowboys," he offered. "He's been in the NFL for about fifteen years, so my mom told him that was enough," he said. "She told him to get out before he got hurt. She's from Chicago so she wanted to be closer to her family. He's going to do some special teams coaching with the Bears," he explained. "My dad bought this restaurant to give him something to do during the off season," he chuckled nervously. "We're remodeling now, so sorry that it's such a mess," he directed toward Grace. "The roof leaks, and the booths need to be replaced, but the food is good," he smiled. "I'm show not looking forward to the winters up north," he continued. "Folks told me that y'all get a lot of snow. But it's been a long time since I've seen snow in person, so I'm looking forward to at least seeing it," he finished.

"You never traveled to any of your dad's football games up north?" Maria asked.

"Naw, my mom only allowed us to go to the home games. The only away games we could attend was ones where we could be back home in under two hours," he explained. "She was always scared that we'd get stuck in a snowstorm and wouldn't be able to make it home and go to school on Monday," he groaned. "Sometimes she'd let us travel to the Monday night football games, cause those are always special. But if the Monday night game was in Chicago, we couldn't go cause my mama has memories of some big blizzard that shut the city down," he laughed. "I can't wait for my first blizzard experience," he said.

"Trust me, it's overrated," Teenie replied. "I'm Tanisha Carlson by the way, but everybody calls me Teenie," she explained. "And this is Rashanda Jordan, Justine Wellington and that's Grace Dudley," she pointed.

Grace smiled softly, lowering her head and playing with the straw in her hand.

"I've been running my mouth like a chucklehead and didn't bother to introduce myself proper. I'm Dell Jenkins," he offered. "My real name is Wardell, but everybody calls me Dell," he explained, tapping his order pad nervously on the table, his eyes darting back and forth to Grace.

"It's nice to meet you, Dell," Rashanda grinned.

"I'll go get your pitcher of root beer," he offered before spinning on his heels and walking into the kitchen.

"He's fine," Teenie whistled.

"You got that right," Justine agreed. "If I weren't so knee deep into AM, I might have to pull out my flirty girl card," she teased. "But I think Dell only had eyes for Grace," she shared.

The straw now bent into quarters, Grace blushed. "He did not," she defended. "He was just being friendly."

Maria leaned into the booth and gripped both of Grace's hands. "Dell couldn't take his eyes off of you, Grace," Maria shared.

"He must smell boyfriend scent on the rest of us, because his radar was locked on you like a missile."

"Really?" Grace asked.

"Really," Teenie agreed.

"Here's what you should do," Maria offered as though reading Grace's mind. "When he comes back, smile at him a lot and see if he smiles back," she coached. "And after you pay the bill, because you are treating, trust fund," she reminded. "Leave something at the table so you have a reason to come back and talk to him while we wait outside," she finished.

"What should I leave at the table?" Grace asked confused.

"Anything," Justine said. "Pull out your lip gloss and just leave it on the table by the window," she suggested.

"But I love this lip gloss," Grace protested.

"You'll get it back, silly," Teenie laughed. "Just leave it, go outside with us and walk back in to retrieve it so you can talk to him."

"He probably won't say anything to you around us because most boys don't want to risk rejection in front of a group of girls," Rashanda shared. "Just leave your lip gloss on the table to give him a chance to talk to you alone."

"Here he comes," Maria whispered. She nudged Grace under the table and smiled at her, watching as she slowly lifted her head and smiled softly at Dell, casually combing her fingers through her long, strawberry blonde hair.

Rashanda giggled as Dell's eyes widened and his jaw fell slack. His eyes locked on Grace's face, he returned her smile with a wide grin. Rashanda pretended to cough to hide the laughter. "I must have a tickle in my throat," she coughed into her hand. "Thanks for the root beer, Dell," she offered.

The girls watched as he walked down the hall. "Even his walk is cool," Teenie observed. "I love guys who have a little swagger in their step."

"Reel him in Grace, you have him on the hook," Maria laughed. "He's like putty in your hands right now. Running your fingers through your hair was brilliant! I thought he was going to faint," she laughed.

Her posture straightened, Grace pulled her compact mirror from her purse and applied lip gloss, carefully finger combing her long hair once again.

"So what does it feel like to be worth that kind of money, Grace?" Maria asked.

"Maria! You're not supposed to ask someone that," Teenie scolded.

"Why not? You can ask any question you want, but the person doesn't have to answer it," she laughed. "Well?" she asked. "How does it feel to be wealthy?"

Grace shrugged her shoulders casually. "It feels the same," she grinned. "The only difference is that my allowance is a lot bigger," she laughed. "And now my parents aren't stressing about how to pay for my college education. They also said that I can get a car when I graduate from high school, so I'm excited about that."

"That's cool!" Teenie squealed. "What kind of car do you think you'll get?" she asked.

"I don't know," she shrugged.

"Get a BMW," Teenie suggested. "I loved driving David's mom's Beemer."

"I was thinking more like a Volkswagen convertible or a Saab. I love the little sporty Saab convertible, it looks like a referee's whistle," she smiled. "But we'll see. I can't touch the bulk of the money until I'm twenty-four and only if I've finished college. That's one of the stipulations. I have to finish college at an accredited four year institution by the time I'm twenty-four years old or the money goes into my grandparents' charitable trust," she explained. "There's also a clause in the will that reads that if I have a baby before I finish college, unless I'm married, my inheritance goes to charity too," she said. "But if I've finished college, and I'm at least twenty-two years old and have a baby, I get to keep the inheritance even if I'm not married," she finished.

"That's a pretty strict rule," Rashanda blurted. "But I guess it's their wealth so they can attach any type of stipulations on it that they want, and rich people often do some weird stuff," Rashanda whistled. "How did Chip find out that you stood to inherit their estate?" she asked. "I know you explained this to the crew, but I was with Ian that day so I wanna hear it for myself."

"Well," Grace paused. "When we visited my grandparents' house in Wilmette, the people that lived there now gave him the name of the law firm that handled the estate sale," Grace shared. "They were really nice and let us walk around the house and tour it," she continued. "I was really shocked, but when my parents explained that they used to live there, and that I was the prior owner's granddaughter, the new owners welcomed us with open arms," she shrugged. "The house was huge and had these beautiful views of Lake Michigan. In fact, the end of the backyard was Lake Michigan," she described. "There were these steps that led to a private beach area. My mom said that the house really hadn't changed much other than the kitchen and bathrooms which were renovated, but the rest of the house was pretty much the same as she remembered. She showed me my mom's room and everything," Grace smiled.

"Was that spooky, walking around the house where your mother grew up?" Teenie asked.

"Not really," Grace shrugged. "My parents were there, and Justine and Chip, so it just felt like we were touring a museum where people live," she said. "My parents kept making comments about a lot of things that they remembered, like some of the window treatments that hadn't been replaced and the details in the woodwork. Stuff like that," she said. "There was an apartment above the garage, and that's where my parents lived when they worked there," she explained. "There was also a third floor maid's room that was like a small apartment too," she shared. "It was a one bedroom apartment that had a living room, bathroom and bedroom. I asked my mom why they didn't stay up there, and she told me that she preferred to be above the garage because it was a larger apartment and it gave them more privacy," she finished. "Plus, she told me that the maid lived in that room."

"They had a full time maid too?" Teenie asked.

"Yup," Grace shrugged. "They were really wealthy and had a staff of people to do everything. My mom was the nanny and cook, my dad was their chauffeur. They also had a maid, a gardener, a pool boy," she rattled. "They had someone to do everything for them," she finished.

"I've never been inside a house that big in my life," Justine gushed. "It was like touring a little castle. And the thing is, their house wasn't even one of the largest ones on the block," she shared. "Some of the other houses were twice as large as the Moore place," she finished.

"Egads, Batman! I wonder how much it costs to heat a house that size?" Teenie asked. "And sitting right on Lake Michigan like that, it probably gets really cold in the winter," she observed.

"Only you would even think of that, Teenie," Maria chuckled. "Rich people don't care about heating bills," she said.

"Well, heat isn't free," Teenie explained. "And I'm always cold, so if I lived in a house that large, we'd have to be able to afford to heat it to at least seventy two degrees during the winter months," she explained.

Maria gently whacked Teenie upside the back of her head. "Let her finish her story, Ebenezer Scrooge."

Justine shook her head at Teenie's pragmatism. "I should have known that Chip was up to something because while we were walking around taking the tour, I noticed that he stayed downstairs talking to the owner and then when we left, the husband gave Chip a business card," Justine added.

"I saw that too," Grace commented. "And I just thought he was getting their number to send them a thank you card for being so kind and allowing us to tour the house," she paused. "But it turns out that it was a business card for the law firm who handled the estate sale when my grandparents died."

"How often do you talk to Chip now?" Teenie asked.

"We talk every weekend, and we still write letters about once a week," Grace smiled. "It's fun getting to know him. He's really cool."

"So now you have two dads," Maria grinned widely.

"I guess I do," she considered. "But Chip is more like a favorite uncle," she corrected. "Anyway, he told me later that he called the law firm and spoke with a trust and estate planning partner who pulled my grandparents' file and confirmed that there was a provision in their will for their grandchild," Grace smiled. "He called to talk to my parents one night and explained what he'd learned," she paused. "That Monday, my parents and I went downtown and met with the lawyers involved," she sighed. "We had to sign a bunch of papers and affidavits, and we had to show my birth certificate to prove that I was in fact Lydia Moore's child. Fortunately, my mother had a copy of my birth mother's birth certificate in a file, so once we produced that, everything moved really quickly," she said. "Chip told me that if there hadn't been a provision in their will for me or my mother to inherit anything, he wouldn't have even mentioned that he researched it."

"Wow!" Teenie smiled. "Why didn't your parents think to do that?" she asked.

Grace twirled her straw and took a sip from her soda. "My parents are older, and they don't even have their high school diploma," she shrugged. "So it never occurred to them that there might be a legal way for me to receive a part of my grandparents' estate. They never considered it," she said. "They didn't grow up with money, they don't understand estate planning law," she shrugged. "At first, they felt really bad for not thinking to look into this on their own," Grace admitted. "But I assured them that I didn't miss out on anything all these years. They've provided a wonderful life for me, and now I can use some of my inheritance to provide for them."

"What a great sentiment," Rashanda said.

"And now you're loaded," Maria whistled. "Exactly how loaded are you, by the way?"

Grace giggled. "Let's just say that I'll never have to work for money," she smiled. "The banker at The Northern Trust who manages my trust fund is really nice and told me that I'll be able to live an 'exceptional quality of life' on the interest alone," Grace said, using her fingers to make quotation marks. "I'm not sure what an exceptional quality of life is," she laughed. "But I'll take her word for it. My parents' house is already paid for, and so is their car, so they don't need anything, and they don't want me spending my money on them, but I'm going to take them to Europe since my mother has always wanted to see the Eiffel Tower," she said. "But other than that and buying a car when I graduate next year, I don't see anything really changing."

"We're going to make sure you start dressing better," Maria laughed. "We aren't going to blow all of your money on clothes, but we'll add a few key, classic pieces to your closet, especially so you're ready to start dating Dell, the waiter," she teased. "And if you need some tips on how to live an exceptional life, maybe you can talk to one of Teenie's suitors since at least two of them lead privileged, exceptional lives," Maria shared. "Your turn, Teenie. What's up with you and your three boys?"

Teenie laughed nervously. "It's Justine's turn to share now," she stalled. "We need to hear about Justine and AM first," she reminded.

"No news there," Justine said. "AM has agreed to apply to medical schools wherever I get accepted for undergrad," she replied. "His number one choice is still Harvard, so I'm applying to a few schools in Massachusetts," she said. "And he's also applying to medical schools in the Midwest to cover his bases," she continued.

"Do you really think you'll still be dating AM after next year, Justine?" Teenie asked as Dell approached the table, carefully balancing two pizzas on a large tray. His gaze shifted to Grace as he moved the pepper and cheese dispensers from the center and placed the pizzas in their place.

"Would you like me to slice the pizza in triangles or squares, ladies?" he smiled.

"Squares," the girls said simultaneously giggling at their

unison response.

"What's so funny?" Dell asked nervously. "Is my fly undone or do I have a bat in the cave?" he asked.

"We're just laughing at how alike we are," Maria shared. "We often finish each other's sentences."

Dell pulled a pizza slicer from his apron pocket and expertly sliced the pizzas into squares. "I forgot to bring out your complimentary garlic toast," he remembered. "I'm supposed to bring that out before the food," he groaned. "It's a new recipe so we're testing it on our customers," he explained. "I'll be right back with that," he winked at Grace.

"Okay, did you see that?" Rashanda asked.

"I did," Grace smiled. "He winked at me," she blushed.

"He seems less nervous than he did when we first arrived," Justine announced. "But to answer your question, Teenie, I really hope that AM and I are still together next year," she sighed. "I really like him."

"I know you do," Teenie smiled. "I just don't want you to get too strung out about your first boyfriend and then if you get your heart broken, you won't have a back-up plan," she coached. "At least Maria has been dating Dante while Todd was at school, so she's not completely crushed about their break-up," she finished, reaching for a pizza square. "There aren't any boys at North Prep that you want to date just to get some more dating experience?" she quizzed.

"Not really," Justine shared. "Besides, Rashanda's parents were high school sweethearts and they're still married," she reminded.

"That's true," Rashanda agreed.

"How's your mom doing these days, Rashanda?" Grace asked. "She's done with her chemotherapy now, right?"

"She is. She's really doing well. Her hair has started to grow back, and she's gone back to work," Rashanda shared. "My mom was such a trooper through the whole chemotherapy, radiation treatments," she said. "We switched her to an organic diet and she even tried the acupuncture sessions that I recommended. I was blown away," Rashanda offered. "She fought really hard and now the cancer is in remission, so we're just praying that she remains cancer free." Rashanda crossed her fingers on both hands and raised them over her head. "And now my mother has turned into a health nut," she laughed.

"Was there a history of breast cancer in your family?" Teenie asked.

"Not that I'm aware of," Rashanda replied. "But my mom did smoke for a few years before I was born. Everybody smoked back then, but the doctors said that smoking usually results in lung cancer, not breast cancer. Ian said that it's difficult to find a cause for breast cancer," she finished. "Our prayer is that she remains cancer free."

"Amen to that," Teenie said. "Let's all add that to our prayer list."

"Would you like me to bring you another root beer?" Dell asked.

"And since I was delayed in bringing out the complimentary garlic bread, your second pitcher of root beer is on the house," he grinned widely, this time staring directly at Grace, all hints of nervousness long gone. "How's the pizza?" he asked.

"It's delicious," Grace smiled fingering the sugar packets.

"I hope you're not planning to eat any sugar, because you look sweet enough already," he teased. "Do you come here often?" Dell asked.

"Not really," Grace giggled. "But I'll have to start coming more often now that I've met you," she replied sweetly

The other girls suppressed the giggles and stared at each other, their eyes bulging widely. Maria and Teenie shared shocked glances as their heads followed the flirting volley unfolding before their eyes.

"Is that right?" Dell asked. "Well, I'll have to give you a reason to come back besides the pizza," he grinned.

"That works for me," Grace replied as he sauntered away, his gait as smooth as the wind; the wink over his shoulder an exclamation point for the unassuming, new heiress.

"You little flirty tart," Maria whispered when Dell was out of ear shot. "You handled that like a professional flirt," she squealed. "I felt like I was watching a mini me at work," she boasted. "I'm so proud of you! I didn't know you had it in you," she offered, bumping Grace's shoulder lightly.

Grace poured herself a glass of root beer. "Well, hanging out with you babes all these years," she paused. "If I haven't learned to flirt by now, shame on me," she laughed. "Remember, I'm in the same grade as you guys, but I'm a year younger so it takes me a little longer to catch on," she reminded. "But he is too cute for words," she exhaled. "I'm definitely giving him my number. Put a piece of the sausage and mushroom on my plate, Rashanda," Grace instructed.

Teenie raised her eyebrow at Grace. "Let's make sure we use your powers for good and not evil, little miss flirty girl," Teenie teased. "You don't want to turn into a mini Maria overnight," she laughed. "Pace yourself."

"Don't hate the player, hate the game," Maria laughed, snapping her finger in Teenie's face. "I didn't make the rules, I just mastered them. And slow down on that pizza, Grace," she cautioned. "Now that you have snared a man, you need to watch what you feed your girlish figure."

"Ignore her, Grace," Teenie encouraged. "Just eat comfort food in moderation, and you'll be fine. You're in great shape."

"Teenie's right, Grace. And I'm glad you're feeling better, Maria," Rashanda said nudging Maria's shoulder.

Maria's sigh was long and loud. "Don't get me wrong," she blurted, her hands in the surrender pose. "My heart feels like it's been shred into a thousand tiny pieces, and I'm still pissed at Todd, but life will go on," Maria sighed again. "I got dumped. Whattaya gonna do?"

"Remember, boys are like buses, Maria. You miss one bus, and another bus will be along shortly," Teenie reminded gently as she patted Maria's hand.

"Yeah, yeah, whatever. Tell that to my broken heart. Your turn, Teenie," Maria brightened. "What's up with you and your boys? And don't be stalling for time by chewing the food in your mouth twenty times like you do when you don't want to share," Maria laughed. "I'm on to that trick, girlfriend." Her eyes roamed the nearly empty parking lot. "And look, it's started to rain again so we have all day. Spill it, chick!" Maria ordered.

Chapter 24

Take a Chance

Nestled in the large bed, the girls snuggled closely, their toes intertwined beneath the heavy comforter. "Tell us another story," she squealed. "And tell us a long one this time. The last story was too quick," she whined, twirling her long hair around her thin finger.

"Yeah, tell us a story, Mom," her twin sister repeated. "I love hearing your stories," she grinned, her tongue caressing the hole from her newly lost tooth. "Will the tooth fairy come tonight for sure, Mom?" she asked.

"Absolutely, sweetie. The tooth fairy never misses you two nights in a row," Mom explained. "But sometimes the tooth fairy has so many people to visit that it takes two nights to get to everyone," she paused. "And since you lost your tooth after three o'clock in the afternoon that means that the tooth fairy might have to come on the second day," she explained quickly.

"How do you know all of this?" Portia asked seriously, toying with her mother's large diamond.

"It's uh, it's in the tooth fairy handbook that you read when you're a mom," she stammered smoothing the comforter nervously, and staring lovingly at her daughter's small hands. She grinned as her daughter's soft fingers gently caressed the sizable emerald cut diamond ring that was now tight on her fat finger. The platinum band no longer swiveled loosely to the left or to the right, serving as her personal weight management tool, her fitness level measured by the looseness of her rings. Now the beautiful adornment sat motionless like a department store mannequin. The last time she'd tried to remove it, she'd needed baby oil to wiggle it from its perch. "What's the theme for tonight's tale?" she asked settling her head against the pillows resting on the headboard. Time to lay off the sodium.

"Tell us how you met Dad again," Portia suggested.

"You've heard that story several times," she reminded. "You guys are just stalling because you don't want to go to bed," she laughed. "I'm so on to you both," the young mom said, tickling the little frames nestled on either side of her.

"Please, Mom," Jeniece pleaded. "I love hearing that story," she whined. "But start at the part where you finally decided to date him," she coached.

Portia tossed a pillow at Jeniece's head. "Not that part, monkey breath. I want to hear how mom met Dad," she whined. "I love that story. Tell the black diamond story, Mom," Portia whined. "Pleeeaaassse," she begged.

"The black diamond story takes too long, stupid," Jeniece retorted, wiggling the loose bottom tooth in the front of her mouth. "We've heard that story too many times."

"Eleanor Jeniece!" Mom shrieked. "You know that stupid is a bad word in our house! You apologize to your sister right now!" she scolded.

"I'm sorry for calling you, stupid, Portia," Jeniece said softly. "And I love you."

"Jeniece, your tooth will probably fall out in a few days,"

Mom assured sweetly. "The tooth fairy isn't going to run out of money so you don't have to wiggle your tooth out tonight," she explained. "And Portia Jane, don't call your sister 'monkey breath,'" she reprimanded. "I heard that. And you know that I don't like it when you call each other names," she paused. "You are sisters, and you're twins, for goodness sake. You two are supposed to love each other unconditionally. No matter what happens, I want you two to be close," she smiled. "Now if the two of you can't behave we don't have to have a story," she threatened halfheartedly. "My back is killing me anyway," Mom shared, shifting her weight against the pillow. "If you're not going to get along nicely, I'll put you to bed without a story and I'll take a nice, hot bath," she threatened.

"Are we having a boy baby or a girl baby?" Jeniece asked, gently rubbing her mother's round belly.

"We don't know," Mom shrugged. "Your dad and I want to be surprised."

"Oh, come on, Mom," Portia whined. "Tori's mom has a baby in her belly and she found out that it was a girl. Why can't you find out? Are you too old to find out?"

She laughed at her daughter's innocence. "No. I'm only twenty-seven years old, Portia-Smortia," Mom giggled. "I'm not too old to find out, we just don't want to find out, sweetie," she explained. "Your dad and I didn't find out with you," she reminded. Her gaze was soft and reminiscent. "It's fun being surprised," she shrugged. "There are so few surprises in this world nowadays that not knowing the sex of God's gift is a great surprise," she paused. "We just want a healthy baby. That's all we're praying for," she finished, stroking her belly lovingly. "Now, do you want a story or not?" she asked.

"Story!" the twins stated in unison. "And start at the part

where you and Dad started dating, not when you met," Jeniece reminded.

Holding her index finger in the air and smoothing their long hair, Mom grinned. "Before I tell you how I started dating your dad, I have to share what happened to the other guys that were courting me," she explained.

"Does Dad know that you had another boyfriend?" Portia asked, her face pinched into a concerned scowl.

"Portia!" Jeniece yelled. "Of course Dad knows that she had another boyfriend, Mom was married to our dad before she married our new dad, genius," she scolded. "Is it okay to call her genius, Mom?" Jeniece asked sheepishly.

Teenie stared at her look alike disapprovingly. "Eleanor Jeniece, that's pushing it and you know it," she scolded. "I know that you don't mean that Portia's a genius in a nice way," she frowned. "And yes, Portia, your dad knows that I had another boyfriend. He had another girlfriend before he met me," Teenie sighed. "Now stop asking questions and listen, because no matter where I am in the story," she paused dramatically. "It's lights out at nine o'clock sharp!" she reminded. Teenie blew the air from her cheeks and let her mind drift back to the summer after her senior year in high school.

∞)(∞

Maria's elbows rested on the table, her hands underneath her chin. "We're waiting, Miss Thang," she teased. "Your love life saga is better than All My Children. Spill it!"

"I don't want to just start talking," Teenie protested. "Ask me some questions or something. Give me some direction so I don't just start rambling aimlessly," she suggested, taking another bite from the lukewarm pizza.

"How's your 'friendship' with David Barton?" Rashanda asked, her fingers serving as quotation marks. "Are you still stringing him along?" she laughed.

Balling her napkin, Teenie tossed it at Rashanda's face, watching as the napkin landed in the empty root beer pitcher. "I am not stringing him along," she protested. "David and I are still friends," she reminded.

"Is he still dating that Patty chick?" Maria asked.

"Well, not anymore," she offered. "Patty interned for some Congressman in D.C. and now she's engaged to him. David thinks she'll probably be married the day after she graduates from Howard and pregnant within a year," Teenie laughed. "The Congressman is in his late twenties and he's supposed to be the next rising star on the Hill."

"What's the Hill?" Grace asked.

"Capitol Hill," Rashanda and Maria replied in unison.

"Was David pissed that she got engaged so quickly?" Grace asked.

"He was relieved," Teenie said. "Patty was pressuring David to give her an engagement ring or at least a promise ring," she shared. "Did I tell you guys that Patty actually took me shopping with her one afternoon and showed me the type of ring that she wanted in case David asked me my opinion?" she laughed.

"So that dingy girl still believed that you were like a little sister to David?" Maria asked. "She's clueless."

Teenie rolled her eyes at Maria. "I think she suspected that he liked me as more than a friend when he was home for Christmas break and David told her that he couldn't go to her family's New Year's Eve party because he and I planned to watch Alfred Hitchcock movies at his house," she smiled. "Patty stopped calling me after that."

"Keep your friends close and your enemies closer," Rashanda quoted. "Some famous philosopher said that, and it's so true. Patty probably knew that David liked you, which is why she tried to make you her best friend," she laughed. "She knew you were the competition."

"I was not her competition. David and I are just friends," Tanisha groaned. "How many times do I have to say that?"

"Run that line on someone else, chick," Maria laughed with her hand in Teenie's face. "So just to recap, David's still pining away for you like a little puppy dog," she panted, her hands now under her chin in the pant position. "But he's a junior in college now, Teenie," Maria reminded. "He's not going to wait around for you forever, girlfriend," she warned. "Is he pre-med or pre-law now?"

"He's pre-med," Teenie said. "He's studying for his MCAT now."

"You can study for that?" Justine said. "AM isn't studying for it."

"AM is only a sophomore, plus he was accepted to Northwestern's six year med program like Ian was," Rashanda reminded. "So if he stays at NU, he won't need to take the MCAT, but if he transfers to another school, he'll probably start prepping for it in a few months."

"He's busy studying so I don't see David that much these days," Tanisha interrupted. "His parents are so excited that he's planning to go into their profession that they've offered to buy him a condominium wherever he gets accepted to medical school," she shared.

"Did any of his siblings go into the family business?" Maria asked.

"His sister is in her last year of residency at Rush Presbyterian," Teenie explained. "She's planning to be an OB-GYN like her dad. His sister is really nice," she added.

"You met his sister?" Grace asked.

"I met his whole family," Teenie said. "I just met them a few weeks ago," she trailed.

The girls stared at her blankly. "Why didn't you tell us that you met his parents, chick?" Maria asked.

"I just forgot I guess," Teenie stammered. "David picked me up from work one day and told me that he just needed to run into his house to get something," she paused. "So I go inside with him so I can pet Mr. Belvedere, and his whole family is there. His mother was expecting me," Teenie explained.

"What were they doing?" Rashanda asked.

"They were just chilling by the pool. His father was swimming laps, and his grandmother was knitting. His dad's mother moved in with them a few months ago," she explained.

"I never met Todd's parents," Maria blurted. "Were David's parents nice to you?" she asked softly.

Tanisha bit her bottom lip, her eyes softened toward Maria. "They were really nice. His mom hugged me as soon as she saw me," she blushed. "And they kept telling me how pretty I was," she said softly. "They made me feel very welcome. But I was mad at David because I wasn't prepared to meet his family," she whined. "If I'd known that he was taking me over there after work I would have worn something cuter that day or at least brought a change of clothes," she sighed. "And I would have brought a hostess gift for his mother or baked some cookies or something," she trailed.

"I'm sure you looked fine, Teenie," Rashanda assured. "Did you send a thank you note later?"

"Of course I did," Teenie said. "So at least his mother knows that I have home training."

"Why didn't he just tell you that he was taking you to meet his parents?" Justine asked.

Slouched in her seat, her back curved like the letter C, her chin almost resting on the table, Maria's voice was monotone. "Because Teenie has a list of rules and would have protested," Maria groaned. "I don't want to meet your parents, David," she mocked in falsetto. "They'll get the wrong idea. They'll think we're boyfriend and girlfriend."

Sticking out her tongue, Teenie rolled her eyes at Maria. "Well, it's true. They kept treating me like I was his girlfriend," she defended.

"Do you think that they liked you?" Grace asked.

"I think so," Teenie smiled. "At first they thought that I was at Georgetown with David," she paused. "So they were surprised when I told them that I'd be a freshman at Yale in the fall," she said. "They thought that I was older than I am."

"I can't believe that we'll be separated in a few months," Rashanda whined, her eyes panning the booth. "Teenie will be at Yale, Maria will be at the University of Pennsylvania, Grace will be at the University of Illinois," she paused. "And Justine will be chasing AM around the globe," she laughed.

"Look who's talking," Justine teased. "I'm going to take classes at DePaul for now, and then apply to Howard next semester," she reminded. "If I get accepted at Howard, AM will transfer to Johns Hopkins for medical school," she added. "Don't make me feel bad about chasing my beau when you'll be at Northwestern watching Ian's every move like a security guard, Rashanda."

"Exactly," Rashanda agreed. "Having the time of my life,"

she grinned staring lovingly at her promise ring. "Hail to thee Northwestern!" she sang.

"You already know the school song?" Teenie laughed. "You're whipped."

"So you're going to go to a historically black college that will have a campus full of fine, smart, black men, and you'll have a white boyfriend," Maria stated.

Justine glared at Maria harshly. "And you have a problem with that?" she asked.

"No problem at all," Maria replied. "I was just making a point. Stop changing the subject, ladies. The spotlight is still on Teenie," she reminded. "So it sounds like there's no update on David Barton other than he's busy studying for his MCAT and you're still stringing him along like a kite," Maria summarized. "Has he at least tried to kiss you yet?"

This time, the look was more a glare than a stare. Her eyes slanted, Teenie balled her fist and waved it in Maria's face. "Well, actually, there is something else," she shared.

"What?" Rashanda asked. "You finally kissed him?"

"No. We still haven't kissed," Teenie corrected. "But we set a date."

"Set a date for what?" Maria asked gruffly, her head now resting on the table like a guillotine.

Tanisha closed her eyes and scrunched her face into a silly grin. "You guys have to promise not to share this with anyone," she cautioned.

"Who would we tell, Teenie?" Rashanda asked. "Every person that we would tell is sitting at this table," she laughed.

"Set a date for what?" Maria repeated, her posture straightening from curiosity.

"We set a date for our first kiss," Teenie blushed.

"That is the dumbest thing that I've ever heard before," Maria groaned slamming her back into the booth. "A kiss should be spontaneous, not scheduled, Teenie."

"I think it's romantic," Justine smiled.

"Me too," Grace agreed.

"Me three," Rashanda echoed. "When's the date?"

"New Year's Eve," Teenie whispered.

"Whose dumb idea was that?" Maria asked. "Let me guess. It must have been yours because that sounds like something that you'd suggest, Teenie."

"Actually, it was David's idea," Teenie corrected.

The girls stared at each other curiously. Rashanda spoke for the group. "How did this come about, Teenie?" she asked.

"He said that we've been friends for four years now and that he's willing to wait until winter break of my freshman year of college," she paused. "And if I haven't decided that I want to be his girlfriend by then, he's going to move on and stop courting me," she said softly.

"Good for him," Maria cheered. "You've been leading him on long enough," she laughed. "Enough is enough."

"Be quiet, Maria," Rashanda said. "How do you feel about that, Teenie?" she asked softly.

"I don't know," Teenie exhaled. "It's kind of an ultimatum, but I guess I don't blame him," she shrugged. "He has a lot on his plate with his medical school applications and MCAT studies," she shared.

"Why did he choose New Year's Eve?" Grace asked reaching for another slice of pizza.

"David said that by winter break I will have met the Yale

roster of available talent, or nerds, as he called them," she chuckled. "He said that by then I should be ready to start a relationship with him."

"I still can't believe that he's still hanging in there," Maria stated. "As fine as he is. Girl, you better snatch that man off the market before I do," she threatened.

Tanisha fanned her fingers across Maria's face. "Anyhoo," she said dismissively. "He's dating a girl who goes to Georgetown now," she said softly.

"Are you jealous?" Maria asked.

"Not at all," Teenie replied quickly. "He knows about Glen," she paused.

"But you and Glen broke up," Rashanda corrected.

"And David doesn't know about Brian Kraft," Maria blurted. "If he knew that you were now dating the hickey giver from camp," she cackled. "I think he might have issue with that."

"Since he knows about Glen, why didn't you tell him about Brian?" Rashanda asked.

Tanisha took a bite from her cold pizza and chewed slowly. The girls stared at her patiently. She swallowed and gulped her root beer. The rain had now slowed to a trickle.

"I thought that might be a little too much information for now," she admitted slowly. "Besides, I don't know where this thing with Brian is going," she whined.

"It's a soap opera," Maria laughed. "Let me summarize it for you. David Barton is warming up in the batting cage. Glen Horton has been placed on injured reserve for his failure to pucker up on demand," she chuckled. "And Brian Kraft has moved into the starting lineup because he has magic lips and claims to be in love with exhibit A," she laughed pointing at Tanisha.

"Nice job, Maria," Justine giggled. "Hearing it explained like that, it does sound like a soap opera," she agreed. "No offense, Teenie."

"None taken," Tanisha groaned.

"Does Glen still call you?" Justine asked.

"Daily," Teenie smiled. "He really wants to get back together, but I don't," she paused.

"And he didn't kiss you because of his religious beliefs, right?" Grace asked.

Teenie nodded. "Right. He's saving his first kiss for his wedding day," she said softly.

This time Maria's laugh was guttural and deep, the pizza slipped from her lips. "That's the second dumbest thing that I've heard in less than an hour," she cackled. "Teenie, you attract the strangest guys into your world," she laughed.

"Continue, Teenie," Rashanda encouraged.

"Glen said that he thinks that I'm marriage material," she paused. "And he's a really great guy, but I can't imagine waiting for him to kiss me until our wedding day," she groaned.

"Even Lori would think that was a bit much," Rashanda suggested. "She was kissing Doug."

"That's what I mean," Teenie sighed. "I feel so bad for him. Glen has never kissed anyone before, but he knows that I have," she paused. "When I met him at the arcade, he was so smooth that I would have never thought that he had a no kissing rule."

"He had on a Malcolm X tee shirt and an earring in his ear," Maria reminded. "I thought he was a thug, not a church boy."

"If he had told you about the no kissing rule when you first started dating him, would you have stopped seeing him, Teenie?" Justine asked.

Tanisha stared at her straw. "I ask myself that all the time," she shared. "And I really don't have an answer to that question."

"She would have dropped him like a hot potato," Maria laughed.

"I'm so glad that you're over your heart break and that my drama is providing folly to heal your wounded heart," Teenie said winding her napkin into a tight spiral.

"This is better than watching All My Children," Maria repeated. "Because it's real life. And it's your life drama and not mine for a change," she grinned.

"But by the time he told me about his rule," Teenie continued. "I really liked him." Staring out the window, she watched the rain pattern. "I think that was his plan," she finished.

"Probably so," Rashanda agreed. "But he's at Morehouse now, right?"

"Uh huh," Teenie nodded. "But he's thinking about transferring to the University of Connecticut next year," she said. "He wants to be near me."

"How do you feel about that?" Justine asked.

"He's a really nice guy," Teenie said quickly. "And besides his no kissing rule, he was a fun boyfriend. He was kind and thoughtful," Teenie listed. "I don't have anyone to compare him against since he was my first real boyfriend, but I think he was all of the things that you want a boyfriend to be," she admitted. "He introduced me to his parents," she said. Maria shifted uncomfortably in her seat, sliding down the booth, her chin rested on the table once again, her spine curved like a capital C. "But it's over and I've moved on now," Teenie paused. "And he knows that I've moved on, so his wanting to transfer to the University of Connecticut to be near me is creepy."

"Sounds like he's a stalker," Maria said. "That'll really make your soap opera interesting, Teenie," she cackled.

"Now how does Brian Kraft fit into the puzzle?" Grace asked.

"I'll answer that," Maria offered quickly. "Brian wines and dines her and provides exercise for her lips," she laughed.

"Enough Maria," Teenie said seriously. "I'm really confused here."

"Do you have feelings for Brian Kraft?" Rashanda asked.

"Of course I do," Teenie said a little too sternly. "I really like him. He's a great guy. You guys met him at prom," she reminded. "And he's saying all the right stuff," she paused. "But he's white."

"Teenie, that's no reason not to like him," Maria offered softly sitting up straight, her posture ballerina perfect. "If you like him, you like him. Who cares what color he is?"

"But I'm worried about what my dad will think," she shared.

"But you said that your parents didn't flip out when your brother Jack introduced Kerri Peck as his girlfriend," Maria reminded.

"True," Tanisha agreed. "But he and Kerri broke up and now that my brother is in college, he's dating a black girl."

"Your dad will get over it," Maria stated cavalierly. "As long as Brian keeps treating you like a princess, your dad will be fine."

"I don't know about that," Teenie sighed. "My dad had some pretty horrible racism experiences back in the day," she shared. "In fact, he still rants and raves about some of the white men at his job. He says that they treat him like he doesn't know what he's doing and they act like they're smarter than he is just because they're white," she finished. "I think he might blow a gasket if I got serious with a white guy."

"My dad complains about the same stuff," Rashanda shared.

"I think it's just the plight of black men," she shrugged.

"I agree," Justine sighed. "And not just black men. Blacks period. We have to work harder to prove we're as good or better."

"You're right, Justine," Maria agreed. "My mother calls it white privilege. She says that many whites have this air of superiority and privilege that stems from slavery. They just think that they're better than people of color because they're white. It's almost like it's programmed in their DNA," she said, shaking her head and scowling. "Not all whites feel that way, but many do," she finished.

Straw in hand, Grace chimed in. "I went into a store on North Michigan Avenue with my mom last weekend and the clerk was very rude and nasty to us," she shared. "I wanted to cuss the woman out, but my mom told me to let it go," she continued. "She said that I should have dressed up to go shopping downtown because blacks always have to dress up in order to receive good service in certain stores," she paused. "My mom was mad at herself for the way that white clerk treated us. Like it was her fault."

"What did you have on, Grace?" Justine asked.

"I had on a pair of jeans and a sweater," she explained. "I didn't look like a bum or anything," she assured.

"It shouldn't matter what you had on," Rashanda commented.

Teenie paused. "I agree, and I'm sure you looked cute, Grace, but my Grandma Bootsy told me the same thing," Teenie shared, her head nodding in disgust. "She always dresses up to shop downtown, and she told my cousins and me to do the same. It's one of those unwritten rules that only apply to blacks," she sighed.

"But there was this white girl in the store with her mom and she had on sweats," Grace protested. "And they weren't even cute sweats. They were tacky, Save Mart type sweats," Grace continued.

"She looked dirty and poor, but the clerks were sucking up to her like she was a Rockefeller," she growled. "I wanted to pull out my bank statement and slap that salesclerk across the face with it," Grace admitted.

"She may have been a Rockefeller, or she may have lived in a trailer park, but she was white," Rashanda exhaled. "It's a double standard. Grace, you're a perfect example. You're half white, but you look more black than white, and you're worth tens of millions of dollars, yet you get treated like a pauper in a store just because of the color of your skin and the texture of your strawberry blonde hair."

"Actually, I'm worth more than that," Grace grinned slyly. "But that's only if you factor in the real estate holdings in my portfolio."

Their jaws slack, Teenie, Rashanda, Justine and Maria stared at Grace in amazement.

"Witch, when we go out, you're definitely paying the tab from now until eternity," Maria stated.

"Amen to that," Teenie echoed. "But the point is that our life experience is different because of the color of our skin," she said. "It's just a fact. Our parents and grandparents experienced it, and Lord knows our great grandparents experienced it, and fought for things to be different and better," she offered. "And in some ways things are better, but that story is proof that we're still feeling it too," she sighed. "Maybe things will be different for our children," she brightened.

"My dad is so fed up with it that he's planning to go into business for himself. He's studying to get his real estate broker's license so he can run his own company. But we're way off topic now ladies," Maria reminded. "We're talking about Teenie's love life." Her hands cupped in a bowl position, she pointed at Teenie. "If Brian is the guy who treats you the best and makes you happy, Teenie," she paused. "I think your dad will be happy for you."

"Plus, you'll be in college so whatever you decide to do won't be in his face," Rashanda suggested. "And you're on full scholarship so it's not like he'll stop paying your tuition if he doesn't like the choices you're making," Rashanda reminded.

Tanisha took another bite of her cold pizza square. "You're right," she paused. "Now that I think about it, I don't think that my dad is going to like any boy that I date. Glen was black, and he scowled at Glen every time he saw him," she laughed. "And Glen never even kissed me."

"Your dad didn't know that Glen wasn't kissing you," Rashanda corrected. "But that's exactly the point I was going to make," she stated. "Dads never want to think of some boy violating their little girl," she paused. "No boy will ever be worthy, white, black, green or purple for that matter."

"Do you ever feel uncomfortable when you and Brian hang out?" Maria asked.

Tanisha bit her lip softly. "A little," she said. "When we hold hands I feel like people are staring at us," she admitted. "And I never felt like that when I held hands with Glen."

"Justine is dating a white, Jewish guy," Rashanda reminded. "Does that happen to you, Justine?" she asked.

Sighing quickly, Justine twirled her straw. "Sometimes it does," she admitted. "When we're on campus, it's no big deal, but when we go off campus together, if we're holding hands sometimes people stare at us and scowl," she shared. "AM notices it too, but he told me that we'll get used to it."

"That's what Brian said, too," Tanisha agreed.

"Teenie, isn't Brian at Brown?" Justine asked.

"No. He's a freshman at Princeton," Teenie corrected. "He got accepted to Brown, but he chose Princeton."

"Where's Princeton?" Grace asked.

"It's in New Jersey," Teenie said. "Princeton is in Princeton, New Jersey."

Maria eyed Teenie carefully. "And New Jersey isn't that far from Connecticut," Maria shared. "How convenient," she laughed. "You'll be able to continue your love fest with Brian Kraft in college," she cooed.

"Does Brian know that Glen wants to transfer to the University of Connecticut?" Grace asked.

Her head bobbled in the affirmative. "He does," she shared quickly. "He's not too happy about it. He wants to confront Glen and tell him to back off," she added. "That's another thing," she offered. "Glen thinks that my black card should be revoked because I'm dating a white guy."

"Well, he was wearing a Malcolm X shirt when you met him," Maria reminded.

The crease from Teenie's scowl spanned the width of her wide forehead. "Well, I'm just saying," Maria defended. "He had militant splattered all across his chest," she chuckled softly, unsure if Teenie's gaze was friend or foe.

"I'm confused. So you told Glen about Brian Kraft?" Justine asked. "But you're keeping him from David. Riddle me that, Batgirl?" she requested.

Her expression softened, Teenie gestured with her hands. "I wanted Glen to know that I've moved on," Teenie defended. "I thought that if I told him that I was seeing someone that he'd move on," she explained.

"How did Glen find out that Brian was white?" Rashanda asked.

"When Glen asked me who the guy was I told him that it was the guy that he saw me talking to at prom," she finished. "I think part of his issue is that he can't believe that I broke up with him to date a white guy."

"Who cares what he thinks?" Justine chimed in. "Glen needs to build a bridge and get over it," she said angrily. "It's none of his freaking business who you date now," she growled. "He knows nothing about Brian, he's just judging him because he's white. I'm so tired of people making judgments based on their own stupid prejudices! Glen's an idiot and you need to tell your father that Glen is stalking you," she barked.

"I wouldn't say that he's stalking me," Teenie defended.

Maria's expression was one of stunned disbelief as she held up her index finger. "You're being stalked, Teenie. Let me spell it out for you. One. You broke up with Glen, but he still calls you every night long distance from Atlanta," she emphasized. "Two. He's unhappy with your new boyfriend. Three. He's planning to transfer to a school in the same state where you'll be attending college so he can be near you," she listed. "Four. He hates that your boyfriend is white. And five. I know a stalker when I see one," she assured, gripping her thumb with her free hand. "He's stalking you, Teenie. It's time to involve Big Poppa," Maria finished.

Chewing on her lip, Teenie stared out the window as the sun slowly melted the clouds away. She watched as a bird flew by the window, a juicy worm dangling from its beak. "If I tell my dad that Glen is stalking me, Jackie will go ballistic," she exclaimed. "And I don't want to get Glen in trouble," Teenie protested.

"You need to involve your dad, Teenie," Rashanda concurred.

"This isn't about getting him in trouble. This is about Glen not respecting your boundaries. You have a new boyfriend," she paused. "So there's no reason for him to still be calling you. Glen needs to move on."

"It's really that simple," Maria agreed. "You need to involve your dad now or hire some thugs to beat Glen up," she laughed. "We can have Miss Grace High Net Worth pay for the beat down. We'll do a casting call to hire the biggest, thuggiest looking guys we can find, and we'll hand pick them," she smiled. "It'll be fun! In fact," Maria paused. "Maybe we can negotiate a two for one deal and have them beat Todd up too," she cackled, the confidence in her voice dulled by the curtain of pain that suddenly veiled her face. "On second thought, I'll pay for that one myself," she whimpered softly. Her demeanor had changed from carefree to melancholy in the blink of an eye. The tears even caught her by surprise. "He's going to pay for his little stunt," she assured. "How dare he dump me while playing theme music in the background? He played theme music!" The tremor in her voice weighed heavier than the weakened confidence in her tone. "Mark my word," she stammered softly as a puddle of tears spilled from her eyes like a tipped pitcher of root beer.

The girls looked knowingly at Maria and thrust napkins in her face. She waved them off and wiped her eyes with her sleeve. Teenie reached for her hand and squeezed softly. Rashanda's arm cradled her friend's shoulder like a shawl.

Their eyes darted from one to the other, searching for words to salve their friend's wound. But there was nothing to say. Her heart had been shattered into a million shards. Only time and new, happier experiences could fill the chasm in her soul. "I'll be fine, you guys," Maria said. "I just can't believe that he would break up with me in such a cruel way," she sighed. "He told me that he loved me," she choked.

Pursing her lips to speak, Teenie swallowed, choking the words that were desperately trying to escape her lips like a convict with possession of the jail cell key. Out of the corner of her eye, Teenie noticed Rashanda's subtle shake of the head discouraging her from stating what they were all thinking.

The words in Teenie's throat fought their way into the air. "I'm sure he loved you," Teenie comforted confidently. "But he didn't love you in the way that you deserve to be loved, Maria. Maybe the way he loved you was the only way that he was capable of loving," she continued. "And maybe that will work for someone one day. But you deserve to be loved better than that," she finished. "You're young. You're beautiful, and you're going to find someone to love you better."

Her eyes staring through Teenie, Maria picked up a soiled napkin and wiped her tear stained face, shielding her eyes for a brief instant. Maria's head resting on Rashanda's shoulder, Rashanda winked at Teenie and gave her a thumbs up. Teenie shrugged and smiled.

Maria's weary eyes were glued on Teenie's nose like radar, her gaze a million miles away. She stared blankly at Teenie as though she were looking through her friend examining her internal organs. Prepared to defend her position, Teenie braced herself for the displaced aggression rant that usually followed any bad Todd experiences, her friend's best interest her only motivation.

The deep voice startled the girls. "Looks like the rain has stopped and the sun is out, ladies," Dell announced cheerfully. "I'll just take these plates out of your way. Can I bring you ladies anything else?" he asked, once again, his question directed at Grace.

"I don't think we'll be ordering anything else, but do you have any tissue you can bring us, Dell?" Teenie asked.

"Sure. We keep a box in the office. I'll go get it," he said.

Maria wiped her eyes again. "There goes my make-up," she laughed softly. "Thanks, Teenie," she offered. "I needed to hear that. I deserve to be loved better than that," she repeated. "That sounds like something that my mom would say," she smiled weakly. "But you're right. I deserved more than I was getting from Todd," she sniffled as Dell set the box of tissue on the table and quietly removed the remaining plates.

"Here's your check," he smiled. "I hope you ladies will come back. Once we're done with the renovations, the atmosphere will be much improved," he assured. "Although you ladies helped brighten things up in here," he spoke directly to Grace. "I'll take care of this whenever you're ready. No rush. You're welcome to sit here and talk as long as you'd like," he grinned. "Grace, can I call you sometime?" he asked boldly.

"Uh, yeah. Sure," Grace stammered quickly. "I'll write my number down for you."

"You can use the pen that's in the tray with the check," he suggested.

Rashanda handed Grace a piece of paper from her purse and watched as Grace wrote down her name and telephone number.

"I'll give you my number too," he smiled. "I'll write it down and bring it out."

"Okay," Grace blushed.

"I'm glad someone's love life is on track," Maria blurted, her voice dripping with sarcasm and envy. "I didn't mean that the way it sounded," she corrected. "I'm happy for you, Grace. Dell seems nice," she offered quickly. "But back to you, Teenie. How are you going to choose between Brian and David?"

"Are you sure you're okay, Maria?" Teenie asked.

"I'll be fine. I don't want to talk about my drama anymore. Who's it going to be?"

"I haven't a clue," Teenie sighed. "That's what you babes are for. Tell me what to do!" she groaned, tilting her head against the booth and closing her eyes. When she opened them, her friends were staring at her expressionless. "I really don't know what to do," she confessed. "I like them both. They're so different, but I like them both. I'm hoping that between now and New Year's Eve, one of them will do something stupid and irk me so I don't have to choose," she laughed. "Or I'm thinking about just kissing David Barton to get it over with and then if he has halitosis or he's a horrible kisser I can dump him," she teased. "You know how important fresh breath is to me," she reminded.

"Teenie, would you really dump David just because his breath was bad?" Justine asked.

"Of course she would," Maria replied. "Teenie is quirky like that. You know how she is."

"Well, even though you haven't kissed him, you've been close enough to smell David's breath," Rashanda paused. "Is it stank?"

"Unfortunately not," Teenie shared. "He's almost as neurotic about his breath as I am about mine," she continued. "He brushes his teeth after every meal and keeps a small bottle of mouthwash in his glove compartment to freshen his breath during the day. He also keeps gum or mints in his pocket," she sighed. "The breath is quite fresh, so I can't dump him for failing the fresh breath test," she sighed.

"That's shallow anyway, Teenie," Justine offered. "You need a real reason to dump either one of them."

"You're right," she agreed. "But it's so confusing. And it doesn't help that Brian is doing all of the right things," Teenie continued. "He's taking me to meet his parents next weekend," she said.

"You met his parents too?" Maria asked.

"Not yet," Teenie corrected. "He's taking me to his house next weekend. He tried to get me to meet them last weekend, but I had to work."

"I can't believe that you are meeting his parents too," Maria groaned softly, her posture slumping into the C curve once again.

"Do his parents know that you're African American?" Grace asked.

"They do," Teenie replied.

"They do? Are you nervous? Didn't Brian tell you that he was worried about what his parents would say if he dated a black girl?" Grace asked. "Isn't that why he didn't call you after camp?"

"But Brian told me that when he told his parents about me they just said that if I'm that special to him then they would like to meet me," she shrugged.

"Are you sure that he told them that you're African American, Teenie?" Rashanda asked.

"Positive," Teenie assured. "We ran into his dad's best friend and his wife when we were having lunch downtown a few months ago," she added. "Brian told me that his parents play couples golf with them every Sunday afternoon, so if his parents didn't know before, then they know now," she said. "They were really nice. They saw us holding hands, and Brian introduced me as his girlfriend," Teenie finished. "They didn't seem surprised when they saw that I'm black."

"Well, it's not like you have five heads," Maria offered. "You're just black. And technically, you're not even black, you're banana yellow to be exact," she laughed. "But seriously, you're going to

Yale on an academic scholarship, you're pretty. You sound like a white girl on the phone," she continued. "So if they close their eyes at dinner they can pretend that you're blonde and blue eyed," she trailed.

"Thanks for the vote of confidence, Maria," Teenie said.

"I'm just saying that you're no different than the white girls he's probably dated. You just have a permanent golden hue," Maria finished. "Brian isn't dating anyone at Princeton?" she asked suspiciously.

"He says he isn't," Teenie replied. "So all I can do is believe him and take him on his word. I don't have the energy to worry about what he might be doing when I'm not with him," she paused.

"I agree. Lori used to always say that 'what's done in the dark will come out in the light,'" Grace added. "I think that's a scripture too. I'll have to look that up in the Bible when I get home."

"You're right, Grace. I remember hearing Lori say that a few times," she agreed. "I don't worry about Ian at Northwestern anymore either," Rashanda echoed. She grinned mischievously. "Actually, I need to tell you guys something," she blurted. "No, never mind. We can talk about it later," she amended quickly. "When are you going to let Brian meet your parents?" Rashanda asked.

"I think I'll wait until after I meet his," Teenie admitted. "Or not. I don't know where this is going. If his parents treat me like gum shoe there's no sense getting my dad all worked up if I decide to break up with him," she paused. "In fact, I might wait until Thanksgiving break to see how things go after my first quarter at Yale."

"Good idea. You might meet someone different," Maria offered. "You might add a fourth stud into the Tanisha Carlson love triangle stable," she laughed.

Rashanda twirled her napkin tightly. "Let's go before it starts to rain again," she suggested quickly, standing up in the booth, her eyes darting rapidly. She plopped back down just as quickly.

"What's wrong, Rashanda?" Teenie asked. "Are you okay? You need to breathe. It looks like you're hyperventilating!"

Rashanda blew the air from her lips loudly, the breath whistling between her teeth, her eyes panning the now empty restaurant. Her smile was faint, her lips trembling as she spoke. "I'm not supposed to say anything," she stammered. Ian begged me not to tell anyone," she paused. "But I can't hold it in any longer," she whispered.

"Dish, chick," Maria insisted. "What's up?"

Ignoring Maria, Rashanda continued. "Ian told me that he's ready to take the next step in our relationship," she shared. "And I'm thinking about doing it."

"What next step? Doing what?" Justine quizzed. "I know you're not thinking about that next step," she blurted.

"Rashanda Rochelle Jordan, I know you're not thinking about breaking our pact!" Maria screamed.

"No, silly! Ian asked me to marry him," Rashanda blushed.

ABOUT THE AUTHOR

A native Chicagoan, JC Conrad-Ellis now lives in the Memphis, Tennessee area with her husband and their three children.

Read these titles, too!

Sunshine on Sunday
Love, Secrets & Pearls

The fifth and sixth books in the Black Diamond Series!

Sunshine on Sunday and **Love, Secrets & Pearls** chronicle the girls' college years and serves as a page turning blueprint that connects the Black Diamond Series' plot dots and explains how the young women became the glorious young women of God that they were destined to become!

Visit JC Conrad-Ellis' website for interactive blogs:
www.blackdiamondseries.com

Follow JC Ellis on Twitter
@dearjcellis

In **Dancing with God's Grace**, the reader experiences the highs and lows of high school arm in arm with Tanisha "Teenie" Carlson and her core group: Maria Wesley, Lori Perkins, Rashanda Jordan, Justine Wellington and Grace Dudley.

From prom, temptation, break-ups and reconciliation, each chapter continues the storyline of a main character and begins to unveil the cosmetic facades that lay behind the girls' carefully made-up images.

As they morph from awkward caterpillars into charming butterflies, their shared experiences impact each others' lives in sustainable ways. Their bond is strengthened when the group provides support through a frightening healthcare scare to one friend while nurturing another friend who is forced to redefine her family structure.

A true love story, **Dancing with God's Grace** proves that the heart wants what it wants even if the want of the heart goes against popular opinion.

Other Books by JC Conrad-Ellis
Boys, Beauty & Betrayal
Camp Colorblind
Chemistry & Chaos
Sunshine on Sunday
Love, Secrets & Pearls

www.ingramcontent.com/pod-product-compliance
Lightning Source LLC
Chambersburg PA
CBHW070740190726
48292CB00002B/358